P9-EGL-552

HE WAS HER MAN

A SAMANTHA ADAMS MYSTERY

SARAH SHANKMAN

POCKET STAR BOOKS

New York   London   Toronto   Sydney   Tokyo   Singapore

This book is a work of fiction. Names, characters, places and incidents are products of the author's imagination or are used fictitiously. Any resemblance to actual events or locales or persons, living or dead, is entirely coincidental.

 A Pocket Star Book published by
POCKET BOOKS, a division of Simon & Schuster Inc.
1230 Avenue of the Americas, New York, NY 10020

Copyright © 1993 by Sarah Shankman

ISBN: 0-671-77563-4

First Pocket Books paperback printing September 1994

10 9 8 7 6 5 4 3 2 1

POCKET STAR BOOKS and colophon are registered trademarks of Simon & Schuster Inc.

Cover art by Tristan Elwell

Printed in the U.S.A.

Novels in the Sam Adams Series by Sarah Shankman

First Kill All the Lawyers
Then Hang All the Liars
Now Let's Talk of Graves
She Walks in Beauty
The King Is Dead
He Was Her Man

Other Novels by Sarah Shankman

Impersonal Attractions
Keeping Secrets

For Walter Mosley and Dallas Murphy

My thanks to:

the tireless booksellers, especially mystery booksellers, who do such a marvelous job for us all; the kind and helpful people of Hot Springs, particularly the staffs of Oaklawn Park and McClard's BBQ, which isn't open on Sundays, but ought to be; Ann Culley and the many other long-suffering friends who cheer me on; everyone at Pocket Books, especially Jane Chelius, my editor; and as always, my agent, Harvey Klinger. I owe a special debt of gratitude to Dallas Murphy, whose advice saw me home.

". . . Some day, somewhere, a guy is going to come to you and show you a nice brand-new deck of cards on which the seal is never broken, and this guy is going to offer to bet you that the jack of spades will jump out of this deck and squirt cider in your ear. But, son, do not bet him, for as sure as you do you are going to get an ear full of cider."

—*Advice given to young Sky Masterson in Damon Runyon's "The Idyll of Miss Sarah Brown"*

1

SAM ADAMS WAS RUNNING AWAY FROM HOME. SHE'D BEEN
driving since dawn, mostly on rain-slick two-lane. You
couldn't take the interstates from New Orleans to Hot
Springs, Arkansas. There were none.

On the other hand, the narrow roads threading
through the little burgs gave her something to look at,
to take her mind off the notion of shooting her boyfriend
Harry, her songwriting barbecuer who'd done her
wrong.

*Harry, Harry, boy toy, Harry, why'd you do what you did?
Didn't your sweet Sammy make you moan? Ain't that what
you said, son? Said, Sweet Sammy, nobody's ever been as good,
nobody, nobody, nobody ever gonna come along, make me kick
you out of bed, darlin' one. Lay lady laid up in my big brass
bed while the rains drip drip honey, musk, sweet sweetwater
over the patios of the French Quarter, cooling everything but
the love I feel for you, old lady, sweet lady, lady who steals
my heart, bends my mind, melts my bones.*

Bull.

In St. Francisville she'd passed moss-dripping live
oaks. Hush-my-mouth antebellum houses in Natchez.
The skies had cleared and the sun peeked out near Ferri-

day, where she'd stopped for three chocolate-covered doughnuts and a cup of not-bad coffee which had picked up her spirits, sugar and caffeine being medicine for the blues. Feeling as bad as she did, she'd grab at almost anything—except, please God, not the booze—to blunt the pain. Then she looked from her doughnuts and spied the photos on the coffee shop wall of Ferriday's three infamous cousins: Mickey Gilley, Jimmy Swaggart, Jerry Lee Lewis. Maybe Mickey wasn't so bad, but the other two . . . Child, don't get her started on the perfidy of men.

Why else was her rearview mirror showing her a face that looked like twenty miles of bad road? And no matter what was playing on the radio, what she heard was a mean low-down version of the My-baby-done-stepped-out-on-me blues.

Finally, four hours, three Cokes, two brownies, and a box of Cracker Jacks later, a road sign announced *Hot Springs, 10 miles.* But the red light flashing on her dash laid odds she wasn't going to make it.

Well, wouldn't you know? Samantha Adams—former crime reporter, forty-one years old, running away from home, running away from a gut-stabbed ego—had managed to run out of gas, too.

But, yo, girl. Heads up. See that red-and-yellow promise of deliverance just up the road? *Gas 'N Grub* said the sign over the one-stop convenience store. *Olive Adair, Sole Proprietress.* Beneath that, *Pearl Adair, Top Dog.* Sam managed the first smile of her long grim day, then wheeled into the Gas 'N Grub.

Inside Olive Adair was saying to her hound, Pearl, "Those girls don't know what they're talking about. Do you think they know what they're talking about?," snapping off the TV, Donahue and the three bottle blondes perched on the edge of their seats like canaries, saying how being a call girl was fun.

Pearl sat back on her haunches and said, "Aooo, aooo," which is what she was supposed to do, and Olive reached behind the counter of the Gas 'N Grub for a package of Cheez Doodles, the big redbone hound's favorite snack. While she was at it, Olive snagged herself a Delaware Punch from the cooler. Pearl, impatient, barked twice.

"Hold your horses," Olive said to Pearl, tearing open the bag. "I'll tell you what, dog, way back when *I* was living the life, no matter what those Donahue girls say, not a single minute of it was fun. Living in town in Hot Springs, yes, but not the work. 'Course maybe it's a little different, the way those girls do it, calling on the johns, you have some control, instead of them walking right in off the street, pointing a fat finger in your face like you was supposed to be thrilled to pieces, you'd won some kind of beauty contest. 'Course, you get down to it, no matter who does the traveling, you close that bedroom door, it's all the same thing." Olive lifted a blue-veined hand and smoothed at the gray curls that had popped loose from the knot atop her head. She was wearing a purple-and-green muumuu she'd bought when she was in Hawaii with her friend Loydell, nothing under it but rolls of pink flesh and a pair of lilac step-ins. "That was the fifties," she said to Pearl, "when I was practicing my profession up at Lola's behind the bank on Bath, right off Central Avenue. Which reminds me, Pearl, we need to figure out what I'm going to wear to Jinx's party this evening. My blue? What do you think?"

Pearl gave her a puzzled look like she wasn't sure. Just about then the bell sounded as a silvery-blue BMW pulled up at the gas pumps. A tall curly-headed brunette wearing a red sweat suit jumped out and reached for the do-it-yourself unleaded supreme. She filled that tank right up, slapped the nozzle back on the pump, and stepped inside to pay.

"Hi!" Olive said. "How you doing this afternoon? Have you ever seen prettier? I was just saying to Pearl here that I didn't think I'd ever seen a more beautiful afternoon, once that rain cleared off. Kind of day makes you think, well, Lord, you finished with me here, I'm about through, ready to come on home to Glory, it looks anything like this."

It was then that the pretty brunette broke into a big boo-hoo.

"Jesus, I'm so sorry," Sam said for the tenth time, sitting on the stool Olive had pulled out from behind the counter. She blew her nose on one of Olive's pink Kleenex, feeling like a fool.

"Honey." Olive patted her on the knee. "You don't need to be apologizing to me. I think that's what's wrong with the world, folks go around holding everything in. Letting it fester. Next thing you know, there's some sucker, been chewing on a world of hurt, somebody flunked him, fired his butt, stole his honey, whatever, he rolls out, climbs up in a tower, jerks open an office door, one of those, pulls out a shotgun, starts blasting away. Usually kills a whole bunch of folks, sometimes even the main one did him dirt, before he puts himself out of his misery. Whole thing could have been avoided, he'd just given in to his feelings, said what was on his mind. 'Course, it's mostly men that does that."

It was those last words that made Sam start up again. "I wish he hadn't," she sobbed.

"Hadn't what?"

"Said what was on his mind. I wish he'd just kept his damned mouth shut."

"Uh-huh." Olive settled her rear up against the counter. "I see. Was he one of those, it made him feel soooo good, sharing his doo-doo with you? Laid a big

4

pile of it in your lap, then walked away, wiping his hands, like Whew! *I* feel a heck of a lot better. Meanwhile, you're sitting there trying not to shoot him. Tell me now, was it another woman?" Sam nodded. How *tired* her situation was. A lover fooling around, well, it wasn't like that page-one news, was it? Olive shook her head and tightened her lips. "Never ceases to amaze me. Wouldn't you think somebody had a woman as nice and as fine-looking as you, he could keep it zipped? But they don't. They never do. It's the testosterone." Olive slapped the counter. She had dainty hands with a petal pink manicure. "Same thing that causes football, strip-mining, shoot-outs, wars, most of the world's miseries short of the rheumatiz. We'd all be better off they flushed that stuff out of 'em on a regular basis. I say, give *them* the monthlies."

Sam was thinking she'd like to give Harry the business end of a .38.

"Now, you tell Olive all about it. You want a drink? It'll make you feel better. I've got a bottle of bourbon stuck back here, or would you rather have a beer?"

"Neither, thank you."

"Cause it's against your religion?"

Sam shook her head.

"Well, if you're an alkie, that don't bother me none. I got a whole raft of friends used to have some serious problems with the booze."

Sam stuck out her hand and said, "I'd be proud to join that club." For she'd been sober twelve years and had grown awfully fond of Olive Adair in the past fifteen minutes.

"Let me get you a soda pop. How about a Delaware Punch? Or you got the sugar, too?"

"Nope." Sam grinned. She didn't have diabetes, and she hadn't had one of the dark red sodas, so sweet they made your face squinch up, since she was in pigtails back in Atlanta. "Delaware Punch used to be one of my all-time favorites. I didn't know they still made it."

"They ain't quite run off everything's that good." Olive plopped a can on the counter. "Now tell me all about this son of a bitch. What's his name?"

Sam took a long swig and shuddered at the sweetness. "Harry. Harry Zack."

"Is he cute? I was always a fool for cute ones myself."

Oh, Harry was a looker all right. The next thing she knew, she was telling Olive about how he was only an inch taller than she was, but he had this slow grin, broad shoulders, strong legs, neat butt, a head of dark curls much like her own, gray eyes. The left one drooped a little.

"Is that sexy?"

Everything about Harry was sexy. Her ten-years-younger boyfriend she'd met at Mardi Gras two years earlier visiting her friend Kitty Lee. She'd spotted Harry at the airport, the minute she stepped off the plane. With that first glance, he'd set her hormones in an uproar. They'd do-si-doed around one another, chased up and down blind alleys searching for a killer, Harry being an insurance investigator at the time. They'd ended up in the big brass bed in Harry's French Quarter apartment, and from then on it seemed they were compatible in most of the ways that are important between a man and a woman.

"So you wanted to settle down and he didn't?" asked Olive.

"Nope. Turn it around the other way." Sam had had her heart squashed one too many times and had decided that semipermanent was the best one could hope for in that game. Certainly all that she could ever commit to. "But I did what I could. I took a leave from my job reporting for the Atlanta *Constitution*. Moved over to New Orleans. Well, almost to New Orleans. I'm renting a house on the north shore of Lake Pontchartrain, about an hour away from Harry."

"So you're close, but not too close?"

Sam nodded. Olive had her number, all right.

"And everything was just hunky-dory, until when? Yesterday, he told you about the blonde?" Olive handed Sam a package of peanuts, which she ripped open with her teeth.

Then Sam said, *"Young* blonde. *Pretty* young blonde. I've met her a couple of times. She was working on the advertising for his restaurant, Harry and his friend Lavert have this barbecue business." Sam took another long swig of the Delaware Punch, then held out the can and looked at it. *"Very* young. Very cute. Very skinny."

"Did you suspect something right away?"

Sam nodded. "Hated her on sight."

"Any woman's got an eye in her head knows. If she says she don't, honey, she don't want to. You Twelve-Steppers call that denial, don't you?"

"Olive, you sure you're not in the program?"

"Nawh. But I been a couple of times. Those friends of mine seemed to be having too much fun at them meetings, I said let me in on this thing. So they did, or Loydell did. She's my best friend. So I saw what y'all are all about. Folks sitting around, telling the most godawful stories about what they did when they was drinking, and everybody else laughing their fool heads off because they'd been there, too, done exactly that same thing. Or worse. That's the reason the thing works, I figured it out. Being with a bunch of folks know exactly where you've been and not condemning you for it, helps you stay clean."

"You got it," said Sam. She most definitely had to get herself to a meeting or three this weekend. Stop pretending she wasn't trying to run away from the pain, driving five hundred miles in one day.

"So," said Olive, "you up here in Hot Springs looking

for a Rent-A-Shooter to kill her, him, the both of them, vacationing, or just passing on through?"

Sam wiped her salty hands on the pants of her red sweat suit. "I'm following my friend Kitty, who flew up for a party. I need the use of her shoulder."

"Well, that's good. That's what friends are for. I don't know what I'd do without my friend Loydell. We talk to each other first thing every morning, make sure we want to go to the trouble of living that day. The day we decide we don't, we're riding up to the top of that tower on Hot Springs Mountain, hold hands, jump off."

Sam laughed. The old lady was a great kidder. *Wasn't* she? Then she backed up to the Rent-A Shooter. "I really hadn't thought about *hiring* somebody to kill 'em, but now that you mention it . . ."

"You're too late by thirty years. Hot Springs used to be a wide-open town till Bobby Kennedy got his drawers in a twist. You name it, we had it. Gangsters, killers, colorful characters out the wazoo, gambling casinos, bookie joints, hot and cold running houses of ill repute."

Having said that, Olive stood up straight. Sucked her stomach in. Pushed her chest out. The pounds and the years melted away. Oh, yes, thought Sam, Olive had been a looker in her day. She wondered what exactly Miss Olive had done for a living in Sin City?

But before she could ask her, the old woman was off on her two-dollar lecture. "It's the waters that first brought folks here. One-hundred-and-forty-three-degree springs, coming right out of the rocks, Indians knew about them. Healing waters, they say, but I think back then it was a relief just to loll around in a big old tub of hot water that you didn't have to fell the trees, chop the wood, build the fire to heat. But once you'd bathed, you needed something else to do."

"Wine, women, and song?" Sam reached for a Hershey's bar with almonds, peeled it, and stuck it in her mouth.

"And gambling, which brought your criminal element. Why, back in the olden days, Jesse James used to hold 'em up right at the edge of town, and that's the truth. There were racketeers fighting over territory, shooting up each other and innocent bystanders in the middle of Central Avenue when it was still a mud trough full of pigs. Then later, we had the Capones. Lots of Chicago mobsters came for the waters. Owney Madden, a bootlegger from New York, he settled here, ran his gambling operation out of the old Southern Club. Now it's the Wax Museum. But, oh, it was something, all right, the old Hot Springs." Then Olive leaned closer. "Though even today, if you want a little action, take your mind off your troubles, there's still some gambling—and I don't mean the Oaklawn track—you know where to look." Then she patted Sam's hand. "You want another pop? How about a sandwich?"

"No, thank you. I've consumed about five thousand calories since I came through that door, and I still have a party to go to." She patted her stomach. "I'd better be getting on." She was feeling a lot better. Nothing like a good cry and a bunch of sugar and salt to improve your spirits.

"Where are you staying in town? You never said."

"At the Palace. That's where the party Kitty came up for is being held. I was invited, too, but I wasn't coming—till Harry turned into a son of a bitch."

"Are you talking about Jinx Watson's party?"

"Why, Olive! Do you know Jinx?"

"Her mother is my friend Loydell I was telling you about. And I'm going to that party, too. I was just discussing with Pearl here what I ought to wear. We agreed on my blue."

Sam grinned. "Well, I'm wearing my red. But not this." She pointed at her sweat suit. "A little red dress with gobs of pearls. You think that'll do?"

"Honey, if you know Jinx, you know it doesn't matter what you wear."

Sam nodded. Oh, yes, ma'am, she sure did know Jinx.

"Then you know she's going to turn up looking like Elizabeth Taylor—or Cher—whoever's the latest version of dressed-to-the-tits. Nobody's going to give you a second look."

Sam laughed. "She and Kitty and I were all together in school at Stanford. Back when Jinx was a beauty queen."

"First runner-up to Miss Arkansas. We thought for a while there Jinx was going to kill that girl what won."

And if she had, and if they'd hanged Jinx, Sam would have thrown a party to celebrate. But that was one thing about giving up the booze. You had to learn to give up hating people's guts. Alcoholics couldn't afford resentment. It was surely one hard lesson to learn. But that didn't mean she had to *like* her old rival. The one who'd been so pretty it'd make you puke. The one who'd horned in on her friendship with Kitty. The one who'd ripped off her best beau.

"I wouldn't exactly say Jinx and I are close," she said to Olive.

Olive hooted. "That's precisely what her momma says. My friend Loydell? The woman doesn't give two hoots for her one and only flesh and blood, but she makes the best of it. I reckon you'll make the best of it, too. In any case, it ought to be *some* party. They say a whole planeload of folks flew in from San Antonio, where Jinx'd been living before she came over for the races and met that man she's marrying. And them Texans know how to party. I myself have been looking forward to this shindig. A fat old lady like me don't get asked much to such fancy goings on. The last doodah I went to was over in Little Rock the night Bill was elected President. Me and Loydell got all dressed up and drove over and stood out in the yard of the Old Statehouse, yelled Woo Pig Soooooeee till we couldn't anymore. It was one of those times just like today, I was saying about it being so beautiful and all, I thought, Lord, I ain't ever going to be happier than I am right now. Take me if you want. But He didn't, so here I am, about to iron my blue dress."

"And I'm glad." Sam reached over and gave the fat old lady a big hug. "I'm glad you stuck around to be with me today."

"Me, too. I swear I don't know what you'd have done without me. Drove off in a ditch and starved to death, I reckon."

"Probably. Now, I've really got to scoot." Sam checked her watch. "Kitty's expecting me, and she's going to be screaming bloody murder if I don't get there in time to have a visit before the party." She hugged Olive again. "I'm *so* happy you're going to be there too. You save me a dance, okay?"

Olive cocked a finger at her. "Now that's an offer I'm holding you to."

TEN MINUTES LATER OLIVE HAD TURNED ON HER TALK show again. Sitting up there now were these eighteen-year-old girl Siamese twins who wanted to marry each other. Olive said, "I can't see as how it'd make any difference, can you, Pearl?" Then the bell sounded, and a four-door silver Mercedes about ten years old pulled up. A slender redhead stepped out and reached for the do-it-yourself unleaded supreme at the very same pump Sam had used.

"Would you look at that, Pearl? Are we having a run of pretty ladies today, or what?" Olive raised up off her stool to get a better look, pulling down her muumuu in the back where it had bunched up. "You see that yellow suit, that's genuine linen. That pretty white blouse is silk, and those pumps—that's real alligator, Pearl. Which reminds me of that Japanese tourist at the alligator farm in town who was carrying an alligator bag from one of them designers, leaned over too far, a big old 'gator snagged her bag like it was his Uncle Elmer he'd always had it in for, chomped it and her wallet, a thousand dollars in cash and a whole bunch of credit cards." Pearl barked. "I already told you that one? Well, you look out at that woman there, she'll keep you amused. Ain't she purty? And rich, got to be rich, driving that big car, you see those diamond studs in her ears, see 'em sparkling way over here? That's class *and* money, Pearl. Bet she comes in here and flips out a gold card. Or a platinum." Pearl barked again. "That's right. That's all the metal you see these days, none of them silver dollars I used to collect. We'd drop 'em in the big slots in Bubbles. Did you know that's what the Yankee gangsters used to call Hot Springs, Pearl? Idn't that cute? Watch out, now, here she comes. Wonder what her name is? Rita? Lucy? Something to match that red hair, I bet."

"Well, hello there," said the woman, breezing in with the same smile you'd swear she used when she had tea with the Queen of England. Olive took a look at the turned-up nose, small white teeth, milky skin, the faintest little laugh lines at the corners of the mouth and eyes—and put her at twenty-eight. Probably be good to fifty. "Beautiful afternoon, isn't it? Oh, my goodness, what a gorgeous dog. Is she a hunter?" asked the redhead, wrinkling up her nose. She had an overripe accent, like maybe she was from Charleston, Savannah, one of those. But she had a West Coast kind of body, slim, strong like a young boy's. She looked like she jogged five miles a day or rode a bike.

"Coon dog," said Olive. "Redbone hound's the best coon dog money can buy. Pearl here belongs to my grandbaby, Bobby." At that Pearl flopped right over, belly up, tongue out, drooling like a perfect fool. The redhead leaned over and goosed her for a minute with long thin fingers, which were pretty, but looked like they knew a few tricks. On her right hand sparkled an emerald-cut diamond that had to be at least four carats, maybe six. She said, "Dogs are so much better than people, don't you think? I used to keep English spaniels. But I can't now, I travel so much." The smile on her beautiful face was a heartbreaker. If it were a record, thought Olive, she'd play it over and over again on rainy afternoons. Then the redhead straightened in one long motion and pulled a bill for the gas from the alligator bag, and handed it to Olive. "Do you mind if I use your ladies' room?" The pretty lady glanced at her gold-and-stainless steel watch, the kind you see in fancy ads in magazines. "In fifteen minutes I'm due at a meeting in Hot Springs, at the Arlington, and I need to freshen up."

"Why, not at all. Please help yourself." Olive heard herself flossing up her inflection as if she were a grand lady with appointments to keep instead of a former hooker/waitress now convenience store proprietor/gas jockey. Though she did have Jinx's party this evening. "You go outside, turn right, around to the side, you can't miss it. But don't you want your change?" Then Olive looked down at the bill she was holding. A fifty. You hardly ever saw one of those.

The woman's smile tucked in at the corners as she nodded at the bill. "I'm hope that's not inconvenient." She stared back down in her bag, then lifted eyes of emerald—just like the cut of that perfect diamond on her perfect finger. "I'm afraid it's the smallest thing I have." Then she did the tiniest little shrug, followed by something with her fanny you'd say was cousin to the hootchy-kootch if she wasn't such a lady and you didn't know that she *really* had to go to the bathroom.

Which set Olive to worrying about the shape the Ladies was in. Oh, she'd emptied the trash like she did every morning, made sure there was plenty of toilet paper and paper towels and pink liquid soap. But she hadn't mopped it. She wished she'd swabbed it down with Lysol and hung some of those little huck towels with the day of the week done in cross-stitch and laid in some of that pink carnation soap her grandbaby, Bobby, gave her for Christmas four years ago, still in the box, Olive was saving it for something special. But Olive handed over the $32.45 in change and hoped for the best, bathroom-wise. "Thank you so much," said the redhead stepping outside.

Olive shook her head. "There's them that has, and them that don't, Pearl. You know that? That's the way God made the world. 'Course there's them that say there's only so much people stuff in the universe and it keeps getting recycled, so there's always another chance, depending on what you did the time before, you could come back a millionaire. I know what *I* want to be next time around."

Pearl sat up and said, "Rowooo, rowooo," like she had a big old coon up a tree and could see the shine of his eyes, *her* idea of nirvana.

Olive said, "Nope. Don't wanta be like that redhead, either, driving that big silver car. I already was a pretty woman, and look how that turned out."

Pearl muttered something deep in her broad chest.

"That's right," said Olive. "*You.* I'm coming back as a coon dog with a momma who owns a store full of snacks and nothing better to do than sit around and spoil me all day. Though, I wouldn't mind having that one's figure again. I used to have me one like that—and a pretty pale yellow suit. Wouldn't that look swell at Jinx's party? I think it'd be perfect, early evening do. . . ."

Just about then, the lady whose suit Olive was coveting was striding back to her car, turning and waving with that stiff little motion like you see beauty queens do, when suddenly she yelled bloody murder. It was the kind of scream that you used to hear from the blonde in monster movies. The kind of scream that let you know the screamer wasn't fooling around. There really was something out there in the dark that was going to scare the bejesus out of you. More likely it'd eat you alive. Olive thought maybe the redhead'd stepped on a snake, so she grabbed her .44 Bulldog from behind the counter, and hit the door running, making sure Pearl didn't escape. "You stay!"

The lady was still screaming. Then she saw Olive with the revolver and threw her arms up in the air. "Oh, my God! Don't shoot, please don't shoot me!"

"Lady, are you crazy?" Olive was looking all around for the snake. Where'd it go?

The lady was jumping up and down hollering. "I've lost my ring! My diamond ring!"

Her ring? That's what all this fuss was about? Then once again Olive saw that emerald-cut sparkler catching the fluorescent lights, and she commenced to joining in the screaming. "Where? How? Tell me exactly what you did."

Now the lady was jumping up and down, shaking her wrists. Then stopping to stare at the right hand like if she looked at it long enough, her ring would reappear. "I took it off in the ladies' room to wash my hands, and then, well"—she started to wail—"I don't remember!"

"Yes, you do. Just calm down. If you get ahold of yourself, you'll see what you did." Olive knew how that was. How you did things automatically. Driving, even. Like when you were thinking about something real hard, you'd start off in your car in Hot Springs, next thing you knew you'd be in Pine Bluff, forty miles away, not remember a dad-blamed thing.

"I was thinking about Dean, Dean's my boyfriend who gave me the ring." The lady broke into some serious tears.

Olive wouldn't have figured her for a crybaby, but you never knew. She could hear Pearl yodeling away inside. Pearl was dying to poke her nose in their business, see if it was something she could chase through the brambles, torture across a bog.

"Listen, lady," Olive said.

"Madeline."

"That's a right pretty name. So listen, Madeline, let's just collect ourselves here. I know we'll find that ring."

Madeline was wiping her eyes, making black smudges on her knuckles. That and the runny nose, she looked like a kid.

"Come on, now. You only went from here to the Ladies. We'll retrace your steps, find it for sure."

So that's what Olive and Madeline did. Olive slipped the revolver in the pocket of her muumuu, and together they examined every square inch of the oil-spotted concrete. They poked at old chewing gum, at gravel, at weeds growing up through a crack. They inspected every last centimeter of the Ladies itself, though Madeline swore that she knew she hadn't dropped it in there. The more she thought about it, the more she remembered shaking her fingers one last time in the sunshine to make sure they were dry before she put on her ring because she was prone to dermatitis, she had sensitive skin. The ring had simply disappeared into thin air.

Well, it couldn't have done that, said Olive. Things just didn't dematerialize. They weren't snatched up by haints. Olive was a practical woman who'd always lived in the here and now, and by God, that diamond was here, and it was here *now*, and they would find it if they just persevered. So they did the search all over again.

Frontwards. Backwards. Sideways. Widening the area each time, but with no luck. Madeline was crying all the while, blubbering like a baby, talking about how much that diamond was worth. A quarter of a million dollars, she said. Insured, of course. But she couldn't report it missing. Not after that robbery that she and Dean had had at his beach house last summer, when the thieves broke in and knocked them around and tied them up and took every last piece of jewelry she had. My stars, said Olive. Dean had given her this ring as a sort of consolation prize while they were looking around to replace things with the insurance money. Not that you could ever replace those pieces with sentimental value. Of course not, said Olive, shaking her head, remembering that pink-gold locket with the little engraved roses, pictures of her first dog, Pokey, inside, that a john had ripped right off her neck forty years ago. Thinking about it still made her mad. But because of that robbery, said Madeline, her insurance premiums were already so high, if she reported this . . . Besides, she wanted the ring that Dean had given her, the very one, not some replacement. Then she broke into sobs so heartrending, Olive almost joined her.

After a while Madeline got control of herself, blew her nose in a white linen handkerchief trimmed with both cutwork and lace, rocked back on those alligator heels, and moaned, "On top of that, now I'm late for my meeting. And it's an *important* meeting."

Olive was sure it was. What other kind of meeting would a woman wrapped in linen and silk and alligator and diamonds and gold and stainless steel and a silver Mercedes be going to?

Madeline reached in her alligator bag and pulled out a little notepad and a gold pen. She scribbled her name, *Madeline Brooks*, and the words *Arlington Hotel, Hot Springs*. "That's where I'm staying."

Olive nodded. Anybody who knew anything about

Hot Springs knew the Arlington. It and the Palace were the two grand hotels left from the good old days when Hot Springs was something. Al Capone had kept a suite there.

"I hate to leave." Madeline turned her head and closed her eyes and threw her naked right hand over her pretty white-silk-and-yellow-linen-covered breast. "But I must. With the hope, of course, that I'll hear from you soon. That you'll call and say that you've found my ring and you're waiting for me to come and claim it and give you your thousand-dollar reward."

Olive gasped. A thousand dollars! Now wouldn't that come in handy? That trip she and Loydell were planning to Morocco.

"Cash," said Madeline. "To anyone who finds Dean's token of affection. Oh, Olive, please, please, find my ring." Tears danced in her emerald green eyes.

Olive had never seen anyone with eyes that color. "Don't you worry your pretty little head about it. Unless the angels have swooped down and carried it off for the Good Lord to wear on His pinky, you're gonna hear from me soon. I promise you that." With any luck, she'd find it right after Madeline left, bring it into town with her on her way to Jinx's party, stop into the Arlington, call Madeline up on the house phone. . . .

"Oh, Olive!" Madeline clasped her to her bosom and gave her a big hug. "I know you'll be my salvation." Reluctantly she stepped into the Mercedes and pulled the door to with that solid kerchunk like a bank vault closing, and waving a sad little Miss America wave, drove off.

3

THERE WERE TWO MESSAGES WAITING FOR SAM AT THE hotel desk. The first one said, Call Harry. That was a laugh. What did he want, to fill her in on a forgotten detail of his trysts with Barbie? And how'd he know where she was, anyway? She handed the yellow slip of paper back to the desk clerk and said, "Could you burn this, please?"

The second message was from Kitty telling her to get herself down to the baths. Now! So she dumped her bags in her room, stripped, grabbed up the mono-grammed terry cloth robe and paper slippers the hotel had so graciously provided, and rang for the cute little gilded elevator, which took her to the spa on the Palace's second floor.

The reception area was a Moorish temple done in tiles of turquoise and maroon. Behind the desk the reception-ist wore a platinum beehive and rhinestone catglasses and called her Honey. She took Sam's room number and pointed her through the pink curtains, straight back to the twenties. The waiting room sported wooden ceiling fans, walls of spanky clean white tile and gray marble, and mazelike floors of pink and white octagons.

Kitty threw herself at Sam from a scalloped green metal lawn chair. "Oooooooh, I am so glad to see you!"

The two old friends kissed cheeks and hugged. The top of the five-foot-two Kitty's strawberry blond head tucked neatly under Sam's chin. She said, "I know. I almost died without your smart mouth running in my ear the past twenty-four hours." And that was true. The visit with Olive had been great, but nothing beat old friends.

"Speaking of dying. I don't know why you didn't fly. Did it rain all the way? I was just sure you were roadkill by now. You all agitated, driving eighty miles an hour."

"I never topped seventy-five," Sam lied. She was famous for her speeding tickets, and her impatience. "The driving was good, I needed to work off some nervous energy."

"Well, sit right down here and tell all." Kitty patted the chair beside hers.

So Sam repeated the tale of woe she'd shared with Olive and had already told Kitty the night before on the telephone, filling in more details. But woe was like that. You needed to twist it around and chew on it several times before you could begin to get the hurt out.

Kitty fell back in her chair, her robe flapping. "I say shoot both the sons of bitches. Him and her."

"Oh, you always say that. But you don't mean it."

"What the hell are you talking about? I never say things I don't mean." Which was a joke. Kitty was in the public relations business in New Orleans. She lied for a living.

Sam said, "Let me remind you that twenty-odd years ago, back in school, when Jinx, this very same Jinx whose *third* engagement party you're here for"—she held up three fingers—"ran off with Frank, my very best boyfriend in the whole world up until that time, you said the same thing. Shoot 'em. *Moi*, I agreed it was a superlative idea. Then, I start chatting up our friends in the Panthers about a gun, what did you do?"

"I said you were nuts. Locked you in our dorm room. Reminded you that all that bourbon you used to consume made you forget the difference between Southern hyperbole and reality."

"So what does that say about my killing Harry and this blonde now?"

"Says you're sober, which means you'd know more about what you were doing, plus you have all that crime-reporting business under your belt. I'd say you could probably get away with it."

Sam laughed. "While I'm at it, you think I could get away with doing Jinx, too? Since I missed my chance the first time around?"

Kitty got that prim look on her face that meant she was going to say something that would make Sam want to slap her. And sure enough she did.

"Now, you know you don't still hate Jinx."

Sam slammed a hand on her forehead. "By God, you're right. How could I forget that? We went over the same ground when you first tried to drag me up here for this stupid party. *You* feel sorry for her—which, of course, is akin to feeling sorry for Attila the Hun because his momma wasn't nice to him. And *I* let go of all my mean, ugly, and vicious feelings about her eons ago. I don't think about her any more often than I think about—oh, say rattlesnake bellies."

Kitty's eyes narrowed. "You're lying through those pearly teeth, and you know it. Otherwise why wouldn't you come to her party? She invited you. I know the invitation came in the mail the same day as mine."

"Jinx probably invited the entire South. And Texas. Especially Texas, since she made off with their lottery."

Kitty had her forefinger ready to point. "*That's* why you let that green-eyed monster get ahold of you again. You're jealous because Jinx won that million dollars, tax-free."

Sam, who had inherited that and more from her long-deceased parents, narrowed her eyes and sniffed. "An engagement party for your third time around, when you're forty-one years old, is tacky, and you know it."

"Since when did you become Miss Manners? You don't give a rip about that kind of thing."

Kitty was right, but Sam didn't let that stop her from trashing Jinx. "I bet she's going to have a long white gown, a four-tiered cake, and six bridesmaids, their shoes and dresses dyed lime or puce or whatever to match the punch. There'll be a video of her getting her ring—four carats. No, six. Jinx wouldn't marry anybody for fewer than six. And a cake at this party tonight with a music box inside playing a recording of Jinx and the groom—what's his name?"

"Speed. Speed McKay."

"Sounds like a pool hustler to me; anyway, a recording of Jinx and Speed, blathering about the day they met."

"Sammy, you're over the top. Your mind's come unhinged over this Harry thing. What you're saying about Jinx, I think this is called displacement. You're furious with Harry, but you're dumping on Jinx."

It was maddening to have a friend who knew her so well. Sam absolutely was doing that very thing. She was losing it, big-time. She sounded like a jealous sixteen-year-old girl. And she *hated* the idea that she was so het up about Jinx's wedding because of her own problems of the heart. Resenting Jinx because she was getting married again just when Harry had strayed. June, moon, croon, puke. She was bored with the whole concept. Maybe she'd find a nice nunnery to check into for a good long sulk, even if she wasn't Catholic.

Just then a short middle-aged black woman all in white—T-shirt, shorts, socks, sneakers—sauntered up to the two women and patted Sam on the shoulder. "Hi, baby, I'm June, and I'm going to take care of you. Come on over here with me." She nodded at Kitty. "Sweet thing, somebody'll be along for you directly."

Back at the Gas 'N Grub, Olive Adair was down on her hands and knees talking to herself. *It's here, I know it's here*. Wiping the sweat out of her eyes. It could get pretty hot in Arkansas in late April. Hot enough to make an old lady think maybe she was about to get sunstroke if she didn't take a break from searching for that diamond ring.

Besides, Pearl was about to have a fit. Howling, Ooohuroo, ooohuroo, in front of the soda cooler as if Olive didn't know how that felt, a woman left lonely, which was the title of her favorite song by Janice Joplin. It was on the album, *Pearl*, she'd named the dog after. Bobby, her grandbaby, hadn't had time to name her before they dragged him off to the slammer.

"Momma understands, sugar." Olive leaned over and gave Pearl a hug, then reached into the cooler and grabbed herself another Delaware Punch. Whew! There was nothing like an ice-cold pop to make an old lady feel better.

Unless it was a thousand-dollar reward. Olive rested back on the cooler and took another swig. "How would that be, Pearl? You and me, we'd throw ourselves in that Sunliner, drive into town, have ourselves a little vacation right here at home." She glanced out at the old black-and-gold retractable hardtop convertible shrouded with a tarp. It was a classic, more than one young hotshot had offered her good money for it, but Olive wouldn't let it go. It belonged to Bobby. He was supposed to be getting out any minute now, she'd been saving the Sunliner for him all this time. Kept it in A-1 condition, too. "Then we'd drive into town and check into the Arlington. No, the Palace. I always favored the Palace, better class of clientele, and I ought to know, having entertained gentlemen from both plenty of times. Get ourselves freshened up, go downstairs, stroll through that pretty lobby, watch ourselves in all those gold mirrors, I bet they make us look slim, take ourselves a table on the veranda, order ourselves a shrimp salad and some real sweet iced tea. Watch the passing scene on Central Avenue. Ask the waiter to call and make us a reservation for a bath and massage a little later."

Pearl barked.

"You like that? Well, then we'd take us a little nap in our suite, get up and dress for the evening. You remember that dress I used to have of lemon yellow dotted swiss? It had the most beautiful collar trimmed in lace, I think that's what Madeline's suit reminded me of."

Pearl said, "Ooooruha."

"No, I guess you don't. That was before your time. Anyway, we'd stroll down Central, go look at us some art. There's all these new galleries now in the old buildings across from Bathhouse Row. Boy, have things changed. Back before air-conditioning, standing out on the sidewalk you could hear the results of the races at Santa Anita, Saratoga, Pimlico broadcast over the loudspeakers came right through the open windows of those same buildings in the hot weather. Pearl, would you *hush up!*"

Then Olive looked around and saw what had the hound so agitated. There was a tramp cutting across the edge of her property, a tall old man in a filthy long-sleeved undershirt and a pair of what looked like green fatigues belted with a rope. He had long white hair under a straw hat, a scraggly gray beard, and a sticky-looking handlebar mustache.

Well, God knows there were plenty of folks poorer than her these days, people who didn't have the luxury of worrying about not meeting next month's rent, worrying about bankruptcy, had already lost what little they had, including their homes, lots of which were pretty pitiful anyway. Things had gotten so bad under those damned Republicans, rich folks sucking off not only all the cream, but purt near down to the bottom of the bottle, you couldn't drive more than five miles in any direction in this country anymore you didn't see people living in shacks, in chicken coops, in that kind of cab-over

trailer that'd fit on the back of a pickup truck, no matter
what there was always a bunch of snot-nosed kids playing out in the dirt, old clothes flapping on a single line.
It'd break your heart. Olive was about to reach back in
the cooler, pull out a cold drink to take out to the old
man, he looked so hot, when suddenly he stopped at
the edge of the pavement, reached down, and picked up
something, his mouth falling open like a black cave. He
stuck whatever it was in his pocket in a godawful hurry,
and looking behind him like a booger-bear might be after
him, took off down the road.

Jesus H. Christ! He'd found the ring!

June led Sam off into a small room with a dressing
area and a tub. "Take that robe off, honey, hang it up
there." Sam felt a little shy, standing there in the
altogether—like maybe she ought to do more than fast-
walking three miles a day, which wasn't doing a thing
for her upper arms, and what the heck was happening
to her waist—but June, who handled naked ladies all day
long, didn't give her a second look.

She pointed Sam toward the deep long tub, sort of like
a horse trough of ancient white porcelain with a contrap-
tion at the end that looked like an oversized egg beater.
"Y'all friends, you and that women you talking to? Unh-
huh. Mozelle'll take care of her in a minute. Ain't nothing like girlfriends. Where y'all from?"

While Sam talked, June gave her a hand into the tub,
and the water was hot, not the kind of hot when you've
overdone it filling the tub and you have to jump out
again before your tootsies parboil, but good hot, and
growing hotter as June opened the tap. "How's that? Tell
me if it's too much."

It was wonderful. Absolutely aces. She could already
feel the tension of the long drive melting away.

Then June scrubbed Sam all over with a loofah and
pink liquid soap out of a plastic jug, chatting away about

what a small world it was. "Ladies run into each other in here all the time. Had a couple last week, had to be seventy years old, hadn't seen each other since high school somewhere up in Ohio. You ain't never heard so much hollering in your life. Liddy, that's the old lady outside at the desk with the sparkly glasses, she called in here, had her fingers on the nine-one-one, thought we'd drowned somebody for sure." June laughed, showing perfect white teeth in a chocolate face so clean and smooth Sam wanted to lick it, see if it'd taste as good as it looked.

She asked June, "Are all the bathhouses like this?"

"Well, strictly speaking, this ain't a bathhouse. I mean, it's a bath, but it's in a hotel. The bathhouses are those eight buildings you see parading on down the hill from here on Central. Only one of them's operating, the Buckstaff. And the Fordyce, it's all fixed up as a museum. You go in there, you want to see yourself some glamorous. It's got lobbies and verandas and ladies' parlors and billiard rooms, a fountain, stained glass, treatment rooms, a gym. Joe Louis himself worked out there. 'Course, the Dallas Cowboys been here. *Big* old boys." June laughed.

"So all the others are closed?"

"No, there's a restaurant called Bubbles in one of them, on the *main* floor." Then June sniffed, like there was more to be told, but her time with Sam was up. She slapped a hot white washcloth over Sam's brow and plopped two paper cups full of hot water on the bathtub ledge. "You drink that, same water inside and out you, holler if you need anything, I'll come back and get you in about fifteen minutes." Then she flipped on the egg beater, and the water bubbled and surged.

Sam stretched out, sighed, and let go. She was tired of conversation anyway. Thank you, God, for hydrotherapy. Was there anything better than hot water pumping over your bare bod? Well, yes, there was. But she didn't want to think about him or his damned brass bed.

"Sammy? Can you hear me?" So much for silence. That was Kitty, over in the next cubicle. "Listen, after the party's over we can snuggle up in my bed, have a serious talk about Harry, what you ought to do. But in the meantime, don't fall asleep, we've got to be downstairs at six-thirty sharp."

"Whoowee!" June's voice floated over the divider. "Y'all must be here for that McKay do."

"I'd say Watson, because we're friends of the bride-to-be." Kitty spoke as if she were being asked which side of the church she wanted to sit on.

I myself am an enemy of the bride, thought Sam. An enemy of long standing.

"Ain't that something," said June. "Miz Loydell Watson's daughter, the one that was on the TV talking about them lottery altars she builds. They work, too, unh-huh. She won that million down in Texas. They say her fiancé, that Speed McKay, he's rich, too. Ain't that the way it always is, them that gots gots. Them that nots nots. It don't hardly seem fair."

"You didn't say he was rich," Sam called to Kitty.

"Are you starting in again?"

"I'm just curious."

"I bet." Kitty wasn't having any of it. "Jinx allowed as how he was comfortable. That's all I know except that he's lived in New Orleans. Not that I ever heard of him before, but I'm sure he's very nice."

Sam grinned. *Not that I ever heard of him* is the kiss of death in New Orleans society, where nobody cares how much money your family has or had, but their great-great-great grandmother better have known yours, or, darlin', socially speaking, you might as well move to Slidell.

"Unh-huh," said June. "There's lots of rich folks here in Arkansas nobody ever heard of. Like that Mr. Sam

Walton, owned them Wal-Marts. Man owned half the United States, before anybody even knew his name. Mr. Don Tyson, the chicken man, Mr. Witt Stephens, natural gas, it's the same thing. Arkansas white folks, they not like other Southern people. They kind of a mix of South and West, more West, some say, they just keep kind of close to themselves, doing business with their own, all of a sudden other peoples figures out they *rich*, you know what I mean?"

"So what does he do, this Speed McKay?" Sam asked, her tone innocent as a spring day.

"Lordy, I don't know," said June. "Breezed into town during the racing season out at Oaklawn. But makes an impression, you know what I mean? Comes in the hotel, *big* tipper. The kind belongs to the Oaklawn Club out at the track, fancy folks. Sugar," June patted Sam on the arm, "your time's up. Let's get you out of there 'fore you pucker." Then she leaned over the tub, gave Sam a hand, toweled her off, and wrapped her in a white cotton toga.

Next June led her out into a long room where a half-dozen mummies lay stretched out on tables. "Now, you want to go in the steam or you just want the wrap?" June was pointing over at an old-fashioned metal cabinet they'd open up and sit you down on a chair, then close it, you with only your neck sticking out. No, thank you. Once Sam had begun working a crime beat fifteen years ago, she wanted her hands free and her back to the wall. "Okay, then come lie down"—June patted one of the padded tables—"and tell June where it hurts."

Well, for starters, her neck, her shoulders, her knees. She wasn't saying anything about her heart. June piled on the hot packs, then tucked another sheet around her tight, slapped an icy towel on her forehead. Sam felt like a big pink noodle, way beyond *al dente*. She said as much to Kitty on the next table, who grunted. Then June was talking to someone. "I don't care what you say, they's

professionals. Gangsters! Friends of Mr. You Know Who.
You *see* them men in them sharkskin suits up in the lobby
the past two evenings? Wearing them big diamonds, gold
rings? Who you think they are, Mozelle? Ice cream
salesmens?"

Sam opened one eye to spy Mozelle, the short round
light-skinned woman attending to Kitty. Mozelle snorted.
"Them's friends of Jinx Watson and Speed McKay come
to town for the big party. That's who."

"Who's Mr. You Know Who?" asked Sam, but no one
answered.

June said to Mozelle, "You think what you want to,
but I'm telling you, they's stuff going down. They was
a jockey riding a favorite, end of Derby week, his horse
lost, and he *died*."

"Girl," said Mozelle, "everybody knows, it was in the
paper, the trainer told that boy to ride that horse one
way, that boy says Uh-huh, then he does just the opposite, which is because he is from one of those countries
down in South America, he didn't even speak good English, dudn't understand what the trainer's saying, that
horse got mad, balked, went down, and fell on top of
him, broke that boy's neck. Sounds like you trying to
make out gangsters had something to do with that. Ain't
even any of those trainers Italian, far as I know."

"Gangsters ain't all Italian," June muttered. "Owney
Madden, lived right here in Hot Springs, big-time gangster in New York during the Prohibition, he was Irish,
born in England. Makes him Irish, just like Mr. You
Know Who. And I know because my Aunt Odessie used
to do their fine laundry, the Maddens."

"Who's Mr. You Know Who?" Sam tried again, but
then from over the top of a massage cubicle came a high-
pitched white country-woman voice. The nasal kind that
can cut through steel saying, "It was the Lord's will that
jockey boy died, is what it was."

June made a face and whispered, "That's Ruby, she's a Foot-washing Baptist."

A fundamentalist sect. Sam had heard about them since she was a child, but she'd never known *exactly* what it was they did. If she could get Ruby to talk with her, would foot-washing make a chapter for her book, a collection of pieces called *American Weird?* Or would that be too irreligious?

Thwap thwap thwap. It sounded as if Ruby were handling a side of beef.

June gave Sam a little wink, then called, "You think the Lord killed that jockey, Miss Ruby?"

"One of His agents did. Nobody saw it, but from what I hear, it was a haint. Witch, warlock. But it all ends up the same thing, transmutation, reconfiguration." *Thwap thwap.*

"How come the Lord did it, you think?" asked June.

"That horse betting. Lord don't like betting. Don't like anybody has anything to do with it. Gambling's an abomination in the eyes of the Lord. That's what I told Loydell Watson, right to her face, her daughter getting ready to marry that McKay man. What I heard, he was out at that track nearly every day betting money on them racehorses. He'll come to no good. 'Course that Jinx Watson got the curse on her, too, taking that lottery money. It's all the same thing."

"Whoowee," said June. "Witches out killing everybody got anything to do with gambling? They got themselves a row to hoe."

"There's no such thing as a witch," mumbled Mozelle. "Even if there was, God ain't got nothing to do with them. Woman's crazy."

"I heard that, Mozelle Williams." Ruby delivered one last thump to her victim, then stepped outside her cubicle. She was pinch-faced with inky black hair, tall, pencil-thin, pushing sixty, wearing what looked like a pink nylon nurse's uniform zipped up to her chin. "And I'm here to tell you you are wrong. Wrong as a person can be, and I get down on my knees every night and pray for your eternal soul."

Mozelle made a sour face. "I hope you don't be setting no witches on me when you doing that."

"I'm setting the Lord on you, Mozelle, that's what. Witches, I told you, sometimes they be the Lord's agents."

"I thought witches worked for the devil," Kitty piped up.

Ruby narrowed her eyes. She knew an infidel when she heard one. Disbeliever. Fun-poker. Heathen. "Check your First Samuel, Twenty-eight, you want to see witches."

"In the Bible?" said Mozelle. "I never saw no witches in my Bible."

"Well, you didn't know where to look." Obviously Ruby did, as she marched smartly over to a desk of chipped green enamel, opened a drawer, reached in deep, and pulled out a white pebble-grain volume stamped in gold, flipped right to chapter and verse. Then she wet her thin lips, peered down her sharp nose, cleared her throat, and read the account of the witch of Endor summoning up the spirit of Samuel at the request of Saul.

"Well, I don't care what you say," said June. "No witch killed that jockey boy. And furthermore, nobody I know ever saw a witch in their whole lives, and I know some grannies who speak regularly with folks done passed over."

"Well," Ruby said. "You wouldn't necessarily know one if you saw it. They take all forms." Sam couldn't wait to hear what they were.

"Unh-huh," said June.

Ruby said, "I know you don't believe me. But listen to this. There was this woman from over near Pine Bluff, her cat was a witch. And what the cat used to do, in the night it would swap spirits with the woman. So the woman would go out, walking in her sleep, and do all kinds of witchy things."

"My Aunt Odessie, she walks in her sleep," said June. "Mozelle, I told you about her. Poor thing."

"Nobody wants to hear about your old auntie. Would you let me finish this story?" said Ruby with what Sam didn't think was a very Christian attitude. "Anyway, one night this woman's spirit is in the cat, and the cat's spirit is in the woman, and lo and behold, the cat got out through a rip in the screen and got run over in the middle of the road. And that poor woman, to right this very day, is in a sanitorium over in Little Rock in an irreversible condition. Can't speak a word. You ask her something, she just meows."

"Ummmmhuh. Ain't that something?" said Mozelle.

Then Kitty piped up. "What I want to know is, when she goes to the bathroom, does the woman use the toilet or the litter box?"

Sam watched Ruby's face turn to vinegar. No doubt about it. Right now the odds of her interviewing this Foot-washing Baptist for *American Weird* stood about a million to one. If she wanted to do some work, she'd poke around, find out about Mr. You Know Who, see if what he was up to might fit the bill.

Back at the Gas 'N Grub, Olive's heart was pounding. "Wait! Wait!" She ran out after the tramp who'd found her ring.

He wheeled with a wild look in his eye. "What do you want?" His voice sounded rusty, like a porch swing that had been out all winter.

"That's mine, what you've got in your pocket."

"I ain't got nothing in my pocket." He wiped at his nose.

"You do, too. You do, and I know what it is. It's a ring! Show me it ain't!"

He stepped back, his eyes slits. "So what if it is? What's it to you?"

"It's mine. It was on my property, and if you don't hand it over, I'm calling the police."

Olive stepped right up close to the bum expecting him to smell like a hog, but he didn't. He was plenty shifty-eyed, though. Real pale gray eyes that didn't give back any light, just like cold cement. She wished that Loydell was here to get a load of this sucker. Loydell had been the matron for almost forty years for the women prisoners, when there was any, at the Garland County Jail. And Loydell knew a real criminal when she saw one. Olive was sure she'd say this fellow was the genuine article. She wasn't going to spend another single solitary minute feeling sorry for him, especially since he was standing between her and a thousand bucks.

"Are you deaf, old man? I said if you don't give me that ring, I'm calling the cops."

He took the ring out of his pocket—it was the very one Madeline had dropped, big old emerald-cut diamond, bigger than any the tourists had ever picked up at the Crater of Diamonds over near Murfreesboro—and stared at it for a long minute. Then he said, "Can you prove it's yours?"

Well. That made her step back a bit, catch her breath. But she knew whose it was, and she knew who was going to get that thousand-dollar reward for it, and if she didn't, it'd be over her dead body. "I most certainly can," she said.

He waggled a dirty finger in her face. "I don't think so. I think if you could prove it, it wouldn't have taken you so long to say. What *I* think is finders keepers, and I'm the finder."

Olive could see the thousand-dollar reward slipping away. If she called the cops and they came, there was that thing about possession being nine-tenths of the law, and this son of a bitch definitely had the ring in his mitt.

Which probably meant he'd get the reward. The very idea made her chest hurt.

"Okay. I'll give you fifty dollars for it. For that you can buy yourself a whole lot of Thunderbird."

"Ha! You must think I'm a fool, I'd sell you a diamond like this for fifty bucks. It's worth at least a thousand. Pawnshop'd give me a thousand, for sure. I'll just walk on up the road, Hot Springs's lousy with pawnshops."

He was bluffing. Olive turned away.

"Okay, okay. Seven-fifty. I'll take seven-fifty."

"I wasn't born yesterday." She said that over her shoulder, walking back toward the store. Pearl was standing right inside the door, her tail wagging, her nose up against the glass. Every time Olive saw that sweet face, her heart turned over. They were right, what they said about dogs. Nobody'd ever loved her as much as Pearl. She turned back to the tramp. "A hundred's my best offer."

"Five."

At that, she'd still clear another five hundred on the deal. But if she'd just looked harder a little while ago, she could have had the whole enchilada. At five hundred, the suite at the Palace would shrink to a single room. Her long weekend of at-home luxury telescope to a couple of days. She shook her head. "Two, and that's my best offer."

"Four."

It looked like three hundred was going to be it. Olive tried two-twenty-five. Two-fifty. But three it was. Three once, three twice, three thrice, she had herself a genuine emerald-cut diamond ring for three hundred dollars on which she could clear seven hundred, after she got the reward. . . .

But wait a danged minute. Who said she had to call Madeline at the Arlington? If the ring was worth a quarter of a million, she could sell it herself, rake in God knows how much. Now she saw herself back at the Palace registration desk, Pearl loping along beside her, herself saying, Thank you kindly, a penthouse suite will be just fine. She was calling room service, inviting Loydell to join her, winning a high stakes poker game, chucking the Gas 'N Grub altogether. . . .

"Lady, you gonna give me the cash?" The tramp was waiting with his dirty hand on the counter, palm up.

"Oh, sure. Just a minute." She didn't have but about a hundred in the register, and she didn't want him to see her reach down under for the cash box. Of course, she still had the revolver in her pocket, could feel the weight of it, if he tried anything funny. He smiled. He had nice teeth for a bum. Then he held the ring out in his right hand for Olive to see again, speed her up. Pearl barked, and he leaned over like he was going to pat her. It was then Pearl lunged at him, snapped right in his face.

"Oh, my God! I'm so sorry," said Olive. Pearl, you bad dog, she was about to say, until she saw that Pearl had snatched the scraggly beard and mustache away. Underneath, the tramp was smooth and tan and clean and not nearly as old as she'd thought.

"You're not a bum! You're some kind of . . . fake. Some kind of phony." And then as she said the words, Olive got it. No indeed, she wasn't born yesterday. In fact, she was so old that she'd forgotten some of what she once knew, what she'd learned living the life. But now she remembered. Bait and switch. A con game, old as the hills. As old as human greed. And she'd been greedy. That's how con games worked. You had to be greedy to get took. She reached for the phone. Now she really was calling the police.

"Put the phone down, lady." His voice wasn't creaky anymore. It wasn't young, either, but it was strong. And mean.

Pearl growled, showing her teeth. She was a big powerful dog.

Shit, Doc Miller said to himself. Mickey'd warned they ought not to take this one last mark before they rolled into Hot Springs. So he'd gone ahead anyway, just to show her. He couldn't stand it when she told him what to do. The lost ring was one he'd pulled a million times. And they'd done it together, the two of them, before. It always played like a charm. Mickey working outside, setting up the mark, pretending she'd dropped the ring, waiting up the road while he made the sting, pocketed the cash, left the twenty-five-dollar paste imitation with the pigeon, the blowoff being "Madeline" wouldn't be at the hotel, the mark would keep calling for the reward, then realizing the pretty lady never was going to be there, probably trying to sell the paste ring for a profit. By then, he and Mickey would be far away. Except, this time they wouldn't. They'd just be up the road, in Hot Springs.

No way, Mickey'd said that. That's how cons screw themselves, not being able to see that some chances weren't worth it. Like stealing two newspapers out of the vending machine. The cops pick you up, some little crap like that, the next time you know, they've run your priors, you're looking at a year in the county jail. For what? A thirty-five-cent paper?

Awh, come on, he'd said after they'd driven by the little convenience store. You turning weird? It's an old lady—and we'll bag enough to help pay the rent. This setup could be expensive, Mick. We don't know what all it's going to take.

What he did know was that this was the one he was going out on. Doc's retirement. His last job, not that he'd told Mickey that. He knew she'd be pissed, it'd queer the deal.

But if it went the way they'd planned, the boys'd talk about it for years. Of course, that wasn't the important part. What was important was getting out, buying himself that new Cadillac, silver to match that new Airstream. Jesus. He'd be in gypsy heaven. His ma would be proud. Of course, she'd been dead these twenty years.

Even more important was doing Jack Graham. That was the icing on the cake. They could pull this deal off, Doc'd have this loot on top of his nest egg—and the place was here, Hot Springs, Arkansas. Adopted home of Jack Graham, who'd never been very far away from Doc's mind since that afternoon Jack had called him out in New Orleans. Beat him up. Broke his nose. Whole bunch of Jack's friends standing around, laughing their asses off. Big Jack, Smilin' Jack, *he* was the one who queered the deal with that horse in the first place, if you asked Doc. Blamed it on him. Made him look small.

Well, Doc had gone to Jack's house and left his calling card, hadn't he? But it wasn't enough. Whatever he'd done, it would never be enough until Jack couldn't smile anymore. That's why Doc wanted to do this now. Pull this job off and put an end to Jack all in one fell swoop.

It was like it was meant to be. That's what Doc's mama would say if she were here. She'd close her eyes, run her fingers through her gold coin necklaces. Not that gypsies believed in the phony magic they sold to the *gaji*, but they believed in signs. And this kind of symmetry was a sign. It was meant to be, marching right into the Jack's territory to pull off this scam, grabbing the boodle while pissing in Jack's yard. If he went ahead and took Jack out, Doc could begin his retirement relaxed.

But none of that was going to happen if he had to do a little sleep-over in the county jail right now.

He grabbed Olive's wrist.

"Owh!" she hollered. "Let go, you're hurting me!"

At that, the dog locked onto his calf, just above his boot, her sharp teeth sinking deep. He reached over to a shelf and jerked up a quart bottle of apple juice, knocked the dog in the head with it, hard. The dog's jaw released, and she tumbled to the floor.

"You son of a bitch!" the old woman screamed. His head snapped. She had his full attention now. Her face was bright red, her mouth trembling. He watched her hand slide down the front of her big purple-and-green muumuu, reach into her pocket and find what he was afraid she was going to find. It was a powerful gun, the Bulldog. It'd blow a man's stomach out, splatter his brains all over the wall. He could see what would happen if he didn't reach his hand out, grab her arm, she was holding it way out, too far from her body, asking for it practically, it wouldn't be hard to twist the gun loose, that part was easy, she was an old woman. The part that he'd forgotten (for a similar scenario had happened before and would probably happen again, obstacles like this having a way of cluttering up the crooked streets of Doc's life) was the sweet shock of release when he knocked her face down with one punch, grasped her fat neck from behind and squeezed. After that, it didn't take long at all.

4

A WHILE LATER MICKEY AND DOC WERE STANDING IN THE big yellow kitchen of the rambling two-story house set back in the woods five miles west of Hot Springs. Built of stone sometime in the twenties, the house backed onto Lake Ouachita, a large blue lake with many fingers. Mickey and Doc had been going at it for some time now, but she hadn't heard anything that made sense.

She said, "Explain it to me one more time, please, Doc. Now, I know I'm stupid. . . ."

"You can cut the sarcasm, okay? I told you, the old lady wasn't going for it." He was rolling up the sleeves of the white shirt he'd changed into, that and some khakis, shucking the tramp duds. "She was giving me a hassle, I decided to blow, and she came after me. I jumped in her car and hit it. Got here five minutes ahead of you, washed up." He peered into the refrigerator. "There's not a damned thing in here except some ketchup."

"Furnished doesn't mean they stock it with Doritos and all that other junk you eat. You wanted that, you should have sent the landlord a shopping list. Though I see you managed some beer. You nab that off the old lady?"

"You can get down off your high horse, okay? What's your damn beef?" He was staring into the knotty pine cabinets now. "Ah ha!" Holding his beer in one hand he pulled out a fresh jar of Miracle Whip and a box of graham crackers with the other. Then he started opening one drawer after another, searching for a knife.

Mickey couldn't stand drawers being left open. Doors. Tops off jars. She went behind Doc now, closing things. "I can't believe you're really going to eat that—and with beer." She wrinkled her nose.

"Look!" Doc wheeled, a cracker thick with salad dressing poking out of his face. "Are you going to ride me all the way through this job? Is that the way it's going to be? 'Cause if it is, I can find another partner like that." He snapped his fingers. "I don't need you, Mick."

"Oh, yeah?" That was a crock. Who'd been in town working the races a couple weeks back, spotted the chance of a big score?

He knew that. "Big deal. Take a finder's fee, you can blow." He crammed another cracker in his mouth, washed it down with the Bud. "I'm telling you, I don't need the grief."

"All I'm asking you is, why'd you take the old lady's Sunliner? It doesn't make any sense. We've run the lost ring how many times, *you've* probably done it a thousand, did you ever take a car before this? Did you ever nab something big like that you'd have to dump, something that'd tie you to the mark that easy? Besides, Jesus, Doc, we're not thieves."

"Ho ho ho." The Old St. Nick laugh didn't work with a mouth full of crackers and salad dressing. "Nope, we're not thieves. We're hustlers."

Mickey sniffed and started turning side to side, her arms up, elbows bent, still wearing the yellow suit. "Con artists, Doc. *Artistes.*"

"Yeah, we're that all right. Fancy schmanzy crooks. All the partners in the world, I got to hook up with a princess—Jesus, could you stop with the Jane Fonda? I'm talking to you."

"And I'm listening. I'm still listening for the explanation to why it was—even if for some insane reason, some bolt of inspiration came down and struck you from the blue—you felt absolutely compelled to take that car, and I'll admit it's something special. I'd love it myself." Mickey was doing toe touches now in the middle of the green-and-yellow tiled floor, still in her alligator high heels. She was proud of keeping her flexibility considering how much time she spent traveling. "What were you doing back there that took so long, anyway? Usually, you're in, you're out, quick as a bunny on the yak. And why it was then you passed me, had to be doing eighty? You didn't toot the horn. I'd have pulled over, you'd have dumped the car, left it on the side of the road. What *was* all that?"

He said in a perfectly reasonable voice, "I wasn't wearing gloves. I needed to wipe it clean. We don't want any screwups, any way the cops can place us here."

Mickey stopped halfway to her toes, bent back up so her body was at a perfect ninety-degree angle from the waist, tilted her face. She used her sweet voice. "Doc, there'd have been no prints to leave if you hadn't taken the car."

He slammed the Miracle Whip down on the cabinet so hard it rang like a pistol shot. "Okay! You're right, I'm wrong. I was wrong from the get-go on this one. So what do you want me to do? Kill myself?" He jerked open the drawer where he'd found the silver knife and pulled out a cold forged steel version, a chef's blade, long and sharp. He held it to his neck. "Okay, Mick. Say the word. Go ahead. I fucked up, I'll pay the price. One slice, the jugular, it'll be a little messy for you to clean up, but so what? Yeah? That's it? That's why you're taking your skirt off? You don't want to get blood all over it?"

"No, Doc." She gave him her slow grin. "That's not why I'm taking my skirt off." She paused. "My blouse." It took a minute to undo the little glass buttons. She was wearing one of those lacy flesh-colored bras that could make a man's heart stop. "My shoes." Those were quick. "My stockings." And those were real slow, her slipping the little rubber nip on the garter, letting the silk slide. Pulling them off over her red-tipped toes. You'd never catch a woman wearing pantyhose who worked a scam that depended on the weakness of men.

Olive had been right, Mickey *was* twenty-eight years old. She'd only been at the grift for four years or so. Before that she'd been a college textbook saleswoman, fresh out of school. But she'd had to give it up. It was too dull for a cute redhead who'd only signed up in the first place to meet some professor whose brains would make up for her gene pool, riddled with incest from too many generations of Savannah blueblood.

She headed for Australia and Adventure, worked as a dance instructor in a disco; and one thing you could say about those big old Aussies was that they were just as macho as any bubba she'd ever met, which in a sicko way turned Mickey on even while she was spending her spare time reading Chaucer in Middle English. The Wife of Bath being her favorite, of course. In truth, Mickey was a genius, with off-the-chart scores in both verbal and mathematical aptitude, though her purest talents lay in the field of psychology, of which she had never read a word, but was a natural.

It was on a steamer trip from Sydney up through the Coral Sea with stops in New Caledonia, the Solomons, and New Guinea that Mickey encountered the Professor, a man of eighty years and vast experience, and realized that *this* was the one she'd been looking for, not to father her kids but to give birth to her whole new life.

The life of the grift, for which she had an innate talent.

On that slow boat to Sulawesi the Professor taught her many a pretty trick. Some of them were variations on the lost ring, cons that depended on an attractive girl looking like she was in a fix. Or she could use her youth and looks to sucker an older, wealthy mark into a hotel room, where they would be interrupted by her partner, the "cop," who would shake him down.

There are a million variations on the con, but among Mickey's favorites was the proposition bet. *Bet I can tie this cigarette in a knot without breaking it*. She was a prop hustler par excellence, with a large repertoire of challenge bets that seemed to give the mark the best of it. *Bet I can light this match and hold it to fifty without letting go or extinguishing it*. Smart gamblers were her favorite target. *Bet I can toss one of these walnuts over that five-story building*. She once snookered ten thousand bucks on a coin-guessing prop from a professional blackjack player who'd just hit it big in a Vegas casino, but those kinds of takes were few and far between.

She was a whiz at cards, too, and could clean your clock at poker. She cheated, of course, sometimes pulling the drunken mitt, where she'd appear to get a little tipsy on wine and expose her apparently losing hand, sometimes using a mirror called a twinkle or flick, a glim or light; but most of the players were so tickled by the notion of a beautiful young woman in evening clothes shuffling the cards while smoking a thin cigar (that was the Professor's idea of cute) they never had a clue, and if they did, maybe that was the price of entertainment.

After the Professor, she'd had a number of partners, all men, all older. But she had never worked with anyone for more than six months. Conversation got awfully boring after that. She didn't want anyone getting too close. Most of all, she'd never found a partner who shared her attitude about the job.

Mickey was always on the lookout for the main chance, whereas the big score is all that most grifters could see. Furthermore, all the grifters Mickey ever knew had spent more time than she cared to think about locked up, which made them age young, and Mickey had no plans to age at all. What she was looking for was a legal grift—like shysters or Wall Streeters—but not so cut and dried. Something with some juice to it. Some sizzle.

Now take Doc. Doc was good, but he didn't have a clue about the main chance. She'd met him three months ago in Boca Raton, and it turned out they'd grown up on the same stretch of the South Carolina coast. He was the best she'd ever known since the Professor, who'd passed away in his sleep at the age of eighty-two.

As grifters went, Doc was a real pro. Right now he was staring at her, slouched back against the counter, his feet wide in his cowboy boots. He was resting his elbows on the yellow formica.

She watched him watch her. He watched her watch.

He took a deep breath. Watching Mickey undress was one of his very favorite pastimes. He really was gonna miss her.

She had one of those faces, Jesus, it was like an angel's. Classy. That cap of red curls above that rounded forehead, smooth and cool, then those wide-spaced eyes of that incredible green, deep and pure with no flecks of gold or brown, just green. That turned-up nose with nostrils that had this cute little pear shape to them. Her mouth, God, her mouth was sweet as a plum. And what Micky could do with that mouth, *say* with that mouth when you got down to the nitty-gritty, he'd never heard a woman say such things. And he'd known some women in his time.

Christ. Why wouldn't he? He was old enough to be her father, easy. Maybe that was part of why she did it for him so much, that old thing about the forbidden, not that he ever would, of course, if he had a daughter, the very thought made him sick; but now there was her back, God, he loved her back, the tender bones of her spine, and though she had definition because she was such a nut about fitness, it was girl definition tapering down to a narrow waist, then flaring, there were those two little dimples, two of his favorite places in the whole wide world. Edisto, Folleys, those Sea Islands, they were great spots, but you couldn't snuggle into them the same way you could into Mickey's sweet places.

It hadn't taken long, staring at her back, then watching the way her little ass moved as she walked up the stairs, before she had him in a bedroom.

"Isn't that nice," she murmured, "a king-size bed."

"Clean sheets." He pulled his boots off. Then he was out of the white shirt and khakis. "Very considerate."

"Very thoughtful."

"Very."

A while later, Doc pretended that he was asleep when Mickey slid out of the big bed, silent as a ghost.

He knew where she was going, dressed only in his white shirt.

He'd known that was the point of this cute little display of gymnastics from the moment she'd given him the slow grin.

One thing he'd never been able to teach Mickey, and

God knows she was a fast learner, was this: Never try to con a con man.

She didn't get it. Just because she had an enormous talent for the grift, and maybe throw in the fact that she was beautiful, not to mention one hell of a great lay, she was always thinking she could pull one over on him.

He'd been working the grift almost fifty-five years, since he was five. His ma, Pearsa Miller, was a Machvanka, a tribe of Serbian gypsies whose good-looking women were the sharpest at the *bajour* or con. Pearsa was among the best. She had to be, tossed out on her own after Doc's father, a tall blond *gajo* carnie, seduced her, and from then on the other Machvanka spit when they called her whore. She'd taught Doc well, there was little about the grift that he didn't know.

So everything Mickey did, she was clear as glass to Doc.

Like he knew she was heading for the Sunliner convertible now, but he also knew it was locked. Both doors, and the trunk especially. He didn't want her to see what was in the trunk. She'd rolled his pants looking for the keys, just like he knew she would. He heard the Damn! in her mind, though she hadn't said it aloud. She'd never find the keys, stashed under some towels in the hall closet.

He eased out of bed and slid into his khakis. He thought about his ostrich boots. Mickey teased him about them, called them his affectation. He smiled. He'd leave them here this time.

By now she was probably out in the triple carport. There was no locked garage, and he hadn't been thrilled about leaving the Sunliner outside, but he'd figured come dark, there was lots of deep water around here, plenty of lakes, he'd just let the car roll off into one. Windows open, it'd go down fast. With any luck it'd be years before they found it, if ever, and by that time there'd be a skeleton in the trunk, and he'd be an old man meandering through the Sea Isles, minding his crab traps, fishing from his john boat, drinking the way he wanted to.

He tiptoed in his bare feet down the hall, down the stairs, past the kitchen, the pantry, the laundry room, a bath, and threw open the back door that opened into the carport.

"Surprise!" he yelled at Mickey, standing there in his shirt in the early dusk, the light softening just a little.

He had to give it to her. She didn't even jump. Instead she turned like she'd been waiting for him to come down and try to sneak up on her checking up on him. She gave him another one of her slow grins. This one wasn't about sex, though. This one was more sly. This one was about winning.

But winning what? She didn't even have the trunk open. She didn't . . . hey, that wasn't even the Sunliner she was leaning against. Her hip was up next to the silver Mercedes, but where was the black-and-gold convertible? What the hell had she done, snapped her fingers and made it disappear? Doc looked around, his head bobbing like one of those celluloid ducks marks tried to plug at the carnival. Now come on, damnit, this wasn't funny.

"I was just wondering," she said, showing him her little white teeth, "where's your car, sport?"

5

As Sam and Kitty approached the Palace Hotel's Silver Ballroom, two footmen in gold knee pants, silver vests, powdered wigs, and golden pumps bowed and threw the doors wide. Before them was a stunning mirrored room, dappled in gold, the ceiling hung with a dozen crystal chandeliers. It was jammed to the gills with swells in full-out formal gear. This was going to be an even longer evening than Sam had thought.

"Good Lord have mercy!" said Kitty.

"Marie Antoinette or stay home," said Sam in lieu of *I told you so*.

But Kitty got her drift. "You were right. I was wrong. Jinx is pulling out all the stops. And we're both underdressed."

Who knew that a party in Hot Springs, Arkansas, even Jinx's engagement party, would call for sequins and bugle beads to the floor—the sort of thing any self-respecting beauty contestant kept at the ready in three or four colors?

But all one hundred of the other women guests seemed to be either from Texas—where women were serious about dress-up—or were former Miss Somebodies. Their big hair was done up with sequins and swirls and bows. Some of them had even dyed their tresses to match their gowns.

Sam was in the simple knee-length scarlet silk sheath she'd described to Olive. Kitty wore seafoam chiffon evening pants and jacket, nice with her red-blond hair. Kitty said, "We look like street people."

"Good. Then everyone else will give us a wide berth, we won't have to make stupid chitchat about Herself, and we can just eat. Jesus, would you look at those hors d'oeuvres!"

A platoon of white-gloved tuxedoed waiters stood in the center of a great circular table serving up chilled lobster, Beluga caviar, truffled pâté, pressed duck, three-vegetable mousse, soft-shell crabs, smoked catfish, skewers of snails and chicken, shad roe with lump backfin crabmeat, grilled spring onions, rare eye-of-the-round tenderloin, and a pan roast of oysters with wild mushrooms, spinach, leeks, and cream—all of which Sam intended to sample.

There was a twelve-piece ensemble playing Viennese waltzes.

Silver cages of turtledoves.

A fountain of Roederer Crystal champagne.

And Sam didn't recognize a single other soul.

But Kitty did. "Oh, look, there's Loydell!" She pointed through the crush toward an old lady in the receiving line. Sam had long been curious about Jinx's mother, who'd now turned out to be her new friend Olive's best buddy, and there she was.

Loydell Watson was thin where Jinx was curvy and pointy-faced. Her iron gray hair was crimped into a series of stiff waves marching back like soldiers in formation from her forehead. And party or no party, she was wearing her sensible shoes.

Which might not be a bad idea, Sam thought. Her high-heeled pumps were killing her already. So you reached a certain age, like Olive and Loydell, you traded in cute for comfortable, stashed the pumps, the pantyhose, all the other folderol, bought muumuus, pants with elastic waists, let it all hang out.

Maybe that's what she was going to do now that Harry was out of the picture. She'd shuck the lacy underwire bras, forget exercise class, race-walking. Not exactly let herself go, but get more comfy. Why not? She couldn't compete with a twenty-two-year-old blonde, no matter what. And those women who worked at it so hard, trying to keep the illusion of youth—well, they were nuts.

Like Jinx, the beauty queen. Kitty had said the last time she'd seen Jinx she hadn't aged a whit, looked exactly the same as she had when she was first runner-up to Miss Arkansas.

Sam turned to Kitty now. "So where is Herself? You think she's going to descend in a swing from the ceiling? Lope in on an elephant? Burst out of a giant cocoon and fly across the room?"

Kitty ignored her and peered at someone around a substantial blonde wearing half an acre of silver and jet beads. "Yes," she said, pointing. "*That* must be Speed, the fiancé."

The big blonde moved, and Sam saw a balding man with a curly halo of salt-and-pepper hair. He was waving his short arms like a helicopter, talking ninety miles a minute.

"Tell me it's for real," she said.

"Hush," said Kitty.

"Oh, be still my heart. Jinx marrying a chubby mosquito. Promise me it's not a joke."

"Shut up, Sammy, or I'm walking right off and leaving you."

Though he was kind of cute, if you went in for elves. He had bright blue eyes and a pink cupid's bow of a mouth. For a little sucker he was built, she would give him that, broad-shouldered and barrel-chested beneath his cream-colored slouch tuxedo right out of the thirties. His tie, tiny black patent pumps, and shirt were black. Sam grinned. "I take back what I said about his being a pool hustler. He couldn't reach the table."

"You lied, didn't you, when you promised to be nice."

"I'm sorry. I'm tired, Kitty. Morose. Cranky. Just put up with me tonight, and I promise, tomorrow, I'll kiss Jinx's feet." That was easy to say, since she knew they weren't scheduled to see the happy couple the next day, what with Jinx's raft of Texans. Kitty had promised the two of them could have a lazy morning, take another bath and massage, pack a lunch, and head for the mountains and a long hike. Nature therapy.

Just then the musicians struck up "A Pretty Girl Is Like a Melody," and through a side door flounced a covey of them, all dressed in yards of floating white organza. A buzz flew around the room. And then the buzz grew as the guests realized that the eight girls—beginning with the tiny one who was no more than three years old and working up to about twenty-one—were blond, blue-eyed lookalikes who all, in turn, looked like Jinx. It was like watching the Breck girl grow older or the Ivory soap commercial where the baby grows into the woman. It was weird, is what it was. Beyond weird. It was bizarre. Sam tried to sneak a look at Kitty, but she was staring off into space. Trying to stifle a major choking attack, if Sam knew her Kitty.

Then, a long beat passed, and the orchestra struck up "There She Is," which Jinx had never been. Miss America, that is. But it was *her* party, by God. And *so* tacky, it was definitely worth the trip.

A drum rolled, a spotlight hit a darkened area at the end of the room, and there she was indeed, Julia Alice Watson MacMillan Barnard about-to-be McKay, just as luscious as ever with the kind of blond, blue-eyed beauty queen looks that were everywhere you turned in the Atlanta and Dallas-Forth Worth airports. Maybe we were talking a contender for *Mrs.* America now, but she still had spaces between the curves. The only thing that was noticeably bigger was her platinum hair. Bigger than Texarkana, Sam would say to Kitty later. Jinx floated into the room with a rhinestone tiara atop her blond chignon, wearing a dangerously low-cut strapless gown of cloth of gold that looked like it had been spray-painted on. Jinx waved to the crowd as if they were her subjects as she made her way across the room toward the reception line.

"Too bad there's no runway," Sam murmured. "I guess they couldn't get it built in time."

Then suddenly, there she was, right in their faces. "Samantha Adams and Katherine Lee, I swear! Come here and let me hug your necks! I'm so proud y'all could come!"

Gag me, thought Sam, with an iced-tea spoon—in the bride-to-be's silver pattern, of course.

6

LATEESHA ROLLINS WAS IN BIG TROUBLE. WHICH IS WHY she was standing in a phone booth at the corner of Malvern and Church about to call her second cousin Early Trulove, who everybody knew was a stone killer, bodyguard to Mr. You Know Who. She was practicing what she was going to say. *Early, I've fucked up bad. You'll come and help me, won't you, pretty please with sugar on top and chocolate sprinkles.*

It had all started last week with what her friend Denice had said about Aunt Odessie's boobs.

Well, maybe it had started because Lateesha had been on the honor roll at Hot Springs High for six semesters in a row and was a soloist in the choir of the Rising Star Baptist Church, which is why her girlfriend Denice was always calling her Little Miss Too-Good.

So when Aunt Odessie, who'd taken Lateesha to raise when Lateesha's momma was killed in a drive-by in New Orleans, heard Denice say, "Yo auntie's got the biggest effin' bazooms in the state of Arkansas," it wasn't half a second before Aunt Odessie, who'd been sitting on the porch with Cousin Early, got on the phone and called Denice's mom, gave her an earful about bad language and home training, and said Lateesha couldn't hang out with Denice anymore. Denice's mom grounded her for a week, and it was then that Denice started in calling Lateesha Little Miss Too-Good for real.

Denice was making fun of her at the Harvest Foods on

Malvern where they both worked after school, saying, Watch Little Miss Too-Good Computer Brain add up yo' groceries, folks. That girl be a robot, for sure. Just because Lateesha had this mathematical aptitude, she could run her eyes over the groceries, add 'em faster than the electronic cash register. Numbers were just her thing, she'd tried to explain that a million times to Denice.

It really hurt Lateesha's feelings that Denice would do her like that, being her best friend since the eighth grade and all. But that was the thing about friends. They knew you better than anybody, so when they decided to dump on you, they could do it the best. Or the worst, depending on your point of view.

But Lateesha had taken just about all the crap she was going to. Now she was going to *show* Denice she wasn't just Little Miss Too-Good. That's why, when Lateesha was out on her bike this afternoon, and she was riding down Lake Loop Road out in the woods, when she saw that super fresh old car parked in that big old stone house's carport alongside a silver Mercedes, that's why something went off Pow! in her head.

She was going to steal that car. The old one. Because it was in her favorite colors, black with a little bit of gold, which were also the colors of Hot Springs High School. She was going to drive it up to Denice's house, and say, Hey, Miss Thang, you wanta go for a spin in my wheels?

That would show Denice and put an end to that Little Miss Too-Good stuff once and for all.

Except she didn't know how.

Oh, yes, you do, this little voice had spoken up. This little voice of the devil. Girl, ain't you watched enough TV to know how to do that thing, smart girl like you?

It was amazing how the devil's voice sounded exactly like Denice's. And the voice was right, too. She did know how. She'd watched this segment on *Prime Time Crime* about these gangs of kids stealing cars in Newark, New Jersey, car-theft capital of the United States, and she most certainly knew how to get into the car, assuming it was locked, which, she cruised up and checked, it was. But it only took her ten minutes to zip back out to the big road, and sure enough, there was a gas station, and she wheeled in and said to the semimentally retarded wormy white boy, all Miss Innocent Do-Goody, Do you have one of those slim-jim things I can borrow, there's an old lady back down the road, got out of her car, locked the keys in, she's about to have a fit? Well, she knew he wasn't gonna loan her shit, black girl on a bike, but he said, just like she thought he would, here, take this here coat hanger, sometimes that'll work; if it don't, just wait for the Highway Patrol, they'll be along directly.

It didn't take her very long at all to work the straightened end of the coat hanger over the top of the window and lower the hooked end to the door handle. She had to fish for a bit, but then there it was! She tugged on it a couple of times, and she was in. Now what? They definitely hadn't left the keys in the ignition. Well, she knew from the crime show if she had some lamp cord with clips at either end she could hot-wire the engine, but she didn't. And she didn't have time to go find any either. Somebody could be walking out of that house any minute, she'd be in juvie so fast it'd make your head spin, and she could just hear Aunt Odessie screaming and praying and praying and screaming. So she started fooling around with the stick, it wasn't an automatic, and the next thing she knew, she must have gotten it into neutral, and the house was up on a hill with this steep drive, the car just started rolling out, backwards, down the driveway, Jesus!, she was flying, she was going to be killed, except nobody was coming when she hit the blacktop, and all she had to do was hold it in the road, still going downhill, which was easier said than done, and then she was losing it, she'd lost it, and the car was bouncing off down this grade and into the woods, where it crashed against the foot of this pine tree.

So Lateesha had scrammed, and now here she was, scared to death. Scared that a policeman was going to come along, find that car, lift her prints off the steering wheel, and come and throw her in the pokey.

Cops around here, cops like that Archie Blackshears who was always lurking around the school, they'd bust a fifteen-and-a-half-year-old in a New York minute. That's what everybody said. Said you didn't want to know what Archie'd do to you once he got you in that jail.

So Lateesha didn't see but that she had but one option, asking Early for help. The phone was ringing. But Early wasn't home. And he didn't have an answering machine either. Not that she'd thought he would. Most assassins probably didn't.

7

SAM HAD BEEN CHATTING WITH KITTY AND JINX FOR ABOUT fifteen minutes, and her smile was beginning to feel like a baloney sandwich left lying on the kitchen counter too long. Jinx hadn't changed a whit. She ran on and on. She never asked a single thing about *you* and didn't even pause for breath, jumping from a room-by-room description of the new house she and the groom were about to build, to where she had her hair done, her latest shopping trip to Manhattan, her engagement ring—which, as Sam had predicted, was a diamond you could use for Ping-Pong.

"And we're honeymooning at this *exclusive* resort in Hawaii. We're flying *first-class* direct to Maui, and then we take this little plane to the resort, where we have our own cottage. The cast of *LA Law* stays there every chance they get, and it's very exclusive and very expensive."

Sam couldn't stand it. "Jinx," she interrupted, "tell me about your altars—is that what you call them? Praying to one of them really won you that lottery?"

Jinx batted her baby blues. "Not praying exactly, but I swear, Sam, you sound so *cynical.*"

Before Jinx could finish, her mother, Loydell, cruised up to them like a royal blue Olds 88 heading for a reserved parking spot. The old lady in her satin dress, tan knee-highs, and sensible black shoes gave Kitty a big hug, said Howdy to Sam, then got right up in Jinx's face.

"Have you seen Olive? She said she'd be here, and she's never late. I've been standing in one spot waiting for her because I'm dying to tell her about that letter I got from our friend Wanda. You remember Wanda? I locked her and Olive up at the same time once, in the same cell. Anyway, Wanda wrote that her sister Nell, who lives in Lubbock, was out in the garage with that no-good husband of hers working on their car, and he kicked the jack, at least that's what it looked like. She was under there twenty-five minutes before the police came, and he was only then just starting to jack that car up again. He was drinking a beer and eating a turkey, mayo, and cranberry sauce sandwich he'd stopped and made. Killed her dead as a doornail. What I say is they ought to just take him out, drop a sledgehammer on him about a hundred times, starting down at his feet making hamburger meat out of him. You know, sort of like that Kathy Bates did in that picture show about that romance writer. Did you see that one?"

"Oh, Mother," said Jinx. She sounded thirteen years old.

Sam had suspected that any friend of Olive's would be someone she liked, and from the minute she'd seen Loydell's sensible shoes she had. The fact that Loydell embarrassed her daughter was just the icing on the cake. "I met your friend Olive just a couple of hours ago," Sam said. "I stopped in her store to buy some gas. What a *great* lady."

Jinx looked at Sam as if she'd lost her mind, but Sam saw no need to tell the Original Floozie that when she'd dissolved in tears over Harry at the Gas 'N Grub, Olive had wiped her nose. In fact, she didn't want Jinx to know about Harry at all.

"Olive is something special," said Loydell. "We go way back. I can't tell you all the things we've been through. Old friends, that's what every woman needs. Push comes to shove, they'll be right there beside you."

Sam caught *her* old friend Kitty's eye. "I couldn't agree with you more." Then, turning back to Loydell, she said, "I told Olive she'd better save me a dance. Any idea what's keeping her?"

Loydell said, "I don't know. But I'll tell you what. I'm going to go and find me a phone, give her a ring."

Jinx reached out and grabbed her mother's arm. "Hold up a minute. Do you think while you're at it you could call up to your suite? Speed said he was just running up to take his allergy pills and he'd be right back down. He ought to be here by now."

Good, thought Sam. That would give her an opportunity to see if Speed was something Jinx had found on sale at Neiman Marcus, ran on batteries.

"Men," said Loydell. "You can't trust 'em. Let 'em out of your sight for two minutes, I tell you, Jinx, he's probably gone off with one of those cute look-alikes you had heading up your big show-off into the ballroom. Probably with the one who's about sixteen. I told you those girls was a mistake."

"Mother! What an awful thing to say."

Sam grinned. Loydell was mean as a snake, a trait that Jinx had inherited. Except Loydell didn't sneak and hide around with it. You got it right in your face.

Now Loydell was saying, "Well, it's beyond me why you'd want to get married again anyway, looks like you'd have learned your lesson by now. First that football player turning out strange. . . ."

Kitty never would say what happened to Jinx's first husband.

"Then Harlan . . ."

That was the second one. He'd gotten himself into some kind of business tight.

"Running out on you with that cheerleader, then losing all y'all's money and ending up in the pokey to boot, cheating all those people. Same mentality as those S&L robbers. Put 'em all on the chain gang, I say. Family values, I tell you, the families I know teach their children not to steal other people's money, that's what they do."

"Moth—urrrr." Jinx hit the word like an electric drill. "About Speed?"

Loydell held up a hand. "Okay," she said. "Hold your horses. I'm on my way."

"And I'm going to run upstairs and take something for my headache," said Sam, seizing the opportunity to make a getaway. What she really aimed to do was get into her pajamas and snuggle up in bed. She'd miss seeing Speed again, but what the hay? Truth be told, she was much more interested in Olive and Loydell. Maybe tomorrow afternoon, when they came back from their hike, she and Kitty could invite the old ladies for tea. Olive and Loydell could fill them in on the local dirt, whatever weird there was, and she'd have to ask them about Mr. You Know Who—now, *that* would be fun.

8

HEADING TO BED, YES, INDEEDY, THAT WAS SAM'S PLAN.
Harry, five hundred miles of rainy bad road, a stomachful of junk food, a reunion with Jinx Watson, she was pooped. But on her way through the Palace's lobby, she was sidetracked.

First, there was the space itself, which she'd hadn't had time before to take in. It was enormous, arching three stories, a magnificent creation of black and gold and silver Art Deco with a little Moroccan around the edges. To the right was a stage and a bandstand with a dance floor before it. The middle area was filled with dozens of small tables occupied by prosperous-looking Southern white folks dressed up in their very best. On the far left wall was a mural of the Oaklawn grandstand as the horses pulled into the finish. Racing was a major industry in Hot Springs, and the Palace's lobby was a favorite rallying spot for the fans. A bar stretched the entire length of the wall beneath the mural. And just in front of the main bar stood a baby grand piano surrounded by stools.

It was the black woman sitting at that piano whose voice had waylaid Sam. As she'd started to stroll by the lobby's edge on her way to the elevators, she'd been stopped cold by the woman's driving left hand and her throaty contralto. Sam hadn't heard anyone she liked so much since she'd first heard Nina Simone rattle the raf-

58

ters of the old Atlanta Civic Auditorium with "Mississippi Goddam."

That's why Sam, who hardly made it a practice to frequent drinking establishments, found herself perched on a stool of black leatherette and curvy chrome pulled up to the side of the ebony grand piano, the only vacant seat in the room. She was sipping a mineral water, Mountain Valley, the local brand.

The room was gorgeous. The music was wonderful. So why, all of a sudden, did she slide from fatigue into anxious depression? Low-down. Mean. Blue. Only halfway through her drink, three songs into the set, she felt like she wanted to crawl under the piano and die. Maybe drag something under there with her and kill it, too.

The lady in blue velvet was singing "Baby, Get Lost," the old Dinah Washington standard about a two-timing son of a gun. Maybe that had something to do with her mood? Intimations of Harry?

Harry, sweet Harry. Why was it when somebody did you wrong, you only remembered the sweet times? Wouldn't it be better to think about the things you hated? Like all those perfectly gorgeous weekends he made you waste, sitting glued to the tube watching football games. Except Harry didn't do that. Nor did he chew with his mouth open. He didn't snore. He didn't insist of having his way all the time, but he wasn't such a pushover that she didn't respect him. He wasn't a whiner. He was both a great story teller and a great listener. He was a passionate and considerate lover. He was unnecessarily handsome. He was a great traveler. Remember that week on the Cape? Atlantic City and that huge round pink bed? Hot days sea-kayaking in Belize, hotter nights beneath the mosquito netting?

So if he was so great, so perfect, what the hell was her problem? Why couldn't she commit to this man? Because he was a cheat, that was why. Yes, Sammy, but when had he cheated? After she had committed to him, or before? Well, she never had said she would move in with him, settle down, so it couldn't very well be after, could it?

Oh, the hell with Harry. The hell with men. She was perfectly fine by herself. She had plenty of girlfriends. Well, she had Kitty. And her sponsor. She *liked* spending time alone. She *adored* her own company.

She slowly checked out the room. Yep, all these people, and she was the only unaccompanied woman in sight, and damned proud of it. Everywhere she turned were couples holding hands. Their heads leaned toward one another like tulips in a vase. People played footsies, and a dozen couples twirled cheek-to-cheek, arm-in-arm, belly-to-belly on the little dance floor. How conventional. How recherché. How passé, all this *dependency*. Couldn't any of these people stand on their own two feet? She certainly could, and she preferred it that way.

Though why she was suddenly blinking back tears, she couldn't explain.

It was the dancing. Oh, Jesus, she loved to dance with Harry. They were like Ginger and Fred, born to fly together across polished hardwood.

Well, they wouldn't be dancing anymore, would they? Vertically—or horizontally.

She bit her bottom lip and struggled for control. Come on, girl, buck up. You're going to end up being one of those old ladies who sits around bars, crying in their beer.

And that would be a rerun, wouldn't it? She'd already gone through that phase, as a young lady. Tall, curly-headed girl, snockered out of her mind. Knocking back the booze. Telling strangers her sad tale—whichever one had seemed appropriate at the moment.

And she'd done more than her share of dancing *atop* the bar. Oh, yes, the young Sammy was famous for her hootchy-kootch. Sometimes she stripped, too. Another form of dancing that you didn't need a partner for—unless you counted Mr. Jack Daniel's or Mr. Jim Beam.

Now the singer was doing the old Simone standard "You Can Have Him."

Oh, no. That was too much. Pushing the edge of the envelope. For the ironic words of the song spelled out every romantic reason in the world why she *did* want him. You couldn't have him at all. She'd scratch your eyeballs out if you even got close, girl. Little blond thing. Oh, shit. She did want Harry. She wanted him desperately. But on her terms. Her way.

For no, unlike the song, she didn't want to give him a baby for every year. She was too old, for one thing. And she'd never wanted children, for another.

Yes, she wanted to run her fingers through his curly hair.

And, yes, she loved that occasional Sunday when they spent all day in bed.

But did she, like the song said, want to meet his every need, bow to his every whim? No way!

She wanted, as Olive had deduced, to be close, but not too close. So, that was a problem. So, it was hard to make that work. But it was all she could manage.

Jesus! She'd been abandoned so many times before, big-time. Her parents killed in a plane crash when she was twelve. Lovers split hither and yon: her first love, Beau; Frank, whom Jinx had snagged; her husband, Jimmy. Sure, by Jimmy's time she'd been a drunk, but she was sober when Sean—who'd for sure been the love of her life, was mowed down in San Francisco by a hit-and-run driver. That was when she'd turned tail and returned home to the South.

Don't think she didn't know she had an intimacy problem. She'd talked talked talked about it at ninety bucks per fifty-minute clip. Talked talked talked with her AA sponsors in San Francisco, in Atlanta, in New Orleans.

What was it Harry had said? *It's not that I don't love*

you, Sammy. This fling had nothing to do with age. Nothing to do with her being younger. And then he'd said that he needed the *possibility* of more commitment.

And sometimes *he* needed to be in control.

Well, screw him if he couldn't take a joke. Being in the driver's seat was the only way she could avoid being hurt. Didn't he know that? That was what Samantha Adams did for a living. She controlled.

Let go, let God, said a chorus of voices she'd heard in the program for the past dozen years.

Well, she let go as much as she could—which wasn't a whole lot. She loved free-lancing, because she called the shots. She lived alone. She controlled her emotions. She controlled her drinking.

Oh, yes, she did that.

Why, she could sit here at this bar and stare at that drink to her left, the one the handsome man who was sitting there had ordered, till the cows come home—and not give it a second thought.

Well, sure, she'd noticed what it was. He'd ordered an extra-dry Bombay martini, three olives, straight up. It was gorgeous in one of those classic V-shaped glasses.

She could smell the gin, that hint of juniper. Taste the salty olives. She closed her eyes. Feel the hit in the back of her throat.

Ummmmmm. Didn't she love that? The clear icy cold draught, that first kapow going down, then the lovely warmth spreading to the tips of her toes. That smooth silky release from all her cares and woes. Yes, indeedy, blackbird. Oblivion was right around the corner. As close as her raising one red-lacquered fingertip as the waitress passed. Pointing at the glass next door, then herself. Didn't have to say a word to tell her, Hit me with one of those.

Now the songstress was working "My Funny Valentine" right down to the nub. Which wasn't making this solo outing any easier for a recovering drunk with a black-and-blue ego and a battered heart.

"What can I get you, ma'am?"

Sam looked up into the face of a young blond waitress. Another goddam dewy blonde, just like Harry's, with the kind of flesh, you touch it, it springs right back.

And the words were right there, on the tip of her tongue: *Black Jack on the rocks with a side of water*.

"Check, please," she said.

Then she held onto the edge of the curved ebony and shut her eyes tight. She'd been joking with herself, of course. She didn't *really* want a drink. So why was she trembling, head to toe?

She was shaking because she knew that old devil Mr. Booze was always lurking around the corner. He always had been, he always would be. Oh, sure, months passed that she didn't even get a whiff of him, his breath that at first smelled like perfume. Whispering promises, Oh, Lordy, hon, don't you know how that drink would feel? *Soooo* good.

She opened her eyes and took a deep breath. The lady in blue velvet was watching her, even as she sang. She gave Sam a slow wink. Was the lady a friend of Bill W's, too, another recovering drunk? Or did she just know a woman in trouble when she saw one? A woman who played piano in public rooms for a living was bound to have seen everything once.

Sam fiddled with her swizzle stick. She didn't even smoke anymore, and what she'd give for a cigarette right now. But the nicotine had been even harder to kick than the booze.

And Harry? How hard was it going to be to kick him?

Enough. That night was history. She was going to her room. Lights out. But where the hell was her check? She stood. Where *was* that blonde?

She searched the room, her gaze sweeping the tables around the dance floor, the bar, then up the curving stairway of gold that rose from the Palace's lobby to the mezzanine above. At the top of the stairway stood a pretty redhead with a short boyish bob, who not only caught her attention, but wouldn't let go.

Now this was a woman who knew how to make an entrance, who paused for a count of ten on the landing, slowly scanning. For whom? wondered Sam. Or was she just letting the room take *her* in: the black suede pumps, the simple black velvet dinner suit, the fitted jacket unbuttoned just enough to show her pearls, diamond solitaire ear studs. Sam particularly liked the little black sequined evening cap with the wisp of wide net that touched the tip of her nose.

Mickey was fond of it, too. The cap was the kind of cute touch that the Professor had loved.

Sam watched the woman's trim ankles scissor down the stairs. Then with a slow sashay, but not too much, she crossed the room and headed toward a table for two just to Sam's right that was emptying even now as she approached.

The lady had probably had good parking karma, too. Sam, still waiting for that check, watched the redhead place her jet beaded evening bag on the empty chair and order a mineral water in a low pleasant Southern voice. She was polite to her waiter, who had eyes only for her, avoiding Sam's salute.

The lady had a pretty smile, too, which she bestowed on the gray-haired cigar-smoking sport who, in half a minute, mosied his chair right over from his table to hers. He looked like a Texan, or a playlike Texan in an expensive Western-tailored suit and alligator cowboy boots.

Sam eavesdropped, as any good reporter would—even a former reporter couldn't resist the old habit—while the man, who introduced himself as Slim, talked of south Texas and goddam, beg your pardon ma'am, spring rains nearly flooding them out, the oil bidness, the godawful silly party downstairs in the ballroom his wife had dragged him to. Sam tipped her glass to that. He spoke of the salutary effects of single malt Scotch following a bath and massage, and wondered what a pretty lady, whose name it turned out was Mickey, might be doing by her lonesome in Hot Springs, Arkansas.

Sam bristled. Was it against the law for a woman to go out in public alone? Lots of women did it, you know. Some by choice. Some by have to.

But this Mickey wasn't offended by the question at all. She smiled as she said, "I'm here to play a little cards."

"Oh, really?" Slim had a big rich laugh. He also had a diamond-studded Rolex that could blind you, diamond button covers on his Western shirt, and a gold cobra-shaped pinky ring with emerald eyes and diamond fangs. "What's your game, you don't mind my asking?"

"Texas hold 'em," said Mickey, then paused. "Among others."

That got a big laugh from Slim. Sam smiled. So Ms. Mickey played big-time hardball poker. She was beginning to think this lady was more than wise. Sam was curious, losing her impetus to pay up and move on, even as the waitress finally dropped her check on the bar. Fine, let *her* wait.

Mickey added, "In my spare time I do card tricks."

Sam looked around the piano to see if anyone else appreciated the redhead's lines and found herself staring straight into the eyes of a small, slight light-skinned black man two seats to her right around the curve of the piano. He was wearing a neat mustache, a navy double-breasted blazer, a high-collared white shirt, and a red foulard tie. She'd seen this man before. Where? When? A good while ago, it seemed. But there was no question in her mind that she had. She gave him a little nod. He nodded back, but gave no signal that she looked familiar to him.

Then the singer launched into "Stormy Weather," and Slim said to Mickey, "So, you came to clean our clocks."

The redhead took a sip of her mineral water and said, "That's about the size of it."

"Want to give me a demonstration? I don't mean a serious game. Just show me one of those tricks you're talking about."

"Oh, I'm sure you're much too clever." Mickey smiled. She had very pretty little white teeth. "You look like a serious player. I wouldn't want to insult your intelligence."

Slim didn't say a word to that, just reached in his wallet and pulled out a hundred dollar bill. He laid it on the table and leaned back in his chair.

Sam turned again to glance at the black man in the navy blazer. His eyes flicked toward the redhead and the Texan, then back at Sam. He raised one eyebrow. Who the hell *was* he?

"I see," said Mickey. She slipped a brand-new deck of cards from her evening bag, handed it to Slim. "If that's how you feel about it, I'd appreciate your doing us the honors, please, sir."

Sam thought, Slim, you have a hundred bucks lying on the table, you don't even know the trick? I think you're about to be fleeced, my man. Then she watched Slim catch Mickey's gaze and hold it for a while like he was reading her mind, turning the pages slowly. Then he gave her a slow grin. "Nobody's doing me any harm here tonight, are they, sugar baby?"

Mickey handed the grin right back to him. "Nope," she said. "*Sugar Baby* ain't doing anybody no harm. Ain't gonna take any of your money, either." She pushed the hundred back toward Slim. Without missing a beat he pulled out its twin, pushed two hundred back at her.

Sam wasn't surprised. It was the kind of thing men did. And the kind of thing a clever woman would lead them to do. Mickey looked like a very clever woman. Sam looked back at the mustachioed black man. What did he think? He was still watching. He gave a small smile.

Then Sam looked back at Mickey, so she didn't see the man whom she couldn't place glance over his shoulder and nod at a big silver-haired man who had paused before the elevators to fire a slender cigar with a heavy gold lighter. The big man returned the nod, message received, then disappeared.

Back at the table Mickey was saying, "Oh, all right, if you insist. Now, here we go, are you ready? Yes? Then would you open that deck and shuffle, please, sir? Good. Why don't you do that one more time? Now, just place it on the table." Mickey didn't touch the cards, which were backed with a scrolling Florentine design of red, blue, and gold. "Here's how it goes. You and I'll take turns. Slip a card off the top of the deck, turn it face up. The first one who turns over a picture card loses. Now, you don't have to turn every card. You can put it aside, face down, if you feel like it might be a picture card, turn over the next one. Or the one after that. Skip as many as you want. Got it?"

"The first picture card turned loses the bet? That's all there is to it?" said Slim.

"That's it. Why don't you go ahead?"

"Ladies first."

"No, no, I insist."

Slim reached for the top card, and without hesitating a moment, flipped it. Three of diamonds.

Mickey carefully lifted a card, just high enough that Sam could see she peeked. Slim had seen her, too, for Sam caught his little start of surprise. Mickey turned the card over. The ace of spades.

Slim drew the ten of clubs.

Mickey peeked again. Sam turned to see if the mustachioed man had seen the cheat. He raised and lowered his eyelids like blinds. He'd seen, all right. Mickey turned the six of hearts.

Slim hesitated on the next one, slid it aside. Next up was the eight of diamonds.

"Good call, my man," said Sam under her breath. Her natural inclination was to pull for the lady, but if the lady was a cheat. . . .

The next card, Mickey peeked again, then slid the card over, face down. Then she picked another, peeked, and flipped the five of clubs.

Slim reached over and turned the card she'd passed on. There it was. The jack of diamonds wearing a handsome face.

"You lose!" Mickey crowed.

Slim was stunned. "What do you mean, *me?*" His voice rose. "*You* cheated. You peeked every time. You saw that was a picture, and you passed on it."

"That's right." Mickey's smile was a killer. "And *you* turned it over. *You* turned the first picture card. *Sugar Baby* wins. You lose."

Slim fell back in his seat. "Well, fuck me and the horse I rode in on."

A bell sounded in Sam's head. Something about a horse. The key to who the black man was something about a horse.

Slim was laughing now. He was halfway between astonishment and indignation. But he was still a gentleman, standing as Mickey stood, checked her watch, gathered the cards, slipped the two hundred dollars and the cards into her bag, and extended her hand. "Thanks so much for the drink, Slim. It's been a pleasure doing business with you, and I hate to win and run, but now if you'll excuse me."

Sam had it. She whirled toward the black man, who grinned, and she caught a glimpse of a gold star embedded in one of his two front teeth. That cinched it. She was right, by God!

He was Early Trulove, sure as shooting, an old jail-house buddy of Harry's partner, Lavert. She'd never really met him, hadn't gotten close enough to shake hands. It had been a year or so ago, she and Harry and Lavert had been out at the track in New Orleans, and Lavert had pointed out Early as he had walked a filly into the paddock. Early had called something to Lavert and grinned—and Sam had commented then on the flash of gold. Early's lucky star, Lavert had said. Wards off the silver bullets. Sam had pressed him for details, and Lavert had said Early was working as a groom for Lavert's former employer, Joey the Horse.

She remembered the day and the man because of the filly Early had been walking. She even remembered the filly's name, Lush Life. Lavert had said, with an insider's wink, Bet her to win. They did, and then in the stretch she'd run herself to death. Died, they said, of a heart attack. But she broke a leg going down, and then kept foundering, struggling to rise again. It was a hideous sight, and Sam hadn't been back to the track since.

She was about to speak to Early, call him by name, when he dropped a twenty on the bar and melted away.

That was it. Call it a night, Sammy. You're running on your rims. She stood, slipped a bill in the crystal snifter for the singer, who gave her a big grin, then wove her way through the crowded tables across the room. She was heading out toward the elevators when she had an attack of good manners.

Well, hell, it wouldn't kill her to take the five minutes to run back downstairs to the ballroom, say good-night to Jinx and thank her for the party, then she could go snuggle into her jammies.

Later, Sam thought that for many a Southern belle, the road to perdition has been paved with good manners.

It's that always smiling, saying yes and thank you, and no, I don't mind one bit, honey, you just go ahead and do what you have to, that has landed many of them in the looney bin if not in jail.

In this particular case, she could have been upstairs asleep, she could have been watching late night TV, she could have been eating a box of chocolate pecan fudge. Instead, she was standing there in shoes that pinched, listening to Jinx.

"I don't know how that Katie Couric does it. I'll tell you, that morning I was on her *Today Show* with my crystal altars, I thought I was going to die. I could no more get up at that time every morning to interview celebrities than I could fly to the moon. I told her. I said, Katie, honey, I don't know about you, but I need to get my beauty sleep."

Kitty said to Sam, "Did you have to go out to a pharmacy for those aspirin? We were about to send a rescue party."

"I got sidetracked."

Jinx took a deep breath and sailed off on another tack. "Don't y'all just love Southern weddings? Aren't they the best? I feel so sorry for Yankees and other foreigners, they don't even begin to get into the spirit of the thing. You know how outrageous I am, and the second time, when I married Harlan, I had fourteen bridesmaids, all his sisters and girl cousins, and I had them all wear shocking pink and black from Valentino. Honey, that was even before New York women discovered black.

"Actually what we did was this Southern wedding in Italy because that's where Harlan's friend, the Italian count, lived, the one he went into the electronics business with. We had a nineteenth-century coach and four horses with roses in their manes carry us from the church to his villa. I had all these little footmen in cute knee pants serving fried chicken wings and potato salad and deviled eggs to the Italians. I had to have forty deviled-egg plates sent from Neiman's. You know you can't get a decent deviled-egg plate north of the Mason-Dixon line, and certainly not in Italy. I mean, I could have done carpaccio and pasta primavera and veal tonnato, all that

Italian thing, which would have been easier, but not nearly as—Sam, are you listening to me?"

"Why do you ask?"

"You don't *look* like you're listening."

Now, that was the perfect opportunity for Sam to say, No, I'm not, Jinx. And what you've noticed with your extraordinary perspicacity are my eyes glazing over from sheer screaming-meemie B-O-R-E-D-O-M—except that wouldn't be very polite, would it, and she had come back downstairs to be polite if it choked her.

Right about then Loydell steamed back into the scene, her mouth a thin line, her blue eyes sparkling. "Loydell Watson reporting back," she said with a smart little salute as if her daughter were a general.

"Very funny, Mother. Now where *is* Speed?"

The bridegroom wasn't downstairs yet? He must have had a even bigger headache than Sam's. Well, of course, he did, and she was standing right there, running her mouth.

"Where is he, Mother? Is he sick? Did he have an asthma attack?"

"I called up there, but nobody answered," said Loydell. "So I went up there, to y'all's room."

"And?" Jinx tapped a satin-clad foot. "What did he *say*, Mother?"

"Nothing. He wasn't in the room."

Jinx sighed heavily. "You are the most contrary old woman in the whole wide world and you are driving me NUTS! Now, I've got to leave my party and go see about him. Christ! I hope he's not stuck in some elevator."

"Nope," said Loydell. "He's not. He's gone."

Sam could feel a little bubble of spite rising in her breast. The fiancé had ditched Jinx. Jilted her at their engagement party. Split. Vamoosed. Oh, this was so sweet. And she was *so* glad she'd come downstairs to say good-night.

Jinx's face had gone white with an even lighter ring

around her scarlet mouth. She said, "Gone? What do you mean gone? Gone where?"

"Well, the note didn't say anything about their destination."

Loydell, Sam thought, you're enjoying this too much. Jinx is going to haul off and slap you in about half a second. Spit it out, lady, before it's too late.

"What note?" Jinx screamed. "What note?"

"The ransom note that was pinned to y'all's bed in that big old expensive room. A family of ten could live in there easy."

"Ransom note? What ransom note? Mother, have you gone crazy?" Jinx looked like she might stroke out any second. "You are the meanest woman I've ever known in my entire life. You're just making up all this crap to ruin my party. You hate me. You've always hated me!" Jinx was about to go into orbit. Even Sam was beginning to feel a little sorry for her.

"Shhhhhhhhh! Not so loud," said Loydell. "I didn't bring the note down because I know better than to mess with the scene of a crime, all those years I spent in the law enforcement, but basically what it said was that if you want to see Speed alive again, it'll cost you a million dollars, and you're not to go to the police under any circumstances, or they'll kill him. Dead."

"Holy cow," Sam said.

"Double holy cow," Kitty added. "If *this* doesn't take the cake."

"So to speak," said Sam.

"DEAD?" Jinx shrieked. "DEAD?"

"Shhhhhhhh!" said Loydell. "No, Julia Alice, I did not say he's dead. But he will be if you don't quiet down. They said not to breathe a word of this. Not to anybody."

Jinx whirled like a comet and raced out of the room as fast as she could in her skin-tight gold lamé.

Loydell went right on. "I don't know that I've ever run up on a man I thought was worth a million dollars, and I've encountered a gracious plenty of 'em in my time. Now, Jinx's dad, he knew some tricks that I guess I'd have paid for on a piecemeal basis, one by one, sort of like them men used to pay Olive, which reminds me, I need to go and call her again." Then Loydell was off in her sensible shoes, her words trailing behind her. "I can't imagine where Olive's got off to. This isn't like her. Not one bit."

EARLY TRULOVE WAS FOUR WHEN HE WENT HORSE CRAZY. At least that's what his momma called it when she'd carried him to downtown Daytona Beach, "to sit on a pony and have his picture took. He wouldn't get off that pony. I say I'm gone beat him with a stick, he say, Go on, this little horsey's mines. The man owned the pony, took the pictures, he just laughed. Say, boy like you, think you'd grow up out in the country, be used to horses 'fore now."

But that wasn't how it was. Early's mom, Valeen, had escaped the green prison of the deep Arkansas countryside, where you could live and die and meet your maker, all the time seeing nothing more exciting than two dogs in a dead heat chasing a squirrel. Valeen had been looking to bust out. And when a cousin, a daughter of Aunt Odessie, wrote her from Daytona Beach saying that there were not only jobs for black folks but a blue ocean and a sandy beach and *real* speed, race cars going around and around like a house afire in the Five Hundred, well, Valeen had started packing.

Grabbed up Early, her only son—named because he arrived at the end of her seventh month, small, but fully formed and raring to go—and headed for Daytona thinking a boy as in-a-big-hurry as Early could probably find himself something to do around the race cars when he grew up, mechanic maybe, he was handy—even if he was black in a white man's world.

But it wasn't cars that Early fixed on. It was that pony, and by the time he was sixteen, Early had migrated due west from Daytona Beach a little over an hour's drive to Ocala and Marion County, which claims the highest density of thoroughbred farms per square foot in the United States. Valeen said, Humph, could have stayed home in Arkansas, I knew horses what you be studying.

It was in Ocala that Early was taken in by Asphalt, a black groom who knew all there was to know about thoroughbreds—and young boys who had the bug. Asphalt taught Early that a horse was something you honored, that you were proud to serve them with the hard, low-paying work because there was glory in it. Besides, if you had the bug and you were black, what were your options? You'd never be a jockey, even if you were a small man with good hands like Early, nor a trainer. And as for owning, well, you might as well dream of being the lord of one of those castles that came with a yacht down in Palm Beach. But you could groom, you could hot-walk, you could travel the circuit of racetracks working with other good people, black and white and brown, good people who honored horses.

It was while he was down in New Orleans grooming for Joey the Horse's trainer that Early had met Jack Graham.

It was Jack who was waiting now behind the wheel of a tobacco brown Rolls when Early stepped out the back lobby door of the Palace Hotel. Jack, the same large silver-haired man Early had signaled to in the lobby only a few minutes earlier. Jack, the boss operator of Hot Springs's underground gambling machine, whom the locals called Mr. You Know Who, a term of both endearment and respect.

"You want to slide over, Jack?" Early hoped that he would. He'd never seen anyone so awful behind the wheel.

"I'll drive," said Jack, giving him his fishy grin.

Early knew that Jack knew how much he hated to ride with him and insisted on driving now and then just for the devil of it. It was those times that Early became a God-fearing Christian again, in fact, wished he were a Catholic, had himself some of those little beads.

They were heading out toward Lake Hamilton and Gardiner Place, one of Jack's two casinos. Jack had just missed grazing a Lincoln Town Car pulling out of a parking place on Bathhouse Row when he said to Early, "She's a looker. Doc's partner."

"What'd you expect? Aren't they always, the women, that is?"

"Yeah." Jack hoisted his big body in the leather seat, which creaked. "Doc always did have pretty good taste in women. I never knew what they saw in him, though. Even less now, he's showing his age. And the booze has got to be eating away his brain."

Then Early watched Jack check himself in the rearview mirror to see if you could say the same of him. Well, you couldn't. For a white man Jack was pretty sharp-looking, in Early's opinion, which probably didn't count for much, his being a better judge of horseflesh or womanflesh.

Jack Graham was about fifty, six foot three, two hundred pounds, maybe two-oh-five, with a powerful body, a nice big square-jawed face, and a nose that hadn't been broken but once. He had a full head of silver hair and bright blue eyes. Take that actor Brian Dennehy, subtract a few years, you'd pretty much come up with Jack Graham.

Jack himself had grown up in New Orleans's Irish Channel, out on Magazine Street, and could trace his lineage in the Big Easy's underworld back to his grandaddy, who was a bootlegger and had worked out the original accommodation with the Italians.

Jack was charming and smooth and bent—all prerequisites for the state's governorship, which he could have taken with a fingersnap, except that *Cut to the chase* was Jack's motto. Why go to all that trouble pretending to be straight when he had the juice to run numbers, cards, shylocking, bookmaking, all at the indulgence of Joey the Horse, who took a healthy cut, of course.

It was a horse named Lush Life, in fact, that had come between Jack and Joey and had brought Early into the picture.

Joey had desired that the filly win the last race of a Pick-Six, which would have resulted in Joey's bagging a half-million dollars and Lush Life not only breaking her maiden but becoming a rising star. Forget the details, the bottom line was Joey passed the responsibility for said scenario along to Jack, who not only understood the subtleties of such a delicate operation but also loved horses. Jack meticulously explained the game plan to one of his men out at the track, Doc Miller, who'd in turn explained it to Speed McKay. They'd fucked up (Speed from stupidity, Doc out of avarice, trying to cut his own angles) so ignobly that the end result was not only did Lush Life lose, but she literally died in the stretch due to the enormous amount of phenylbutazone pumped into her— bute not having been part of Jack's game plan at all.

Early had been broken-hearted. He'd loved that filly. Nonetheless, when he came stumbling into his backside barn after the race and found three of Joey the Horse's men about to club Jack's brains out, he thought three against one plus the tire iron was chickenshit odds, no matter what the big silver-haired man had done. So he'd mounted a horse named Caliban and, with a ferrier's tool, whacked each of the three upside their heads as neatly as if they'd been polo balls.

Jack had reached in his pocket on the spot and counted out five thousand dollars in hundred-dollar bills as a thank you. A few months later he'd called Early up, said, Come guard my body, be my man-of-all-trades, I'm going into the casino business. I'm up in Hot Springs, that being where Joey the Horse has decided he'll allow me to continue breathing.

Early wasn't sure. It would be tough to trade in the dawn smells of freshly farrowed track, manure, new-mown grass for cigarette smoke and booze in some casino room where you never saw the light of day. Especially after the time he'd pulled in the state pen in Angola, Louisiana, for a seriously dumb mistake, Early didn't fancy anything that felt like lockup. But, on the other hand, Hot Springs was home. His birthplace.

Jack said, "Oaklawn's up here, you know. Awfully sweet track. We'll buy us some horses, run 'em. First one, we'll call her To Lush Life."

That did it. Early had hung up his manure-caked rubber boots and overalls, got himself fitted for a neat navy blue double-breasted suit complete with bulletproof lining. He'd taken a quick course in target shooting, for which he found he had a natural aptitude, as he did for the martial arts, and he began to shadow Jack Graham, who quickly set up undercover casino operations in Hot Springs as if the town were ripe for sin. Which, not having had much to speak of since the feds shut down all the fun back in the sixties, it was.

And things had been good, except Jack had been steaming since the day Lush Life was put down. It wasn't even so much his exile. He said the mountains were a nice change from the swamp. It was that that perfectly beautiful filly had died for no good reason, Doc's cupidity not being a good reason.

That's what Jack had said to Doc when he'd called him

out on the matter. Jack wasn't one to blindside you with a tire iron. He'd called him out like a man, the last day he was in town before he shipped out for Hot Springs. Early hadn't been there, but he'd heard it wasn't much of a fight, at least not on Doc's part. Jack, who'd grown up with knocking around the ring in the Irish Channel, had stepped right up to Doc and started punishing him with his jab, put a couple of combinations together before he staggered him with a short left hand to the head. Doc fell facedown like a redwood. When he got to his feet, he didn't say a word, but there was murder in his eye.

Jack had brushed himself off and gone on his rounds to say his good-byes around town.

But that night when he got home, Jack found his two beloved Irish setters, Yeats and Maude, to whom he'd promised a big yard and long runs in the Arkansas hills, decapitated with their guts pulled out and strung around the bushes in front of his house like Christmas lights.

The pain had gone deep. Jack had truly loved those dogs.

But he was a patient man, and he knew how to bide his time. He'd gone on along to Hot Springs and set up his casinos, of which Joey the Horse got his twenty percent. One out on Lake Hamilton at Gardiner Place, a handsome former mansion now a superb restaurant with full-tilt gambling in the gigantic basement, which you could reach through an underground tunnel that led right from the marina where you could pull your boat up. Another in the old Quapaw Bathhouse right in the middle of town on Central Avenue.

Jack had been very busy—and very successful. He'd pat his pocket and say, "Early, I've got the sixth tailbone of a black cat in there, brings me luck." But it wasn't any Irish Channel mojo that made the man so good. He knew what he was doing, he wasn't afraid of work, and he was a good guy. People liked him. Early liked him a lot.

So things were going great, just rolling along, until that day just a couple of weeks ago, To Lush Life's running in the sixth, and Jack's in his favorite spot, way over at the top of the grandstand, you can see the horses making the last turn. Early's up in the Oaklawn Club with the white linen napkins and the roses on the tables, which he likes to do every once in a while just because he can, Jack gave him the membership as a little perk. All of a sudden Early spots Speed McKay. He can't believe his eyes, but it's the little man all right, romancing this curvy blonde, a couple of years on her, but you could tell she'd been the real article in her prime, and Speed's saying to her, "I once knew a another filly named Lush Life, just Lush Life without the To, but she was a lazy nag, couldn't go the distance, dropped dead rather than run."

Early wants to pull out his gun, pop the stupid little son of a bitch right there. Damn him! But the Oaklawn Club wasn't exactly the place to do that, not that he would really, he just *wanted* to so bad he could taste it. As soon as the race was over, To Lush Life won, bless her sweet heart, paid ten to one, he ran to find Jack.

"I want you on him like a fly on shit," had been Jack's response. Early knew that Jack was hoping that where there was Speed, there'd be Doc. So Early had spent the past few weeks following the little man, watching him romance the blonde. It wasn't long before he reported to Jack that their little Speed McKay seemed to be getting himself engaged to the ex-beauty queen who had won herself a million dollars in the Texas lottery not all that long ago.

"You don't say?" Jack had smiled and told Early to keep on keeping on. So Early followed them to the gate when the lovebirds flew off to the Bahamas and to New York, though he hadn't gone on either trip. Jack said he was interested in what was happening here at home. Like Speed renting a big stone house out on Lake Ouachita. Early kept watching, and one thing he noticed that was real odd was that the bride-to-be never showed at the lake house. Never set foot in it. Never drove by. Never bought even a lamp for it. Now wasn't that strange, that she wouldn't take an interest in their lovenest?

"Let Speed go, watch the house," Jack had said.

Which is how Early came to see Doc and then Mickey drive up to the big stone house yesterday.

Jack had said, "So who's the woman?"

Early did some backtracking through friends of friends in New Orleans and found out that Doc and Speed hadn't been working together for a long time now, that Doc had been partnered with this Mickey Steele for a few months. And he was almost sure she was the woman he had seen Speed having lunch with at the Carousel Club the week before.

Now Jack, behind the wheel, puffed on his little cigar and goosed the gas so he almost hit a Toyota that was halfway through a left turn. He said, "What's Doc's angle, Early? He has to know I'm here. Got to know first chance I get, I'm going to even the score."

Early peeked through his fingers. "I don't know what they're up to, Jack. Like I told you, Speed rents the house, then these two show up. I drive by, I see their Mercedes sitting in the driveway pretty as you please. Doesn't make sense to me."

Jack agreed. "And you actually saw Doc? You're sure it was him?"

Early nodded. "I parked down a way, sneaked back on foot. Got up close enough to see Doc sitting in the kitchen, drinking a beer, eating a big bag of potato chips, sour cream and chives."

"We wait long enough, he'll have a heart attack. The man always was stuffing his face with junk."

Though Jack himself was carrying a few extra pounds, it was what he called goodweight. Made of the finest ingredients, gumbo and crawfish étoufée and lamb stew, he ordered the baby lamb direct from a grower in Marin County. He had a man in southern California who air-shipped his restaurant produce, the best grown on God's green earth, from the Chino Farm twice a week. Jack himself was a most extraordinary cook.

Early said, "Well, you can't say that about the woman. Doc's partner's a runner. Up and down the hills. Wears those little shorts."

"Interesting." Jack blew a smoke ring. "And cards are her speciality?"

"She's a righteous player. Wouldn't even have to cheat to make a decent living on poker tournaments. Except she likes to cheat."

"Well, you know, lots of them do." Jack grinned. And then the grin faded, and he said, "You know, what bothers me is Doc's not stupid like Speed. Mean as a five-foot rattle snake with a six-foot poker up his butt, but clever."

And that was as far as he went. Jack never mentioned the animals. Never said a word about Lush Life or Yeats or Maude. He blew another smoke ring. "Do you think it's possible, Early, this has anything to do with Joey the Horse? Maybe Joey's decided he wants to muscle me out up here now that things are going so well, sent Doc to do the job."

Early shook his head. "Joey loves you, boss. That's why he told you to come up here, because he couldn't bear to kill you. So why would he change his mind now? Besides, you think Joey'd pick those two?"

"Nawh. If Joey were in the same room with Doc and Speed, he'd step on them like they were waterbugs. He wouldn't send those bums to do me. The man has more respect than that. Besides, you're right, he loves me too much."

Early glanced over at Jack. The big man's mouth was turned down at the corners, like he tasted something rotten. Early really liked Jack. Actually, he'd grown to love the man. Which meant he liked to see him happy. "So, what do you think, Jack, you want me to shoot 'em?"

At that Jack Graham wheeled the big heavy car right off the road into the parking lot of a Kentucky Fried Chicken, cutting in front of a pickup truck that squealed and fishtailed, but stopped, the driver inside glad he'd listened to his wife and had that five-hundred-dollar brake job.

"What do you mean, shoot 'em?" Jack looked like he was going to blow up, like he might explode all over the inside of the Rolls.

Early was confused. Wasn't he a bodyguard, for chrissakes? Wasn't that what Jack had been talking about for months, doing Speed and Doc?

Though to tell you the truth, at first Early didn't think he wanted to. He was nervous about it, lay awake nights thinking how that would be. He knew it'd be nothing like that time he'd got real thirsty after a track kitchen meal of white bread and chicken wings, swaggered in the front door of the liquor store with his finger poked in his jacket pocket like it was a gun, and said Gimme y'all's cash and a six-pack of Bud. The liquor man had laughed, busted his arm with a baseball bat, next thing Early knew he was doing thirty-seven months at Angola in West Feliciana Parish, compliments of the Louisiana State Penal Authority. But that time hadn't been for real. No gun.

And, of course, if some sucker who'd got pissed because he'd just gambled away the farm came waving a pistol, hollering about blasting Jack six ways to Sunday, now that was something else again. But if somebody, even Jack, just picked out a person, said, Kill that mother, he'd have a hard time with it.

On the other hand, Early'd got to thinking about Lush Life, that sweet filly, pretty little girl who never had an evil thought in her head, and he got to thinking about people getting away with mistreating all kinds of animals, not just horses, and he said, Hell, yeah, I could kill those rotten sons of bitches. Point me at 'em.

And now Jack's saying, "Did you think I was going to *kill* them, Early? I'm not a killer. I'm a businessman."

"Yeah, uh-huh," said Early, not knowing what to think. Which way to look. Trying to cover his butt. "I was just saying that in a manner of speaking, you know. Shoot 'em. Like mess 'em up. Heh heh heh. But I knew all the while what you had in mind was just teaching 'em a lesson, right? Like stealing Doc's woman? Maybe Speed's, too, that blonde? I told you, didn't I, she's first runner-up to Miss Arkansas?" Early was trying to change the subject, fast.

And it worked. Or something did, as suddenly the big man relaxed back into the leather seat.

Jack's moods reminded Early of when he was living down in New Orleans, a big storm would blow in over Lake Pontchartrain. One minute it wasn't there, next thing you knew, skies dark as pitch, hundred-mile-an-hour wind was throwing water and trash all over you, you figure you're dead, then it was history. Leaving you wondering, did you have a little nightmare there or what?

Jack was saying, "Was. Jinx Watson *was* a beauty queen. A long time ago, Early." Then Jack rotated his big head, and his neck creaked. "But what the hell, none of us are as young as we used to be."

Whew. Early eased back a bit in his seat, too. Jesus Christ, was he confused. What did the mob do if it didn't kill people? On the other hand, Jack wasn't the mob. He was Irish, anybody could see that, with a business accommodation with the Italians.

"I've always thought," said Jack, as if he were reading Early's mind, "that killing people was crude. There are better ways to teach them a lesson."

Awh, shit. Now the man was going to make him do

torture. *That's* what he meant by bodyguarding. Wrapping folks in chains. Mashing on their toes. Wrenching their arms out of the sockets. Early didn't go with that kind of stuff. You going to do somebody, you ought to go in and just do them. Don't be messing around.

Jack was saying, "And the more you know about them, the easier it is to find their soft spots."

Early wasn't sure exactly what Jack was talking about now. And wasn't sure he wanted to know.

"That's why I think it would be a good idea if I had a little chat with Miss Mickey Steele."

Just a chat? Whew. "Good idea, Jack. Great."

Then Jack floored the Rolls, and they screeched back onto Highway 7, missing a tractor-trailer rig by millimeters. That did it, first thing in the morning, Early was going over there to St. Patrick's Church. See if he could buy himself some of those beads.

10

WHICH IS EXACTLY WHAT EARLY WOULD HAVE DONE IF he'd been able to get a decent night's sleep.

But unh-uh.

Because what's the first thing he sees when he gets home to his Lake Hamilton condo a little after midnight—Jack had said to go on home, things were copasetic in the casino, he was going to bed himself—but his second cousin Lateesha sitting on his doorstep. In a thousand years he wouldn't have thought that'd be the ending to his evening.

Early said, "What are you doing way out here, girl? Aunt Odessie knows you out in the middle of the night, she's gonna beat you with a strap."

Which Lateesha didn't think was a very good beginning, so she told him quick an abbreviated version of her stealing the car and its crashing backwards into that stupid old pine tree.

"Stole!" Early said, the gold star in his teeth flashing in his porch light. "I can't believe it! Girl on the honor roll like you, soloist at the Rising Star—"

"Screw the honor roll."

That was when Early jumped back like she'd slapped him, that kind of talk.

"And don't give me that look. It's all that Little Miss Too-Good stuff that got me into this mess in the first place. I am sick to death of everybody expecting me to be an angel all the time. Screw that!"

Early got this mean look and said, "I can't stand it when women use bad language. I'm going to take you in the house and wash your mouth out with soap." Lateesha thought that was an awfully wimpy thing for a stone killer to say. But, on the other hand, even stone killers were just folks.

But when she said something about the car being a Sunliner, Early changed his tune quick. He got all fired up and hollered, "What are you waiting for, girl, let's go!" They jumped in Early's old red Caddy, the kind with the big tail fins, and ten, fifteen minutes later, it not being all that far between Lake Hamilton and Lake Ouachita, they were out in the woods pulled in behind that Sunliner.

Early had taken one look, said, "Oooohweee! Cherry baby like this'll be worth twenty thou down in Miami. South Beach, those movie star, modeling folks got lots more money than sense, *love* this kind of vintage flash. Retractable hardtop, Lordy mercy, they'll be falling all over themselves handing me the scratch."

Lateesha didn't know what he was talking about, but she did know she was watching a man who had more than a passing familiarity with the concept of hot-wiring. Early didn't need any lamp cord with metal clips on it either. In sixty seconds, he'd reached over with one hand and slammed down the sprung trunk without even looking in it, grabbed a funny-looking screwdriver out of the gym bag he'd grabbed out of the Caddy, jumped in, and had that sucker up and running.

"Just follow me," he'd hollered at Lateesha, and she did. Fifteen-and-a-half years old, she'd taken the classroom part of drivers' ed, but not the practicum, though like most kids, she'd been driving since she was old enough to see through the wheel. And this Caddy, it moved like a dream. They cruised back toward town on Albert Pike, then Early signaled right, and she followed the Sunliner's taillights right into the back driveway of the deserted mansion on Orange the kids called the Ghost House.

It was a down-at-the-heels Victorian four stories tall, if you counted the cupola on the top, the Tower Room, where all the murders took place, murders the kids made up as they went along. The Ghost House had once belonged to a white railroad magnate; now this part of town was black and a bit down on its luck.

Lateesha couldn't imagine what Early was doing, but he pulled the Sunliner right up to a big yawning garage made of sheetmetal in the Ghost House's backyard. The doors were open, and Lateesha could see it was filled with cars, pieces of cars, and a backhoe.

"Come on, girl," said Early, getting out of the Sunliner and waving at her, but Lateesha wasn't setting foot out of that Caddy. The ghosts were one thing, but the dogs that had set up to yowling were another. Lateesha had already had enough dealings in her young lifetime with great big dogs with hungry slobbering jaws, thank you very much.

Then Early tooted the horn and out of the house came the tallest man Lateesha had ever seen in real life, forget the basketball players on TV. He must have been at least seven feet, scrunching down through the doorway. If he hadn't been black, Lateesha knew she'd have screamed for sure, thinking he was Frankenstein. Or Lurch. Definitely one of those creepy critters—and BIG. He yelled, "Shut up, dogs!" And they did.

"You did good, girl." That was Early patting her on the head. Now the big man reached for her hand, she was sure he was going to munch it for a midnight snack, but he had the gentlest touch, it was absolutely amazing, and Early said, "Lateesha, you know Fontaine, don't you, your cousin June's husband?"

Well, the truth was, she didn't even know Early all that well, her growing up in New Orleans, his traveling all over the country following the racing before he and Mr. You Know Who moved to town. Now June, she'd met her, she worked in the baths over at the Palace Hotel. But Lateesha was sure she didn't know Fontaine. It wasn't like she'd forget him, was it?

"Glad to meet you, missy," said Fontaine. He had this deep Roto-Rooter of a voice, just like you'd expect.

Then Early and Fontaine stepped off to the side and talked together like men do, Fontaine peering down, Early, barely five foot four, looking like he was about to get a crick in his neck.

Fontaine nodded his head like he did business in the middle of the night all the time, saying, "Nope, parts, they wouldn't bring you nothing. But, sure, it's hot, you gone have to paint it, you want to drive it all that way to Florida. I know, it's a shame, but I'll do it for you turquoise and white, that'd be jake." Then a couple more Uh-huhs and You got its. Whatever it takes. Why I'd appreciate it. Nuh-unh, that's more than fair. The next thing Lateesha knew, they'd left the Sunliner, she and Early were both back in that Caddy headed for Aunt

Odessie's, and Early was saying, "Honey, don't you worry your pretty little head. Early's gonna take care of everything."

Well, that might be true. But even if she was only fifteen and a half years old, Lateesha knew that this thing had suddenly zigzagged off from being her show to being Early's. Furthermore, somebody was making more than a buck out of it, and it sure as hell wasn't her. Which—even if Early was a stone killer and even if he had pulled her wagon out of the ditch, so to speak—didn't sit well with Miss Lateesha Rollins at all.

11

ABOUT FIVE HOURS LATER, SHORTLY AFTER DAWN, SAM woke up full of beans and raring to go. Which was rather a shock, since she hadn't gotten to sleep till after three. But there she was ordering herself some room-service coffee, sitting back and sipping it, thinking about what she might do with this jump on the day. The first thing she wanted to do was go and see about Olive. The last thing was to get embroiled again with Jinx and the kidnapping.

She'd had enough of that last night. Though she had to admit that the screaming and carrying on in Kitty's room until the wee hours had had a certain salutary effect. It had certainly kept her mind off Harry. That is until Jinx had chunked a Coke can at her, screaming, "I know why you want me to call the police and get Speed killed! Because you're jealous that you don't have a boyfriend of your own! Lost him to a younger woman!"

Sam had caught the Coke and hurled it back at Jinx, missing her by millimeters. But her killer look at Kitty, the blabbermouth, hit its target. So did her reply. "Yes, indeedy. Another woman, Jinx, another sleazoid blonde, just like you."

It had been a tacky evening, all right. With Kitty chorusing now and again, "Excuse me. Could we get back to the subject? A man has been kidnapped here. Hello? Yoohoo."

Finally, without making a phone call to the police or any other authorities, they'd chucked it in, Kitty and Jinx collapsing in Kitty's room, God bless the child who had her own.

Now after a couple cups of coffee, Sam felt exactly the same way she had last evening: Whatever Jinx chose to do about her purloined fiancé was her own affair. Sam herself was more concerned with making sure her new friend Olive was all right. Had she ever shown up at the party or not? She looked up Loydell Watson in the phone directory, and was about to give her a jingle when her phone rang.

"Hello?"

"Hi. It's me, Harry."

Sam dropped the receiver into the cradle like it was a snake. Her head was buzzing. The blood in her veins was backing up. She was stunned. She stared off into space for five full minutes. What did he want? Why was he calling? Now that he'd turned her world upside down, why didn't he leave her to sort through the debris? Did he think she was going to say, Oh, I understand, if I hadn't been afraid of commitment, you wouldn't have been screwing around.

Then she stood. She absolutely was not going to think about Harry. She was going to keep moving in a forward direction. She made herself focus on Loydell's number, and she picked up the phone.

Loydell answered on the first ring. "Oh, Sam, I'd

hoped you were Olive. It's about the right time for her to call." Loydell sighed. "I guess I'll drive out to her house. I was going to last night, but I don't see so good in the dark, I'd probably drive off in a ditch, then there'd be two old ladies for the police to look for."

"Did you call the police?"

"I did. But I don't even want to waste my breath talking about them. I'll tell you, the police ain't what they used to be. Used to *help* folks. Don't get me started." Then she paused. "I guess you wonder why I'm not asking about Jinx's fiancé."

Sam didn't know exactly what to say. It wasn't as if Speed had been number one on her Hit Parade either. Actually, she felt a little ashamed.

Loydell continued, "I know I ought to call Jinx and see what's happening with her fiancé being snatched up. But frankly, I have to tell you, compared to Olive, I just don't care very much. I had a hard time working up any enthusiasm about the little man from the get-go. Not that I have anything against him personally, though I never trusted him any further than I could throw him. Of course, that's pretty much the way I feel about most people." She paused. "Including Jinx. I guess that's a terrible thing to admit, not caring much for your only child, but I swear, we've had about as much in common as a Martian and a Venutian from the minute we first spied one another. That child popped out, took one look at me, and set to squalling so loud I wanted to slap her, and it's been pretty much that way ever since. And, don't mistake me, it's a two-way street. We're just oil and water."

"Well, Loydell." Sam didn't know what else to say. She'd felt exactly the same way about Jinx, but it was strange, hearing her mother say these things. Especially because Loydell seemed so warm.

"It's kind of a tragedy," said Loydell, "our feeling that

way, but you know, you play what you're dealt in this life. On the other hand, you take Olive."

Sam could hear the tears building in Loydell's voice.

"We met on the first day of first grade, sixty-six years ago, and we loved one another on sight. Not that we were always best friends, you understand. In fact, there were years that went by that we hardly spoke. It wasn't that we were mad at one another, just that our lives took off in different directions. Olive's got real different there for a while when she was working in one of those old cathouses up here behind Central. Just a block down from where I live right now."

Sam thought back to Olive telling her about the hot times in old Hot Springs. Olive *had* had more than a passing familiarity with the naughtiness of those days.

"There were those," said Loydell, "who didn't speak to Olive ever again after that. I, personally, have no use for those people. Hypocrites, with their thin little mouths." She stopped and took a deep breath. "Well, listen to me rambling on. That's what happens when you get to be an old lady. But all of that's to say, I'm desperate to know where Olive's got off to, but I don't plan to put one iota of effort into Speed McKay's search and rescue. And them that don't like it can go suck eggs."

Sam laughed. "Well, I'm happy to help you look for Olive. Why don't I drive out to her place?" Proceeding, full steam ahead in a forward motion. Not stopping to think about Harry. Not stopping for Go.

"Oh, good. Sugar, you do that, and I'll call the hospital, and if Olive's not there, I'll zip around to our favorite haunts, see if maybe Olive stopped somewhere, like maybe went for a bite of barbecue at McClard's and had a stroke out in her car. For all we know, she could be sitting, stove up, out in a parking lot somewhere. Let me get going here, you call me later, and in the meantime, maybe she'll show up."

"I'm sure she will, Loydell."

"Sure." The old lady laughed. Sam could tell it was an effort. "I bet she's been shacked up with some young man, now she's too embarrassed to show her face, missing the party. She's sitting over in the Pancake House trying to make up a good story."

"I bet she is," said Sam. "Or I'll catch the two of them still in bed back at her house. Now, let me dress and get moving."

Which is how Sam came to be walking into the Gas 'N Grub at eight A.M., saying to the young man who was standing there, "Hello. Do you happen to know where the older lady who works here might be?"

She was thinking, Jesus, was Loydell right or what? Could she have spent the night with this young hunk? Except the kid was young enough to be Olive's grandson.

Then, sure enough, the young man in the plain white T-shirt, khakis, and white running shoes reached over and touched Sam's arm lightly with his fingertips like he wanted to show her that he wasn't going to hurt her, not now, not ever, and said, "Ma'am, that old lady's my grandma, I'm Bobby Adair, and she's who I'm here to visit, and I'm real worried about her. She ought to be here, and I don't know where she's got off to. It's gonna be up to me and Pearl here to find her. That is, the Hot Springs cops don't lock me up first."

That was certainly an interesting train of thought. And obviously Pearl was of the same opinion, for when Bobby said the dog's name, the redbone hound began to shake her head with its long lovely ears and bawl like a baby.

"You can see Pearl's real upset," said Bobby. "When I got here, just a little while ago, she was carrying on like this. I got the feeling she's been doing it for some time. I was just about to see if I could start her tracking Mamaw. Are you a friend of hers?" Then he gave Sam a long look, taking in her white linen jacket, navy-and-white striped T-shirt, jeans, loafers. "No, you don't look like you're from around here."

Bobby Adair himself was an innocent-looking boy of about twenty-five years, five-ten, clean-featured, with a brown crew cut and clear blue eyes that seemed to look straight through your head, watch the picture show you were running in there. He had a nice tan and a very good build, which made Sam wonder aloud if he'd just come home from someplace like Venice Beach in California. But then, why would he be talking about the Hot Springs Police?

"No, ma'am, I haven't been to any beach. In fact, I just yesterday afternoon late got out of Cummins, that's the correctional facility for stone-bad motorscooters down between Pine Bluff and McGehee. Not that I'm that bad, but the reason they sent me there is related to your other question about the Hot Springs Police."

Working the crime beat, Sam had met more than her share of cons, ex-cons, and pre-cons, but she had to tell him he was the most polite member of any category she'd run up on.

"Well, yes, ma'am, I believe in politeness. Which is why I sent away from prison for a membership and joined the Graciousness Society which is headquartered in Elberton, Georgia. I look forward to their bimonthly newsletter which gives tips on how to make the world a kinder and gentler place. For real. Not just giving lip service to the idea, like some people I might mention. I have my Graciousness Society card right here in my wallet, if you'd like to see it."

You know, thought Sam, maybe she ought to give up on writing *American Weird*. Because, more and more it seemed, weird wasn't weird at all. It was the norm, like the dysfunctional family. It's just that now there was a name for it.

She said, "Could you go back and do the part about

the Hot Springs Police Department again? It's early, and I'm tracking a little slow."

"Well, they never took kindly to my assaulting Archie Blackshears," Bobby said in his nice polite voice, like you'd asked him the time and he'd checked his Timex and was pleased as punch to be sharing it with you.

Sam said, "Cops usually don't take to people assaulting one another."

"Well, I didn't hurt him nearly as bad as he had coming to him. But you're right, even if you just mess somebody up a little, they take it real hard. Especially when he's one of their own."

"Archie Blackshears is a cop?"

"Yes, ma'am, he is. And he's a good cop, I always gave him that. But he's a bad person. A very bad person."

Sam nodded, trying to figure out what it was this very polite angelic-looking self-admitted cop-assaulter might mean.

Bobby helped her. "He was very good at doing his job without busting too many heads. I used to see quite a bit of him, he was my girlfriend Cynthia's daddy."

"You assaulted your girlfriend's dad?"

"You'd have to have been there," Bobby said without an ounce of irony, looking her straight in the eye. His mouth seemed to hold itself in a naturally sweet expression. "You'd have to have seen how he did her when he got to drinking."

Oh, yes. Having once been a member of that worldwide organization of folks who took leave of their senses behind a few belts, Sam was well aware of the possibilities. Her personal specialties had been mostly self-destructive, but she knew lots of drunks, men especially, who went in for other forms of abuse that involved their tongues, fists, feet, and other people's more tender regions.

She said, "So you told Archie to stop, and he didn't?"

"That's right."

"But you didn't shoot him. We're not talking about a gun here?"

Bobby smiled sweetly. "At the time I didn't know what it was I'd picked up. I really wasn't thinking. Cynthia had a broken arm and was bleeding sideways out of her squashed nose. Archie was charging me like a big old bull, so I just grabbed for something. It turned out it was this great big trophy he'd won for target shooting. I think it was that little pistol on the top that knocked the hole in his noggin."

"You hit him with the trophy in self-defense?"

"Well, the cops, they said he wasn't armed."

"And?"

"You know, I never was sure. I mean, the thing happened in such a blur. I was so mad, seeing Cynthia like that, and I'd seen Archie with a gun so many times—I didn't really think about it. I just hit him."

"What'd Cynthia say?"

"At the trial she said he wasn't armed. And other than that, well, she's never spoke to me again personally. She let it be known she didn't want anything to do with me."

It could happen. Thank you very kindly for saving my life, now hit the road. It could have been that way. And then, on the other hand, it could be that *none* of this was true. Sam had known enough cons to know that almost all of them had convenient and colorful imaginations. If he even *was* a con—but it was your rare bird who'd claim to be and wasn't.

"The way I figure it," said Bobby, "you do what you've got to do. What I had to do then was stop Archie from doing anyone any more harm. What Cynthia had to do, well, I know the whole thing had to be hard for her. And what I have to do right now is figure out why my Grandma Olive's not here, not in her little house there up the hill, my car she was keeping for me's gone, and Pearl here's about to have a fit."

At that, Pearl started up her bawling again, Owwwr-huuuuu, Owwwrhuuuu, so loud and pitiful Sam had to cover her ears.

"What makes you think she didn't just go off to run an errand, leaving Pearl to guard the store?" Sam doubted that seriously, but she wanted to know Bobby's theory.

"With the door open? She'd never do that. And she'd never take my Sunliner either. You know the car I mean—retractable hardtop convertible coupe? This one's a black-and-gold sixty-one, you saw it it'd make your heart beat faster. She'd take her old Rabbit if she was going somewhere, and it's still sitting up at her house. Furthermore, the cashbox's clean. It's like somebody came in here, snatched her up along with every last red cent. And I found this." He held up a ring.

Sam reached out and took it from his hand. She said, "I don't remember her wearing this yesterday. I stopped to buy some gas and had a nice long chat with Olive."

"It was kicked up in a corner underneath the counter. Tell you the truth, I don't think this thing looks good."

Sam had to agree. She stared at the ring, thinking. The diamond looked like a pretty good fake to her, but if someone had robbed Olive, would he know that? Toss it on the floor? Or, in some flurry of activity that she didn't want to think about, had it just been overlooked? This could be an important piece of evidence. Or it could be nothing. But it was certainly worth hanging on to.

Pearl sniffed the air and howled again. Then she ran to the door and hurled herself against it.

Sam said, "I know what you said about the police, but if you think something's happened to your grandmother, well, to tell you the truth, the main reason I came by this morning is because she didn't show up last night at a party we were coincidentally both going to."

Sam looked around the store, checking for traces of blood, but the place looked squeaky clean. "Anyway, I know you don't want to go to the police, but don't you think you ought to report it if you really think something's happened to her?"

Or maybe you know for sure. Maybe you robbed her and stuffed her in the broom closet. That could have been what happened. What did she know? She certainly didn't know who this young man was. Not really.

"I *just* got here," he said as if he could read her mind. "Ten minutes before you. Tell you what, would you like to see my parole papers?"

Before she could answer, Bobby had reached in his back pocket and pulled them out. There was even a photo ID. Yep, that was Bobby Adair, all right. Not that that proved he was Olive's grandson. Not necessarily. But probably he was.

"And, like I said, *I* go to the police, they're gonna have me locked up in about five seconds. Probably say *I'm* the one who made my grandma run off. And the terms of my parole, I'm not even supposed to be here. Not supposed to be within fifty miles of Hot Springs or Cynthia or any of her daddy's cop friends. But I had to come and see Mamaw. She's the only family I've got, her and Pearl. And I thought I'd try to see Cyn."

With that, Bobby Adair opened the door of the store. Pearl took off like a shot, toenails scratching the pavement, nose low on the ground, high in the air, down in the dirt, headed straight down Highway 70 toward Hot Springs like they were holding a reservation in her name at the Palace Hotel. And before Sam knew it, she had handed Bobby her car keys, and she was riding shotgun down the road after Pearl in her own BMW. She was swept away with the passion of the hunt, her head hanging out the window following Pearl's bawling as surely as if she and Bobby were running through bogs and bushes behind a grand champion about to chop on a big boss coon.

She and Bobby weren't saying much. In particular, he hadn't said a word about her palming and pocketing that fake diamond ring.

12

LOYDELL KNEW IN HER BONES THAT SOMETHING AWFUL HAD happened to Olive. Not because of some cockamamie voodoo like that stuff that Jinx went on about, those stupid altars she built out of rock crystal. Like crystals were something special; as if you couldn't go out to a million places around Hot Springs and dig them up yourself. Nope, Loydell didn't hold with any of that bullshit, that's what she called it. She'd tried to stop cursing so bad once she'd got sober, but so far, thirty years, she hadn't been able to.

However, there were lots of advantages to stopping with the booze, other than the obvious ones, like she wasn't going to die of cirrhosis and she wasn't falling down drunk all the time. Sobriety had really improved her disposition, and furthermore, she was more in tune with her gut. Though sometimes, she still didn't want to hear what it was saying. And her gut said this business about Olive was bad. Real bad. So, while she was going to go through the motions of finding Olive, she knew that there really wasn't any point. Her gut told her that Olive's spirit had left this earth, had gone on without her. Despite their best laid plans, Olive had soloed into the Great Beyond.

That's why she was still sitting at her blue breakfast table in her little yellow house on Exchange with a piece of toast loaded with blackberry preserves halfway to her face. There was no hurry to go out and beat the bushes looking for Olive. She might as well have herself another cup of coffee.

She hadn't explained all this to that nice woman Sam because she didn't want her to think she was just another dotty old lady, the kind who didn't know shit from Shinola.

She sat staring off into space, thinking about Olive and how much she was going to miss her. She felt a tiny twinge of guilt, but just a tiny one, about not caring more about Speed's disappearance. Well, if she and Jinx hadn't always been so distant, it'd be easier to care about her fiancé, but given the way things were, it was sort of like when you read in the paper about the troubles of people who lived in some far-off place. It was hard to make them seem concrete.

At that, Loydell remembered her toast, and took another bite. Wasn't that something, when you started forgetting what you were doing in the middle of a meal?

Why, just the other day, her mind had drifted off halfway through her bath; when she came to, the bubbles were gone, and the water was cold. She'd been thinking about herself and Olive getting dressed for that election night party over in Little Rock. They'd taken turns going to one another's houses, pulling out all their clothes like they were in high school again. Fixing one another's hair. Olive had gotten her all up in this purple velvet number that came down to the floor. Loydell had said she was going to trip and break her neck, and Olive had said, So what? And then they'd laughed and laughed.

They'd laughed because who cared about a broken neck when you already had made provisions for your own passing? They didn't mention it to most people because there weren't many that had the gumption to think about things like that, which was perfectly ridiculous considering that dying was the one thing that everybody on earth had to do sometime.

And Loydell certainly didn't say anything about their

suicide pact—their plans for chucking it all in at seventy-five, if not before—when she'd called down to the P.D. last night. She got Archie Blackshears on the phone. She asked him to send a patrol car out to check on Olive.

She knew better. She also knew better than to try to report Olive as a missing person. It was one hell of a lot harder to be missing than you'd think.

Archie had said, "Well, Loydell, Olive isn't a minor, is she?"

"She's seventy-two years old, same as me, Archie, as you know very well. I didn't say she was missing. I said I was worried about her and just want somebody to drive by her house."

"Well, is she mentally incompetent? If she's not a minor or mentally incompetent or in need of some life-supporting medication, we can't do a thing. Stand to get sued for invasion of privacy. She has the right to go off, do anything she wants to."

"I know that, you idiot!" Loydell had slammed down the phone.

She'd thought for a few minutes about going next door and seeing if Archie's daughter, Cynthia, was home, get her to drive out to Olive's. Cynthia and Olive were real good friends, even after all that mess with Bobby Adair—Olive's grandson and Cynthia's boyfriend—being sent up for trying to kill Archie, which he didn't, in the first place, and if he had, it would have been a blessing, is what they'd said, you asked most folks. Actually, she and Olive both loved Cynthia like she was a grand-daughter, and Loydell had been pleased as punch to have Cynthia move in her rent house next door when Cynthia had left Archie's house right after they sent Bobby to the pokey over at Cummins. Loydell found it cozy, having Cynthia around. But last night Cynthia's lights had been out, and finally Loydell had gone to bed. Not that she'd slept much.

Now Loydell had finished her breakfast and made her

way out to her two-door ice blue Chevette. She was talking to herself. Saying, Cops! Like I said to Sam, they sure don't make 'em like they used to. Now they're just a bunch of big old lazy overgrown boys mostly, like to dress up and carry guns. In cahoots with the big lawbreakers what make the money. Spend half their time sucking after what they can get from the drug dealers, don't have the time anymore to help your ordinary taxpaying, law-abiding citizen. Why, she bet that even if Jinx had the good sense, which she didn't, to call the Hot Springs P.D. about that Speed McKay, they wouldn't do a thing. Well, maybe they just might if she went down there, sat and crossed her legs with one of those little bitty skirts she wore like she was still sixteen years old. They might, once they'd got their eyes full. Then Loydell opened the door of the Chevette, stepped in, and was getting settled behind the steering wheel before it dawned on her that there was a young man standing in her driveway, leaned over knocking on the window on the passenger side.

"Jesus H. Christ!" said Loydell, who'd never thought that the Man Himself was listening to every word. If He did, she was sure He'd have already died of boredom.

"I'm sorry, I sure didn't meant to scare you," said the man, squatting down. He was a beanpole, tall but no bigger around than herself, and Loydell was a skinny little old woman, shrinking by the day. The man was a study in brown. Brown hair, brown eyes, dressed all in tan, suit, shirt, tie. Close your eyes, not much remained of him on your eyeballs.

"What do you want, son? I've got places to go," said Loydell.

"I was just wondering . . . could you roll this window down, please, ma'am?"

Loydell did. She didn't have the patience to try to make out what he was saying through the glass.

"I'm doing a market survey for Beckel & Sally, a shoe

manufacturer out of Kansas City and . . . well, we're curious about the fit of ladies' shoes. You know, for years, manufacturers didn't give a rip about whether or not women's feet were comfortable."

"You can say that again," said Loydell looking down at her sensible black oxfords. "I order these out of a catalogue from a store in Indianapolis that specializes in comfy. All those years I stood around jails, well, you can bet I didn't do it in high heels."

At the mention of jail, the young man seemed to rock back a bit, and then he said, "Ma'am, I think that's awfully interesting. Would you mind if I . . . ?" He laid his hand on the door like he was going to open it.

"Make it snappy now," said Loydell. "I don't have all day."

"I can certainly appreciate that." He was sitting beside her in the Chevette before you could say Jack Robinson. He wasn't a bad-looking boy, a little nervous maybe. "Ma'am, would it be too much of an imposition if I took a look at one of your special-order comfy shoes? It would help our research immeasurably if we knew what it was women really wanted."

"Son." Loydell laughed. "You figure that out, I'll tell you, you can do better than the shoe business." She reached over and untied her shoe with the sensible two-inch heel, the lug sole, the layer of shock-absorption just like those running shoes, the good arch support, your high-quality black calf uppers with the attractive stitching and the little diamond-shaped holes so your toes could breathe.

"Ummmmmh," said the young man, breathing deeply himself, snuggling her shoe in his right hand like it was his heart's desire. "Oh yes, ma'am, this is something all right." Holding her shoe closer to his face, like he really wanted to get a good look.

But though Loydell realized she'd been a fool letting him in the car in the first place and giving him her shoe, she wasn't fool enough to let him keep on sniffing, getting himself all worked up.

Because that's exactly what he was doing.

The man was some kind of shoe-sniffing pervert. Loydell, with her years of experience in law enforcement, knew it took all kinds, but that didn't mean she had to put up with it.

She said, just as sweetly as she could, "Excuse me," which the young man hardly heard, he was off in toe-sniffing heaven, just like he'd done some kind of drug. She reached right over him and snapped open her glove compartment and pulled out her little .22 Jaguar Baretta, one of the perks of having been in law enforcement, and said, "Son, I'm gonna give you about two seconds to drop that clodhopper and get the hell out of my vehicle. I'd run you on down to the department, get them boys to lock you up, but I've got serious business on my mind."

She'd say one thing for the young pervert. He knew how to move.

13

YOU KNOW THAT EXPRESSION, THAT DOG WON'T HUNT? Bill Clinton used it in a speech up in New York during the Democratic Convention, and the Yankees said, What's he mean? As if they wouldn't know, they gave it a minute's thought. Anyway, Pearl was the opposite of that dog. Hunting was what she wouldn't stop. When they got to the city limits, that long stretch of strip shopping centers, Jack in the Boxes, and gas stations that have mushroomed at the edge of every American town, Sam was afraid the hound was going to be run over in traffic, so she got out and ran along behind her. Bobby brought up the rear, slumped down in the BMW and wearing a baseball cap he hoped would keep him incognito and out of the clutches of the Hot Springs P.D. Even though she did her share of exercise classes and fast-walking, Sam thought she was going to roll over and die by the time they came to the old part of town.

Hot Springs had begun as a single row of buildings on either side of a creek that flowed through the narrow mountain valley. Now that creek was Central Avenue, and the buildings on one side were the eight phantasmagorical bathhouses built in the twenties; on the other stood a row of nineteenth-century structures now housing art galleries, candy shops, stores that sold tourist bric-a-brac. On both sides of the street, the mountains sat right on backdoor steps.

Pearl loped along the sidewalk, pausing to take a whiz at one of the five-globed cast iron lampposts in front of the bathhouses. A little girl wearing a Mountain Valley Water T-shirt called, *Here, doggie, doggie, doggie*, to Pearl from a wooden rocker on the Fordyce Bathhouse's front porch. But the dog trudged on.

She loped uphill past the Palace and Arlington hotels, both of which were snuggled in at Hot Springs Mountain's feet, past dark green magnolias heavy with creamy blossoms that smelled of musk, sweet dreams, and chivalry long-dead. Just past the Arlington, Bobby tapped the horn, slowed down, and Sam rolled into the BMW's cool leather upholstery like a batter sliding into home. Her brain was gone. Her only thoughts for a good five minutes were, Breathe in, breathe out.

Pearl, her pace steady as a metronome, climbed on out the north side of town, up a two-lane mountain road past a pottery, a flea market, rock shops, billboards for crystal mines where you could hunt for your own, past stone mansions and falling-down shacks and mobile homes, headed on up toward Hot Springs Village, where snowbirds perched in condos, and finally turned off at Mountain Valley, where the bottled water came from. Pearl went right on humping through mile after mile of Weyerhauser pine forests posted with little signs that said when the new trees had been planted. Bobby was hunkered down behind the wheel, looking more worried by the minute. Sam agreed, this was looking bad. What would Olive be doing way up here on this lonely mountain road broken by only an occasional mailbox? Nothing good. Sam shook her head.

Finally they came to the edge of Lake Ouachita, as serene a blue lake as you'd ever hope to see. Sam was entertaining visions of stripping off her sweaty clothes and jumping in for a dip, when Pearl nosed up a little gravel road and stopped.

She sat down in the middle of the road, her big neat head turning this way and that, her pale eyes mournful. Then she lumbered up and switched back and forth in circles.

They got out, and Bobby patted her on the head. "Which way, girl? What's the matter? You came all this way and got lost?"

Pearl's pink-brown nose checked the air, sniffed the ground, and then with fresh resolve she took off again, down the gravel road.

When she came to a little clearing through brush and shrub, she snuffled into the base of a big pine tree that had a fresh raw cut low in its bark oozing resin. There Pearl took her stand and began to chop. "Yo yo yo yo," she sang. "Hunuruhu hoo hoo hoo hoo."

Sam had gone coon-hunting once in north Alabama with Uncle George when she was a girl. It had been fun, following the bawling dogs through the woods, wearing the heavy boots and coveralls, smelling the bacon and woodsmoke, listening to the men bragging and joking and telling tales. That is, until the moment she'd heard this very same sound, this chop on tree, and they'd come up on the dogs. The men had already said that the coon had run a good race, and once it was treed they'd pull their dogs off. But one man got carried away and shot the coon, which screamed as it tumbled into the dogs' slobbering jaws. The shooting was a blessing, at least. But listening to Pearl chop, Sam again saw that coon ripped to bits of bloody fur and bones. She turned her head.

"Hi," said the pretty redhead in bright yellow running shorts who was standing there on the side of the road like a mirage. Except Sam knew she was real because she'd watched her fleece a man named Slim out of two hundred dollars in the Palace lobby the night before. "Did your car break down?" asked Mickey. "Do y'all need some help?"

Mickey stayed to watch Sam and Bobby, who'd introduced themselves, tromp all over the woods. They'd said they were looking for Bobby's car, an old black-and-gold Ford Sunliner, that had disappeared.

With Doc's help, of course. Mickey knew that, and she knew the man had screwed up. He'd been getting reckless lately, not paying attention to details. And now, lookahere, they're being tailed by a dog. The very dog that belonged to the woman they'd run a game on the afternoon before, and for what? She'd asked Doc about the take, he'd just grunted and opened another beer.

He was losing it. And this boozing was definitely getting on her nerves.

"So what you're saying is, you think this dog is tracking the car?" Mickey asked. "Isn't that kind of weird, that the dog would track the car?"

Bobby said, "There's nothing weird, ma'am, when it

comes to dogs. Why, I could tell you some stories, but then I bet you've read the same ones, things like dogs walking by themselves cross-country, like from Ohio to Montana, left accidentally at gas stations, rest stops. Dogs are wonderful creatures."

"Lots better than most people," said Sam, thinking of Harpo, her little Shih Tzu whom she'd left back in New Orleans with Ma Elise, Kitty's grandmother. Harpo, her ever-faithful true love, who thought she hung the moon. She was the center of his universe. And then she thought of Harry, and his wandering gaze. Good old Harry. The son of a bitch could call her for the next hundred years, she wasn't talking to him.

Mickey gave Sam a smile. She remembered Sam, of course, from the bar last night. Mickey always kept tabs on her audience, checking for cops—and prospective pigeons. Sometimes they'd be panting while they watched, they were so anxious to part with their money. This Sam wasn't one of those. But Mickey had noted her, sitting alone, drinking bottled water. She hadn't looked like a woman cruising, though there'd been something going on with the black man.

"You think that car's hiding off down there?" she called when they followed Pearl down into a little ravine. She followed. "You can see the tracks up by that pine. They're faint, but don't you think those are tracks?" But they didn't lead anywhere from there. It was as if the car had been driven in, parked up against that pine tree with the fresh cut, like maybe the car had hit it, then pulled out.

That seemed to be what Pearl thought, too. The dog came snuffling out of the ravine, circled around for a while, and then Mickey could see she was thinking about heading up the hill, up to the old stone house where the Sunliner had sat in the carport. That wouldn't have been pretty.

But then Pearl circled again, and whatever it was she

was smelling, it seemed to be stronger going back the way she'd come. Though she stopped several times and looked back over her shoulder at the little clearing beneath the pine tree. Then up at Mickey. Like Mickey knew what the hell was going on.

That's what Mickey'd asked Doc when she got up to the house. What exactly the hell is going on?

Doc was sitting on a stool in the big yellow kitchen drinking a beer. He looked rested, wearing a baby blue shirt with his khakis and boots this morning. The truth was, Doc was a good-looking man, if you liked the dark, dangerous-looking type. He still had all his teeth and his hair—with only a little silver at the temples. But there were those long lines from his hawklike nose to the corners of his thin mouth that Mickey thought said something about his disposition—which was generally sour. Tall and sinewy, he was in good shape, for his age. His lanky body seemed to thrive on hot dogs, Cheez Whiz, cigarettes. Last night, when they'd run into Hot Springs, they'd stopped at a grocery store on the way. Mickey had bought two bags of vegetables and fruit, leaving behind the white bread so soft you could wad a whole slice up into something the size of a marble. Doc had stocked up on junk.

He didn't answer her question now. Instead, he asked one of his own. "Where've you been?" As if he couldn't tell looking at her in her running things. "I thought we agreed we'd stay put. You could have bumped into somebody."

"I did." Mickey smiled. "Ran into some very interesting people who were looking for an old black-and-gold Sunliner. They had a hound with them I've met before. Seems the hound is a very smart hound, tracked that car way over here from that convenience store where you picked it up. Hound thinks the Sunliner spent some time down the road up against a pine tree."

She didn't add that the woman named Sam had caught her act with a mark from Texas in the lobby of the Palace the night before. Because she wasn't supposed to have sat down. That wasn't in their game plan.

But for the first time in her whole professional career, Mickey had the jitters. Well, it wasn't her usual routine, this kind of scam. It'd made her nervous, and she, who could lie with the best of them, stare down a boss gambler like a bull in a field, she'd gone all to pieces walking around the hotel until she'd spied the easy mark, Slim, near the piano bar. Running her game, an old standard even a baby could do, was like singing herself a lullaby. It had calmed her right down.

But it had exposed her more, too. She knew that. On the other hand, Doc wasn't exactly following the original plan himself. They weren't supposed to be stopping to bag any convenience stores. And something had happened there he wasn't telling her about. She knew that. She just hoped it wasn't something serious that was going to bring them both down. Bring *her* down, that's what she was really worried about. The hell with him.

Mickey was concerned. She didn't like the way things were going at all. As soon as this thing paid off, she was splitting for California. She'd had enough of Doc and his mysterioso routine. Besides, he was a mean drunk, and recently he was drunk more than he was sober. She didn't need this. She had plenty of relatives who were drunks back in Savannah.

"Oh, yeah?" said Doc. "The hound thinks the car hit a tree?"

Mickey stared at him. He stared back. That was the thing about a man who'd been working the con as long as he had. You could wave a .38 in his face, he wouldn't blink. He'd made a life's work out of lying, fooling people, holding that smile, that grin, that firm handshake, how do you do, my name's Jim, Bill, Bob,

Mac, Slick, let me tell you a little story—he never gave up a thing.

Instead Doc cast another question out like it was a fancy fly on a line headed for a cool stream full of trout he'd spent the afternoon catching and releasing: "Hound say where the car is now?"

14

NOT FAR BACK DOWN THAT MOUNTAIN ROAD, PEARL seemed to become discombobulated. Sam said, "Bobby, it looks like her nose is worn out. I think we ought to stop and put her in the car."

They did, and Pearl stretched out in the back seat and immediately began to snore.

Then they took a shortcut Bobby remembered, and it wasn't long before they were back at the Gas 'N Grub.

"Maybe I ought to reconnoiter for a while," Bobby said when they pulled up in Sam's BMW. "I haven't had any sleep for a while now. Think I'll take me a little nap up at Mamaw's house, then get cleaned up, start looking again."

And maybe take a little peek around the corner for Miss Cynthia Blackshears, the young woman he'd done two years' time for, see if she'd changed her mind about speaking to him—that's what Sam thought.

She said, "I'll leave you then, but let me use the phone before I go and see if Loydell came up with anything." Loydell wasn't home. "Well, I guess I ought to get on back to my friends."

Friend, singular, was what she hoped. As in Kitty alone, as in, please God, let Jinx be off rustling up the ransom money, or, better yet, talking to the cops. She wrote her room number on the back of her card and handed it to Bobby. "Let me hear from you later today, even if you haven't turned up anything."

He said he would, and fifteen minutes later Sam was standing in the Palace's lobby staring at two messages.

The first was a fax from Harry. Damn his eyes! She scanned down the long page to his signature at the bottom. Love, Harry, indeed. If he'd loved her, he would have given her more room. Or less. Oh, hell. She jammed the sheet, unread, in her jeans pocket.

The second message was an invitation to join Kitty and Jinx for lunch at McClard's Barbecue on Albert Pike Avenue, if she wasn't too busy.

Olive, Harry, and now Jinx—what she was was oh for three. But she'd never in her life passed on a pork sandwich.

Given her familiarity with Harry's barbecue business, Sam could tell from the driveway that McClard's was the real thing. It looked right, a sort of funky 1920s low squat stucco building, both its parking lots jammed with a mix of Cadillacs, Chevrolets, and pickup trucks. Eleven-thirty in the morning, there was a line of folks waiting out the door. And most importantly, the air was sweet with a mix of pig and pepper and hickory smoke.

She peered through a big plate-glass window, and Kitty waved from a booth of red plastic, Formica, and fake wood.

It smelled even better inside. Sliding into the booth, she said to the waitress in khakis and a maroon jersey, "A sliced pork sandwich with beans and slaw, Diet Dr Pepper, thank you, ma'am." That taken care of, she could concentrate on visiting with Kitty. And Jinx, if she had to.

"Where the hell have you been?" Kitty growled. She clearly didn't feel as cute as she looked in her white slacks and the Elvis sweatshirt Sam had brought her back from Tupelo—where she and Harry had gone for a BBQ cookoff, back in the good old days last year.

"Sweetheart," Sam said to her, "maybe you need to have another cup of coffee." But Kitty didn't let up with the steely glare. Sam raised both hands to the heavens. "Okay, you really want to know, I was out running with a young man and a dog. What can I say? I can't seem to stay away from either one."

Flippant, she'd decided, was the right approach. They'd think she was joking, and she for sure didn't want Jinx to know about Bobby Adair. The woman was perfectly capable of calling up the Hot Springs Police and turning him in for breaking parole, just to make Sam mad.

She turned to the former Miss Hot Springs—who was done up in an hour's worth of big hair and makeup, a microscopic black skirt, teetery high-heeled black pumps, black stockings, and a bright blue silk blouse that made the most of her considerable cleavage—and patted Jinx's hand. "What have you done with *your* morning, sugar pie, other than get yourself all pretty?"

Jinx didn't say a word. She reached in the biggest black patent leather purse Sam had ever seen, pulled out a pair of movie-star sunglasses, and slapped them on. Then she turned back to her grilled cheese sandwich, which spoke volumes about her IQ, her taste, and her lack of qualification as a human being, as far as Sam was concerned. Anyone who would order grilled cheese in a place that smelled this good ought to be put out of her misery.

"I take it that you all did not have a very productive morning," Sam offered.

"No, we did not," Kitty sighed. "Though God knows we tried."

"Well, do tell."

Kitty looked at Jinx, who was otherwise engaged, staring back at a large young man in the next booth who was wearing a gimme hat that said Peterbilt across the front. He'd had a forkful of chili spaghetti halfway to his mouth when he'd spotted Jinx and frozen.

"I'd forgotten that she had that effect on men," said Kitty. "You should have seen the look on Kitty's friend Bo we went to visit this morning—like a deer caught in the headlights."

"And who's Bo?" asked Sam.

"President of the Hot Springs Amalgamated Savings Bank."

"The bank's open on Sunday?"

"It is if your name is Jinx and you went to high school with Bo."

"I see."

"I imagine he had a lot more hair and a lot less gut back in high school, but that didn't keep him from being hot to trot, I'll tell you that. He couldn't wait to get Miss Jinx into that big old private office of his."

At that Jinx turned and pulled the sunglasses down a tad on her perfect nose and said to Kitty, without stopping to breathe, "Bo begged me to go to the homecoming dance with him our senior year, but I didn't. I already had a quarterback and a nose guard duking it out for the honor. Anyway, he's called me at least once a year ever since then, no matter if I was married or not. He's *always* been married, since he knocked that Darlynn Millsaps up his freshman year at U of A. But, anyway, I guess he's still a little sweet on me. That's why he was willing to do me a tiny little favor."

"Which was?" Sam asked, knowing, a bank, it had to have something to do with the ransom money, but she wanted to hear the straight poop from Jinx.

Who was still giving her the freeze. As if Miss Beauty Queen herself hadn't been the one who'd chunked the first Coke.

"Okay," said Sam. "I'll bite. He loaned you a million dollars on your signature alone, with your virginity as collateral."

Jinx took a miniscule nibble of her grilled cheese and chewed it with rapt concentration, as if Sam weren't in the room.

"But wait a minute," Sam said, "I'm being so stupid. You *have* a million dollars you won in that lottery. Tax-free. So what were you doing at the bank?"

The silence was broken only by the waitress who arrived with Sam's order. "Anything else I can get y'all, y'all just holler."

Sam wasn't letting any kidnapping or any ransom negotiations or any beauty queen stand in the way of food that smelled this good. She dug in. The white bun was warm, the meat was beautifully smoked tender white pork shoulder, the sauce an absolutely perfect blending of spicy sweet and piquant with a big hit of hot.

"Listen," she said when she'd eaten enough to be sure she was going to live, "this Q was worth the trip, so if neither of you wants to talk with me, that's okay. I'll finish this, and then maybe another one, or maybe two, and then I'll be on my way. Olive still hasn't turned up, and I've got plenty to do looking for her."

"Oh, hell," Jinx said finally. "What difference does it make? You might as well know."

Kitty gave Sam a look: Wait until you get a load of this.

But while Sam was curious, she remembered she really didn't want to know too much. She certainly didn't intend to get snookered into this kidnapping problem of Jinx's. "Look, don't do me any favors. It's none of my business. You're right. You should handle this the way you want to. Tell you what, I'll get another couple of sandwiches to go, and I'm out of here. You carry on."

"Oh, shut up," said Jinx. "You're dying to hear about how screwed up this whole thing is, and you know it. I swear to God, I wish I'd never come back to Hot Springs. I am so *mad* at Speed."

An interesting attitude, thought Sam. Blame the victim. But she didn't say it.

"He encouraged me, you know, to do this whole thing up right. *I* said I wanted to have this big blowout of an engagement party. He said, Go right on ahead. So I did. I already paid the caterer and the country club and the wedding planner and ordered my gown from Vera Wang, who does those to-die-for dresses up in New York. I flew up there to pick it out and for my fitting, and they're doing a super rush-rush, which is twice as expensive, but Speed said, So what, sugar pie, you want it, go on ahead. No problemo. Speed says that all the time, no problemo." Jinx wadded up a little piece of white bread and popped it in her mouth. "I used to think it was real cute, his saying that, No problemo, back when we met."

'Which was how long ago?" asked Sam.

"A month. Thirty-two days, to be exact."

"And what exactly is it that you're mad at him about?"

Kitty's look told her they were about to get to the good part.

"Well! He said, Go on ahead, do this, do that, and I did, writing checks left and right—"

The light dawned. "So *you* were paying for all this."

"Speed had a little temporary liquidity problem. Something about the yen and German marks and the float. You know what I mean?"

What Sam knew was that she could smell fish in the air, and there was none on the menu.

"So I went ahead doing what I wanted to do, knowing that Speed was going to make it all good. After all, the man is rolling in it."

"*Was* rolling in it. Maybe," said Kitty. "Perhaps. We're not sure."

Sam said, "You ladies want to spell this out for me? I'm a little slow."

"Oh, hell!" Jinx was exasperated, and more than a little embarrassed, Sam could tell, airing her dirty linen in front of Sam. "We went over to the Hot Springs Amalgamated because that's the bank Speed said handled all his big-deal international financial transactions."

"Let me guess. He's bust."

"Not only that, he never had it, never was," said Jinx. "Bucks up, that is. And only because I am a close personal friend of Bo do I know this, otherwise I would still be in the dark, and I'll tell you what, I'm glad I found this out before I married the man. This kidnapping has its up side, I'll tell you that. It sure saved *me* a lot of grief."

Sam hit herself on the ear. Could she be hearing this right?

Jinx said, "Don't give me that look, like I'm an ax murderer or something. I meant what I said. If he hadn't gotten kidnapped, I never would have gone to the bank to see about taking the ransom money out of his account. Though why I wouldn't have checked up on him anyway is beyond me. I ought to know better. You can't trust anybody anymore. The world is absolutely full of people pretending to be something they're not."

Sam decided to let that one go, though it was awfully tempting.

However, Jinx was only getting warmed up. "He *never* had a pot to piss in, or at least not in recent memory. Bo, that's my close personal friend down at the bank, he said Speed had had about five thousand when he blew into town. It went up and down, depending on his luck at the track, but the man was a fake. He's a common gambler. I asked Bo, and he looked it up, and said none of that stuff he told me about was in his portfolio. He didn't even have a portfolio."

"Oh, dear," said Sam, making only a minimal effort to keep the sarcasm out of her voice.

"No portfolio. No house in Carmel. No condo in the hills above Monte Carlo. No cabin cruiser. No polo ponies. No apartment in Manhattan."

"Wait a minute. Didn't you say you were in New York buying your wedding gown?"

Jinx's eyes narrowed, and her mouth drew tight as a rubber band. "Yes, I did, and yes, we were. And we stayed at the Plaza because he said he was redoing the apartment, it was too tacky for me to see."

Sam didn't have to ask whose American Express card the hotel bill had gone on. "So he's bust."

"That's right. The man has *nada*. Nothing. Zilch. Zero. He's a fraud and a fake and a liar and a cheat." Then her blond head fell into her carefully manicured hands. "Oh, God. I don't know what I'm going to do."

"Well, gee, I think that's terrible," said Sam. "That he misled you to think he was rich when he wasn't, but I guess the part I don't understand is why you were dealing with *his* finances in the first place. I thought you were going to the bank to withdraw the ransom money from *your* account. From that million you won in the lottery."

At that, Jinx burst into tears. She sobbed so hard the man in the Peterbilt hat got up and came over and handed her his red bandana handkerchief. "You let me know if there's anyone you need beat up," he said with a grin that was missing a couple of teeth.

Jinx blew her nose on the bandana without even saying thank you to the man, then handed it back to him, wet. "I can't take the money from my account because I don't *have* any money," she wailed.

Sam found that difficult to believe. "You mean you already spent a big chunk of your lottery winnings?" It hadn't been that long ago that Kitty had pissed her off, calling her on the phone and waking her out of a sound sleep at the crack of dawn to see Jinx and her damned altar and her damned million dollars on one of those early morning TV shows.

"I mean it's *all* gone," Jinx sobbed. "Practically every last cent. I spent the last of it on this wedding—that's not even going to come off." A fresh torrent coursed down her cheeks.

"Sugar, you want to get married, I'll be more than happy to hitch up with you." That was the Peterbilt man again, who was still standing there with his damp handkerchief in his hand.

Jinx whirled, facing the man nose to nose. "Would you please mind your own business and buzz off!"

He said to no one in particular, "I'll tell you what, some women, the only way to treat 'em is you snatch 'em bald-headed." And then he stomped off.

Sam said, "You really spent a million dollars in six months?"

Then Jinx sniffed and went wide on defense. "Well, I still owed a lot to begin with, from when Harlan went bankrupt and then got hauled off to the pokey, leaving me without a red cent. You can't imagine how quick the bills pile up."

Sam said, "Were you making anything off your altar business?"

Jinx sniffed, "Yes, I was beginning to. But I was trying to get connected in higher circles in Dallas, and with those people, you have to keep up, or they don't want to do business with you. You have to have a house in Turtle Creek, and you have to have it done by the right decorator, and drive the right car, and go to the right exercise trainer, and wear the right designers, and there are all those dinner parties, well, I'll tell you, it made me tired, which is one of the reasons I gave up and bought a new house in San Antonio, where I still had a life. . . ."

Sam got the drift. Jinx had blown it, the whole ball of wax. Little of which was in retrievable assets, except maybe the houses, and real estate had taken a nosedive in Texas like everyplace else.

"So you came to Hot Springs for the races, ran into Speed—who looked like the real thing, bank account-wise, the answer to your prayers."

"He did! He couldn't do enough for me. Long-stemmed roses every day, a dozen, two dozen, sometimes three. We flew down to the Bahamas one weekend. We'd go to dinner, no matter which place I picked, there'd be a bottle of my favorite champagne, roses on the table, a little note already waiting. It was like I'd think of something, and there it was. He was like a magician."

Right. Doing tricks. Dazzling the lady. Making her think what wasn't was. Just like she was doing. It looked to Sam like both of them got scammed.

"So you were marrying him for his money, which he didn't have?"

"Well, I *loved* him."

Both Kitty and Sam laughed at that one.

"I did! I did, too!"

"I'm hearing an awful lot of past tense, as in not any-more," said Kitty. "Ever since our little trip this morning down to your friend Bo's bank when you discovered he was bust."

Jinx stuck out her bottom lip. She'd had an awfully cute pout back in school. All she had to do was look like she was going to tune up for a good cry, boys would be falling all over themselves running to get whatever it was she wanted. But now? There were faint little lines when she pursed her mouth like that. A couple of years more, she'd want to avoid that maneuver at all costs.

Jinx said, "It does make him less attractive. And he was fooling me all the time, pretending to be something he wasn't. Why would I marry somebody like that?" She paused, reached over, and took a sip of Sam's Dr Pepper.

"Besides which, if I'm bust, and he's bust, well, what's the point?"

Indeed.

"So, I guess that's that," said Sam. "You're calling off your engagement."

"That's right." Jinx tapped her golden fingernails on the Formica twice for emphasis.

"In absentia," said Sam.

"What do you mean?" said Jinx, narrowing her eyes again, as if Sam were trying to pull a fast one.

"I mean you're giving Speed the boot even though he's not around. Of course, when the kidnappers get in touch, I guess you could tell them that the engagement's off, let them pass the word along to Speed."

Jinx was mulling that over. She looked like she thought that was a pretty good idea.

Kitty couldn't stand it any longer. "Good Lord, Jinx!" she exploded. "Don't you think that's kind of cold, his kidnappers giving him the Dear John news? The man's *life* is in jeopardy."

"Now, we don't know that." Jinx held out her left hand, the one sporting the huge rock. "Most of the time, these kidnappers are bluffing."

"Bluffing! What the hell are you *talking* about?" Kitty was getting loud. People were staring. Sam was pleased as punch.

"Oh," Jinx said, "I bet when they see they're not getting any money, they'll let him go."

Sam said, "So you've definitely decided you're stonewalling on the ransom?"

"Well, I'm not giving them any money, if that's what you mean. I was going to buy them off with Speed's, but seeing as he doesn't have any . . ." Jinx toyed with a straw wrapper, trailed off.

Sam said, "Then you might as well call the cops. Let them take it from here."

"Well," Jinx said slowly, "I guess I *could* have. But I didn't."

"What do you mean you didn't?" said Sam, realizing Jinx hadn't finished the story.

"What are you talking about?" said Kitty.

Jinx turned to her. "I guess I didn't tell you this part, but after we went to the bank, I went back to our suite at the hotel to freshen up, and one of those kidnappers called and got real pushy on the phone, and I said they could take Speed and shove him. Whatever they wanted to do, I said, they weren't getting a penny from me, he was their problem."

15

WELL, IF JINX DIDN'T TAKE THE CAKE. SAM WAS WALKING out to her car in the parking lot around to the back of McClard's. Telling the kidnappers Speed was their problem, good God!

She was talking to herself, Jinx and Kitty having gone on ahead while Sam stayed behind to sample the lemon meringue pie.

Lady, she said, struggling to wedge her hand into her jeans pocket for her keys, you're going to weigh two hundred pounds by next week, if you keep this up. But better fat than drunk.

Would Jinx ever get fat? Nawh. She was much too vain. Wasn't that woman something? Crimminee, Sam couldn't get over her brushing Speed off like that. It would serve her right if they made him into mincemeat. *Then* she'd feel guilty.

Except she wouldn't.

Sam was about to unlock her car door when a tobacco brown Rolls-Royce pulled right up behind her blocking her exit.

"Excuse me, ma'am," the silver-haired driver said, powering down his window, "but is this your pretty little BMW?"

Sam smiled at the handsome man with the lovely baritone, hoping he hadn't noticed her talking to herself. "Why, yes, it is." Then she had second thoughts, but, hey, this wasn't New Orleans, where they held you up on your doorstep. This was Hot Springs, and the man *was* driving a Rolls-Royce.

He was saying, "I've been looking all over for one that model and color. I'm sort of a collector, and they didn't make very many of those." Now he was opening his door. "I know I'm keeping you, but if you have a minute. . . ." He was out of the car.

"That's fine."

"Mind if I take a look?"

"Go ahead." She kept smiling, hoping she didn't have barbecue in her teeth. "But I warn you, it's not for sale. I love this little baby. My car and my dog, they're not negotiable."

The man laughed and walked away from her around toward the front of the car. He had a great rich laugh. He really was quite handsome in his beige gabardine slacks and well-cut navy blazer. White shirt and striped silk tie. And he was tall. A lot taller than Harry, who wore torn jeans half the time. Like the child he was. Spoiled rotten child, never knew when he had enough.

"What kind of dog do you have?"

"A spoiled rotten Shih Tzu." Then she laughed. "I guess that's redundant. I'm Sam Adams." She offered her hand as the big broad-shouldered smiling man stepped right up to her.

He took her hand and held it tight. "Sam Adams, huh? Then I'm Kris Kringle."

That was the last thing she heard before he threw his left arm around her neck in a choke hold, compressing her carotid artery. Her world faded to black in a count of five. Fifteen seconds more, she was buckled down, limp and prone in the backseat of the big car, and they were rolling.

When Sam came to, she was sitting on a low stool. Her back was propped against a post, one of four of what she slowly realized was a boxing ring. She was lashed to the post with a soft cotton rope looped several times around her waist.

The large square room was mostly in gloom. She couldn't see into its edges, but the overhead lamps lit the ring like a stage.

The light cut into her head like a knife. She closed her eyes. From somewhere out in the dark, she could hear the rat-a-tat-tat of someone punching a speed bag. Rat-a-tat-tat. The rhythm was smooth. Otherwise, the room was silent, except for the booming of her heart.

Panic rose in her throat like bile. For this was an old nightmare recast. The year before she'd been abducted by an escaped con, someone she'd helped put away. With the help of an elderly hunter, she'd lived to tell the tale of that one, not that she talked about it a lot. However, the chances of a savior traipsing into this boxing gym seemed slim to none.

She struggled, tried to stand against the rope. It had a little play to it, but she wasn't going anywhere.

Rat-a-tat-tat. Rat-a-tat-tat. The bag didn't stop, didn't miss a beat as, out of the dusk, a voice said, "It's not nice to lie, Miss Steele."

She thought it was the voice of the silver-haired man,

though she wasn't positive. But the words he spoke gave her hope. This was a case of mistaken identity. She'd tell him who she was. He'd let her go. Plain and simple.

"Hey," she called. "Kris Kringle, is that you? Listen, we've got a little problem here. My name's not Steele. You've nabbed the wrong woman. I told you my name. I'm Sam Adams. Samantha Adams? Tourist? Just here for the weekend, up from Louisiana?" She raised her inflection at the end of each fact the way Southern women often did, looking for agreement.

Rat-a-tat-tat. Rat-a-tat. "So you said. But we both know that's wrong, Mickey."

Mickey? Who the hell was Mickey? She didn't know any Mickey. And then it dawned on her. Yes, she did. Mickey was the name of the red-haired con woman she'd watched in the Palace lobby last night. The one she'd seen earlier today out by Lake Ouachita.

"Is the Mickey you're looking for a redhead? A pretty redhead about five-four?"

"No." Rat-a-tat-tat. "She's a pretty brunette. Tall. Curly-headed. Wearing a pair of red boxing shorts."

She looked down. Son of a bitch! She was. Red shorts and the white T-shirt she'd had on with her jeans—and white athletic shoes. On her hands, Jesus, how could she have not noticed, was a pair of boxing gloves. The bastard had undressed her, at least her bottom half. What the hell else had he done? Her mood jumped from panicked to pissed.

Sam had never been one to bite her tongue. "Listen, jerk. You've got the wrong woman tied up here. I'm Sam Adams. I can prove it. Why don't you check my driver's license? Assuming you can read. And assuming you kidnapped my purse, too."

The speed bag stopped. The big silver-haired man, it *was* him, walked into the light. His shorts had been washed so many times it was hard to know what color they'd been. With them he wore a blue T-shirt that said

Bubbles, black boxing shoes, and a big grin. "I've seen your license. It's a good one. Real, too, probably. That's no sweat, a license in another name. I bet you have a dozen." Then he climbed into the ring at the corner diagonal to hers and leaned back against the ropes casually, like a man would who was sure of his place in the world. His shirt was blotchy with sweat.

God, he was big. Carrying a tad too much gut, but still, he was muscular and strong. She'd admired his bulk in the parking lot, but that was then. Now it just meant he could snap her neck in no time at all. One good swing with a glove, he'd knock her head right off. Her stomach flip-flopped at the thought of what the ring and the boxing getup must mean: He was some kind of sadistic looney who liked to dress up his victims before he beat them to death. A rich sadistic looney who drove a Rolls-Royce? Why not? As she knew so well from her years of working the crime beat, there was no end to the varieties of mayhem and destruction of which human beings were capable, and in that arena, clothes bespoke the man not at all.

He was talking again. "Jerk? Is that what you called me? Now, Mickey, or would you prefer Miss Steele, *Ms*. Steele, you ought not to go around calling people names. Especially people who are holding all the cards."

He *did* think she was the redheaded Mickey who was clever with the cards. Couldn't he look at them and see they were two different people? Was he stupid or what? Was she going to die because he was color-blind? Now, wouldn't that be a joke? A very bad joke, the thought of which was royally pissing her off. "Look, *Mr*. Jerk. I don't appreciate your kidnapping me, necking me out, stripping me, and tying me up, do you understand? I especially don't appreciate the fact that you're too dumb to know you've got the wrong woman. I am not who you think I am. You're under the misapprehension that

I'm a grifter named Mickey Steele, right? Mickey who's handy with cards? Well, I've met her. But I'm *not* her."

The big man smiled. It was the same nice smile she'd seen earlier in the parking lot, but she was hardly in the mood to be throwing bouquets. He stood and ambled straight over to her, and then before she had time to think about what he was doing, he'd pulled her to her feet. The rope slipped up the back of the pole. He pushed himself right up against her. It was a full body press, his chest to her breast, his belly, his strong thighs. He pressed against her hard, like a lover.

"You lousy son of a bitch!" she screamed into his neck. She'd be goddamned if he was going to rape her—not while she was alive anyway.

She'd take a big bite out of the soft flesh of his throat, hoping against hope to hit his carotid artery, his jugular. Then with any luck, he'd pump scarlet like a gusher, all down her front. It wouldn't be pretty, but when it was over, he'd be the dead one. She opened her mouth wide and pulled her head back as far as she could, knowing she had only one chance to sink hard and fast and deep, hoping she wouldn't puke.

But her target was gone. He'd untied the rope binding her and suddenly jumped back. Now he was dancing on his toes, gloves up. "Are you mad, Mickey? Huh? What do you say? Mad enough to punch?" He tapped her softly on the cheek with his right glove. "What do you say, huh?"

Oh, you bet she was mad. "The name's Sam," she spit. Then she swung hard with her right. She missed him by a mile and twirled in a circle. Shit!

He laughed. "Come on, Mick. You can do better than that. You're punching like a girl." He gestured with one glove. "Come on, now. Get in closer. Keep your elbows close to your body. Keep your chin down. Bend your knees. Make 'em soft. Now jab!"

She jabbed, but he blocked the punch with his glove

and shoved her hand back toward her. Then tapped her a smart one on the chin. It wasn't even all that hard, but the blow snapped her head like a whip. Her chin hurt like hell.

"Hey!" she said. "That wasn't fair!"

Then she heard herself, and her stomach flopped. What did she think this was, some kind of game? A situation that called for chivalry? This was no gentleman going easy on the little lady, teaching his sweetie how to box. This was a sadistic son of a bitch who was going to beat her to death, no matter what. And this, no doubt, was his idea of foreplay.

"What do you mean fair?" he laughed. "Didn't I let you go first? Who got in the first two punches, Mickey?" Then he tagged her with a left to the body.

Shit! That hurt, too. Her ribs were probably smashed. He *was* going to pound her to pieces. She squinted and tried to see out of the ring, into the gloom. Was there any way out of here?

"No exit, Mick. Not a prayer. Give it up. Now, look back here." He was gesturing at her with his glove again. "Come on, give me your best shot. I know you've got the stuff. Anybody who teams up with Doc's got to have some moxie. The man's a killer."

Sam stopped dead and dropped her gloves. "Who the hell's Doc?"

"Don't give me that crap, Mick. Get those gloves up. Now keep moving. Move. Up on those toes. Dance."

She did as she was told. She sure as hell wasn't going to stand there and let him punch her like a weight bag.

He was dancing, too, moving backwards clockwise. He was light on his feet for such a big man. "Obviously," he said, "I don't have any beef with you. Just tell me, what's on Doc's mind?"

"What I'm telling you is I don't know any Doc."

She tried one with her left, which he blocked. Then she tried to sucker-punch him in the gut, sneaking her right underneath. But he was too fast. Fast and light on his feet. Her hands were beginning to hurt in the heavy gloves that smelled like a refrigerator gone bad.

He said, "Doc's got to know I'm here. So what's the deal?"

"I don't *know!* I don't know Doc. I don't know what the hell you want me to say." She could hear herself getting whiny. God, she hated that. She punched again with her right and missed. She *really* wanted to smack him. She moved in closer. She could smell his sweat, or was that her? Could he smell her fear? Did it turn him on?

"Tell me, Mick, did Joey send him?" Then he added, like he was talking to himself, "I don't think he did. Joey wouldn't do that."

"*Joey who?*" She was starting to sound like a fishwife.

"Don't tell me you don't know Joey Cangiano." Now he was dancing forward, closing in on her, taking the lead around the ring as if they were doing the fox-trot in boxing shorts. "Come on, Mick. Joey the Horse?"

Hey, she did! "*Sure*, I do! I do know Joey. Joey from New Orleans?" Joey, head of the Big Easy's wise guys, former employer of her friend Lavert, Harry's best friend and partner in the barbecue business. *That Joey the Horse?*

"Good girl." He smiled. "See, I knew you'd come around."

"But that doesn't mean I'm Mickey!" She jabbed with her right, and this time her glove sneaked past his block and popped into his gut. *Jesus*, that felt good! She grinned. She was pumped.

He grinned back. "You want to hit me again? Huh? A little contact, does that loosen your tongue?" He lowered his gloves, and she danced right up and took her best shot. She popped him one on the jaw. Yes! She felt like Rocky.

"The power comes from your hips, Mick, not from

your shoulders. Rotate your hips and throw your full power into your punch."

She swiveled her hips to the right like he showed her and landed one on his shoulder that had a real pop to it. That was better than good. That was great! There was something very satisfying about this boxing business.

As long as you were the one doing the punching.

They were bouncing and bobbing and weaving now in a pugilistic tango. "So," he said, "Joey sent Doc to do me?" He shook his head and looked sad. Genuinely hurt. His voice grew softer. "That's really disappointing."

"I didn't say that. All I said is I know Joey."

"Okay. That's enough." And with that, he stepped right into her again, pinning her arms to her sides. She struggled, but he had no trouble backing her into the corner once more. He pressed his wet body against hers, which was just as damp. He pulled her arms behind her. She couldn't fight back. Her arms were exhausted, overcooked spaghetti. Her hands were meatballs.

Using the same rope he'd pulled from the corner post, he trussed her up. But she was freer this time, tied neither to the stool nor the post. And her feet were free. One chance, Sam. Do it. She stomped as hard as she could on his foot. He didn't even flinch. But when she raised her right knee higher, he jerked clear and stepped around behind her.

He wrapped her into a warm embrace. His lips moved against her ear like a kiss. "Good thing you didn't kick me in the balls, Mick. You'd be very very sorry."

And what would be the point? The pain wouldn't kill him, only make him mad. And then what?

"Do you sleep on your back or your tummy?"

"What are you talking about?"

"Back or tummy?"

"None of your business. What makes you think I'm going to sleep anyway?"

"You will after a while." Then he jerked the rope and she fell to the mat, hard. "Now, back or tummy?"

"Stomach." She spit the word. She'd banged her head, it hurt, and she'd failed. She was no closer to getting free from this maniac than when she'd regained consciousness. She was still tied up. She was a dead woman.

Then he gently rolled her over, pulled off her boxing gloves, and pushed a cushion under her head. He threw a soft blanket over her and patted her on the fanny. "Sweet dreams, Mick. I'll turn out the light."

And he did. She groaned. The room was dark as a tomb, she was scared, and she had to pee something awful.

16

DOC WAS TRYING TO KEEP HIS DREAM IN HIS MIND: THE SEA Islands off Georgia, South Carolina, his gypsy wagon, the silver Airstream. He even tried picturing the beach and the surf. But none of it did any good. Speed McKay was driving him nuts.

They were sitting in the kitchen of the big stone house on the edge of Lake Ouachita. "So, Doc," Speed was saying, "as long as we're here, got a little time to kill, what do you say we play some cards? Want to play a little gin rummy? Huh?"

Doc had said to Mickey earlier, I'll run into town and make the phone call to the bride-to-be, pay phones being the only kind they used, avoiding a trace in case Jinx hadn't paid attention to what they'd told her about the cops.

Now Speed was saying, "What do you think, Doc? A little gin to kill the time before my darling bride-to-be comes through? Of course, poker's my game. I've played in Hong Kong with gold bullion in little red silk bags, had to fight my way out of a back room, knives, swords, hatchets, sharp things flying everywhere you looked. It wasn't pretty. I wouldn't kid you about that, Doc. No shit. Just giving you a friendly warning, before we deal the cards. Only a friendly piece of advice."

As if Doc hadn't heard this routine a thousand times before. Or it seemed that way. Actually, he and Speed had only worked that little time together, maybe a month or so, for Jack Graham down in New Orleans. It was one of the few jobs Doc had ever held, seeing if he liked the track. He didn't. Even though the action moved around—Florida, Louisiana, Arkansas—up the East Coast, it was still too confining for him. Maybe his ma had been right; she'd always said, Forget the *gajo* in you. Gypsy blood will out. Whatever it was, he sure didn't like staying still. And he hated being cooped up like this, especially with Speed. He'd told Mickey that from the beginning: He didn't know if they could all work this scam together. The little man made him crazy. Mickey had said, Don't worry, I'll hang out with him.

But when Doc had said that about his running into town, making the call from the pay phone, Mickey'd snapped back, You and whose army? If I don't get away from that little motormouth son of a bitch, I'm grinding him up, we can ship him back to this Jinx by the pound, she can make spaghetti sauce.

In the end, they'd tossed for it. She'd nixed Doc's using his own coin, knowing that he had a pocketful of the Heads I win, Tails you lose variety. So they flipped with hers, his knowing it was gaffed, too, but also knowing that he didn't want to leave her alone with Speed.

It wasn't that he didn't trust her.

Okay, so he didn't trust her.

The truth was he didn't trust anybody. So what if Mick hadn't screwed him over yet, in the months they'd been together? He'd known lots of hustlers with more patience than that. For all he knew, Mickey could see their whole time together as a temporal and floating version of the big con.

Just like he did.

The difference was, there was no doubt in his mind that when push came to shove, he was the one walking away with the fat score. Add that to the stash he'd been building all these years, he'd never have to pull a *bajour* again.

And what the hell? He was getting old. Tired. It was his turn. Mickey was young—and female. She had plenty of time before she hit forty and wouldn't be fresh and pretty enough to pull the big fish.

And Speed? Speed didn't count at all. Though Speed had turned them on to the possibilities here and provided the bait, well, that's what Speed was. About as important to Doc as an earthworm.

"You want me to make us something to eat before we deal?" Speed was standing now, halfway to the stove. Earlier they'd been drinking tea. Strong tea, the way Doc's ma made it, and sweet with jam. Pearsa had used sliced oranges, peaches, plums, strawberries, whatever fruit was in season. Or jam, when nothing was. Doc liked it with jam.

Mickey was always after him, saying it was a wonder he had any teeth at all. The truth was, he had strong white handsome teeth with never a cavity.

Now he sipped from his cup, leaned back against his chair, adjusted the shoulder holster and the Hardballer .45 he'd been carrying since the three of them had waltzed through the door last night, Speed crowing at the top of his lungs, We're gonna be rich! Mickey didn't like the gun, but what did she know?

Of course, he hadn't told her about Jack Graham. He

hadn't mentioned a word about their mutual hate-on. He'd known he'd have to finish it since he'd left those mutts in Jack's yard. It was Jack or him, and Jack had started it. Jack's the one accused him of fucking up, called him out like he was some kind of kid. Hell, he had years on the man, eons if you were talking experience. In any case, the big score was one thing, but the stronger attraction to Hot Springs for Doc was Smilin' Jack. Doc was itching to do that sucker, have their shit over and out.

Now he was watching Speed. The little man had thrown open every knotty pine cabinet door in the kitchen, every drawer, and he was standing in front of the refrigerator, it open, too, of course, and the freezer, frigid air curling out like fog, the power cutting on. It really was a good thing Mickey wasn't home. She'd have broken Speed's fingers, slamming those doors closed. Which, come to think of it, wasn't such a bad idea.

Just listen to the little man now: "Well, sir, you don't have much choice in here in the way of foodstuffs, no sir, you don't. But we're not going to let that stand in our way. No siree, we won't. I was raised in the got-a-lemon, no problemo, make-lemonade school of being grateful for what God gave you. Be glad you're not in one of those forsaken countries, and God knows I've been in plenty of those, Africa, Southeast Asia, you name it, we soldiers of fortune went where we were needed, break your heart to see people standing around starving to death, drinking their own slops. You know what I mean?"

Doc didn't bother to answer. He just tapped his left boot, trying to keep himself from kicking Speed's teeth down his throat.

"So, we've got some leftover Kentucky Fried chicken, I can pull off the skin, dice that up with a little mayo, some fresh-ground pepper, and, yep, here's some celery, have a nice chicken salad. I can do that. No problemo.

If we had some good oil, I could make us some homemade mayo. But we don't. And no good bread, but no problemo, we can toast up these English muffins. You know where English muffins came from? I'll tell you."

Doc stopped him before he did. "Speed, I knew you were an operator. But I never realized you could cook."

"Oh, yes," said Speed. "Yes, I certainly can. Man of many talents, my dear old mother used to say, bless her heart. Mother taught me many things. But one of my favorites is her fried chicken. Do you know how to make fried chicken, Doc? It's easy as can be. Yes, it is. No problemo, you've got the basic ingredients. Let me tell you while I whip up this chicken salad."

Doc pushed back from the table. "Excuse me. I'm gonna run up and get some cards while you do that. When I come back down, I'm gonna kill you."

17

THE LIGHTS SNAPPED ON, AND SAM JOLTED OUT OF SLEEP and darkness. Where was she?

Then she tried to move her arms, and she remembered. She was lying facedown in the boxing ring, trussed like a stupid chicken.

She called into the bright silence, "Hey! Kris Kringle, is that you? Are you here?"

Nothing. Well, if he hit her again, she was going to pee all over the mat. But, who knew, that kind of thing might be right up his alley. Jeetz, she hoped not.

What was this place anyway? She wanted to know.

She had to know. Suddenly her location seemed terribly important. She grunted and rolled herself over, and she was staring up into the lights. Her eyes adjusted slowly to the glare, and she could see a few details. Could that be stained glass in the ceiling? She made out what looked like the figure of a swimmer in the colored glass. The panel was surrounded by a double crown molding of creamy plaster. You saw this kind of detail in buildings from the twenties, in the lobbies of big hotels. But did either the Palace or the Arlington have a gym? She didn't know.

But wait a minute. Today, yesterday, somebody had said something about a gym in Hot Springs. A gym and boxing. She closed her eyes and willed the words back. *A gym. Joe Louis himself worked out there.* Joe, the Brown Bomber. People in Harlem had danced in the streets when he won the title. What was there today that would make folks do that? Nothing. The days of that kind of joy were long gone. But wait. wait. She was drifting off. She probably had brain damage from that lick on the chin. Now, who had said that about Joe Louis? The voice, yes, that was June talking, June with the skin so rich and smooth it had reminded her of chocolate. They'd been talking about the baths and—yes, that was it. She had it. June had said one of the bathhouses—Sam slid over the name that was out of her grasp, trying not to stop the flow—had been made into a museum, and that was the one with the gym where Joe Louis, and who else, yes, the Dallas Cowboys had trained. The Forsythe. No, Fordyce! She was in the Fordyce Bathhouse!

Maybe. And maybe she wasn't. And if she was, so what? She was still trussed, ready for the oven. Or whatever fate the big man had in mind.

"Mickey, it's very important for me to know what Doc's doing in town."

What? She could have jumped out of her skin, if she

hadn't been tied up, his voice coming out of the darkness at her like that.

"I understand that just because you're partners doesn't mean you know everything about Doc. But I'm sure you're in on whatever's going down here. Just tell me what that is."

"I told you, Kris, I don't know any Doc. And I have to pee something awful."

"Oh. I'm sorry." He really did sound sorry. "I didn't think about that. Wait right there."

Sure.

But he wasn't joking. He was back in a few minutes with a five-gallon stockpot—which made her think. Maybe this wasn't a bathhouse after all.

"I'll untie you, and then I'll walk away over here and turn my back."

"That's your best offer?"

"That's my only offer."

"How do you know I won't hit you in the head with the pot?"

He laughed. "It's a thought."

The release was sweet even if the cold rim of the pot made her shiver. Too bad she didn't have any tissue. But maybe she did, in her jeans pockets.

She asked.

He held the jeans up, pilfered through the pockets. "I suppose if I were any kind of gentleman, I'd let you do this yourself."

"A gentleman wouldn't have taken my jeans in the first place."

"I wouldn't be so sure of that. Here, this is all I can find." He was holding up Harry's fax, handing it to her.

She unfolded it and read a line. . . . *sure you're having a great time there without me, but I* . . .

"Perfect," she said.

18

DOC WOULD BET THAT SPEED MCKAY WAS TALKING BEFORE he had teeth. No way before that. Doc would bet you, any odds you wanted to name, Speed McKay was talking the minute he saw daylight. And not just talking. Giving instructions. "Excuse me, Dr. Obstetrician, I think if you'll use a sailor's half-hitch on that suture, you'll find that it much more efficient in the long run. Now, let me give you a brief rundown on knot-tying. Back at the dawn of time. . . ."

Though Speed had made a pretty good chicken salad sandwich while he was explaining how to make Southern fried chicken. Now, while Doc was dealing the cards, Speed had moved on to pigeons.

"You know what Jack's taken up? Pigeons. He's got a slew of 'em over at his place. They're descendants," Speed was saying, "of Owney Madden's birds. You know who I'm talking about, Owney? A little man with the biggest set in New York City, running beer, 'shine, got himself in a pinch with FDR."

"You want to skip the history lesson and play cards?" said Doc.

But Speed, once he was started, wouldn't or couldn't stop, unless you hit him with a club. Doc remembered the eyes of race horses glazing over when Speed talked to them. That's how long-winded the little man was.

"It didn't look good when Governor Roosevelt wanted to run for President, having somebody like Owney full-throttle on his turf. No sir. FDR got the man exiled here to Hot Springs. Now, Owney had raised pigeons from the time he was a boy in Leeds, looked after his dad's birds. Kept 'em atop the Cotton Club in New York City. Yes, he did. That Owney, did you know at one time he and Frank Costello had a regular flotilla of boats, ships, tugs, they even had some submarines fighting off the Coast Guard, bringing in booze? They used the pigeons to deliver the all-clear signal, so they could off-load those boats."

Doc didn't believe a word of it, even though, actually, Speed was telling the truth.

"But these birds, that's what I was talking about," Speed said, as he picked up the king Doc had just discarded, "they came down from pigeons that Owney was given by Governor Earl Long—one of the Louisiana Longs?"

Doc turned a queen, which gave him three ladies, a four-card run in clubs, two aces, and a deuce. Two cards in, he could have knocked with four, but why do it? The way he cheated, his gin card would be in the next pull.

Speed kept the next card he took from the deck, discarded Doc's winning ace, and said, "Gin." Four kings, a diamond run, three deuces.

The little bastard had suckered him even when he'd stacked the deck! How the hell did he do that? Nobody suckered Doc Miller. Nobody.

Speed scooped up Doc's twenty bucks, saying, "With your pigeons there's racers and fancies, you know, the ones you use for aerial shows. Tumblers, what they do is fly straight up, then tumble down. Rollers, you train for flying for distance—up. They go so high you can't see 'em anymore, then plummet. I'll tell you, I love those birds. Thoroughbreds and pigeons, they're better than any broad."

The phone rang twice and stopped. Then rang again. Doc picked it up. He said, "She said what? When did you talk with her? Then why did it take you so long to call? What are you saying? I don't believe it. Listen, get back here. What do you mean, don't tell you? I'm telling you, something's screwed up. You get back here, and we'll talk about it."

19

NOW THEY WERE BOTH SITTING ON THE FLOOR, LEANING up against the side of the ring. Sam had promised she wouldn't try anything if he didn't tie her up again. He'd brought her a bottle of cold mineral water. She was actually feeling kind of cozy, like he was looking after her. She wondered if Patty Hearst had felt this way when Cinque let her out of the closet.

He was smoking a cigar. "So how do you know Joey the Horse?" You'd have thought they were sitting across from one another at a sidewalk café, on a first date, he rolled the question out so casually.

She explained how her friend Lavert used to work for Joey as a chef and chauffeur. How Joey had sent Lavert to cooking school in France and Italy, Lavert having picked up his basic culinary skills jailing in Angola, the state penitentiary. She noticed how she left out the part about Lavert being Harry's best friend and partner.

"Lavert's a big black man? About six-five, six-six?"

"That's the one."

"I've eaten his grub. The man's a genius in the kitchen. I'd *forgotten* about Lavert." Then, more to himself than

139

to her, "Maybe I could get him to come up here, cook in my place."

"Your house, do you mean? Or do you have a restaurant?"

He didn't answer that.

So she said, "I first met Lavert in New Orleans when I was still working for the Atlanta *Constitution*. I used to be a reporter. Sam Adams, reporter. I still have some business cards in my wallet, if you want to see them. Along with my driver's license. My Social Security card. You could call the paper, ask them. They'd ID me." Though the way some of the staff had felt about her by the time she left, they'd probably hang up. Hell, let her rot.

"A reporter, huh?"

"Yes, and—" Then she remembered something else. "You know, last night, boy, talk about a small world, I saw somebody else here who knows Lavert. I don't really know him, but I saw this man, a black man named Early Trulove, who—actually, I think Early used to work for Joey, too. He groomed horses for him. Or worked for Joey's trainer, I'm not sure."

He was staring at her. "Where did you see Early?"

"At the piano bar in the lobby of the Palace. The same place I saw Mickey, the woman you've mistaken me for."

"Where were you sitting?" He was getting excited. His face was flushed.

"Like I said, right at the bar with Early. He was a couple of seats over from me. I was going to speak to him, but he left."

"Jesus H. Christ!" He stood up.

"What?"

He was walking in a circle, shaking his big head. "We got our signals crossed. Jesus! I thought he was fingering, I thought *you* were the—oh, shit."

She was beginning to get the drift. "*You* were in the Palace lobby last night?"

He shook his head and nodded at the same time. "I can't believe this."

"Well, listen. If it makes you feel any better, I've had a difficult time with the concept, too. Being grabbed out of the parking lot, knocked out, tied up, battered, etc. It hasn't exactly been a stroll through the park."

He wheeled, reached over, and gave her a hand, pulling her up. "Jesus! This is a—" He was brushing off her shoulders.

"Fuckup. A fuckup of the first water, I'd say."

He closed his eyes and pinched his forehead like he had a terrible headache. Then he opened them again, and there it was, that same brilliant blue. He said, "Who the hell *are* you?"

"I've been telling you for I don't know how long. Sam. Samantha Adams. But more importantly, who are *you?* And where the hell are we?"

"Oh, Christ." He stuck out a big hand. "Jack Graham. This is the top floor of my restaurant, Bubbles, it's in the old Quapaw Bathhouse, listen, I can't tell you how *sorry*—Jesus, can I—I'll make this up to you somehow."

"Hey. Mistaken identity? Kidnapping the wrong woman? It happens to the best of us. But there's one thing you can do."

"Name it."

"Close your eyes."

He smiled uncertainly, then shuttered those china blues.

Sam rolled her neck and shoulders until she felt pretty loose. She softened her knees and danced back a step or two. Then, like he told her, hands up, she pulled back her right, rotating her hips through her swing, and threw all her power behind it. She was bare-handed, so her fist throbbed like crazy after she landed her punch.

But his nose hurt worse.

20

~~~

"WHAT?" SAID SPEED, WHEN DOC GOT OFF THE PHONE.
You could never read the man's face. He did that stony
thing. But he knew Doc had to be fooling around with
Mickey, pulling his leg. Or, Speed wondered, maybe
they were jerking him off. Pretending something had
screwed up, so they could do him out of his third. Well,
they could fool around all they wanted to, they were
nuts if they thought they were pulling his chain. "So,
Doc? Something went wrong?"

"Nope. Everything's just hunky-dory."

Doc looked like he was figuring out something. Speed
didn't like that. He didn't like it when Doc was figuring.

"It sure sounded like something was wrong. You don't
look happy."

"I'm telling you it's nothing. Mickey said the car keeps
stalling on her. I tell her all the time, buy a Cadillac, if
you want a good car. But, no, she's got to drive that
damned Mercedes." He poured himself another cup of
tea. "Women."

"They're all crazy," Speed agreed.

Doc laid a hand on his shoulder. "Did you think I
was talking about the deal? Nawh. The deal's copasetic.
Mickey said your girlfriend's coming through." Now all
of a sudden, he's wearing this big smile. "Piece of cake,
Speed."

Speed relaxed. "Right. Piece of cake. That's what I said
from the minute I ran into Mickey at the track, been two,

three years since I saw her down in Sarasota, told her about Jinx and her lottery dough, how I'd flimflammed Jinx into thinking I was Mr. Gotrocks, marrying me, but the sticky part being the prenup she wouldn't back off of."

"I know, Speed." Doc still smiling, but sounding a little impatient. Like he'd heard all this before.

Well, he had. But that didn't mean that Speed didn't like telling it over and over. He liked to talk. Talking helped calm his nerves. And he'd been real nervous since he'd left New Orleans. It hadn't been pretty, that chapter. What was a guy supposed to do, his whole life he'd been connected, a first cousin to Joey the Horse, who'd given him odd jobs despite the fact that his dad was Irish from Magazine Street—just like Jack Graham. One little screwup, that Lush Life thing, which was all Doc's fault anyway, and he's out. Just like that. Like he wasn't family.

Joey said it was Speed's own fault, but Speed didn't see how he figured it that way. Joey had told him to work with Jack, and Jack had told him to work with Doc, and he figured Doc knew what he was doing. Jesus!

He went back to his story. "Jinx'd get a *big* hunk, we divorced. That's what that prenup paper said."

Doc said, "Not that it made the least bit of difference, since you ain't got the proverbial pot. A big hunk of zilch is zilch."

"Hey! I had my hot streaks. But the part that was the kicker, in the case of her death, all her money goes to her kid. That didn't seem fair to me. Does it seem fair to you? Huh, Doc? I said to Jinx, it's like you don't trust me."

"Why should she trust you, Speed? You're only marrying her for the bucks."

"Yeah, but I told you she doesn't know that. I wined her and dined her and danced her and romanced her. Hey, the woman thinks my heart is doing flip-flops. And she's nuts about me. You never saw a woman so nuts about anybody. She worships the ground beneath my feet. She'd do *anything* for me."

That's what she'd said. But then, he'd heard those words before. Joey used to slap him on the chops, just playing, and he'd say, Speed, I'd do anything for you. Then when he screwed up that one tiny thing, Joey said, Walk. Walk if you want to live. Just like that. The man was cold.

Doc said, "Yeah, uh-huh. The woman'd do anything for you except cancel the prenup." Then he took a long swig of his tea.

"Yeah, but Mickey, she's always been a smart girl, she came up with the plan, saw the way around it just like that." Speed snapped his fingers. "The phony nab. Jinx, she loves my little butt, she'll cough up the mill for ransom, we split it three ways, we're outta here. So tell me, what exactly did Mickey say just now, about the money? Said she's coming through with it, right? Just like we planned. Right? No problemo?"

"Why don't you ask her yourself?"

Speed had been so busy talking, he hadn't heard the car drive up. But there she was, Mickey, standing in the kitchen door. She wasn't smiling. You'd think she'd be smiling. Speed turned back to Doc. Doc was smiling. So, it must be like he said, Mickey was on the rag because the Mercedes stalled on her.

He'd jolly her up. "Hey, I heard about your car. But you got back here all right, right? Bringing us some of the good news, right?"

"Wrong," Mickey snapped, swinging into the room. Moving up on him, so close he had to look up to see her face. He hated that. He hated people making him feel short. She was saying, "Wrong, wrong, wrong, Speed. The lady you were so sure about? Your Jinx, the sure thing? Well, little buddy, Jinx said to tell you to go fuck yourself. And fuck Doc. And fuck me. We're all fucked here, Speed. We went to a hell of a lot of trouble, and now we're coming up with empty." She flipped her hands palm up.

Speed turned back to Doc, who was still smiling, Doc, who was strolling over to the counter where Speed had made the chicken sandwiches. Doc, who was picking up the chef's knife he'd used to chop. Doc, who was strolling back over to the table where the gin hands lay, face up. You could see Speed's winning hand. He knew Doc didn't like that.

But Doc was still smiling. A kind of sharky-looking smile. Not real pleasant. Not the kind that warmed your heart.

"She's joking, right?" said Speed, backing away a little. Doc was making him nervous. "Mickey's just joking."

"No joke," said Doc. Then quick as a wink, Doc reached over and pinned his right hand to the table, reared back with that chef's knife and hacked off the first joint of his little finger so neatly the horseshoe diamond ring didn't even fall off.

He stared down at his finger lying there on the table. He couldn't believe it. He was spurting blood like a frigging fountain.

Then he looked up at Mickey. She'd screamed once. Then she'd gone all white around the mouth.

Now he heard himself yelling at Doc. "What? What the hell'd you do?" The room was moving. "It doesn't even hurt. I can't feel a thing." He looked up at Doc, who was still smiling that awful smile. "Why'd you chop my damned finger off?"

The con man leaned into his face and crooned, "You know that old saying, don't you, Speed? Never play cards with a man named Doc?"

21

"FONTAINE FONTAINE, WHERE ARE YOU?" LATEESHA couldn't believe she was being so bold, standing right in that giant's yard, hollering out his name. But if he was her cousin June's husband, it wasn't like he was going to bite off her arms. Was it?

From deep inside the house, somebody answered. "Whaddyou want?"

It didn't sound like Fontaine. It didn't sound like anybody she'd ever heard before. Probably the ghost of one of those people who'd died up in the tower. Lateesha shivered in the middle of the afternoon of a warm spring day.

"I want to see Fontaine. I need to talk to him about something important."

"He ain't here."

"Well, where's he gone?"

"Gone to his day job."

"And where's that?"

"You don't know that, girl, you ought not to be coming around here hollering out his name in the first place." And then the door creaked open, and the tiniest little old man Lateesha had ever seen was standing there, his bottom lip all puffed out with snuff.

Lateesha had seen this little old brown apple doll before. She just didn't know where.

"You that girl stays with Odessie?" said the old man, opening the screen door and spitting around Lateesha into the orange daylilies.

"Yes, sir, I am."

"Then I'm your great-uncle, Sweet William."

"Yes, sir." So that meant she'd seen him at family reunions. Like last year when Aunt Odessie got to be the Big Momma and ride in the carriage with the white horses. Lateesha still had her family reunion T-shirt. She wondered if they'd given Uncle Sweet William a kid's size, how'd he look in it?

"You want to see Fontaine, you just go on over to Greenwood Cemetery. You'll find him."

"Greenwood?" Lateesha didn't like that idea one bit, even on this sunny day. Haints and goblins and who knew what? Besides, once when she was ten and was up here visiting from New Orleans, she was over in that cemetery playing with her cousins, and one of them was running around, his foot went down into this hole in the ground, and when it came back out, it didn't have a sock or a shoe, just these long scratches all around his ankle where this buried-alive person reached up and grabbed him. That's what Aunt Odessie said. Said that'd teach 'em to be playing where they ought not to.

Lateesha asked, "What's he do over to Greenwood?"

Sweet William leaned back his head and laughed this little old man silent laugh. He didn't have a tooth in his head. "You'll see. Now go on. You're keeping me from my programs. I likes to watch my programs every day. Weekends I watch things got balls in 'em. Today I'm watching basketball. You like basketball, girl? No? I used to tell Fontaine he ought to go try out, he's so tall, but the boy was too lazy. Now it's too late. He's too old. Not as old as me though. You know how old I am?"

No, Lateesha didn't, and she didn't mean to be rude, but she didn't care either. What she cared about was telling Fontaine that she had first dibs on that Sunliner, she being the one who'd gone to all the trouble snatching it in the first place, and she didn't appreciate Early, even if he was a stone bad killer, just stepping in and grabbing it all up. If there was anybody who was going to make the big bucks off that car, it ought to be her.

"Or you could talk with June," Sweet William was saying. "June's got more brains than Fontaine any day. She the one tells him what to do most of the time. If it's important, ain't that what you said, you ought to be talking with June anyhow."

Lateesha thanked Sweet William kindly and walked on back around into the side yard to check on her Sunliner. She hadn't noticed the sign over the garage door last night. FONTAINE BODY WORK. Well, it had been pretty late, and there'd been Fontaine and those dogs scaring her half to death. Now she could see the dogs, four huge black-and-tans, lunging at their fence, dying to get a piece of her.

She stuck her tongue out at them and opened a corrugated steel garage door that looked like somebody had just cut it out of the wall with a blowtorch and slapped a couple of hinges on it, which made her a little nervous about the quality of Fontaine's work. She wasn't sure she wanted him touching her Sunliner at all.

It was dark inside the garage. Dark and spooky, but not so dark that Lateesha couldn't tell that Damn! That Sunliner had up and gone.

22

"GET OUT OF MY WAY, PLEASE," SAM SAID TO JACK. "I don't want you to walk me back to my hotel." It was only a hop, skip, and a jump up Central Avenue, anyway, and if he thought he was getting off that easy, he was crazy. "Go soak your nose in some ice," she said, grabbing up her jeans and stomping out the back door of the Quapaw toward the Promenade. She was wearing her jacket, her T-shirt, his red satin shorts, and carrying her jeans.

"Give me your keys, and I'll have your car picked up and delivered," he called as she climbed the steps to the red brick lane that wound its way along the mountainside behind the bathhouses toward the big hotels. He sounded awfully nasal. His nose was swelling. Good.

"Are you crazy? My keys? I'll see you in court, mister."

"Please, I'm *so* sorry." He was halfway up the steps. "Listen, I'll make this up to you. I'll do anything. Anything."

She paused. A marker from a big-time crook? She said stiffly, "I'll think about it."

"Great! Remember, *anything*. I mean it."

She waved him off behind her. But now she couldn't wait to get back to the Palace and tell Kitty about the latest Perils of Pauline. She knew what Kitty would say: And he tied you up? Jeetz, you have *all* the fun. She jogged all the way back to the hotel.

But back at the desk, the clerk handed her a message

slip along with her key. If this was from Harry, well, he'd better watch himself, now that she had that old one-two punch under her belt. She was of half a mind to call him up and give him what for. Men! Who did they think they were, anyway? She bounced on her toes as she unfolded the message, only to read:

Sorry, kiddo, but a brunch guest choked to death this A.M. on a boeuf béarnaise in Her Majesty's Grill Room. Must fly back home and smooth the waters. We'll have to move our hike to Audubon Park. Not the mountains, but there's café au lait and beignets at the end of the road. P.S. Jinx could use a shoulder to cry on, good buddy. P.P.S. Don't faint at the floral offerings in your room. Harry's been real busy with the FTD. You've not died, and it ain't your funeral. Kisses, Kitty.

What? No, she wasn't dead, but she could have been, easy. And now there was no one to share her adventure with. Crap. And be nice to Jinx—was Kitty nuts? She'd give Jinx a shoulder all right, that conniving bitch, a stiff one.

Speaking of shoulders, hers hurt like the dickens. Those boxing gloves were heavy. She really was out of shape. But, how lucky for her that there was the spa, the whirlpool, the hot packs, a massage—right there on the second floor. She'd race in and do it all, then catch up with Loydell. See what the latest was on Olive. Ask the bellman to take those damned flowers and deliver them to the nearest hospital. (Didn't Harry know that that's what flowers reminded her of—hospitals, death, desertion by the ones who'd loved her most?)

She was thinking about Olive as she began to undress in the spa's anteroom, and suddenly she remembered. Olive's ring! Had it fallen out? Was it still in her jeans? She grabbed them up and felt through her pockets.

Yes! That was a relief, the ring hadn't slipped out along the Promenade. Or when Jack took off her jeans.

She stood there in her underwear, thinking of Jack pulling off her jeans. Pulling up the red satin shorts. Pulling off her jeans. She flushed. She had a fever. Or maybe this was how hot flashes started.

Nope. She was too young.

The answer was simpler.

She was going crazy. She was standing around in her underwear in Hot Springs, Arkansas, fantasizing about a man who'd kidnapped her, tied her up, stripped off her jeans, dressed her up in little red shorts, and punched her around.

Well, he hadn't really punched her around. And she'd certainly gotten her licks in.

But anyway you looked at it, this had all the elements of a feminist's nightmare—and she was wallowing in it and getting hot. She was a descredit to her gender.

Though, now, wait a minute. It was perfectly understandable if you thought about it logically. She had been dumped by her younger lover for a baby Barbie. Yes, and therefore, she was feeling old and ugly and invisible. And then this handsome older man came along and kidnapped her and tied her up and . . . Kiddo, give it a rest. There's nothing wrong with you that a hot tub and a cold shower can't fix.

Doc Miller had explored every inch of the basement under the old stone house on the hill, the servants' quarters, a woodshop, a wine cellar, a root cellar. There was a fully outfitted rec room with a billiard table, Ping-Pong, a couple of old pinball machines. The knotty pine walls were dotted with the heads of long-dead deer, caribou, elk. Their glass eyes shone in the lamplight.

Speed McKay's eyes shone, too. They were filled with tears that brimmed over and tracked down his cheeks like quicksilver. Doc hated to see a man cry. And today he really wasn't in the mood. He poured himself another tumbler of Scotch and leaned back on the leather sofa that was stitched with cowboys and horseshoes. Speed was sitting across from him in a chair upholstered with a colorful serape.

Speed was talking.

You cut the man's finger off, and he was still talking. You cut his head off, he'd probably still be talking.

The only way to shut him up was chop out his tongue, and even then it'd probably flap a path across the floor, lick at your shoe.

"I don't know why I came down here with you," the little man sobbed. "Don't know why. Now you're just going to do more terrible things to me. I never did anything terrible to you. I never did, Doc. I was always nice to you."

"Nice? *Nice?*" Doc reached over and grabbed himself another couple of ice cubes. "What the hell does *nice* have to do with anything? And, you came down here because I poked a knife in your back."

Speed sobbed and held up his right hand. A towel, soaked with crimson, was wrapped around it. "This wasn't nice. Not nice at all. Mickey didn't think it was nice."

"Don't kid yourself. You think Mickey gives a rat's ass about you? She's in this for the dough, just like me. If I know her, she hasn't given a second thought to you, she's upstairs right now figuring out some other scam to make the trip to this burg worthwhile."

Speed brightened. "How about Jack? I know the kidnapping part fucked up, but we can still hit on him. Lean on him hard, get a bunch of money out of him. You know, make him suffer for the way Joey treated us. That was all Jack's fault." And then the little man looked down at his hand again and started to bawl.

Doc thought out loud. "Mickey doesn't know Jack. Though, you know, that could be interesting, putting her on to him. Maybe we could rig something in one of his casinos, still make a big score."

"Yeah, we could!"

"Not *you*, jerkoff. Jack knows you."

"Yeah, but, I could help set it up, no problemo, run interference, you know what I mean?"

"I know you don't know what the hell you're talking about. And I don't much have any use for you at this point." Jack grabbed up the kitchen knife that was sitting on the coffee table, drew back, and hurled it across the room at a dartboard.

Speed flinched and laughed. The hysteria was creeping in. "Gee, Doc, that was pretty good." His voice was out of control. "Bull's-eye. Pretty neat. Heh heh heh."

"You wet your pants that time, Speed?"

"No. No way. Nuh-uh. I didn't wet my pants. I knew you weren't going to throw that knife at me."

"Tell you what, little man. Why don't you just get up and walk out of here? There's nothing holding you."

"I—I wouldn't run off and leave you like that."

"You think I'd kill you, don't you?"

"No, I don't think that. I really don't."

Doc leaned back into the sofa, stretching his long legs out in front of him. "You don't even like to hear me say those words, do you, Speed? Like, if I say them, it makes the possibility more real, doesn't it?"

"I don't know what you're talking about, Doc. I really don't. I really don't know what it is you mean when you say that, but I'll tell you, I think we ought to start working a plan to do something about Jack. We could hold up his casino. We could hold him up on the road with his receipts. We could poison his pigeons. He's crazy about those pigeons."

"Two out of three, Speed. You win, you walk. You don't, you don't. That make sense?"

"I don't know what you're talking about, Doc. What are you talking about? I mean, if you want to play something, gin, whatever, sure, no problemo, but I don't understand what these stakes are you're talking about."

"Don't worry. I'll show you. Now, here we go." Doc pulled a book of paper matches from his pocket, tore out a match, and holding it by the very bottom, turned his hand over so the match was inverted. "I'll bet you I can light this match and hold it in this position while counting to fifty without letting go of the match or extinguishing the flame. Here." He handed the match to Speed. "You try it, then see if you want to bet me."

"I don't want to. You're gonna make me burn my good hand. I only have one good hand." He whimpered and held up the blood-soaked mitt.

"You don't have a lot of choices here, Speed. You know what I mean?"

Cowed, Speed took the match, struck and lit it and held it in the inverted position Doc had showed him, for about five seconds before he dropped it.

"Ouch! I knew you were going to burn me."

"So? You think I can hold it for fifty? Without letting go or putting it out?"

"No. No way you can do it. I know you can't do it."

Jack lit the match. "One, two, three," he started counting slowly, all the while moving the hand holding the match back and forth over a distance of about eight inches. "Eleven, twelve thirteen." The match burned, but because of the motion, it burned very slowly, and the flame was pulled away from his hand. "Thirty-eight, thirty-nine."

"You didn't say anything about moving your hand," said Speed. "I don't think you said a word about moving your hand."

"Forty-nine, fifty. No, I didn't, jerk. If I'd told you how the prop worked, that would have been stupid, wouldn't it? And I'm not stupid, Speed." Doc poured himself another Scotch. "Now that's one for me. Let's go for two."

"I don't think I want to, Doc."

"Fine. Then just get up and leave. No one's holding you here."

Speed sat staring at Doc. Sweat poured off the top of his balding head. Gray strands were glued to his scalp. He leaned forward a little, as if he were going to do it, get up and walk out, but then he fell again into the chair, sank back, defeated. He was too afraid to move. Doc was the cobra, Speed the mongoose.

"Okay, good." Doc rubbed his hands together. "I guess that means you want to try again. Now, here we go." Doc ripped another match out of the book and flipped it up into the air as if it were a coin and let it land on the table. Then he ripped and flipped another. "You see, Speed, one side's gray, and one side's brown. That's the way paper matches always are, different colors on each side. Now, I can make whichever color I want to come up."

"I know there's a trick," Speed sighed.

"No. No trick. Come on, let's give it a try. You call."

"Gray."

Doc flipped, and the match came up gray.

"All right!" Speed crowed.

"You want to do it again?"

"Sure."

"Call."

"I'll take gray again."

The match was brown.

"Okay, so we're even."

"Can I see the matchbook, Doc?"

"Speed, Speed, Speed, baby, you don't trust me? I'm shocked." But he handed the matchbook over.

Speed inspected it carefully and satisfied himself that the matchbook wasn't gaffed, that all the matches were indeed two colors. "Okay, let's do it again."

They did, and the little man won. "So, that's one to one, right? You won the lit match thing, and I won this."

"That's right." Doc smiled. "But, you know, I bet I can make a match land on its *edge* instead of one of its sides."

"Can I see the matches again?"

"Why, sure."

Speed ripped out five matches and flipped them one at a time. All of them landed on a side, two brown, three gray, which were the odds of pure chance that Doc was playing with when he suckered Speed with the come-on.

"Tell you what," said Doc. "You win this one, you win the whole magillah. I can't make the match land on its edge, you get up and walk out of here, I won't do a thing to stop you."

"Swear to God?"

"Swear on my mother's blessed soul, may she rest in peace." At that, Doc downed another two fingers of Scotch.

"Deal."

Doc picked up a match, and as he started to flip it, he bent it in the middle with his thumb into a V shape. It landed on the edge every time. Time after time, as Doc flipped it over and over, and Speed cried. Great big tears rolled down his face, and he was sobbing aloud, but he was silent once Doc stuffed a rag in his mouth and taped it. He also bound Speed's hands behind him with strapping tape. And then he marched him outside and down to the boat dock.

Five minutes later, Mickey came down to the kitchen wearing clean white sweats with a towel wrapped around her head. Doc was cleaning up, putting away what was left of Speed's chicken salad, the plates, cutting board, knives, mopping up the spatters of blood from Speed's stump.

"Ummmmm, you smell good," Doc said to her. "You have a bubblebath?"

She ignored him and pulled a jar of apple juice out of the refrigerator. She poured herself a glass, drank it, and started to head back upstairs, when she paused and looked around. Her eyes narrowed. "Where's Speed?"

"He's outside."

"Outside? Doing what?"

"Trying to win a little wager."

She turned and faced Doc. "A little wager?"

"Yeah, I bet him a hundred bucks he couldn't swim out to the float and back."

"So, why aren't you watching him?"

Doc smiled.

Ruby was kneading Sam's shoulder with bony fingers that *hurt*. This wasn't quite what she'd been looking for, but shiatsu and pressure-point release didn't seem to be part of the Foot-washing Baptist's repertoire.

"So how'd you get into this business, anyway?" she asked Ruby between her grunts, making conversation.

"My chicken died. I used to run the Tic-Tack-Toe Chicken across the street over by the Ohio Club. Tourists paid a dollar to play with her, she beat 'em nine times out of ten. But when the gambling went, lots of the tourists did, too. Chicken wasn't worthwhile." Then she grabbed up Sam's right leg like she might just wrench it off at the knee.

"Why, Ruby, I thought you didn't believe in gambling."

"The chicken wasn't gambling. You didn't win anything if you beat her except the satisfaction that you'd won. You could go back home to Texarkana and tell all your friends that you were smarter than a Rhode Island Red." Sam laughed, and Ruby whacked her in the thigh. "Anyhow, the massage is more in line with my beliefs. Humbling yourself in the service of another. That's what it's all about, you know. Just like Jesus wasn't too stuck up to wash another's feet, we do it, too."

"That's what it means, foot-washing? Y'all wash each other's feet to show your humility?"

"Every Sunday," said Ruby slapping her hard on the butt. "Now turn over."

If Ruby was an example of humility, Sam wasn't sure she had a handle on the concept. She was about to ask Ruby to describe a service when, from over the top of the cubicle, she heard June talking to someone. "Now, Lateesha, that's Fontaine's business. You want to know about that old car, you go talk to Fontaine."

"That *old car* I left with Fontaine is a vintage Ford Sunliner that's worth twenty thousand dollars. That's what Early said."

Sam sat straight up on the massage table, her towel falling to the floor. Forget foot-washing. Forget modesty. That young voice had said the magic words.

June said, "Whoa, child! Twenty thousand dollars?"

"And, furthermore, that's for real. I know because I got on the phone this morning and called a dealer over in Little Rock, and he said that was about right, if the car was in its original shape."

"How'd you know to do that?"

"I looked in the ads in *Car and Driver* till I found one in Arkansas. Listen, June, we're wasting time. The man said the car ought not to be repainted, and that's what Fontaine's taken it to do, and I want you to call him and stop him. You do that for me, and you help me sell it, I'll give you a piece of the deal."

"Well," said June, "Lateesha, that sounds mighty good, except there's complications."

"If you're talking about Early, I'll take care of Early."

Sam thought Lateesha sounded awfully sure of herself to be so young. Having grabbed a robe, Sam was perched now on an empty table out in the big wrap room, soaking up their every word.

June said, "Well, I'm not exactly talking about Early, though I'd say we need to give some thought to him. The man's not going to be happy about you snatching this deal away from him."

"It's not his deal, it's mine because I'm the one who found the car in the first place, and I say finders keepers."

"I'd say losers weepers," Sam spoke up, "if you're talking about the Sunliner that belongs to Olive Adair out at the Gas 'N Grub."

23

"MAN, YOU LOOK LIKE SOMETHING THE CATS DRUG IN," said Tate to Early Trulove, who was working on his third beer. Tate, the owner and barkeep of this saloon, which was also home to the best burgers in Hot Springs, had played in a sandbox with Early before Early's mom, Valeen, had carted him off to Daytona Beach. Thus, Tate's entitlement to personal commentary.

Early looked up at his tall friend with the shiny bald head, reminded him of an eight ball. "Don't it just frost you when you get blamed for something that ain't your fault?"

"Thelma does that to me all the time. But then, what you gonna do?" Tate opened his palms to the heavens.

"I'm not talking about any woman." Early shoved his empty bottle toward Tate. "I'm talking about *the* man."

"Oh, well, then."

Early heard what Tate was really saying: What do you expect?

"Justice, I expect justice," Early was saying, the little gold star twinkling in his mouth. Then a little slip of a white girl—lots of long dark hair, not much over five feet, didn't weigh a hundred pounds soaking wet, but with good strong hands—stepped up to the bar with a round tray and said, "Ordering two Buds and a margarita, salt and rocks, please, Tate."

"She'd make a good jockey," Early said to Tate after he'd filled the order and she'd walked away.

Tate leaned over the bar. "You think you've got the red ass now, try messing with Cynthia, you'll find out what trouble is." Then he jerked his head down toward the end of the bar where two white men in uniform sat. Tate's was across the street from police headquarters and was a hangout for the boys in blue as well as other locals. Tourists rarely wandered in, though it was only a block off the main drag. Tate barely moved his lips as he added, "Cynthia's Archie Blackshears's kid. The fat one on the right's him." The one with the pig face and the straight black bangs down in his face. Add a mustache, and that's what Hitler would have looked like, if he'd been a fat redneck.

Early started, "Ain't he the one who—?" He didn't even get out the question before Tate gave him that squinty look that meant, Shut your mouth.

Early did. But that didn't mean he was happy about it. Early wasn't in the mood, not that he was ever in the mood to watch what he said in front of a white man. Or to a white man. Like only a little while ago, Jack Graham had started in yelling at him, saying he'd fingered the wrong woman, that wasn't Mickey Steele he'd been sitting with at the piano bar. Early said, I already *told* you the Steele woman was a redhead. When I nodded, that mean, Yeah, *this* redhead. Not any stray woman with some other hair color who happened to be sitting within six miles of my nodding head.

He's said that much back to Jack. But then Jack kept going on about it, and if Jack'd been black, Early would have said, You stupid s.o.b., you don't listen half the time. But he couldn't say that. Even as much as he and

Jack got along, and Jack gave him respect, he couldn't say that.

Or at least he didn't think he could.

But maybe he ought to, once, test it. See what happened.

Though would that be about black and white, or about Jack being boss? See? It wasn't that simple.

Tate had dropped a quarter in the jukebox, and James Brown was hollering at the top of his lungs about feeling good. Tate leaned over and said to Early, real quiet. "Yeah, Archie's the one used to beat Cynthia up till her boyfriend knocked out his lights. She moved out of his house, started working here, saving up to go away to college. Archie, he hangs around here to see her, but she ain't spoken a word to him since that night her boyfriend beaned him—two years ago." Then all of a sudden, Tate gave Early the old nod and wink. Something worth checking out had just checked in.

Early stared in the backbar mirror until into it strolled the reflection of a tarted-up white hooker type, the likes of which he hadn't seen since New Orleans and Bourbon Street. White-blond hair, scarlet lips, even a beauty mark.

"Can I help you, miss?" asked Tate.

"Oh, no," she said, tucking herself into one of the booths that ran along the wall opposite the bar. She tugged at her short black skirt. "I'll just make myself comfortable right here. Is there waitress service? I'd like to see a menu."

There was something peculiar about this woman, thought Early, still looking in the mirror. In addition to the fact that she was dressed like that—the little white jacket with the big shoulders, the tiny skirt, the fishnet stockings, the high heels, the long red gloves—in middle of a Sunday afternoon. His ma, Valeen, had told him stories about how a long time ago, a madam in town named Maxine used to drive her dolled-up ladies up and down Central in an open convertible. Advertising the wares. But that had been back when the town was something. This was Southern small-town Sunday afternoon, all the white folks lying down taking a little snooze after the exertion of one helping of Baptist fire-and-brimstone, two of fried chicken and potato salad.

"Hi!" Cynthia the waitress was saying to the floozie. "Can I get you something?"

Early turned from the mirror to look directly at the two women: the tarted-up bimbo in the booth and the pretty young waitress in the black T-shirt and black jeans standing with one hand on her hip, the other resting on the wooden tabletop carved with the intertwined initials of folks who had long ago swapped spit, probably couldn't remember one another's names today. Early wanted to hear the bimbo speak again.

"Hey, boy, what you looking at?" That was Archie Blackshears.

Uh-oh, Tate grunted.

Early whipped his head to the right. Was that cracker cop talking to *him*?

"Yeah, you. What you think you looking at?"

"Now, Archie—" started the cop who was with him.

Archie shrugged the man off. "I said, what you think you looking at, boy? I know who you are, don't think I don't. You think just 'cause you's away from here for years, you come back, all dressed up in your fancy clothes, that changes things? Think that means you ain't still a nigger?"

Early was halfway down the bar, waving his beer bottle over his head before Archie's words had stopped reverberating. Before his brain had connected with what might come next. Before Archie's daughter had shut her mouth after speaking to Archie for the first time in two years, yelling, "You get the hell out of here!" But not before the hooker had flown from the booth to the end of the bar and leaned herself up against Archie Blackshears. She was around to the side of him, caressing his fat neck with a red-gloved hand.

"Honey," she was saying, "you don't need to get yourself all riled up. Besides, you want Bobbie Sue to sit with you, you can't be ugly. Bobbie Sue don't like ugly."

"I don't give a shit what Bobbie Sue likes." Archie was all red in the face.

"Now, sure you do, sugar." Bobbie Sue nibbled on his fat earlobe, in case he needed a hint.

All of which gave Tate time to jump over the bar and get a headlock on Early, whom he dragged into a side room. He slammed the door behind them.

When Tate looked out again, the cops were both gone, Bobbie Sue was drinking a beer at the bar with her legs crossed, showing plenty of muscular thigh, and Cynthia was standing next to her saying, "I am truly not believing this!"

"Come on out, Early," Tate called behind him. "The Klan's done packed up and gone home."

"Do you know who this is?" Cynthia said to Tate with her hands on her hips. Early was standing behind him, checking forward and aft, ready to tear limb from limb anyone who looked at him sideways.

"Now, Cynthia, honey," said Bobbie Sue, "you just watch your mouth. You never know who might be listening." She mimed Early, craning her neck to check out the joint.

"Oh, Jesus," said Cynthia, "there's only those three goobers in the back room, and they're so shit-faced they don't give a rip if you're a transvestite or a Transylvanian."

"Well, that's okay, darlin'," Bobbie Sue said, her voice dropping an octave when she hit the endearment. "I'd *be* a Transylvanian if I thought it'd make you talk to me again."

Tate said, "Good God have mercy, it's Bobby Adair!

Idn't it?" Then Tate leaned right over in the blonde's face. "Bobby, idn't that you in there "

"Who's Bobby Adair?" asked Early, feeling all-of-a-sudden wrung out, his adrenaline crashing head-on into confusion like a train wreck at an unmarked crossing. Was Tate saying the bimbo was a transvestite, is that what it was?

Then Cynthia began to laugh. She had a mighty big laugh on her for such a little girl. She was absolutely hee-hawing, leaning back against Bobby or Bobbie Sue, whichever it was, tears running down her pretty face. Then Tate started in, and then Bobbie/Bobby said, in a normal young-man voice, "Oh, God, I'd have given the world to have laid a big wet one on Archie full on the lips, got him to put a little tongue in it, then ripped off my wig, said, Arch, you french pretty good. I would have, too, but I was afraid he'd ID me, I got right in his face. He liked that ear nibbling, though. He did."

Early had to ask, "What's with the costume, Bobby?" He stuck out his hand. "And who the heck are you, anyway?" They introduced themselves.

Tate wanted to tell the story of the young lovers, Bobby and Cynthia, and Bobby coming to Cynthia's defense, knocking Archie in the head with his own shooting trophy when Archie was beating up on her, but first, Tate insisted, they had to have a round on him.

"Bobby did all that for you, and you haven't spoken to him since?" Early said to Cynthia when Tate had finished. "Girl, you're cold."

Cynthia put her chin up in the air. "I hate violence. I never did think violence solved a thing, so I decided never to speak to either one of them again."

"You're saying you'd rather that son of a bitch, excuse me, I know he's your daddy, but you'd rather he beat you to a bloody pulp, killed you maybe, then my man here"—and Early grabbed Bobby around his shoulders, which is what was filling out that little white jacket, not shoulderpads—"would come to your rescue with that shooting trophy and save your life."

"Well, now wait a minute," said Bobby, scooting around on his stool, adjusting himself in the fishnet pantyhose that were binding something terrible. "Actually, having had some time to give the matter serious contemplation, *and* having become a member of the Graciousness Society of Elberton, Georgia, the goal of which is to reinstill politeness in our rush rush rush workaday world, I'd say I could have handled that situation better, without the shooting trophy."

Cynthia's smile said, So there.

Bobby continued, "Now, Early, you noticed how, just then, when you were about to bash Archie's head in—an impulse I fully respect and can certainly identify with—I used my wiles instead of resorting to violence again. Violence simply begets violence, in my opinion."

"Oh, Bobby!" said Cynthia, throwing her arms around him.

"Shit," said Early. "That was easy, using your wiles, you dressed up like a girl, and besides, it wasn't you he was calling nigger."

"That's true," said Bobby, wiping the beer off his mouth with the back of his glove, smearing his lipstick. "That is true. Wiles wouldn't be so easy if I were in my jeans. Or if I were you. I guess I need to think about that a bit."

"And should we assume," said Tate, "that you're wearing that getup in the first place because you were afraid you might run into Archie when you came looking for Cynthia."

"Correct," said Bobby. "And, of course, I wasn't sure how Cynthia might react, if I just walked up to her with my naked face. Not to mention, I can't let *any* law enforcement catch me within fifty miles of Hot Springs. Terms of my parole."

"That ain't right, man," said Early, shaking his head.

"And you know, it occurs to me that you put yourself in an awful lot of jeopardy, snuggling right up to Archie like that to save me from committing murder. He could have recognized you, man. I'm telling you, I owe you a big one." Early reached over and grabbed Bobby's red-gloved hand again.

"No, you don't owe me a thing," said Bobby. "Any human being with a shred of graciousness would have done exactly the same thing."

"Nawh, now, I do," Early insisted. "There's anything you want, you tell me." Early lowered his voice. "I got connections."

Tate's eyes rolled. Jack Graham, the same connection Early was bitching about earlier, now he's bragging on him.

"Well," said Bobby, "I *am* real worried about my grandma."

"Olive?" said Cynthia. "What's wrong with Olive?"

"I can't find her," said Bobby. "When I got out to her place this morning, there's Pearl, worrying and whining. No Mamaw. Pearl and I looked her for a while with this real nice lady named Sam who came along, but we didn't find hide nor hair of her."

A woman named Sam? Wasn't that who Jack said he'd mistaken for Mickey Steele? But Early didn't want to think about that now. "Who's Pearl?" he asked instead.

"Pearl? Well, Pearl," said Bobby, his voice softening the same way it did when he spoke Cynthia's name aloud, which was the last thing he'd done for the past two years right before he went to sleep, "Pearl's my dog. I left her with Mamaw when I got sent over to Cummins. Pearl's a redbone hound. Anybody can find Mamaw, she can."

"You think maybe Olive went off with Miss Loydell?" asked Cynthia. "The two of them are always traipsing off places together. Though Miss Loydell hasn't said anything about their going off until June. I water her plants, keep an eye on things, when she's away."

"Nope," said Bobby. "I talked with Miss Loydell just a little while ago. She's looking for Mamaw herself, said she didn't show up at a party she's supposed to last night. Said she asked your daddy"—he turned to Cynthia—"to drive by her house and check on her, but she doesn't think he did."

"I'm going to kill that man," Cynthia said. Then she looked embarrassed, considering what she'd said about violence not two minutes earlier.

"You think we ought to go get Sweet William's black-and-tans, you want to hunt for her?" asked Tate. "They're the best trackers in the county."

"I don't think so," said Bobby.

"It wouldn't be any trouble at all," said Early. "And I know Sweet William wouldn't mind. He's got so old, he doesn't run those dogs nearly as much as he ought to."

"What I'm saying is, thank you very kindly, but Pearl's the best tracker in the county, and if any dog can find Mamaw, it'll be Pearl that does."

Tate backed right off. "I certainly didn't mean to be casting aspersions on your Pearl." You could brag about your breed and bad-mouth another, but you never wanted to say something about a man's *specific* dog. You might as well call his baby daughter ugly.

"No offense taken," said Bobby. "I'm just saying that Pearl's daddy, Louisiana Red, was some kind of talented dog, and Pearl's inherited his genes, of course."

"Now, Bobby, tell us about Louisiana Red," said Early, signaling Tate for another round on him and taking on the role of host.

"Don't y'all think we ought to get going, look for Miss Olive?" asked Cynthia.

But the men were already slipping into serious dog-bragging mode. "Well, you know redbones are superlative coon dogs," said Bobby.

"Nothing finer than the sound of a redbone bawling when he picks up the scent of coon," agreed Tate, trying to make up for even mentioning Sweet William's black-and-tans in the same conversation as a redbone.

"That's right," said Early. "Nothing finer, except of course when they start to chopping when that coon is treed."

"Y'all going to sit around talking about dogs when you ought to be out hunting Miss Olive? I'm telling you," Cynthia said to her reflection in the mirror since there was no one else to say it to, "men are nuts."

"Now, hush, sugar," said Bobby, patting the stool beside him with a red glove. "Sit down here and listen, if you want to hear this man-talk."

"Sure, sure, girlfriend." Cynthia patted him right back on his fishnet-covered knee.

"And Red," said Bobby, already too far in to stop, "was more superlative than most. In fact, not only could Red outhunt any coon dog in the whole free world—bluetick, redbone, black-and-tan, brown-and-black-and-white treeing Walkers, brindles—Red could cook."

"Tell it, Bobby," said Early the way you do when you're encouraging a good preacher or a baaad jazzman. "Tell it about the cooking dog."

"It was a sight," said Bobby, "in fact, it was a privilege, to witness Red out hunting with my Uncle Clyde in the fall. That was the best time, when the coon season was open, you couldn't get arrested for jumping the gun, and the woods are starting to dry up a little bit, so there's kindling."

"I 'spect it's good for a dog to have some kindling, he's going to do his cooking out in the woods," said Tate. "Red do cook in the woods, don't he, or he set himself up in the camp with the ladies, womping out chili and sausage and eggs and french fries and steak served up on them red-and-white checked tablecloths?"

"He cooks in the woods," said Bobby, ignoring the

innuendo of exaggeration. "Now, you know, Red always was straight on coon from a pup up. That dog lived and breathed coon. You could put a fox in front of him, he'd look at you like you'd gone nuts. Cat. Chicken. He wasn't interested in anything in the world except coon."

"And the culinary arts," said Tate.

"Tate, you better leave this man's story alone," warned Early. "Give him another beer."

"Well, that's true, what you say about the culinary," said Bobby, leaning back and taking such a deep swig on his beer that his blond wig slipped back an inch or two, giving him a particularly slatternly look. "And the way Red got into that, he was on this real rough old coon one night, coon had been around the block more than once, had led Red up and down a creek, over and under a dozen fences, in and out of a well."

"A well?" said Cynthia. "It must have not been very deep."

"Oh, it was deep, all right," said Bobby. "Forty foot, but that didn't faze Red a bit. He was in and out of it so fast, he didn't even get wet. It was the train that slowed him down."

"The train?" asked Cynthia.

"Yep. See, that coon, when he got out of the well, he took off for this railroad bridge, and Red's right on his tail, closing in, when the Midnight Special comes roaring through."

"And made raccoon pancakes, and that's where Red got the inspiration for his cooking," said Cynthia.

Bobby went on like she hadn't said a word. "And at the last minute, the locomotive's bearing down on them both, going a hundred miles an hour, when the coon bails out over the side trestle, doing one of those perfect swan dives a hundred feet down into the water, barely made a ripple, and Red, he goes the other way, the dog jumps as high as he can in the air, when he comes down, he falls right into the exhaust pipe of the kitchen car of that train, and that was one hot dog for a minute, I'll tell you, landing smack on the griddle, but he jumped right off that sizzling iron and into the head cook's heart."

Cynthia was fanning herself. "It's getting awfully thick in here."

"Yep," said Bobby, "that cook knew a redbone when he saw one, and he kept Red right by his side all the way to Nashville. Taught Red everything he knew."

"Is that where the cook lived, Nashville?" asked Early.

"No, that's where Red skipped off the train, took a run by the Grand Ole Opry, heard himself righteous human bawling and chopping. Though my ownself I'd still rather hear a redbone hound giving out that mountain music on a crisp November night than have George Jones singing in my living room. Anyway, then, after he'd got himself an earful, Red came back on home, and that was when he commenced to cooking."

"Red just walked home from Nashville to Hot Springs?" asked Cynthia.

Bobby looked at her like she'd gone stupid. "It's only about five hundred miles. Any redbone worth his salt could do that in a breeze."

"Now what exactly did the dog cook?" asked Early.

"Well," said Bobby, "if Cynthia would stop interrupting"—and he reached over and patted her on the cheek—"I'd tell you."

"Go on ahead," said Cynthia. "My mouth is zipped. Of course, anytime y'all get through lying and want to go look for Miss Olive, I'm your woman."

"Just a minute, darlin'," said Bobby. "I'm almost through. Now, here's what happened. When Red gets home, Uncle Clyde's so happy to see him, he invites all his friends to go on this big hunt, and he's clean forgotten it's Aunt Vandy's birthday and he'd promised to take her to the HoJo in Little Rock for fried clams. Well, she gets her nose out of joint, and says, Go on, all of y'all.

But don't come looking to me for grub. Y'all can all starve to death in those woods for all I care. Hope you do, in fact."

Bobby looked at Cynthia, who just nodded at the mother wisdom of Aunt Vandy. Then he went on. "So off they go, Clyde and a whole mess of his friends, bringing six dogs apiece with 'em and about a case of sipping whiskey."

"Now we're talking hunting," said Tate.

"And it's one of those nights that nothing's going right. It seems like it takes them three hours before they hear the first bawl. Plus it's started to drizzle just a little bit, and the leaves are getting slippery, and what with one thing and another, old boys are starting to fall down, and Merle Moore, I remember this, Clyde said he fell in a bog, and it took four of them and two ropes to pull him out. 'Course, Merle weighed a good three hundred pounds. But it's getting late, and the boys are taking not only drunk but tired and hungry, and Clyde's starting to think Vandy's put a curse on them."

"Sounds like it to me," said Tate, thinking of his Thelma.

"Anyway, all this while, before they heard the first bawl, those dogs have been all over the county. They've been up ridges, through fields, down a waterfall, rooting through the mud, treed themselves a four-point deer."

Bobby paused a second, but no one rose to the bait.

"And then, finally, finally, those old boys heard the sweetest sound ever heard to man, well, almost the sweetest, depending on whether or not he has a loud or a quiet lady in his bed."

At which, Cynthia, silent as a shark, grabbed a newspaper off the bar and slapped Bobby in the head with it.

Bobby didn't flinch. "That sound I referred to, of course, was the sound of sixty hounds all chopping a good hundred barks a minute apiece. And the boys took out running like their pants was on fire, and before long they came up on this little clearing in the piney woods, and they couldn't believe their eyes."

"Are we getting to the climax, or is this the denouement?" asked Cynthia.

Bobby went right on. "Because those dogs had treed themselves five coons at once in five separate trees."

"Jesus," said Tate reverently, which let Early know that it was time to cut the bartender off. Anybody who believed a word of this story was definitely drunk.

"And it didn't matter if those coons were up in those trees with their little hands over their eyes or not, which is what they'll do to keep them from shining in the hunters' lights, sooner or later, they all were shot. Shot clean. Because the dogs, following Red's lead, just stepped back when their masters got there, like they were saying, Take it, Mr. Bubba."

"Instead of chewing the live coon down to little bits of gristle and fur, which is what y'all usually like to see the dogs do?" said Cynthia.

"But the best part"—at this point Bobby stopped and stood, his wig slightly tilted, his lipstick smeared—"was that in the center of the clearing, there was a fire that the dogs had already made by means of running around and around and around so fast that they created sparks which lit the kindling under the wood which they'd stacked. And out to the edge of the fire buried in the dirt were sweet potatoes that they'd dug and collard greens that they'd pulled out of those fall fields they'd rambled through, washed them off in the waterfalls, steaming now in a wrapping of pine needles."

"Holy shit," Tate said reverently.

"Well, that's not what Vandy said." Bobby shook his head sadly as if he had to tell them something that was going to break their hearts. "Clyde got home and told her how successful the hunt had been, and what a superlative leader and provider Louisiana Red had been, and how proud of him he was, and Vandy said, If that dog had any kind of grit, he'd of made you some cornbread to eat with those greens." Bobby paused dramatically for a count of ten. "So the next time Clyde took Red out, Red did that very thing. He tacked homemade cornbread with cracklings on to his menu."

At which, the three men almost beat each other to death, pounding backs, slapping hands. Cynthia sat there, silently sipping her beer.

And when the hooting and the howling were finally over with, and the tears had been wiped, and the noses blown, and the final harump harumped, Cynthia said, "I know y'all think that's real funny because of Vandy, right?"

"Now, Cynthia," said Bobby. "That's not the point of the story. The point of the story is that Red was a superlative dog, which means Pearl's come from some superlative stock."

"Well, all I've got to say is my grandma used to have a dog that would make Pearl look like caterpillar snot."

"Ooooooooooh, watch out," said Early.

"I think I'm going to go on in the back room and see about some, well, some *things,*" said Tate.

"You most certainly are not," said Cynthia. "I sat here and listened to Bobby's incredibly boring story about the incredibly boring sire of his incredibly boring Pearl, and now I'm going to tell about my grandma's dog."

"I thought you were in a Godawful hurry to get out there and find Olive," said Bobby.

"I am, and we're going to, but this is only going to take a minute, and then we'll be on our way." Cynthia sat up straight on her bar stool. "Here it is. My grandma had this cold-nose black-and-tan gyp named Rosie. Now, in case you don't know what a cold-nose hound is, I'll tell you. It's a hound who can pick up on a cold trail that's hours or even days old—which is what it sounds like we need this very day, since you, Bobby Adair, have been wasting all this time letting Olive's trail get cold when you ought to have been out there looking for her instead of in here drinking beer, which is not worming you back into my good graces."

"Yes, it is," said Bobby. "Because you're talking to me after two years of not." He squeezed her upper arm, and she shrugged him off.

"Anyway, Grandma used to like to brag about her Rosie, which lots of folks thought was unseemly, especially because she was a woman. Until one rainy Sunday down at the store, this farmer's saying as how he was feeding his cows in his upper pasture, up near the woods, and he saw an old gray wolf chasing a jack rabbit."

"Wolf's not good near your cows," said Tate, who himself had never lived outside the city limits of Hot Springs.

"So the farmers all said, Dove, that was my grandma's name, Dove, she was one-half Cherokee, this Rosie of yours you're always saying is such a good cold-nose hound, why don't you take her up to Farmer Jones's upper pasture and see if she can find that wolf. Dove said she thought that was a good idea, she'd do that very thing.

"So all these old boys loaded themselves in their pick-ups, just sniggering and poking each other to beat the band, 'cause they figure they've called Dove's bluff.

"They're all standing around watching while Rosie circles the area where the wolf was last seen. Then after a couple of zigs and zags and circles and going this way and that, Rosie lets out a long bawl, puts her nose to the ground, and takes off down a draw and into a bottom.

"The old sons, they're following Rosie by horseback and pickupback, laughing all the time, making fun. And there's Dove, walking by her lonesome just as proud and silent as her full-Cherokee grandmothers through those swampy woods.

"Late that evening, sure enough, Rosie overtook that wolf. But he wasn't a big old gray wolf. He was just a whimpering little old wolf pup.

"So, what you got to say for your Rosie, now? The old sons laughed and pointed and sniggered.

"And Grandma Dove, she looked straight at 'em with those big brown eyes of hers, and she said, Rosie has backtracked so far and so fast that she caught that old wolf back when it was still a pup." With that, Cynthia stood and drew herself to her full five feet. "And that's the truth, boys, if it ever was."

They all chuckled, and then Bobby slipped off his stool, too, and threw his arm around Cynthia's waist. "I concede anything and everything to the power of this wonderful young woman whom I love more than life itself."

"Hear, hear!" Tate and Early raised their glasses high.

"And now," said Bobby, pulling off his blond wig and throwing it on the bar, "anybody who wants to join me is welcome, I've got to saddle up and go find my grandma and my Sunliner that disappeared along with her."

Sunliner? Early couldn't believe his ears. Did Bobby who'd come to his rescue, who'd saved him from killing that fat policeman, did he say *Sunliner*?

"DID YOU SEE ANYBODY IN THE HOUSE YOU TOOK THE SUNliner from?" Sam was asking Lateesha as they made their way in Sam's BMW down the narrow gravel road into Greenwood Cemetery. They were looking for Fontaine.

"Nope," said Lateesha. "I didn't see a soul. There was another car in the carport, though. A silver Mercedes. A big one, about, oh, I'd say seven years old."

Lateesha held up as many fingers, each of which bore a ring and was polished a different color. In fact, Lateesha was a kind of Rainbow Coalition all by herself. Her hair, done in a hundred little braids, was intertwined in a scarf of fuchsia and gold. Her blouse was peacock blue, and her micro-mini was the same fabric as her do-rag. The thin shapely legs that stretched for years from beneath her tiny skirt were covered in bright orange tights. Her high-top tennis shoes were purple.

She lit up the cemetery as they passed slabs of black granite, praying angels, ancient oak trees, until finally they came to a green cement-block house surrounded by rhododendrons.

Just as they pulled up, Fontaine stooped through the doorway. "Good Lord," said Sam. He was the tallest person she'd ever seen close up.

"I told you he was a giant," said Lateesha. "He could pop your arm off and eat it for breakfast. That's why I'm glad June wrote us this note." She was clutching it in her hand. "Though he was really nice when I met him before."

Sam stepped out and introduced herself to Fontaine, and they exchanged pleasantries, he in a voice that made the earth rumble beneath their feet. Sam said, "I understand you're the chief caretaker here."

"That's right," said Fontaine. "Been looking after the grounds, the folks, digging holes, oh, fourteen, fifteen years. There's some nice people buried here. All white people, of course. But some nice white people."

Sam stared down at her shoes, not knowing what else to do. White Southerners of a liberal bent spend a lot of time inspecting their footwear.

"Some famous ones, too," said Fontaine. "Like Owney Madden, you know who he was?"

Sam nodded. "The bootlegger who was exiled here from New York."

"That's right!" Fontaine was pleased that she knew so

much about his most famous charge. "Now tell me, what can I do for y'all?"

"You can do this, Fontaine," said Lateesha, stepping up with June's note and handing it to him.

Fontaine read it slowly, then started over and read it two more times, and then he said, "Well, I'd be happy to oblige you ladies, but I'm afraid I can't hand that car over to you like my wife says here I ought to."

"Why not?" said Lateesha. She stepped even closer to Fontaine, about to get in his face—that is if she'd been tall enough. Sam reached out to grab the back of her skirt.

"Well . . ." Fontaine pulled at his khaki work cap. "I'd love to, but, you see, that car's already gone."

"We brought you the car at two A.M., and here it is"— Lateesha checked her watch—"thirteen hours later, and you're saying it's gone. You told Early you were going to paint it. Now I for one don't think you painted it and dried it and got it on the road, which was not your job in the first place, but Early's, not that it was his car to begin with, in that amount of time, and I hate to call you a liar, Fontaine—"

"And she's certainly not doing that," said Sam, stepping right in front of Lateesha. "But you see, we're awfully concerned about the car because it belongs to Olive Adair, who seems to have disappeared."

"Yes, ma'am," said Fontaine. "I hear you."

Oh, great. Now he was going to yes ma'am her from here to next Sunday, agreeing with everything she said while not telling her a damned thing.

"And, you see, if we could put our hands on the car, then that might be helpful in finding Olive," she said.

"Yes, ma'am."

"And also might be helpful in *somebody* getting their twenty thousand dollars," said Lateesha.

Sam could see that she might have to shake Lateesha

to rid her of the notion that she was owed something for the car that she had nabbed.

Fontaine stared at Lateesha, then turned back to Sam. "Yes, ma'am. I can see what the problem is, but I just don't see as how I can help you."

"You could tell us where the car *is*, for starters," said Sam.

"Like I said, it's gone."

Okay. She was just going to have to go find Early Trulove and get him to talk to Fontaine, and if *that* didn't do any good, then she'd ask Jack Graham to talk with Early, since Jack certainly owed her something. But, by God, she'd gotten this close to that Sunliner, she was going to find it and find Olive, if it killed her.

"Come on, Lateesha." She grabbed the young girl's hand.

"I sure wish I could be more help," said Fontaine.

"Oh, you do not!" said Sam out the window of her BMW. She was just about to back up, when Early Trulove and his red Cadillac came cruising into her rearview mirror. There were two other people with him; now all of them were stepping out, Jesus, was that Bobby Adair in makeup and full drag?

"Yes, it's me," said Bobby, shaking her hand. "Please, forgive the way I look. It's a disguise."

Sam nodded, wondering what the hell *he'd* been up to.

"Good to see you again, Sam. I was telling Cynthia and Early, may I present Cynthia Blackshears, Cynthia, Samantha Adams—whom I mentioned to you before—and Early Trulove, about your helping me look for Mamaw."

Sam eyed Early, and he eyed her. Did he remember her from the piano bar?

"Miss Adams," said Early. "Good to see you again."

"Oh, so you've met," said Bobby, then pushed on. "Now, Early tells me that his friend Fontaine—" He

turned and looked up at the man who towered over him.
They shook hands. "That Fontaine has been taking care
of my grandma Olive's car, actually, it's *my* Sunliner that
Mamaw was keeping for me while I was away."

"Early." Fontaine shifted his huge body from one foot
to the other. "I need to talk with you a minute. If y'all
could excuse us, please."

The two men stepped off, back up toward the little
green building with the attached shed, and Sam wondered what kind of double-dealing they were up to,
when she saw Early suddenly step back at something
Fontaine had said. No! Early said, raising one hand to
the heavens. My God! Dear God! And then he sat down
atop the nearest tombstone and dropped his head in his
hands. Whatever Fontaine had said, the man was obviously stunned—unless he was one hell of an actor. Sam
had seen an awful lot of good actors in her time.

"What?" said Lateesha, closing in on Early.

"*What?*" said Bobby.

"Folks," said Fontaine, "I'm afraid I'm going to have
to ask you all to leave."

"No way!" said Lateesha.

"Forget it!" said Bobby. "This has something to do
with Mamaw, you'll have to kill me first!"

In the end, after a lot of screaming and harsh words,
it was Lateesha and Cynthia who were sent on their way
and Sam and Bobby and Early who stood and watched
as Fontaine drove the backhoe over to a plot way in the
back of the cemetery and dug up the Sunliner, which
he'd buried whole, thinking, understandably, that what
he'd found in the trunk was Early's doings.

Fontaine, who was a whiz with the backhoe, dug a
long slow grade for the Sunliner, and then he hooked a
couple of big chains to a tractor and pulled the car up
the grade. When they opened the trunk, Bobby went
crazy. He attacked the Sunliner with his fists and his feet
and finally with his head—as if that old car that he'd

so loved had been responsible for Olive's death. Finally Fontaine and Early wrestled him to the ground, and Fontaine picked him up and threw him in the red Caddy, Early saying, Bobby, we've got to call the cops, and you don't want to be in the neighborhood.

Sam was left alone to say a prayer for Olive, whom she'd only seen that once, late the previous afternoon—which now seemed, and in many ways was, some other lifetime.

THE CEMETERY WAS QUIET EXCEPT FOR THE TWITTERING OF birds. Sam sat, keeping Olive company, a little distance away from the Sunliner, under an ancient oak tree. The tree shaded the grave of a child who'd died in 1908 at the age of six. Alice Ann Barnstable, she'd be over ninety, if she'd lived. And if she had, Alice Ann would have seen the advent of rural electrification, indoor plumbing, automobiles, faxes, jet planes, satellite communication, mankind's stepping on the very face of the man in the moon—and yet, not much people stuff had changed. Folks still went to bed hungry. Fathers got drunk and beat their womenfolk. Men killed one another, out of rage or greed, or because they were sick s.o.b.s.

"Tell me his name, Olive," Sam said aloud, her voice floating among the graves.

She had no doubt the killer was a man. Women hardly ever strangled their victims, and when they did, it was not with their bare hands.

The bruises on Olive's neck were brutal, with clear impressions of fingernails. And Sam would bet anything, if she pulled back Olive's eyelids she'd see tiny red dots, minute blood clots actually, in the lids' lining, which were presumptive evidence of strangulation.

Sam had witnessed more than her share of crime scenes in the years on the beat. You saw enough of them, you became an expert on things that you'd rather you never even heard of.

She picked up a pebble and pitched it across three graves. Jesus, man was a miserable creature.

Dogs were a hell of a lot better. Cats. Name any of God's other creatures, they killed for food, not for whatever rotten excuse the miserable bastard who'd done this to Olive had given himself.

Olive, funny fat Olive, was never going to get to go to Morocco with Loydell. And Sam was going to have to find Loydell and tell her that. Hell.

Well, better her than the cops, and at least Loydell had AA, she could find some strength in that. Not that Sam herself had been to any meetings lately. Wasn't she going to do that, call up and find a meeting the first thing when she hit town? Well, it wasn't as if she hadn't been busy. She looked at her watch. From the time she'd met Olive yesterday, till now, was just about twenty-four hours.

Then she heard gravel spinning, and she stood. Over a little green rise flew a chrome angel. It was perched on the hood of that brown Rolls. Behind the angel, she saw the big silver head of Jack Graham. He was wearing a Band-Aid on his nose.

Early jumped out from the passenger side, and he was saying something about putting Bobby in a safe place and how Jack had helped them figure out a story so they didn't all go to jail over the Sunliner. Fontaine was unfolding himself slowly from the backseat. But Jack was already walking toward her with his arms wide.

She didn't think. She didn't say to herself, This is a very shady character, Mr. You Know Who, the same man who grabbed you, tied you up, made you go two rounds. She needed a big hug, and he had one.

"So, what you're saying," said Archie Blackshears, who along with his partner had answered Fontaine's call, "is that you were poking around back here a little while ago, and you saw that a big grave had been dug, and you didn't do the digging."

"That's right," said Fontaine.

"And so you decided to dig it up and see what was in the grave."

"That's right."

"Why didn't you call the police right then?"

"There wuddn't any reason then that I could see to do that."

Archie rolled his eyes at his partner. "So you took it upon yourself to dig up this big old plot, and you found this car."

"That's right, I found this here Ford, but I'd have to differ with you about the taking it upon myself part. It's been my job for the past fifteen years to make sure that everything in Greenwood Cemetery is on the up and up. This fell into that category."

"But it wuddn't so suspicious that you called us."

"That's right. I didn't figure it was against any law, burying a car. Especially since this space don't belong to anybody in particular anyway. Folks don't buy plots at the back of the cemetery while there's room up front. Most folks want some company underground just like they do on top. Though," Fontaine pushed back his khaki cap, "it was inconvenient for me, of course. Big job, digging up a car. Even with a backhoe."

"And then you opened the trunk of the car?" said Archie.

"That's right."

"And why did you do that?"

"Because it smelled pretty ripe. I thought I ought to see what was causing that."

"And you didn't think you ought to call the police first?"

"I had the keys. The keys were right there in the ignition. I didn't need to bother y'all then. Could have been a load of fish in the car. Bunch of potatoes. Like that."

Archie hitched up his pants. "But when you saw what it was, *then* you decided to bother us?"

"Right. 'Cause then I figured y'all'd want to be bothered. Dead white lady in the trunk. Starting to bloat."

"Do you know this lady, Fontaine?"

"Well, she looks an awful lot like Miss Olive Adair runs that Gas 'N Grub out on the edge of town."

"Do you know Miss Adair?"

"Not personally, no. But I've stopped in her store."

"And you have no idea how she came to be in the trunk of this car in your cemetery?"

"I'd say somebody put her in it and buried her here. That's what I'd say. That's right. You ask me, that's what I'd say."

Early was navigating the Rolls up the curving mountain road toward the house where Lateesha had found the Sunliner.

"I hated leaving Fontaine with all that in his lap," said Sam. She and Jack were sharing the backseat.

"I know," said Jack. "But I couldn't see any other way to do it."

He reached over and patted her hand. He was agreeing with her, comforting her, and making her uncomfortable, too. She didn't know this man, and what she did know of him was not exactly the stuff you'd put on a résumé. He was a very clever, very attractive big-time crook with whom she suddenly found herself in cahoots.

"But look at it," said Early from the front seat, not

turning around on this snaky road. "Fontaine volunteered, didn't he, once he heard the story? Did we twist the man's arm, or did he step up of his own free will and say, Seems to me we do this any other way it's gonna be hard explaining away Bobby Adair, who ain't supposed to be in town in the first place, then Lateesha and your's—you know, my's—stealing the car? Keeping you out of it, too, Sam. 'Cause how come you didn't call somebody about Bobby breaking his parole? 'Cause he said he was Miss Olive's grandson, right, but what you *should* have done was sicced the police on his butt."

"In for a penny, in for a pound," Sam said. How had she gotten herself in this mess in the first place? "You think Fontaine's going to be okay?"

"He'll be fine," said Early. "The big man knows how to handle himself. Besides, what they gonna say—he killed Miss Olive and stole her car and buried 'em both in his cemetery, and then decided to dig 'em up and call the police? Man did that, he'd get off on insanity, 'cause he'd be crazy, once he was home free, go and unearth 'em."

"He's got a point," said Jack.

"Right there," said Early pointing, "is where Lateesha and I found the car."

"Then Pearl was right," said Sam, peering down off the road through the brush. "This looks like the place she led Bobby and me, the same place we ran into Mickey Steele early this morning. Or, rather, she ran into us."

"And according to what Lateesha said, yep, there it is," said Early, slowing to a crawl, but not stopping as they passed the gates of the big stone house set back from the road.

"It's the same house?" asked Jack.

"Sure is," said Early.

"Do I have to fill in the story for myself?" Sam asked Jack. She knew only what Jack had told her after she'd popped him one good—that he was anxious to talk with Mickey because she was partners with some people he thought were out to do him harm. Serious harm.

"Okay," Sam continued, since nobody else spoke up. "Lateesha stole the Sunliner from this house, ergo, from Mickey and this Doc Miller who you say is her partner. So does that mean you think they killed Olive?"

"I don't know about Mickey," said Jack, "but it certainly wouldn't surprise me about Doc."

"Is he a con artist, like she is?"

"Of the first water."

"Somehow I don't think of con men as being killers."

Jack shrugged, but he didn't say anything. Okay, so this Doc was a con man and a killer.

"So, how about the other partner?"

Jack gave her a look.

"You said you wanted to talk with Mickey because you thought she could tell you something about her partners who are after you—you did say partners, plural, didn't you?"

"Early, would you pull over here, please," said Jack, pointing to a sign at the edge of the deep blue lake that read SCENIC OVERLOOK. "Come on," he said to Sam. "We'll just take a little stretch, and I'll explain it to you."

The path down to the lake was edged with wildflowers. Jack stooped and picked a few as they walked. Finally he said, "Yes, partners plural. You don't miss much, do you?"

"As a reporter, I got paid to listen up. So, tell me, who else?"

"Mickey and Doc are up to something with a man named Speed McKay."

"Sweet Jesus," she breathed. She stared out at the deep still lake. What a can of worms. Then she looked Jack in the eye, watching for his response. "Did you know Speed was kidnapped from his engagement party last night?"

The man had a great double-take. "You're kidding."

"Why would I joke about a thing like that? Actually, I was thinking maybe *you* were responsible. Seems like your kind of thing."

Jack shook his head. "Give me a break."

"Simply judging on past behavior."

"Point taken. Now, you want to tell me about this kidnapping?" He said the last word in quotation marks.

Sam kicked a rock down into the lake. "In the middle of the party, Speed went up to his suite, the one he was sharing with his fiancée, Jinx Watson."

Jack nodded.

"You know Jinx?"

"I know who she is. Go on."

"Well, I know her better than I want to, believe me, but anyway, I left the party downstairs and went up to the lobby, which is where you and Early saw me—"

"Yes." He smiled. What was that smile?

"And I went back down to the party and heard that Speed had been kidnapped. It seems that Jinx's mother Loydell Watson—"

"I know Loydell. In fact, she and her friend—Jesus, that's right, *Olive's* the one who's Loydell's friend, the two old ladies used to come into Bubbles every once in a while for dinner, play a little poker. Loydell likes the slots. What? What are you staring at?" He looked down at his front. "Do I have soup on my shirt?"

"There's a casino in Bubbles? In the Quapaw—along with the gym?"

"Yes, Sam. Starting at the top, it goes gym, Bubbles, casino in the basement. Have I somehow misrepresented myself? Did you think I was a Sunday school teacher, or what?"

"No. I'm fully aware that you're a crook who tortures women. I just wasn't sure—"

"Sammy, Sammy. I've apologized." She stepped back. Sammy was what Harry called her. "What I'm trying to do is show you I'm actually a good guy. I may not pay all my taxes, but other than that—I'm on the side of the angels. And I'm on your side. Now, you know my thinking you were Mickey was an honest mistake. I would never have grabbed you otherwise."

"Oh, no?"

He grinned. "No way. Not like that." Then he handed her the little bouquet of wildflowers he'd gathered. "So, go on. What were you saying about Loydell?"

Why was she was beginning to think that Jack was way ahead of her, that he was only waiting for her to drop the other shoe to confirm what he suspected? She watched a hawk swoop down, dive for a fish, and miss. He rose again into the open sky. "Loydell came down from Jinx and Speed's suite, where Jinx had asked her to go look for Speed. Speed was upstairs to take an allergy pill or something, and Loydell didn't find him, but she found a ransom note."

"How much?"

"A million. Which Jinx should have had, because she won that much—"

"In the Texas lottery."

"You knew that, huh? Listen—" She turned with her hands on her hips. "Why don't *you* just tell *me* the rest of the story?" She stepped back, and he grabbed her as she began to tumble off the path backwards. It was a long fall down to the water. "Thanks," she said. "I'm okay." But she was shaky. Heights were not her favorite thing, and this was turning out to be the longest day of her life, and hardly entirely pleasant. . . .

Jack tucked her arm firmly under his and said, "Let's head for that flat spot and sit for a minute." There, he spread his handerchief on a big rock. "What else, Sammy?"

"The only other thing I know, which I had just found out at lunch right before we ran into each other in the parking lot—"

Jack smiled at her circumlocution.

"Is that Jinx doesn't have any dough. She's spent it all, a lot of it up front on this wedding—that isn't coming off, by the way, even if the kidnappers let Speed go. It turns out Speed didn't have a dime. Jinx checked his financials out with a banker friend this morning, and Mr. McKay was a fraud."

Jack laughed. "No shit."

"You like that?" She was warming to the story. "Wait till you hear this. The kidnappers called after Jinx discovered Speed was broke, and she told them to go take a flying leap. Said she didn't care what happened to her former fiancé."

"So, what do you think was really going down here?"

"Jinx was marrying him for his money, which he didn't have. And he was marrying her for hers—no, wait. I heard your tone when you first said 'kidnapping.' There never was one, is that it? The whole thing was a fraud?"

"Could be."

"Mickey and this Doc and Speed set Jinx up with this *phony* kidnapping, thinking she's going to spring for the big ransom. But the joke's on them, because Jinx doesn't have any money, and doesn't give a rip about Speed. So, it's a hoax that's gone wrong?"

"I'd say so. They're con artists, Sam—Mickey and Doc. Speed's kind of a screwup, a hanger-on. Somehow he just fit into this particular scenario, would be my guess. But setting up swindles, that's what the two of them do for a living. They run scams, play games to steal other people's money."

Sam shook her head. "I never covered bunko. Murder was more my beat."

They both fell silent for a minute, thinking of Olive crammed in that car trunk like a sack of rotting potatoes.

Then Jack said, "Your classic con artist will do anything, bait and switch, the smack, hot seat games, clipped card. I understand cards are Mickey's speciality.

But a con man's a con man. They can't stop. Big score, nickle and dime stuff, switching price labels in the grocery store, snitching two papers out of the vending machine, taking one back for a refund, a con just can't resist conning. They'll do setups, bet you how many watermelons in a load, after already buying off the farmer, the lost ring, the drunken mitt—there's a million of them."

Something fell off a shelf in Sam's mind with a loud bang. "What did you just say?"

"There's a million scams."

"No, right before that."

Jack thought back. "Setups, watermelons, lost ring—"

"Stop." Sam held up one hand like a traffic cop. "Tell me how the lost ring works."

"Well, it's one of the oldest in the book. Not all that profitable—though, like I said—con artists will take some ridiculous chances sometimes for not much payoff."

"Just tell me, Jack." This was it. She knew this was it. "You've got something, don't you?"

She shrugged. Maybe.

"Okay, the outside man, that's the one who sets up the con, is usually a woman, though you can do it with two men in a bar with a men's room. But let's say it's a woman, a well-dressed attractive woman who's—uh oh." He stopped.

"What?"

"Who's driving a luxury car—like Mickey." He took Sam's arm. "You tell *me*. What do you have, Sammy?"

"Just go ahead, okay?"

He shrugged. "She stops in a place, a gas station usually."

"Like Olive's."

"Like Olive's. And she goes to the ladies' room, comes out, and pretends she's lost a diamond ring. She and the attendant look for it, no dice, can't find it, they abandon the search, she gives the attendant the number of a hotel where she's staying to call her for a reward if the ring is found. A few minutes later a tramp, who's the inside man, comes along, finds the ring. He and the attendant haggle over the ring he's pretended to find, which is a piece of junk, the bum sells it to the attendant for whatever he can get. Usually a few hundred bucks."

"And the beautiful woman driving the Mercedes never arrives in the hotel."

"Right. And the two crooks are across state lines before the mooch realizes he's been stung."

"Except in this particular case, they only got this far." She motioned back over her shoulder, up the road toward the big stone house.

"Let me see it, Sammy."

She slid a hand down in her jeans pocket and pulled out the fake diamond Bobby had found on the floor of the Gas 'N Grub. It sparkled in the late afternoon sunlight like the real thing.

"I want the bastards, Jack."

"No problem, babe."

26

INSIDE THE BIG STONE HOUSE ON THE HILL, MICKEY WAS saying, "You chopped off his finger because he said *no problemo* too much? And then you drowned him?"

"I never said that. Do you see his body floating out there?"

"No. Probably because you weighted it down with rocks. You're losing it, Doc. No, you've lost it. We've been talking for two hours, and I've heard nothing but bullshit."

"Come on, Mickey." He was standing behind her in the bedroom where they'd made love yesterday.

Correction, Mickey thought. Where she'd screwed him, trying to stay one step ahead before he screwed her. But she'd given up. There was no winning with Doc. He was clearly over the edge. She was booking while she still could. She dumped the drawerful of lingerie straight into her suitcase.

He said, "You don't give a shit about Speed. What are you getting on your high horse about?"

Mickey whirled. "*What*? You want to know what? I'll tell you, Doc. I spot Speed at the track, a two-bit hustler, he yaks to me about his bucks-up fiancée, the beauty queen, I yak to you, you say you know the guy, we can cozy up, flimflam him, make away with a big stash. Fine. We make the plan. Then you *have* to, have to, have to, stop and pull the penny ante score at that store. But something's queer, Doc. Something you don't come clean on. You've got the old lady's car. Then her grandkid's up here looking for the car. The next thing I know, the beauty queen says, Fuck you, so now there's no score. You had to know that, Doc. You had to know Speed couldn't be trusted to set up a dogfight, so you had to be working some other angle. Something I didn't know about. Then I walk in, and you're chopping off Speed's fingers."

"Finger. One little finger."

"And now you've got him out there doing some kind of mermaid routine? I don't buy it, Doc. Because something's stunk here from the very start. There's something else been on your mind the whole time, and I don't know what it is, and furthermore I don't want to know. I'm out of here." She slammed the suitcase.

"You're not going, Mickey."

"Yes, I am." And then she whirled, holding her little revolver close in to her body. "Get in the closet, Doc."

"Mickey." His tone was warm syrup. She'd heard it lots of times before.

"If you don't get in the closet, I'll kill you. And if you give me any trouble, I'll kill you."

He walked in the closet. She slammed the door and turned the key.

"And if you start kicking while I'm standing here, I'm shooting you straight through the door."

Then she pushed and pulled and tugged, thank God she was in such good shape, a huge chest of drawers in front of the door. It was almost as tall as she was and one *heavy* mother. She figured that way it would be harder for him to kick his way out, he'd bang up against the back of the chest, maybe break his toes. Anyway, it would give her enough of a head start to get the hell out of Dodge.

27

EARLY WAS SITTING IN THE ROLLS. JACK HAD WALKED SAM off down the hill to sweet-talk her. Early was thinking about Fontaine and the cops, thinking about Bobby Adair in that blond wig and that little black skirt, thinking about that fat pig calling him a nigger, thinking about the fat pig's daughter, which, give it up, Early, you were, too, looking at her like he said—checking out Bobby in his blond doo-dahs, but checking out the little brunette as well. Not so much for her own sake, because he preferred dark meat *any*time, but he was looking at her and thinking, man, you need to get yourself a little woman. A strong little well-put-together woman like that, looks like she could ride ride ride.

Then Sam stepped up to the car. "Jack'll be here in a minute, he had to take a whiz." Early hadn't heard her coming, he almost jumped out of his skin, and the next thing he knew, that Mercedes flashed by like a silver bullet.

Sam jumped in the passenger side, shotgun, yelled, "Punch it!" So what was he going to do? Holler, "Hey, Jack, get on back up here to the car, there goes the con girl Mickey?" Mickey'd be in Memphis eating herself a plate of barbecue by the time Jack dragged his slow fat butt up.

So Early did what any reasonable man would do. He punched it.

Sam would say one thing for Mickey Steele. The woman could drive.

Early'd slid right up behind her silver Mercedes, she'd signaled him on by. "Pull even with her," Sam'd said to Early. He'd looked at Sam like she was nuts, you couldn't see a thing, two lanes of curving mountain road. Thick pine forests marched up on the mountains on one side, dropping sharply to the deep blue lake on the other. "Nine chances out of ten," Sam assured him, "nobody's coming the other way. Eight out of ten she's not going to push us off the shoulder."

"We live through this," he said, "*you* get to drive for Jack." Then he pulled even with the Mercedes.

"Now you nudge *her* over into the wall," Sam said. They were on the lakeside, Mickey hugging the hill.

"I'm barely holding this mother in the road as it is!"

"Do it!"

Early pulled the brown Rolls closer to the big silver car. There was only an inch or two between them, and the road was treacherous. Sam looked over at Mickey's white knuckles gripping the wheel. Mickey turned and looked at Sam, wide-eyed. Sam could see the small flicker of recognition. Then Mickey lifted her left hand from the wheel and saluted Sam with her middle finger.

Sam laughed. "She's a pistol, all right."

Then Mickey stomped it and pulled ahead, straddling the center line, weaving back and forth so they couldn't pull up on her. She was slamming into the curves, fishtailing, sliding, but hardly flashing her brake lights at all.

"We're all going to die," said Early. "Gonna be one big roadkill stew."

Then SLOW! STOP AHEAD! screamed a big yellow sign.

"How far is it?" Sam was leaning over, practically in his lap.

"I can't see! All I can see is her rear end!"

The road rose again, then twisted down the mountain in a series of S-curves. Up ahead was a little clearing, and there was the stop sign, a BIG ONE, and there was the crossroads, and there was a loaded lumber truck, the long pine timbers bending and bouncing off the back like batons, the truck with the right of way, hauling on through, and there was Mickey, tapping her brakes, one, two, three.

"We've got her!" Sam clenched her fist. "She has to stop."

Of course she did, except, right up on the muzzle of that huge beast of a truck, Mickey stomped the gas, and the Mercedes flew right past its teeth. The trucker didn't even brake. It was that fast. He just kept going. Sam could see his lips moving. "I bet he wet his pants," she said to Early, as they sat there, fully stopped, and the tall truck passed like a freight train before them. They couldn't see to the other side. But one thing was sure. Mickey wasn't going to be waiting for them.

*   *   *

"I'll go in with you," Archie's partner said.

"Nawh," said Archie. "I'll do it by myself."

"Now, Archie, I don't think so." T.J. stepped out of their blue-and-white patrol car in front of the little wood-frame house where Cynthia lived on Exchange. "You know Cynthia won't talk to you. And you really ought not to be with her by yourself."

Archie wheeled. "What the hell does that mean?"

But before T.J. had to answer, Cynthia and Loydell stepped out on Loydell's front porch next door, right up to the edge of the porch that was bordered with red geraniums.

"Y'all came to tell me something about Olive, I guess," said Loydell. "I appreciate your doing that, Archie, I sure do. Let me sit down here in the swing before you say it." And she plopped her skinny body down. Cynthia stood, her arms crossed, her mouth tight.

She'd been telling Loydell about Bobby coming into Tate's and then how they'd all been out at Greenwood Cemetery, herself and Lateesha shooed away by Early after he and Fontaine got real serious and down in the mouth about that old Sunliner of Bobby's they'd found. Early gave her and Lateesha each ten bucks, told them to take a hike over to Central, they were way out by the track, but they could call a cab to get back home.

Well, of course, all they did was sneak around the back way and hunker down in some bushes. They saw the whole thing. Fontaine digging that old car up with the backhoe, then pulling it out with the tractor. The carrying on about what was in the trunk. Bobby losing it. Early and Fontaine dragging him off somewhere. Sam staying with Olive.

Loydell had known in her bones, of course, that Olive was dead. So it hadn't been such a shock as it might have been, though she hated the indignity of her friend being treated like that, like a sack of cow manure or something.

Now she had to muster all the strength she had not to let on to Archie that she already knew about Olive. Because then there'd be that part about Bobby. And she knew Cynthia had never stopped loving Bobby, and she cared about him herself, for that matter, Olive's only grandson.

Archie zipped through the news of Olive's death like he was delivering a weather forecast, might be showers tomorrow, mess up that picnic you'd planned, and then he got to what he really wanted to say. Couldn't wait. In fact, he was rubbing his fat hands together in front of his gut, his legs spread wide in that way that Loydell had always found particularly offensive.

"Actually," said Archie, "what we come to warn you both about is that Bobby Adair got out of Cummins yesterday, and we've already been out to Olive's place and found a bunch of his stuff and lifted some of his prints, and so we've got an APB out for his arrest, parole violation at the very least, but I think we've probably got enough to hold him for Olive's murder."

Loydell flew up out of the swing so fast it banged against the side of her house. "What in the hell are you talking about, Archie Blackshears? Bobby Adair loved his grandma to death."

Archie grinned. "Well, I wouldn't go around saying *that* if I were you, ma'am. You know, it just goes to show you never know, don't it? I just thought you ladies"—he tipped his hat—"Miss Loydell, Cynthia, honey, would want to be apprised that Bobby's on the prowl around here somewheres. Keep my doors and windows locked if I were you."

Then he nodded at Loydell and his daughter. Cynthia didn't say a word, but she made a low sound in her throat so that if she'd been a dog, Loydell thought, you'd throw a muzzle on her fast.

* * *

There was the road straight ahead. There was a turnoff to the right and another one to the left. There was no sign of the silver Mercedes in any direction.

"Which way, boss lady?" Early asked.

One out of three were not great odds. Which way would Mickey have headed? The sun was a red ball low in the sky behind them, just about to dip below the horizon. "Right," said Sam. "Turn right." Her general operating procedure in life had been when in doubt, head south, and do it full out. In any case, there was no point in pussyfooting, thinking they might turn back, have another go at her.

This road was another curvy two-lane blacktop just like the one they'd been on, except it was lined with pine forests belonging to Weyerhauser. Little signs said the trees had been replanted in 1982 and 1983.

"There! Turn there!" Sam pointed at a gravel road that headed off into the woods. A dirt cloud was still rising.

"It's probably another logging truck," said Early. But he turned. Then he said, "Did you see that sign?"

"About the trees?"

"No. Jameson's Crystals, two miles ahead."

Sam drummed on the dash with anticipation. Frustration. Impatience. She hated the thought they were flying in what could be a dead-end direction, while back on a road somewhere else, a road they didn't take, Mickey was laughing her ass off, the wind blowing her red hair as she made her getaway.

Reporting could be like that, when you were on a hot story, and you decided, Okay, that's the lead I'll follow. That one, plucked from a multitude. And if it turned up dry, it might be too late to go back. Your other sources could have clammed up. They could have walked. They could be dead.

They passed a mobile home. A satellite dish. A little girl in a pink dress playing out in what passed for a yard. Hey, little girl, did you see a silver Mercedes roaring past? Unreliable witness. No time to ask. The cloud of dust still billowed before them, floating just above the road like red-brown smoke. Somebody was minutes ahead. Too bad, Sam flashed, they didn't have Pearl.

And, okay, if this turned out to be a dead end, Doc and Speed were probably still back at the house. But she wanted them all. And Mickey had been right there, right in her grasp. Once again she could see Mickey raising her left hand. Flipping her off. Sam wanted her bad.

The road signs were coming fast and furious now, warning them that this was their one big chance, not to be missed, to buy crystals at Jameson's. Or you could buy a permit and dig for your own.

"Why the hell else would you come out here?" Early asked.

They passed another mobile home. A bunch of black-and-white chickens clucking. One of them marched right out into the road. It missed being free-range fricassee by a tail feather as Early swerved.

Then there was a little frame shack. This had to be the world-famous Jameson's. It looked like a hot dog stand that somebody had hauled out in the woods, except that it was covered with shelves that were littered with quartz crystals. It was as if the little shop had turned itself inside out. But there was no Mercedes. No sign of life.

And then the road ended.

"What now?" Early braked to a halt.

Sam slumped. The end of the line, and they'd come a cropper. "Back around. Pack it in, I guess."

"Go pick up Jack?"

Jesus, she'd forgotten all about him.

Early started to back around, and as he did, Sam saw that a rutted path road continued on behind the shack.

"Wait," she caught Early's arm and pointed. "Go there. Go back there."

In another quarter mile the woods ended and the earth dropped off into a man-made crater a half-mile in diameter. The huge red hole in the earth looked like a strip mine. It held a couple of dump trucks, a backhoe, a grader.

And, perched right at the edge, sat a silver Mercedes.

Sam said, "Pull right up on her ass and bump her."

Early turned and stared.

"What? I said bump her!"

Early pulled up, gave the Mercedes a good whack. The silver car jumped within inches of the precipice.

Mickey's head spun in the driver's seat, and then her hand came up.

"Duck! She's going to shoot!" Early yelled.

Sam scooted down in the brown leather only a few inches. She wanted to see. "Hit her again, Early. Hit her!"

He slammed her. The Mercedes's front was edging over, going, going, and in the last instant before it was gone, Mickey flung open the door and jumped. She landed onto solid ground, rolling and tumbling.

Sam was out of the Rolls and stomping on Mickey's right wrist before Early got his seat belt unlatched.

"Get the hell off!" Mickey screamed.

"Drop the gun!" Sam yelled.

"What gun?"

What gun, what gun, what gun? The echo bounced back from the other side of the rock crystal crater, the big ugly gouge in the earth.

Sam looked down and saw only a fresh manicure, her own foot, a slender arm, and a pretty face. Mickey was saying, "Jesus, that was one hell of a waste of a good car."

28

THEY FOUND JACK CALMLY SMOKING A CIGAR BY THE SIDE of the road exactly where they'd left him. "Hi," he said and climbed in the backseat with Mickey, whose wrists and ankles they'd bound with a rope. He took one look at her and said, "Absolutely, Early. She's most definitely a redhead." Sam liked that, his assumption that they had a good reason for deserting him in the middle of nowhere, and sure enough . . . Then he said, "Now, why don't we run over to my place and have a little chat, unless someone has a better idea?"

Mickey did, but her vote didn't count.

Fifteen minutes later the four of them were sitting around a big oak table in Jack's kitchen in his redwood and glass lake house. Jack turned from chopping celery and peppers and onions for a crayfish étouffée and asked Mickey didn't she agree everybody would feel better, find it easier to talk, with a little something in their stomachs.

Mickey said she'd felt just fine until these two, nodding toward Sam and Early, had tried to drive her off the road. Pushed her car into a ravine. Knocked her down and tied her up.

Jack said, "Oh, Sammy, tell me it isn't so."

He was joking, but Sam herself was feeling like this thing was snowballing, totally out of control. It just kept accumulating more debris, involving more people, as it rolled along.

First, if what Jack thought was right, you had the lost ring scam at the Gas 'N Grub. Were Mickey and Doc both responsible for Olive's death? She still didn't know.

Then there were Speed and Doc and Mickey and the phony kidnapping, about which, at this point, no one gave a rat's ass. Lateesha, the fifteen-year-old-honor-student-car-thief, Early, and Fontaine.

And Bobby, how about Bobby Adair, the most polite ex-con in the state of Arkansas, maybe the whole South? She hadn't even asked Early what they'd done with him.

But right now the player she was looking at was the lovely Miss Mickey Steele. She was sitting there, they'd cut her loose, drinking a cup of coffee like she was taking a break from shopping on Fifth Avenue. Sam was thinking about how to frame the first question when the phone rang.

Jack grabbed it. "No," he said, "you did the right thing. Put her through." He tucked the phone under his chin while he added rice to a pot of boiling water and stirred. He dropped a lid on the pot and said, "Loydell! Hey, darlin'. No, not at all. I'm sorry I wasn't here earlier. So tell me." He listened for a bit, Sam and Early and Mickey listening to him listen. "Unh-huh. No. No, you don't worry about it. My man Early took care of that. He brought him to me. Yes, sweetie, Bobby's with me. No, I know he didn't. Well, we'll cross that bridge when we come to it. You and Cynthia, you just stay cool. Yes, I'll let you know. Don't worry about a thing."

He hung up and motioned to Sam with the crook of a finger to follow him through a swinging door into a dining room where stood a handsome bird's-eye maple and ebony Biedermeier table and chairs for twelve. Sam looked up at Jack, waiting to hear what he had to say, and he leaned over her, propping one hand against a cream-colored wall. It was like being enclosed in a tent of Jack.

He said, "You could hear that was Loydell. It seems

that that asshole, pardon my French, Archie Blackshears called Corrections and found out Bobby was sprung yesterday, they've been out to Olive's, found his gear, and they've lifted his prints from Olive's Rabbit they found parked in front of Tate's Bar."

"When he showed up in the cemetery, I never thought what he might be using for wheels. He probably took the bus, hitched, or something from Cummins, then of course he'd use Olive's car."

"Well, Archie's got an APB out on him. They're going to try to hang Olive's murder on him, no doubt about it. The fat man told Loydell so himself."

"Jack, I don't know *for certain* Bobby didn't do it."

"Yeah, but what does your gut tell you?"

"Tells me no way. I *like* the kid, plus it's sort of like Early said about Fontaine getting away with an insanity plea if they tried to pin Olive on him. It doesn't make much sense, does it, Bobby'd kill his grandmother, put her in the trunk of his old car, and then, what? Give the car to Mickey and Doc? And then pretend to go looking for the car? He'd have to be nuts. He's awfully polite, but I don't think he's crazy."

They exchanged small smiles. It was sort of nice, Sam thought, being up under this man-triangle. She, part of the right angle of the wall and the floor, Jack, the diagonal.

"So what's the plan?" she asked. "We're gonna beat up on Mickey till she tells us about Olive, then we take her to the cops downtown, the *sane* cops, assuming there are some who aren't set on pinning this thing on Bobby, and we save Bobby's butt?"

"Sounds good to me."

"So who gets to go the first round, me or you?"

"You bring your gloves?" He tapped her gently on the chin.

She reached up and touched the tip of his nose with a forefinger. His eyes were beginning to go black and blue above the Band-Aid. But she didn't say she was sorry for belting him.

"Come on, tiger." He winked. "Let's go get her."

Mickey didn't flinch when Sam told her that they could put both her and Doc at Olive's store (which wasn't exactly true, but so what), put Olive's car in the carport of the house where she and Doc were staying, put Olive's body in the car's trunk—which is where they'd found it.

Mickey said, "I don't have a clue what you're talking about. You must have the wrong person."

"Don't think so," said Sam, pulling the queer diamond ring out of her pocket and holding it in front of Mickey's turned-up nose. "Doesn't this belong to you?"

"No. Never saw it before." Her voice was even. Sam had to give it to her, the woman had nerves. "But if it's connected with someone's death, don't you think you ought to call the cops? Or are *you* the cops?"

"Nope," said Jack. "We're the vigilantes. You know, the guys in the gray hats. The kind of guys who could understand your running a few card scams on the *turista* mooches—"

Mickey favored them with a wintry smile.

"Even you and Doc doing the hokey-pokey with Speed McKay, trying to shake down his fiancée."

Mickey took another sip of coffee. She held the cup steady.

"But, you see," said Sam, "back to the original topic. That's Olive Adair, in case you forgot, and she was strangled and stuffed in the trunk of her grandson's car. You remember her grandson, don't you, Mickey, you met him and his dog, Pearl, up near your place? But, then, you'd met Pearl before, at Olive's store." Sam leaned over in Mickey's face. "Anyway, just to make ourselves abundantly clear, con games and shakedowns are one thing, but we draw the line at murdering old ladies. Particularly old ladies we like."

"Ah, hell, Sam," said Jack, throwing up one hand. "The woman's right. We ought to call the cops, turn her over to them. They'll pick up Doc. She'll say he did it. He'll say she did it. What the hell do we care?"

"A better idea: Why don't we just shoot her?" said Sam.

"I like that," said Early, who'd been so quiet they all turned and stared at him. "Hell, Jack, they were gonna kill you anyway. The three of 'em. I say, hit 'em first. We'll start with her, then we'll go do Doc and Speed."

Mickey sat up. "Kill you? Why would I kill you? I don't even know who the hell you are."

"Jack Graham, Mickey. You know, Smilin' Jack from New Orleans. Don't tell me Doc never brought me up. Gee, that'd hurt my feelings."

Sam watched Mickey's gaze focus on the middle distance. She was figuring the odds on something. It didn't take her long. When she spoke, her voice was softer than it had been before, and slower. "I heard Doc and Speed mention you, Jack, between themselves. But Doc never talked to me about you. I'll admit I was curious, so I asked around about you a little last night at the hotel. You run the games in town?"

"Good," said Jack. "Very good, Mick."

She turned and gave him her full attention. "So what I'm hearing is that your concern is you think Doc's here to do you?"

"Yep. That's where I came in, anyway. It's gotten a lot more complicated since then, but, bottom line, you could say the two of us are not wild about one another. Of course, the way I see it, I'm a reasonable man. Doc's not. Neither is Speed, for that matter."

Mickey shrugged. "Little sucker never stopped talking, drove you nuts." Then she looked at the trio of captors, slowly, one by one. "You guys aren't really going to shoot me, are you?"

You bet, they all nodded as one. Sam, for punctuation,

pulled Early's Walther out of her jacket pocket and handed it to him across the table. "Could you make it look like a suicide, Early, plant a gun?"

"Sure, but I don't see any reason there'd ever even be a body to find," said Early, looking over at Jack. "Do you?"

Jack waggled a finger, No body.

"What are you going to do? Burn me up? Drop me in acid?" Mickey stared at her hand drumming on the table as if she were considering what her pale flesh might look like when they got through. She turned to Sam. "Are *you* a cop?" Then she answered her own question. "Nope, of course not. You're too intelligent." She leaned back in her chair. "What do you want, guys? Lay it out for me."

"Just tell us what happened," said Sam. "From the top."

So Mickey did. She took a deep breath and told them about meeting Speed at the Oaklawn track. It was sheer coincidence that he and Doc had had some business together down in New Orleans. The little man telling her about this woman he was going to flimflam out of a million bucks, but there was this problem about a prenuptial agreement.

"Jeetz. I didn't know Jinx was that smart," said Sam.

"So, we came up with the kidnapping scam, not knowing that she was broke. You weren't part of the deal," she said to Jack. "Honest to God." Mickey had the grace to smile.

"So you rented the house, went back and picked up Doc somewhere. . . ." Jack made a rolling motion with one hand: Cut to the chase.

Mickey walked them through the lost ring scam and how Doc queered it. How he ended up with the car, and then the car disappeared.

"I knew we were screwed. I knew he wasn't coming clean. I sort of guessed what had happened to Olive, but I didn't really want to know."

She told them about Doc chopping off Speed's finger.

"Jesus!" Early flinched.

Then there was the business about Doc and Speed swimming to the float.

"You think he's dead?" said Sam.

Mickey nodded. "It'd be my guess."

"So, Doc's gone psycho?"

Mickey thought for a minute. "Well, I guess you've got to be crazy to be killing people, but I bet something went wrong in the store, Olive picked up the phone, pulled a gun, he panicked."

"And Speed?" asked Jack.

Mickey shrugged. "I don't know. I mean, like I said, *anybody'd* want to kill him, they hung around him long enough, but—I don't know. Maybe you're right, Jack, about your being the real reason he's here, some kind of vendetta. . . ." She trailed off, waiting for Jack to fill in the gap, to explain what the thing was between the two of them. Jack let it hang, and Mickey went on. "I mean it could have been a *really* big score, if we'd hit that million, but now that I think about it, it was when I said the deal was going down in Hot Springs that Doc's eyes really lit up. Hey, what do I know? I used to sell psychology books for a living, but I never read what was inside."

Yeah, thought Sam, then a lot must have seeped through the covers.

Mickey continued. "There's always been something strange about Doc. He's half gypsy, did you know that? He doesn't talk about it very much, but his mother was one of those real old-timey fortune-tellers who traveled from place to place wearing the big skirts, her life savings in gold coin necklaces. He still uses some of her tricks."

"You don't say," said Jack.

"Yep. Has lots of her ways. *Including* he carries his nest egg with him. Just like his mother with those gold coins, Doc doesn't believe in banks."

"The man carries around a bunch of gold?" Early perked up.

"No." Mickey smiled. "In Doc's case it's not gold. It's one perfect diamond. A *huge* sucker. Flawless. Doc says it's worth half a million, easy. Maybe more. It should be in a museum."

"He *wears* it?" Early was aghast.

"Oh, no. It's unset. To tell you the truth, I don't know where he keeps it. He's pulled it out a couple of times when he was drunk, playing with it, showing off. He talks about it like it's his baby. He calls it Little Doc."

Jack laughed. "Little Doc? The guy's crazier than I thought."

"But you don't know where he keeps it?" Early really wanted to know.

"No, and don't think I haven't sniffed around. But Doc hasn't stayed in the game as long as he has without a few tricks up his sleeve. He's a master of the sleight of hand. He's so good, sometimes *I* think it's magic. Boom, you see it. Boom, you don't."

"And where is our Doc now?" asked Jack.

"In the house up on the lake. Locked in a closet, with a *big* old heavy chest of drawers in front of it."

"Dead or alive?" asked Early.

"Alive when I last saw him. I was just trying to give myself a little time to split. Of course you all put a crimp in that plan." Mickey drained her coffee cup. Jack poured her some more. "But let me tell you all one thing. If you think that there's any way in hell I'm ever going before a court of law and testifying to any of this business with Olive or Speed, you're dead wrong. And don't start with me about plea bargains. Don't start with me about anything. Because here are the choices." She ticked them off. "One, I testify against Doc, and the son of a bitch walks, I'm dead." She raised a hand before anybody else could talk. "It happens all the time. Some technicality, some little screwup, they spell Doc's middle name wrong, they forget to tell him he has the right to lie to his lawyer, whatever, the next thing you know, he's out, and I'm dead. Two, let's say he actually serves some time. But there's not enough time in the world that he's going to forget, so when he gets out, I'm dead again. Three. They fry him. Now, what do you think the chances are of that really happening? And even if they do, even if they do . . ." She dropped her voice. She'd have made a hell of a trial lawyer, thought Sam. She'd have the jury over on its back, legs up. "I'm still going to spend the rest of my life watching my rear, because I *know* that silver-tongued son of a bitch, and he's good. He's very very good, and he'll convince some poor sick bastard he's jailing with that the way to salvation, the way to redemption, hell, the way to five hundred bucks, is to hold me down and carve his initials in my boobs and pour Drāno down my throat. So, I'm not singing, lady, gentlemen." She nodded at each of them in turn. "I'm not saying one official word. And, furthermore, you guys have obviously stepped in some kind of doo-doo, or you wouldn't be here talking to me. Now, I've told you what you wanted to know. Beyond that, forget it." And with that, Mickey leaned back in her chair and crossed her arms across that pretty bosom that she thought Doc had evil designs on.

At which point, Sam and Jack excused themselves for another trip to the dining room, and this time there was no cozy Jack-tent.

"You heard what she said, Sam. Mickey's not going to testify, so what's the point of going to the cops?"

"Do you believe her story?"

"Sure. Don't you?"

"Yes. So what you want to do is ignore the fact that we know for sure Doc murdered Olive?"

"Not ignore. I just don't see any point in involving the authorities if they can't make the case without Mickey."

"That's nuts, Jack. Nuts."

They went back and forth until finally they were each leaning against the back of a chair, facing one another, panting, and Jack played his trump card. "You forgot about Bobby, Sammy."

"What?"

"It doesn't matter what we do, doesn't matter if Mickey sings or keeps her mouth shut, if Archie Blackshears wants to frame Bobby, he'll frame Bobby."

"I don't believe that."

Jack's drawled, "You've been in the big city too long, darlin', you forgot what small-town Southern justice is like."

"Jesus Christ, Jack, this is the United States of America at the end of the twentieth century."

He gave her a long look. She knew he was right.

"So? What?" She raised her arms to the heavens.

"Let's go ask Miss Mickey Steele if *she* has any ideas."

Mickey did, of course. She had the beginning of a plan. And then they all four pitched in and played with it for a while, and when they finished, it had more than one rough spot, but it just might work.

29

DOC WAS WIPED. THE DAMNED CLOSET WAS TOO DEEP FOR him to lean back against the wall, get some purchase for his feet. But too short for him to get any kind of running start. And whatever Mickey had pushed up to the door was jammed against it, so it was like he was trying to kick through the door *and* through the chest, trunk, whatever the hell it was, all at once.

Now he was sitting on the floor, sweating, a bunch of wire hangers poking him in the butt. He was too old for this shit.

Maybe Mickey was right. Maybe this was what came from making things too complicated.

Maybe he should never have gotten into this Speed rigamarole in the first place, just cruised into town, popped Jack Graham a couple of times, bebop bebeep, moved on down the road.

That's what his ma had told him when he was a kid: Part of it's knowing what to do, the other part's knowing how to skidoo.

Part A, she'd let him sit behind the curtain in the *ofisa* and listen when she was working a *bajour*. Her favorite was the one with the egg. It worked every time with the kind of lonely sour middle-aged woman who'd already given up on life, was now on the lookout for which brand of cancer was going to eat her. Pearsa would find proof of the cancer in a devil's head she'd plant in an egg the woman had brought from her own kitchen. The source of the cancer would be the woman's money, which was cursed, of course. She'd bring the money to Pearsa to have the curse removed, and that is when Pearsa would do the switch.

Part B. "And then you *move*, little one," said Pearsa. "You grab your bedroll, your tapestries, your zodiac, your candles, your hot plates, and you haul your sweet little ass down the road quick."

See, he hadn't done that. Things had gotten too complicated. The kidnapping, that scam was screwed from the beginning, he should have known better than to kick in with anything Speed McKay had his pudgy little fingers on. And that fat old broad pulling that gun, the car, then the car disappearing. He was still worried about that Sunliner. His prints were all over it. And there was the body in the trunk.

Just then, he heard somebody coming down the stairs.

Hallelulah! Mickey had changed her mind, come back to spring him. Now, what was he going to do about her? He wasn't real thrilled, her knowing about the car, say things got sticky. . . .

"Hello? Hello? Anybody down here?"

Hell, that wasn't Mickey. That was a black man, sounded like a big bass drum.

"Hel-loa? Looking for the folks own a gold-and-black Sunliner? Is that y'all?"

Shit. It was the cops. They'd found the car. Now they were looking to find him. Well, maybe they wouldn't. Chances were they wouldn't. He'd be perfectly still.

"Well, hell," the big black voice was drawing closer. "I guess they ain't here. Serves me right." The man was talking to himself. "Taking that old Sunliner in the first place. I knew I shouldn't of. I knew it. Took it home, my baby made me feel so bad, I was bringing it back, when—God, how am I gonna tell them that?"

Tell him what? What was the man talking about? Doc wanted to ask him, but he didn't want to blow his cover. Not yet.

"Laronda says that it was the Lord put that hound in the road. Said it was my test, seeing if I was truly sorry that I'd done so wrong, stealing that car. Swerving like to miss that hound, me flying right off in the lake like I was driving one of God's chariots, thought I was about to come face to face with the heavenly host. But God saved me to make amends. Yes, He did. Let me roll down that window, struggle on up out of that Sunliner done stuck itself in the bottom of that lake. Coming to the surface, I felt like I'd been baptized again, bathed in the holy waters. Now, is there anybody heah? Anybody heah? Anybody within the sound of my voice?"

Doc couldn't believe it. The Sunliner was sunk to the bottom of a lake? God, he was one lucky sucker. "Over here," he hollered.

*   *   *

Jinx had moved back to the Palace minisuite she'd occupied since she'd blown into Hot Springs for the races six weeks earlier, staying with her mother not being an option. When Sam and Mickey knocked on her door, she was giving herself a fresh manicure.

"I couldn't just go around wearing that gold polish," she said, waving nails that were now carmine. "People would think I was trash. And I've had just about enough humiliation for one weekend, thank you, without that. How do you do?" She nodded at Mickey, whom Sam had introduced as a friend of a friend she'd happened to run into in the lobby, she just happened to be a private eye. "Y'all just throw those clothes on the floor, make yourselves comfortable on the bed. A *private eye?* Sam!"

Sam said, "Now, Jinx, I've thought about it, and I know you're right, everything you did was right, but wouldn't you like to see those guys who were putting the muscle on you squirm just a little? I think it was so lucky, my running into Mickey. I told her how stressful this had been for you. . . ."

"You can say that again. I'll tell you, it's *awful,* you've got a whole town full of guests for your engagement party, and then you have to say *something* about why your fiancé just disappeared right in the middle of it. You can't very well tell them he was kidnapped, if the kidnappers told you not to. Of course, things are different now, but . . ."

"Why, I think that's just *terrible,* your having to face this alone," said Mickey, sliding right into junior high school pajama party mode. Oh, she was good, thought Sam. Very good. "So what *did* you tell them?"

"I said he died," said Jinx, not missing a stroke with her nail polish.

Sam slid Mickey a look. "He died? Don't you think you might have to explain that later?"

"Well, the way I figure it, those kidnappers aren't just going to turn him loose. It's not like he's going to show up in the next five minutes. They'll probably try again to get some money from me, wouldn't you think? And by that time, all the guests'll be gone back home. Most of 'em are already gone anyway, the weekend being over and all." She held her left hand out, appraising her work. "I've been getting calls of condolence ever since I got back from lunch. Which reminds me, Sam, what happened to you? I thought you were going to meet us back here, *I* had to drive Kitty to the airport." She let that sink in for a minute. "I'm surprised you didn't go with her, to tell you the truth. Can't imagine that you'd hang around here. It couldn't be because you gave two hoots what happened to me."

"Well, I did find a thing or two that grabbed my interest. Which brings me to the—"

"Jinx," Mickey jumped in. "Sam was telling me about you, and she mentioned your winning that million dollars with your lottery altar. And I couldn't believe it! I mean, I *saw* you on TV! And here you are!"

"Did you? Really? Well, isn't that nice?" Jinx was showing those dimples that came with the smug little grin that drove Sam wild.

"I would just *love* to hear how you got into making your altars." Mickey's voice was all breathy as if she'd just graduated from a crash course in Southern Belle Stupid. She shot a look at Sam that said, Let me do this.

Have at it, Sam shrugged.

Jinx settled importantly back into her chair as if she were a research scientist about to explain a new cure for cancer. "Well, right after my first divorce, I didn't know what I was going to do, and I was visiting this girl in Houston who'd been a Miss Texas, and she got me a job modeling with Neiman's. It wasn't quite six months before I met Harlan, and we got married and moved to San Antonio. We moved into his family castle in the historic part of town, and I started remodeling." Jinx's scarlet lips began to tremble.

If Sam remembered correctly that was the same Harlan who had taken up with the Houston Oilers cheerleader, divorced Jinx, and then had the nerve to lose everything, including her alimony, in a scam that had to do with selling shares in his electronics business after it'd already gone down the tubes.

The way Jinx put it was, "And then Harlan and I split up, and he didn't do right by me at all."

Mickey reached over and patted Jinx on the arm as Jinx started to sniffle. Sam wondered if Mickey were going to blow her nose for her, too, since Jinx couldn't, what with her wet polish.

"There I was, tossed like a dust mop out of that big old house I'd slaved over for years, making it perfectly precious for him." Her eyes were still watering, but then she glanced down at the gigantic diamond in her engagement ring, and that seemed to cheer her. Sam had noticed Mickey eyeing the ring, too. She probably had it appraised to the nearest decimal point and was scheming to make off with it. "I didn't know *what* I was going to do. I didn't have a cent, I mean, I was practically on welfare, thank God, Harlan Jr. was off in school, and Harlan's folks would see after him. Of course, *I* could have starved to death, for all they cared. And I couldn't come home to Mother. She didn't have any money, and she's never liked me anyway. Always thought I put on airs." Jinx paused, and then she laughed. "Which I did. How else would a poor little girl from Hot Springs ever get anywhere in the world?"

Give Jinx two points for insight, though getting a job would have been an interesting alternative. . . .

"Anyway," Jinx said, "that was about the time New Age finally drifted down to Texas, and people were running around looking for their auras and sitting in sweat lodges, driving the local Native Americans absolutely nuts, and crystals were starting to come on big. Well, Jinx, girl, I said to myself. Crystals are what you grew up with, Arkansas being the largest producer of natural crystals in the entire world, and some of the very biggest crystal fields being right down the road from here." Jinx waved that diamond again. "But all those crystal necklaces that you saw in New Age stores were so tacky. And one of the things I had kept from my art major days was making jewelry. I always did like pretty things. And, I thought, Jinx, you know how Texans love big. Texas women, they are fond of big men, big oil wells, big hair"—she patted her own—"and big earrings. So, I started making these Arkansas crystal earrings that'd jerk your lobes down to your shoulders and selling them only to the most expensive stores. I had that old Neiman's contact, from when I'd modeled there."

"And it took right off," said Mickey.

"Honey," said Jinx, "they were killing each other for my earbobs, and I was paying the rent on my tacky little two-bedroom townhouse, keeping gas in my car. But I had to do better than that. I knew I had to grow out or grow up, but not having a lick of business sense, I wasn't sure which. Anyway, one day I was in one of those San Antone taco places having me a breakfast burrito and some coffee, when I looked up, and there behind the counter was this altar with all those *milagros*. You know, miracles. Like little tin legs and arms and hearts and whatever ailed you, you put it on the altar and it'd be healed. And I said to myself, Jinx, this is it. I went right home and stayed up for forty-eight hours straight, and when I came out, I *drove* to the Houston Neiman's carrying my first crystal altar. Carried it in to the buyer and said, Honey, this the only one in the whole wide world, and you folks are lucky enough to have it on consignment."

"And it worked?" Sam said.

"They sold it for ten thousand smackeroos before I got back to San Antone. Of which I got seventy-five percent."

"Wow!" said Mickey. "So you went in and started mass production."

"No, see, that was the thing about getting the top dollar, was the exclusivity. And the next thing I knew, that Houston rich bitch who'd bought that first one, well, she had a young singer friend who was busting to make it in the Austin music scene, and she'd told him about her altar, and the next thing I knew, she was paying for me to do a custom job for him. Word of mouth. That's how it works for your really exclusive product."

"Well, that was awfully generous of her," said Sam.

Jinx smiled. "You don't know how generous an old bored-to-tears Texas woman can be to a cute young man in a pair of tight jeans."

"And he made it big, that singer?" said Mickey.

"Yep," nodded Jinx. "Bless his precious heart, he did, made it mega-gold, one of those ten-years-and-one-night-of-singing-honky-tonks overnight success stories. And in the very first interview he gave, he said he owed it all to this altar I'd made him."

"And your phone started ringing?" asked Sam. She was beginning to warm a little to this story. She'd always been a sucker for Horatio Alger, rags-to-riches tales, even though she'd bet that at Jinx's lowest ebb she'd still had closets full of sequined frocks.

"You bet. And I was whipping out these custom altars as fast as I could, when all that hoopla started about the Texas lottery. How it was going to be bigger and better and—well, you know Texas. And the cute thing about the first one was that you didn't have to wait twenty years for the payoff. It was going to be one million dollars, cash on the barrelhead, *after* taxes, one fell swoop. Overnight, you'd be a millionaire, guaran-damn-teed, as many folks as came up with the six numbers, no having to go divsies."

"So you made *yourself* an altar." Sam was remembering some of this from the *Today Show*.

"And I won." Jinx almost snapped her scarlet finger-tips, but caught herself in time. "Just like that. Me, little old me, and only me. The only one. It was the altar that got me on the TV, of course."

"And then?" Mickey asked.

"I just kicked back. I mean, I would have felt awful if I was making these altars for people and they didn't work. And it was a fluke, of course, that Austin cowboy singer and then me. I just couldn't take people's money in good conscience, especially when I didn't need it. And to tell you the truth—" She held her hands out and stared at her nails, which were about dry now, her diamond sparkling. "I didn't really like all that running around, dealing with taxes, all that stuff. I was never cut out for it." She sighed heavily, the weight of the world on her shoulders. "Now, I'm busted, and I have no earthly idea what I'm going to do next. See if I can find me a *really* rich man, I guess." And then she stared at her image in the dressing table mirror, did a little face-lift with her palms, assessed the net worth of her goods.

"Well, darlin'," said Mickey, "that is truly one of the most inspiring stories I've ever heard." Sam stared at her. Mickey sounded like she really meant it. "And it tells me, for one thing, that you have what it takes to make those kidnappers squirm. Why, actually, now that I think about it, I think *they* ought to pay *you* something for all your trouble on this thing. They owe you."

"Really?" breathed Jinx.

"Well, it makes perfect sense," said Mickey. "If you had gone to the police, and they had been caught and arrested and found guilty, why, they most certainly would have gotten fines as well as jail sentences."

"You don't say," said Jinx. Sam could see the wheels of larceny turning, turning.

"Why, sure. Sometimes the judge makes them pay a *huge* sum, that way, if they get any money from publishing their stories, well, it goes to the victims, which in this case would be you."

"I'll say." Jinx stuck her bottom lip out.

"So, even though you didn't go to the police, you're entitled to something. A lot, actually. Why, even more, since they didn't have to go to the pokey." Mickey leaned forward. "We ought to go after it."

"How do we do that?"

"Well, the first thing we need to do is have you set up a meeting with the kidnappers, and you tell them that you've changed your mind about ransoming your honey and you'd love to spring him, but you don't have the jack. However, your mother does."

"My mother wouldn't give me ice water in hell," said Jinx.

"Yes," said Sam, "but would she give you that one flawless diamond she's had squirreled away all these years?"

"She doesn't *have* a flawless diamond." Then Jinx frowned. "Does she?"

"Getting you out of that closet, shoving that chifforobe away, it was just like rolling the stone away from the cave where they laid out our Lord," said Fontaine, who'd introduced himself to Doc as Frank.

"Well, Frank, I was sure glad to see you," said Doc, thinking what a stroke of luck this was. He could have starved to death in that fucking closet, but what was *really* great was that the Sunliner was at the bottom of the lake—and so was the fat old broad. Which is exactly what he'd thought he'd do with 'em in the first place. Now, he could get on with things. *Except*, he needed a car. And there was the matter of Mickey. Who knew what that bitch was up to?

"So," Fontaine was saying, "my baby, that's Laronda, she was right. 'Cause I can see, you're not mad at all. She said you wouldn't be. I don't know how she knows that, but Laronda, sometimes I think she's some kind of seer. You know what I mean?"

"I do," said Doc, trying to keep the wolf out of his smile. Oh, yes, he knew about seers, all right. Did Laronda see that Doc was thinking about knocking this big sucker in the head, taking whatever wheels he might have, get him at least to where the automotive pickings were better?

"She said you wouldn't mind one bit, 'specially since I brought you a replacement. She said, Just you wait and see. Said she bet you'd like it. Said she wanted to see the smile on your face, so that's why I let her drive the car we brought you. Let's go on out to the driveway, you want to see it?"

"You brought me a car?" Doc was shaking his head. Maybe there was something to this Laronda.

"We sure did. Got it off Miss Jinx Watson." They were climbing the stairs, walking down the hall. "I work for her mother, Miss Loydell, some of the time, and Miss Loydell said Miss Jinx was going to give this car to her fiancé, Mr. Speed McKay, for a present, but Mr. Speed, he's carried off by some 'nappers."

Doc couldn't believe what he was hearing, but he knew what his line was. "Are you saying this Speed McKay was kidnapped? My God!"

"Yes, sir, he was. It was a turrible thing, and Miss Jinx, she's just lying and wailing in her bed, says Miss Loydell, saying over and over something about how she went and done the wrong thing, if she just had it to do over again, she'd do it right. I don't exactly know what that means, but anyway, Miss Loydell said Miss Jinx couldn't stand to hold on to this car that she was going to give to Mr. Speed, and so I made her an offer, and she took it."

At that, Doc couldn't keep from laughing aloud. Oh, this was so rich.

"And I guess Laronda's right about the car making you

happy," said Fontaine. "Come on, let's go let her hear you laugh."

Then they rounded the corner of the carport, and there was a two-year-old dark blue Mercury Grand Marquis— which Jack Graham had bought from Fontaine's body shop an hour ago. Lateesha was sitting up tall in it, looking real pleased with herself.

She stuck her head out the window. "Now, look at that face, isn't that a happy man," she said to Fontaine. "Didn't I tell you? Why *anybody'd* be happy to have a nice car like this instead of that old hunk of junk, *excuse me*, sir, I'm sorry for casting aspersions on your car."

"No harm done," said Doc.

"Well, I ought to know better. God Almighty doesn't like aspersions." And then she leaned back in the Mercury to give a better listen to the gospel singing on the car's radio.

Thank God, thought Doc, the song was ending, and an announcer was starting in with the local news. Doc couldn't stand that religious caterwauling, though he had to admit this was something, repentant Holy Rollers bringing him wheels. Didn't God work in mysterious ways? Praise the Lord. And, thank you, Jesus.

"Eight o'clock, that man says it is. We ought to be getting on home, don't you think, Frank?" said Lateesha. "Quit bothering this nice—"

"Wait!" said Doc, craning his head toward the Mercury's window to catch the announcer's words.

"—tentatively identified as Michaela Steele of Savannah, Georgia, the woman was killed instantly. The truck driver said she was traveling at a high rate of speed and didn't attempt to stop at the stop sign—"

"Jesus!" said Doc. He staggered back from the car. It was too good to be true, Mickey out of the way, but still, it was a shock.

"Oh, that was a turrible thing," said Fontaine. "Happened late this afternoon, why, not that far down the road from here. They say there wasn't hardly much left of her, smashed a big silver Mercury."

Mercedes, Doc started to say. This is a Mercury, Mickey was driving a Mercedes. But he caught himself in time.

"Just goes to show you," said Lateesha, ejecting the tape they'd made—Early doing the announcing part with a clothespin on his nose—from the tape player and slipping it in her purse, having first made sure that Doc wasn't looking her way. "You just never can tell when the Lord's gonna call you to be with him. Now, Daddy—"

"Yes, baby?"

"We've done what we came for. Now let's be getting on home. Let this nice man here get his rest. We've caused him enough trouble."

30

IT WAS LATE WHEN SAM FINALLY GOT OFF THE PHONE WITH Loydell. The old lady could have gone on for hours. I want to *get* that bastard, she kept saying as they roughed out the next day's scenario. It was only when Ruby, the Foot-washing Baptist, knocked at Loydell's door that finally she let Sam go.

Now Sam was running herself a hot tub, hoping to unknot from what had been, hands down, the longest day of her life.

She poured bubblebath and slipped in, spread a washcloth over her face, rotated her ankles, wiggled her toes. Ruby, Ruby, was foot-washing in the name of the Father, the Son, and the Holy Ghost any better than this? If it was, Sam wasn't sure she wanted to know about it.

Except maybe for her book, for *American Weird*.

Drifting in the bubbles, Sam let her mind ramble over some of the weird she'd collected in the past year. Competitive barbecuers. Bikers for Jesus. The Civil War Reenactment Bungee Jumpers. A mail-order voodoo doll business in Tuscaloosa.

And what had she found here in Hot Springs? A sweet-faced ex-con who was a member of the Graciousness Society. A former beauty queen/lottery winner who peddled crystal altars. A den of con artists. A gambling entrepreneur nicknamed Mr. You Know Who who nabbed ladies and interrogated them with boxing gloves.

Entrepreneur? Who was she kidding? Jack Graham was a crook.

Or was he? If he were running the same operation in New Orleans, he'd be a local hero. On a riverboat, in Las Vegas, Atlantic City, or if he were a Native American calling bingo numbers on a reservation, he'd be a professional. Legality was sort of a floating crap game, wasn't it? Just like morality.

And why was she lying in a tub of bubbles in the middle of the night in Hot Springs, Arkansas, defending, if only to herself, Jack Graham?

Because she found him attractive. Because he seemed to think she was, too. Because she was needy, hurting, looking for anything to blunt the empty feeling she'd had inside since she and Harry had had their little heart-to-heart. Half a bottle of Jack Daniel's used to fill her empty spaces quite nicely, but now she looked around for other things to latch on to. Chocolate was a winner. Good food in general. Movies were way up there. She could spend a whole weekend watching videos, sometimes running her own retrospectives, like the Jeff Bridges canon. Settle down with Jeff, a barrel of buttered popcorn, a box of Texas Millionaires, the time passed real easy.

And there you had it. Like Jeff, Jack Graham was a big good-looking man, and he knew his way around a crayfish étouffée. Probably a pot de crème, too.

So far, daydreaming about him was doing the trick. When her mind drifted onto Harry, it didn't feel so much like biting on a sore tooth. She hadn't thought about a drink since last night. Hadn't thought about an AA meeting either, and that wasn't so smart, was it?

Well, this had been one hell of a merry-go-round, this thirty-six hours. That was a feeble excuse. Tomorrow she'd find a meeting and go. First thing. But tonight, there was a screening of Jeff's *Jagged Edge* just beginning. In fact, she was climbing out of the tub right now, rolling the TV around, she could watch Jeff from her bubblebath.

Back in the tub, she ran another couple inches of hot water and snuggled in with a towel behind her head. On the TV, Jeff had this great place in Marin County. Sometimes she missed northern California. She'd always miss Sean, which is why she couldn't go back there. Not yet, anyway. The phone rang. Damn. There was no extension in the bathroom. She made more puddles.

"Yes?"

"Hi, Sammy, it's Harry."

Harry, who'd carved up her heart, like Jeff was about to do to his wife on the TV.

"What exactly is it that you want?"

"I want you to talk with me."

"There's nothing to say."

"There's a *lot* to say. We have too much together to just walk away from, dearheart."

"That's not what you—"

"Please, don't. Let's please don't get into that again. There's no excusing what I did. I know that. But I'm sorry. I love you. Can you believe that?"

"Nope."

"Come on, babe. Cut me some slack here. Until four days ago, you'd have had no doubt."

"That was then."

"Sammy, look. I'm not perfect. I screwed up. I know I hurt you, and I'm sorry."

"I'm sorry, too. But I can't pretend it never happened."

"But can you understand that your refusal to make any kind of commitment to me makes me nuts? Leads me to do things I might not, otherwise?"

She didn't want to hear about her fear of intimacy. She was sick of hearing about it. "So your affairlette is *my* fault? We're back to that again?" Somebody was knocking at her door. Good. An excuse to get off the phone—as if she needed one. "Harry, it's late, I'm exhausted. I'll talk to you when I get back to New Orleans."

"No!"

On the TV, Jeff was telling Glenn Close he was innocent. He'd loved his wife. He'd *never* have hurt her, much less killed her. And he was coming on a little to Glenn. Watch out, Glenn. The knocking continued at her door.

"Who *is* it?"

"Room service."

"Harry, I'm hanging up."

"Do not hang up this phone. Do not."

She slammed down the receiver.

Room service? She knew better than to fall for that old ax murderer ploy. Good thing the chain lock was on. She stood right at the door. "I didn't order anything. You have the wrong room."

"No, I don't. I know it's late, but I thought you could use a piece of pecan pie and a glass of milk. Or some hot chocolate. Or a crème brûlée and some decaf espresso. Cereal and bananas. You name it, I've got it."

Forget you, Harry. Move over, Jeff. It was Smilin' Jack.

* * *

Doc was lying in his bed in the big stone house up on the hill above Lake Ouachita, feeling like the King of the May.

The old lady and the car were at the bottom of the lake.

Mickey was dead, not that he'd exactly wished that on her, but it certainly made things tidy.

He had wheels.

The beauty queen wanted to give him some cash.

And then there was Jack.

He took another swig from the bottle of Scotch he'd taken to bed, held it out, and looked at it. Johnnie Walker Black Label. Black Jack. Blackjack. Jack. Deal the cards, sucker. Doc held all the aces and all the pictures. No doubt about who was going to win.

Sam grabbed a robe and unlocked the door. Jack was splendid in his tux, holding a silver tray piled with goodies. The pecan pie, hot chocolate, crème brûlée. "What on earth? How did you—?"

"I own a restaurant just next door, don't I? And people in the hospitality business are very hospitable to their friends." He clicked his heels and did a little bow worthy of the most elegant maître d'.

"Do come in." Sam opened the door wide. "What a treat." Then she looked down at the hotel's terry cloth robe. "Though I'm hardly dressed for the occasion."

Jack's smile said, Oh, yes, she was.

"He did what?" said Loydell to Ruby, who was sitting in her kitchen. They were sharing a late-night pot of Constant Comment.

"I told you. He marched right into the service just as pretty as you please. Nobody had ever seen him before, but that's one of the things the Lord teaches, isn't it, welcoming the wayfarer and the stranger?"

"What did he look like?"

"Young," said Ruby. "A beanpole, tall but no bigger around than you. All in brown. Brown hair, brown eyes, dressed all in tan: suit, shirt, tie. Take him out in the desert, he'd disappear like one of those lizards."

"Uh-huh. And when y'all commenced to the foot-washing, did he have some kind of fit?"

Ruby's eyes narrowed to slits. "How do you know, Loydell Watson? Is this some kind of trick you played on me? If it is, I want to tell—"

"Don't be telling me anything, Ruby, and don't be pointing that bony finger in my face, either. This same boy got hold of me this morning in my car—"

"Got hold of you! What are you saying, Loydell?"

"Well, not hold of *me* exactly. He got hold of one of my shoes, and the next thing I knew, he had his nose stuck up in it and was sniffing away like it was Evening of Paris cologne. It was *very* weird."

"Weird? Disgusting, I'd say."

"That depends on your definition of disgusting." And then Loydell started thinking about Jinx's daddy and that wild thing he used to do with his old silk ties and her in their iron bedstead, that thing that used to make her squeal like a pig stuck under a fence. Horace had taught her tricks that'd show those Olympians on TV a thing or two about balance, endurance, and doing clever things with your various body parts. Of course, that had all been a long time ago. Jinx wasn't more than two years old, that time he said he was going out for a pack of cigarettes, and the thing was, the man didn't even smoke. She didn't see hide nor hair of him for another sixteen years, till they had that drought, and the water went down in Frenchman's Creek, and they found him and that Sartor girl, or what was left of them. Dental records was how they could tell. Horace had the worst teeth of any man Loydell ever knew. And the most vivid imagination, once he got naked. She still missed him.

Ruby was saying, "He was washing Sister Ivy's feet,

and he got to sniffing and snorting and carrying on, I'll tell you, it was the worst thing I've ever seen in my entire life."

Loydell couldn't resist. "Now, honey, are you sure it wasn't the best?"

Ruby drew herself up so tall she looked like her backbone was going to shoot right out the top of her head. "I most certainly do not. This is what I get for coming here instead of going straight to the police. But Ivy insisted on it, and after all, it was her feet, and she said because you used to work for the police department we ought to come and ask you how to proceed. Don't think we don't know that there's those who make fun of us, deride us, call us names—just because we happen to be strict interpreters of the Word of God."

"Well, at least you don't do snakes," said Loydell.

Ruby's mouth was so tight, if it had been a green bean it would have snapped. She picked up her purse.

"Now, now, Ruby, don't get yourself all in a lather. Sit down, let's talk about this. I think you did absolutely the right thing, coming over here and asking me. Because if you marched down to the police and started talking about this toe-sniffer, those old boys would be hee-hawing from now till the middle of next week. Toe-*sucker*, they'd have it in about two minutes, put out an APB for him, and the boys in blue from here over to Little Rock'd be wetting their pants."

"What's an APB?" Ruby relaxed her posture just a tad, though she wasn't anywhere close to sitting back down.

"An all points bulletin. That's when you want all the law enforcement agencies around to look for somebody."

"They wouldn't have to look for him. I left him sitting right in my kitchen."

"Well, Ruby, I swear. What on earth makes you think he's going to be there when you get back?"

Ruby didn't answer.

"Ruby?"

Ruby opened her mouth about a millimeter. "I left Lulu watching him."

"Who on earth's Lulu? Your guard dog?"

Ruby took her own sweet time, but finally she said it. "My mountain lion."

Jack had a great laugh. Sam had rerun Jinx's adventures in the crystal altar business, and he was still wiping the tears off his face. "So, Jinx went for the idea, the meeting with Doc? You think she'll do okay?"

"Went for it? She's chomping at the bit. We'd have to tie her up to keep her away. Mickey thinks she's a natural."

"Mickey ought to know."

"I guess. I never thought of Jinx exactly that way, but I suppose that's what she's spent her whole life doing, conning people."

"And conning herself?"

"I don't know that I'd go that far. I don't think the woman has an introspective bone in her body."

"A great gift for a grifter, wouldn't you say?"

Sam laughed, then helped herself to another bite of pecan pie. "This is *so* good."

Jack wiped a bit of whipped cream off her chin. "Glad you like it. It's one of my specialties." Then he told her about Fontaine's call, the big man checking in. "He said his Stepin Fetchit routine went smooth as silk. And Lateesha was something else. Now *there's* someone with the gift. I'm telling you, another ten years, when that child grows up, gets through college, grabs herself an MBA, she's going to be the president of American Express or something like that."

"I thought we were talking about the grift, Jack."

"We are." He smiled. "You think they're different, the guys, ladies, dressed up in suits with the briefcases? You think they're not on the come?"

"You think everybody's on the come."

Jack shrugged. "This is America, isn't it? The land of opportunity?"

"Maybe." She reached for the crème brûlée. "So, you think Mickey's going to hang in here, or she's going to split?" Right now she was in her own room, just down the hall.

"Oh, she'll hang all right. She's having fun. And she's afraid we'll call the cops if she doesn't."

"We *are* calling the cops after we con the con man. Remember, Jack? That's what we agreed. We spirit Bobby away safely, we sic the cops on Doc."

"Yeah. For all the good it'll do."

"Why are you so certain that Archie's going to get his way, pin Olive on Bobby?"

Right this minute the baby-faced ex-con was upstairs in the gym over Jack's restaurant, snuggled into a sofa bed with Pearl for company. Bobby was oblivious to everything that had happened since they'd found Olive.

"You know, Sammy," said Jack, "cops are a strange breed. You talk to any of them, they'll tell you they do what they have to do to make their cases. Lie, cheat, steal, cook up evidence, kill—there's a hell of a lot more honor among thieves. And you can take that to the bank."

"You're not saying Doc's cleaner than Archie, are you?"

"No way. They're two of a kind, even if we don't know for sure if Archie's killed anybody. But I'd lock 'em up together. They'd be great cell mates."

"Wouldn't that be wonderful?" Sam licked the last of the crème brûlée from its little round crock. "Listen, how's Bobby doing? Did you see him? Poor thing. I know he's destroyed over Olive."

"I went up and talked with him right before I came over here. He's taking it real hard. He truly loved the old lady. And he'd been looking forward to seeing her again after those two years in stir. She wrote him every week, kept him sane. Did you know that Cynthia hasn't spoken to him or written to him, not a word since the day he conked Archie in the head?"

"Uh-huh."

"But when I saw her at the cemetery, looking at him, I thought she had stars in her eyes."

"So?"

"So? You're saying this makes sense?"

"Uh-huh."

Jack shrugged. "Well, of course it does. I'm just a big dumb man. Don't know what a whole lot of nines are. Right?"

"Very funny, Jack." She reached for the hot chocolate.

Doc couldn't sleep. He'd drifted off, and then the next thing he knew, he was wide awake again. Sometimes the Scotch did that. Lately, in the mornings he'd been throwing up.

But this wasn't Scotch. This was anticipation.

He'd been thinking about Jack for such a long time. And now the time had come.

He sat up and turned on the light. His mouth tasted like a garbage dump. He reached down, grabbed the bottle of Scotch, took a big swig, and gargled. That was better.

He leaned back, propped up against the headboard. He picked up the remote control and punched on the TV to a movie with Jeff Bridges playing like he was Mr. Suave, but Doc had seen this one before. Underneath that thousand-dollar suit the man was wearing black jersey like a cat burglar. Carrying a Buck knife.

Now, that was a possibility. There were all those knives downstairs. Good ones, too, look how that one had done the job on Speed's pinkie. But then he'd have to get in real close. Jack had Early working for him now, guarding his butt. That could be a problem. He took another slug of Scotch.

There was always his gun. Hardballer .45, made a big
old noise, and it'd blow a hell of a big hole in Jack, too.
He wouldn't have to get as close with it, but it'd still be
too close if Early was packing.

He needed to think about this. Doc reached down,
rooted around under the bed until he found Little Doc.
He held him in first one hand and then the other, rubbed
him against his brow, kissed him. Little Doc was what
he called his diamond. You could name a big piece of
ice anything you wanted to, just like a kid. Hope. Star
of India. But he'd read once that Elvis called his penis
Little Elvis because it was his favorite thing in the world,
and if that concept worked for The King, who was he to
argue? Little Doc it was, fifteen carats of absolutely perfect, flawless stone. It had taken him years of buying
smaller rocks, always trading up, until he had worked
his way to Little Doc.

His ma, Pearsa, had taught him when he was a little
kid never ever to put his money in banks, stocks, bonds,
any kind of property the cops could get their hands on.
You wanted something small, portable, and indestructi-
ble. Diamonds fit the bill.

And the bonus with Little Doc was that he came with
his own magic.

Little Doc was better than a crystal ball, better than
one of those Eight Balls, better than those phony crystals
they dug up out of the ground around here, that was for
sure.

He'd picked up one of those crystals. It didn't do a
damn thing. You picked up Little Doc, you could feel it
vibrating in your hand. The sucker had powers. You
asked a question while you were holding it, it's not like
you *heard* it speak to you, Doc wasn't stupid, but you
did know the answer. You just knew it. It was like it
was written in your head.

And what Little Doc was saying right now was, Wing
this play. Go with the flow. Forget the knife. Forget the

gun. You'll know the tool when you see it, at that moment, and not before.

Okay, then. Doc turned his attention to Jeff Bridges sweet-talking that blonde. He was conning her into thinking he was her loverman instead of her killer. But, hey, could the man be both? Doc was too tired to think about stuff like that now. He flicked the movie off and pulled up the covers. He liked what Little Doc had had to say. He tucked the diamond under his pillow as if it were a tooth, and the Good Fairy was going to bring him a surprise. He was drunk enough to sleep now, but not too drunk to remember there'd been lots of happy surprises this evening, hadn't there?

He switched off the lamp and said to the dark room, Enjoy your last night, Jack.

Jack had pulled off his black silk bow tie and draped it on the arm of his chair.

Sam had picked it up and played with it while they talked about New Orleans, about the people they knew in common, restaurants, jazz, restaurants, neighborhoods, restaurants, cemeteries, restaurants. Food was bigger than football in the Crescent City, and football was BIG.

Jack knew a lot more people than Sam, but then he had lived in New Orleans forever—until the recent unpleasantness with Joey the Horse. Sam had only been in her house over on the north shore of Lake Pontchartrain, close but not too close to the city and Harry, for about a year.

She smoothed the strip of black silk through her fingers. "Do you miss it?"

"I didn't think so," he said. "I thought the mountains were a nice change. It's a lot cooler up here. Quieter."

"What do you mean, didn't? When did you change your mind?"

Jack looked at her, looked at his watch. "Oh, about twelve hours ago."

She blushed. Then the blush climbed up her chest, out of the terry cloth up her throat. The more she blushed, the more she blushed. She hated giving herself away like a sixteen-year-old kid.

Smilin' Jack just grinned.

He looped the black silk around her wrist and tied it in a bow. Then he took her hand and kissed her fingertips, and she felt all those feelings that sounded so clichéd when you tried to describe them. So she didn't. She told herself to shut up. She relaxed back into her chair, her naked body inside her terry robe still damp from her bath, her belly full of chocolate and whipped cream and pecans. She felt Jack's clean-shaven cheeks and his lips and his tongue and his silver hair against her chin as his mouth found a hollow in her throat and made itself at home.

Jack picked her up and flew her around the room. What a treat for a tall woman who was used to carrying not only her own suitcase but her own weight.

Way later, when he smoked his cigar, it smelled to her of incense. She fell into a dream of tented silks, bells, satin pillows, sweetmeats, and sweeter kisses. Jack played the sheik role. Sam got to be the purloined maiden.

31

"YOU LOOK AWFULLY PERKY THIS MORNING," LOYDELL
said to Sam.

"I'm feeling pretty perky, too. How are you feeling?"

"Well, not *too* bad." Loydell poured herself a cup of
coffee from the bottomless coffeepot that is a universal
feature of AA meetings. "Considering that I just lost my
best friend in the world."

"I know," Sam said and gave her a squeeze, then did
a double-take. The little old lady was a lot wirier than
she looked.

Loydell bowed up her right arm. "You felt that muscle?
I keep in shape over at the Y. Got into that weight training couple of years ago when they brought in the machines, I never looked back." Her smile faded. "Maybe
if I'd been able to get Olive to join me, she'd been able
to defend herself, wouldn't be where she is today."

"Maybe," said Sam. Then she turned to say hello to
that morning's speaker. He'd talked about waking up in
detox in Seattle only to be told he was wearing a red
dress and a hat with a petunia when the medics found
him. Everyone had laughed. Folks in AA laughed a lot.
Sam was glad she'd made this meeting. It, like every
meeting she'd ever been to, made her feel blessed to be
alive and sober and able to laugh.

"In any case," said Loydell, "that sucker idn't doing
the same thing to me. This time, *he's* going to be the one
hurting."

"Now, Loydell. We're not burning him at the stake, though we'd all like to. We're just giving him a serious dose of his own medicine before we turn him over to the police." Sam lowered her voice. The meeting room in the basement of St. Patrick's Church was clearing out, but there were still people around. "Remember?"

"Whatever you say."

"Loydell," she warned.

"Just get on along. Shoo!" Loydell waved her hands as if Sam were a stubborn shoat hogging the trough. "You do your part. I'll do mine. Me and my secret weapon."

Loydell chewed on those last words like Hannibal Lecter savoring the memory of the big Amarone with which he'd washed down a dish of roasted human liver and fava beans. It was a thought that stripped away Sam's morning-after glow, sent a chill up her spine—and got her moving.

This was a dangerous game they were playing. She needed to keep that in mind. Damned dangerous. If they screwed up, Doc could hurt someone bad. Kill someone. Deprive someone of the joy of one more night like the one she'd just spent, which would be a real pity.

When he'd talked with Jinx, Doc had kept it brief. He didn't want any state troopers rolling up to the phone booth while he was still on the line.

"You want Speed back?"

"Oh, yes! Yes, yes, yes. Give me another chance, I'll do anything, just tell me—"

"Shut up and listen." Then he'd told her where and when to drop the cash. "Bargain basement price is half a million in unmarked twenties and hundreds." She started up again, but he didn't want to hear it. He wanted off the line, and he had a doozie of a hangover. "Anybody else shows at the drop, my partners'll make sure Speed's dead, you're dead, your mother's dead.

And the dying won't be easy. You got that?" Then he'd clanged down the receiver.

Now Doc was watching the drop spot. Was it safe? He closed his eyes and waited for the answer from Little Doc.

So far, so good. Doc had taken the bait. Seven minutes ago he'd rolled out of the carport in the dark blue Mercury.

"He'd be back by now if he'd forgotten something," said Sam from the trees behind which she, Mickey, and Lateesha were watching. Lateesha had absolutely refused to go to school while this real-life adventure was still in progress.

And she did come in handy. They needed all the players they could get. Early was to be Doc's tail. Fontaine was going about business as usual in case the cops came sniffing around his story. Cynthia was in place at Tate's in case Archie got his wind up, thought she might know of Bobby's whereabouts. Loydell was at home waiting to hear from Jinx what role she was to play. And Bobby was tucked away in the gym above Bubbles, oblivious to the identity of Olive's killer, oblivious to everything that was going down. The best course, Jack and Sam had decided, if he was to stay out of harm's way.

So here was Lateesha playing lookout. Sam said Go! and she took off on her bike armed with a cellular phone so she could call inside the big stone house on Lake Ouachita should Doc reappear. They didn't want him to catch them searching for that sparkler that was his nest egg, his talisman, his deadly lodestone.

"What the hell?" Doc couldn't believe it. He was staring into the gym bag Jinx had left in the dumpster behind the deserted Texaco station on 270 right before it branched off into 227. He'd liked the spot, the same one he and Mickey had picked out a couple of days ago, because the gas station was shut. So there was no one around, but it didn't look *too* closed. If somebody saw you pulling in or out, it wouldn't look suspicious.

But what difference did it make if anyone saw you or not, if all you ended up with was a gym bag full of cut-up newspaper and a note, written in a loopy hand with little hearts for the dots over the *i*'s, that said, "I'm really sorry about this, but I just don't have the money. Can we talk it over?"

Talk? What was there to talk about? Doc was fed up with this kidnapping scam. It had been snakebit from the get-go, and the longer he mucked around with it, the worse it got. Give it up, man, he said to himself. Move on to the Jack part. Then get the hell out of this godforsaken place, make tracks over to the coast, start shopping for your Caddy, your Airstream, your john boat.

And he would have done that very thing, if there weren't a blonde, a stark-naked blonde, walking toward him, make that a *stacked* stark-naked blonde. In fact, a natural stacked stark-naked blonde, which was something you didn't see very often anywhere.

"Hi," she said, rotating her hands back and forth at the wrists like you would to show a dog that they were empty, you didn't have anymore of whatever it was he wanted. "I thought this way you could see that I'm not armed." When she was within three feet of him, she started turning slowly in a circle. "Hi, I'm Jinx Watson, not carrying a thing," she said in this Betty Boop voice, "and I'm awfully sorry about the money, but like I said in the note, I just don't have any, and I can't get any, and I know this whole thing has been a terrible mess, my not ever really doing what I ought to, but what I came to tell you is that I really do want my sweetie back, and I'll do anything, anything. . . ." She shrugged, which made her boobs, which still looked pretty good, bobble up and down.

Doc ripped his gaze away to check out the perimeters of the parking lot.

"Oh, I didn't bring anyone with me, if that's what you think."

He really hoped she wasn't lying, but so far he still felt safe. He looked back at her face, which wasn't bad either. "So what's the deal? You think you're gonna screw Speed out of this?"

"Oh, no." She shook her head, and there went her boobs again. "Goodness gracious, no. What I hoped was that once I had your attention, you'd listen to me a minute. See, I really do have a plan. My mother, her name's Mrs. Loydell Watson, and I know you must know something about her because you said you'd kill her along with me and Speed if I didn't do this right, well, she used to work for the police department—"

"Great," Doc growled. He started walking back toward the Mercury, then turned. "Listen, if you say a word about this to anybody, the deal's the same. You're both history. As it is now, you didn't pony up the ransom, it's only the Speedster's dead meat." Which was the truth, come to think of it.

"Noooooo!" Jinx screamed and threw herself down on the cracked pavement of the parking lot and started kicking her legs. It was quite a sight. "Nooooooo! You have to listen to me."

"Jesus. Don't do that." He walked over and grabbed one of her flailing arms and pulled her up.

Now she was standing flush against him. She smelled sweet—and expensive. Like Mickey used to smell. He was going to miss old Mick. But, what the hell? A bird in the hand. . . . Doc grinned.

Jinx grinned back just a little, enough for him to see she had a real mouthful of beauty queen teeth. Capped, probably. She was still snuffling. *"Please* don't kill Speed. Please."

"You love him that much?"

"Oh, I do. I do."

"Then how come you told us to take a hike when we talked yesterday?"

"I wasn't thinking straight. And I didn't have the money, but now . . ." She flailed her hands up and down again and did a little dance, but this time she was so close that she bounced right on his chest. "Listen, you have to listen to me. My mother, Mrs. Loydell Watson I was telling you about, I don't know why I said that about her working for the police, she's been retired a long time, and that doesn't have anything to do with anything."

Doc wondered how this broad and Speed had ever spent two minutes together, they both had such serious diarrhea of the mouth. If he had to be with the both of them in a room, he'd blow his brains out, or theirs. Of course, maybe they spent all their time doing other things.

"You want to get to the point?"

Well, she did and she didn't. Jinx wanted to get to the part Sam and Mickey had coached her on, the part where she told Doc about her mother having this big old diamond that she wouldn't give to Jinx, and did he have any ideas about how they might get it away from her? Like steal it, or something?

However, the other part of her assignment was to keep Doc busy as long as she could right now. And they hadn't explained how any of this was going to work, what the big picture was. That really burned her up.

Sam was treating her like she was stupid, just like she always had. Back in school, that's why she stole Sam's boyfriend, and she'd tell her that if Sam ever came down off her high horse long enough to ask. She'd say, Because you acted like I was some kind of Arkie hillbilly, lame-brained as a turkey, didn't have enough sense to close my mouth in the rain.

She'd gotten into Stanford, hadn't she, and she hadn't

done that with her tits, either. Though, today, this doing-it-in-the-buff business was her own idea.

"The point?" Doc said again.

"Well, have you ever heard of Murfreesboro?" And then she was off and running into this long story about Crater of Diamonds State Park over by Murfreesboro, about thirty-five miles away, where you could go and pay a fee and hunt for diamonds. Real diamonds.

She watched Doc's eyes light up, which was nice, because otherwise he had this scary kind of face with that hawklike nose and those long grooves from his nose down to the corners of his mouth that she didn't think came from smiling.

Then she looped around and got into the geology of this part of Arkansas, and how the hot water that came out of the ground at 143°F, and the quartz deposits, and the diamonds, well, they all came from the same place. Folks said it was seabed that had been squashed down and then pushed up to make the mountains that had worn down, and that gave you your hot water and your quartz and your diamonds. Then she was off on Thomas Jefferson, who had thought hot water was such a great thing, so great that he'd sent an expedition to check out Hot Springs, though it wasn't called that then when the U.S. bought themselves all this hot water as part of the Louisiana Purchase. As a result, Hot Springs was set aside in 1932 as a reservation for use by all the people, or our first "national park," though that was before national parks. That was interesting if you think about Bill Clinton being so drawn to Jefferson, *named* Jefferson, in fact, and he'd grown up here, went to Hot Springs High School. . . . It was when she got to the high school part that Doc grabbed her by the neck.

"Shut up!" he yelled. That was when she got scared. Very scared. After all, this man was a desperate kidnapper, and what had she been thinking about, letting Sam and Mickey talk her into this in the first place, not to mention her being with him in the altogether. He was so mad he was sputtering: "Why are you . . . what is this . . . *diamonds?*"

Oh. So she told him, with his hands still on her neck, told him the hooey about Loydell having found the biggest triple-A quality diamond ever in the history of Murfreesboro, and that was saying some, because they'd found some big ones.

At that, Doc let her drop. He stood back and grinned that wolfy grin. And then he said, lowering his eyes, "Bigger than those?"

Which was a stupid question, but she knew what he meant. So she let him take her hand and lead her over to the Mercury and into the back seat, all the while thinking: Sam wasn't so smart, and she was going to figure out what Sam and Mickey were up to. For one thing, Jinx didn't believe for a minute Mickey was a private investigator, but Mickey was nice to her and furthermore the prettiest woman Jinx had ever seen, aside from herself, of course. But Jinx was sick and tired of being treated like she was some kind of blond joke.

"Anybody coming, Lateesha?" Sam was sweating all over her cellular phone. She and Mickey were taking a break from searching the big stone house. They were standing in the kitchen taking turns drinking cold water out of the faucet, being super careful to leave no traces.

"Nope. Not a peep," said Lateesha. "Y'all find it yet?"

"We've about given up. Doc must have it on him. I'll check back with you in a few." Then Sam dialed Early. He answered on the first ring. She said, "How's it going?"

"Well, it's interesting."

"Is Jinx still with him?"

"She's with him, all right."

"You sound strange. What are they doing?" Sam waved Mickey over to listen, too.

"It's kind of hard to describe."

"She's banging him, isn't she, Early?" said Mickey.

"Uh-huh." Early sounded like he wasn't really paying attention to them, which he wasn't.

Mickey hung up, then turned to Sam, "See? I told you she was a natural."

"That's just great. But we still don't have the diamond."

The two women plopped down on stools facing one another. Mickey said, "Patience, my friend. Patience."

"It's never been one of my long suits."

"I'd never have guessed. Okay, if it's not here. . . ."

"Maybe it's in the car."

"Could be. But I doubt it. Doesn't feel right. It's not going to be in something that somebody else could just get in and drive away."

"So you think he carries it on him? Wouldn't you know that? Wouldn't Jinx see that?"

"No, I already told you. It's not a piece of jewelry. It's unset."

"I know. I was just reaching. If it's not here, at least we think it's not here, and it's not in his car, and it's not on his body, then what does that leave?" They sat and stared at one another. Then Sam said, "You must have thought about this a million times. Now, it can't be in his clothing, unless he wears the same clothes every—"

Mickey jumped straight up off her chair. "Jesus, I've been so stupid! What have I been thinking?"

32

"IT WAS ROBBERY IS WHAT IT WAS," ARCHIE SAID TO TATE, who was standing behind his bar, and Cynthia who was carrying a tray full of Buds. "Robbery gone sour, plain and simple."

Cynthia turned on her heel and marched away.

"Now, darlin'," said Archie, following right in behind her. "I think you ought to face it. That Bobby Adair's just as rotten as I always said he was. Killed his own grandma over the money in her cashbox, well, I'd say that's pretty low. Even for white trash."

At that, Cynthia stopped. She pivoted like she was doing some routine she'd learned in step aerobics class and stared straight into her daddy's piggy little eyes. "Excuse me?"

"Yep. Wuddn't even but about three hundred dollars. That's what Olive kept in that box. About three hundred dollars. Idn't that a shame, boy'd kill his own grandma for that?"

"Did you say white trash?"

Archie shifted his weight and settled back into himself, hitching up his pants. "You know, sister, now that we've done gone and proved that that boy is the homo-cidal maniac that I always said he was, I'd think you'd be studying on using a more respectful tone with your daddy. Yep. Maybe even apologizing. Saying you're sorry and begging to be let to move back home."

Cynthia's big brown eyes became firey little slits.

"What do you think *you* are? What do you think *I* am? Have you rewritten our family history so that suddenly we are no longer the descendants of generations of sharecroppers from the Delta?" Cynthia jerked her thumb in a generally easterly direction toward the Mississippi and the part of Arkansas where cotton was still grown. "And if sharecroppers aren't white trash, then I don't know what is, except we had the honor to also have some Cherokee blood, have you forgotten that, Daddy Dearest? A fact that I am proud as heck of, though you always thought it was the same as being black, which is what everybody else around here thinks."

"I don't," said Tate, polishing his bar. "Never did once confuse myself with any Native Americans."

Archie turned and was about to give Tate a piece of his mingy little mind, when he took note of the fact that Tate held a wet rag in one hand and a baseball bat in the other, and *maybe* he could shoot him first, but then again maybe he couldn't.

"Excuse me, Tate. No offense intended, but you know what I mean," Cynthia said.

"Yes, I do." He nodded.

"Tate," said Archie. "I'd appreciate it if you'd just keep out of this."

Tate was very tempted to tell Archie that *he'd* appreciate it if Archie would get his fat butt out of his bar and never come back because, frankly, in addition to his own paternal fondness for Cynthia, he thought Archie stunk up the place.

But then Archie made the mistake of saying what was really on *his* mind. He started, "Anyway, well, I was thinking, and . . ." Then he shifted his weight again and did this funny little motion like maybe he had ants in his pants. Or maybe he was embarrassed, which would be a signpost of his humanity, the first that Cynthia had ever seen.

"What do you want, Archie?" she asked, still holding

the beers. Cynthia had developed considerable upper body strength working in Tate's, and she was giving serious consideration to using some of it on her father right now. Jesus, she wished there were some way she could prove he wasn't really related to her, that there had been some kind of terrible mixup at the hospital, when he said, "Well, what I wondered, I've been looking all over town, and I haven't seen hide nor hair of her, is, well, do either of you know where I could find that cute Bobbie Sue? You know, that frisky blonde I met in here yesterday? Tate, you were talking with Early Trulove when she came in. . . ."

It was then that the phone rang, and it was Sam saying she and Mickey were over at Loydell's, Jinx had called with Doc's plan, and they'd just about worked out the last few details of this thing and wanted to tell her her part.

Cynthia nodded, Uh-huh, uh-huh, while Tate said, "Well, sure, Archie, if you want to leave me your number, I think I can put you and Bobbie Sue together."

33

"YOU'RE A GOOD GIRL, PEARL." SAM GAVE THE HOUND A final pat on the head as she and Jack turned to leave Bobby in the gym above Bubbles.

"I *do* trust you," said Bobby, "but I don't understand what makes you think it's going to be safe for me to come down."

"Later," said Sam, meaning that's when she'd explain. Right now, she needed to get moving.

"How *much* later? Pearl and I are going crazy up here."

Owwwrhuuuuuu, said Pearl by way of reinforcement.

"We have to work a few things out," said Jack.

"Do you know who killed Mamaw? You better not, and not tell me. I'm warning you," said Bobby, shaking a finger in Jack's face. Olive's death had pushed him beyond politeness. This, Sam suspected, was more what the old Bobby was like, the Bobby who'd beaned Archie with his shooting trophy.

"No, we don't," lied Sam. "Don't you think we'd tell you if we did?" She wasn't sure exactly what she thought Bobby would do if he knew about Doc, but she didn't want to find out. Bobby could just cool his heels a little longer, until Doc was safely behind bars.

"Okay, okay," said Bobby. "I'm sure you're doing the best you can to protect me here. Keep me out of trouble with the parole board."

Oh, son, thought Sam, if you only knew. The parole board was small potatoes compared to the manhunt that Archie was amassing to find his young butt. The last they'd heard, Archie was inflaming the local boys and the state troopers with tales of grandmother-raping in addition to robbing and killing. There were no depths to which the man wouldn't stoop. But just you wait, Archie Blackshears. Just you wait 'til this whole thing is over, and those old boys get an earful of you loving up to Bobby Adair in drag as Bobbie Sue.

Now Jack was tapping on his watch. "Come on, Sammy, we'd better scoot. We'll be right back to you, Bobby, as soon as we can."

"I'd appreciate it."

"You've got everything you need? You're not about to starve to death?"

"No, sir. You've got yourself some wonderful cooks, I'll tell you that. I'm pounding away four or five hours on the speedball, the bag, working it off." He paused. "And it keeps my mind off Mamaw."

Sam gave him a hug, a Keep the faith, and started out. Jack shut the gym door and locked it, then caught up with her on the landing. "Wait." He took her by the arm and pulled her around. It was a small landing. "Sammy, I've been giving it some consideration, and I think you've been right all along. Look, we'll just call the cops, tell them about Doc, hope for the best. Hell, I'm sure there's some physical evidence at Olive's place, they'll be able to pin this on Doc without Mickey's testimony." He put both hands behind her waist and drew her closer. "I don't know what I'd do if anything happened to you."

"The same thing you were doing day before yesterday, Jack. Serving great eats in Bubbles, ripping off the suckers downstairs in the casino."

"Lady," he said, "we don't rip off anybody. Fools come in the casino, they know the odds are against 'em, want to have a little fun giving us their money, what can we do? Though, you know, it's funny, since the second I met you, the take in the casino has doubled." And that was the truth. Jack couldn't explain it, unless Sam was some kind of good luck charm working for him, which was the kind of thing the suckers believed. Jack didn't like to think of himself as a sucker. Then his voice grew tender. "Is this what they call love at first sight?"

"Lust, Jack. They call it lust. It's the thing you've spent your whole life confusing with the other thing."

"The other thing? You can't even say the word."

"I most certainly can, and furthermore, I've experienced it many times."

"Experienced what?"

"Listen, I am not going to continue this ridiculous conversation with you another second. I've got to get out to the front and watch for Doc. Is your man in place?"

"He's there, Sammy. He's there. Now, look."

"You're sure he knows what he's doing?"

"Jethro is the best in the business. He's worked for Joey the Horse for years. I told you, I called Joey, he flew Jethro up in his own plane. He's here, he's ready, and he's good. But I still think we ought to call it all off. I have a bad feeling about this thing. I really do."

"Jack, this was *your* idea, and we're doing it."

He took a deep breath. "I'll never understand as long as I live."

"Understand what? Women? It's easy, Jack. All you have to remember is we're these inscrutable, yet cute, deerlike creatures who are motivated by whims and estrogen and flights of fancy that no man could ever begin to decipher."

"God, give me strength," he murmured.

"God has nothing to do with it. This is what *you* wanted to do, Jack. *You.*" She poked him twice in the chest. "And now you want to change your mind. Well, that's the sort of thing they accuse women of, you know that, don't you? Can't trust them in positions of power because they're always wishy-washing all over the place. Well, you're the one wishy-washing here, my man."

"Jesus H. Christ, Samantha! I'm trying to tell you I love you."

"You do not love me. You don't even know me."

He gave her a look.

"One night in the sack does not constitute knowing even if it was a very nice night." She paused. "A very very nice night. However"—and she held up one cautionary finger—"not only do you not know me, you do not want to know me. I am strong-willed, irreverent, mouthy, and independent as heck; whereas you are a traditional, macho Irish gangster who needs some bimbo on your arm for show and a sweet-faced little Bridget home in the kitchen. And I am neither of those." She paused. "Though I must say that the fact that you're not at all uptight about sex surprised me, given that Blessed Virgin/whore stuff you all carry around."

Whereupon Jack placed one hand on each of her shoulders, pushed her against the wall, and kissed the bejesus out of her. Jack was one of the all-time world-class kissers, and he kissed her and kissed her and kissed her until she was actually seeing stars and thought she was going to faint.

When they finally came up for air, he said, "So, who's the guy back in New Orleans, Sammy?"

She was going to say, Nobody. She was sure that's what she was going to say, but her eyes slid, and she hesitated just a second too long.

"Oh, shit." Jack turned his head, but not before she caught the pain in his eyes. It looked like the real thing.

34

DOC'S PLAN. FIRST, HE AND JINX WOULD RUN A VARIATION of the priest and the jeweler scam on Loydell and nab her diamond. Then he'd leave Jinx in his car with the motor running, and he'd dash into Jack's restaurant, pop Jack, take off, ditch the beauty queen, be on his merry way to the South Carolina coast, a very cushy retirement, and sweet dreams.

To that end, he and Jinx were cruising Central, searching for a parking spot. Headed down from the big hotels, they tooled along Bathhouse Row.

"There's the Quapaw." Jinx pointed. "Bubbles is on the main floor. The casino's in the basement."

Doc stared across the street at the long white stucco building. Big mullioned windows with blue awnings marched across the length of the front. Above the red tile roof of the second story was perched a gold and blue dome stately enough for Kubla Khan.

"You made the reservation?"

"Yes," Jinx said. "Exactly like you told me to. I said I was bringing in a high roller from San Antonio who specifically wanted to meet Jack. They said he'd be there. But I don't understand. . . ."

"And you don't need to."

There it was again. Boy, she had had just about a bellyful of that dumb blonde routine.

"And you know exactly how the flimflam works?"

"You told me forty-two times."

"Yeah? Well, I could tell you a thousand and forty-two, you're an amateur, there's every chance you're gonna screw up."

"I'm not going to screw up."

"Well, you do, you're never going to see that bridegroom of yours alive again."

"I've got it, Doc." Then she pointed. "Look! There's somebody pulling out."

That, thought Doc, was a piece of luck. A good omen. Just as they approached, a red Cadillac driven by a man wearing a huge cowboy hat, that's all you could see of him, was exiting a spot right across the street from Jack's restaurant.

Early's timing *was* impeccable, but then, as Jack said, that's why he paid him the big bucks.

"And Mother's house is right around the corner and up the hill on Exchange," said Jinx.

They climbed out of the Mercury, and Doc locked it. He passed on feeding the parking meter.

"You're going to get a ticket," Jinx said, adjusting her little pink shorts suit with the yellow daisy trim. She was wearing matching pink stiletto sandals with daisies on the toes. She'd redone her manicure and pedicure to match.

Doc just gave her a look. Then he took her arm as they started down the sidewalk past a row of art galleries, souvenir stores, and coffee shops. "You think you can do this? You understand about the bank?"

"Yes, I understand, Doc."

Doc wasn't sure. He wasn't sure she could pull this off at all. But what the hell? What did he have to lose? If the scam fell apart, he'd just do Jack, climb back in the Mercury, and ride ride ride. Of course, he'd have to switch the Mercury pretty quick for another car, which was a shame because he liked the glide of the big boat. It reminded him of those great gas guzzlers from the late fifties, early sixties. He'd had a two-tone purple Bonneville, those loooong tailfins and acres of chrome. Now, that was a car. Like the Sunliner, which was less luxe, though still a beauty. It was a shame, that old sweetie sitting at the bottom of a lake, but them was the breaks.

"Well, hi!" Jinx said suddenly. "How're yeeeew?"

Doc looked up, and Jinx was hugging a tall, curly-headed brunette, he'd put her in her late thirties. She was dressed like him, in khakis, with a white shirt—though she was wearing an expensive-looking blue-and-white seersucker jacket, and Doc was sporting an off-the-rack navy blazer and an ugly red-and-navy tie. The brunette was saying, "Why, *I'm* just fine. But how are *yew*?"

"I'm holding on." Jinx shook her head, and her curls swayed.

"I know it must be hard. Speed just dying on you like that. It's so awful. I just don't know how you can bear it."

Speed dying? What the hell was the broad talking about? Doc gave Jinx a hard look, but she didn't see it because just then the tall brunette hugged her again, and Jinx stepped backwards off the curb.

"Owh!" she screamed. "Oh, my God!"

Damn! Doc thought. She'd sprained her ankle. Well, hell, wasn't that par for the course? No way this town was good for anything except killing Jack. He wasn't going to make a penny here. Why didn't he just give it up?

"I broke the heel right off my shoe!" Jinx cried. She was dangling her high-heeled sandal.

"You just come right on in here into Frank's and let me buy you a new pair," said the tall brunette. "This is all my fault."

"Dr. Dolittle," said Jinx, "do you mind?"

It took Doc a second to realize she was talking to him. Dan Little was the bogus handle he'd told her to use. Blondes, Jesus.

"I don't know what I'd have done without the doctor. He's been so kind," Jinx said to the brunette whom she introduced as Samantha. Sam bustled them into the shoe store, whose windows were draped with silver tinsel and gold bunting.

"Hello, ladies, sir. Welcome to Frank's," said a cute young girl right inside the door of the old-fashioned high-ceilinged store. It still had its original pine wainscoting and a tin ceiling that was festooned with gold and silver balloons. The river of dark hair that flowed down the young girl's back was two inches longer than her little silver skirt. Her hair bounced around as she said, "I don't know how to tell you this, but *you*," and she rounded on Doc and threw her arms around him like he was her long-lost love, "are the one-hundreth person who's walked through our doors since yesterday morning, and that means you are the winner of our Diamond Jubilee door prize!" She was fairly squeaking with excitement. "Yes, sir," she crowed, "this is the one-hundreth anniversary of Frank's Shoes, and you are the hundredth one! Aren't you thrilled?"

Jinx was grinning at him like she'd forgotten what the hell they were doing here, and this shoe business was the main event. But on the other hand, now that Doc thought about it, a Diamond Jubilee, it had to be a good sign.

The little brunette was pulling him by the arm over to a chair cushioned in brown velour. "The prize is any pair of shoes of your choice, for free! And I can see from your boots that you have excellent taste, and we just happen to have a pair of genuine alligator Luccheses that I bet are going to be exactly your size. Eleven A, am I right? You have an elegant foot there, sir, if you don't mind my saying so. So long and narrow. Now, would those alligator boots interest you?"

"What's the catch?"

"Oh, there is no catch, sir." Her big brown eyes grew larger. "You are definitely the one-hundreth customer of our Diamond Jubilee. But if you don't think you'd like the alligator boots, you just tell me what you want. By the way, my name's Cynthia."

Alligator Luccheses had to be worth seven, eight hundred, hell, maybe a thousand. Doc, who'd never even passed a tip left on a table for a waiter without palming it, couldn't resist. "Well, sure. The boots'll be fine. Thank you kindly."

"I'll sit right here beside you," said Jinx, slipping in on his right. "And Samantha'll sit on your left. How does that feel? Being bookended by a couple of pretty ladies?"

Now Doc was sure of it. Jinx had completely forgotten what they were doing in town. Well, let him grab these boots, slap some kind of shoes on her, he'd get her out on the street and remind her, quick.

A young salesman was approaching Jinx. He was a beanpole, tall and no bigger around than a pencil. He reminded Doc of a mobster in New Orleans who had one of those spaghetti names, but they called him Bennie Brown because of his brown hair, brown eyes, and he always dressed in tan: suit, shirt, tie. Just like this young civilian who was asking Jinx how he could help her. Do you have anything like these, she held up her broken sandal, seven-and-a-half B? Why, sure, he said and took off for the stockroom.

The woman named Sam was chatting on, telling Doc every last detail of a dinner party she had given the night before, describing each dessert down to the last lemon drop. Then Cynthia, the young brunette, was back and holding up the most beautiful pair of boots he'd ever seen. "I'll take them," said Doc. Then he punched Jinx in the arm. "We'd better get going, don't you think?"

"I've got to try my shoes on." She poked out her bottom lip. The woman had absolutely no sense of priorities. Like they didn't need to get on to Loydell's, down to the bank, over to Bubbles. She said, "Aren't you going to try on your boots?"

"Nope," said Doc. "Eleven A, they'll do fine."

"Oh, wait," said Cynthia. "Actually, these are a half-size smaller, but sometimes that'll do, you know, so why don't you try them? If they don't fit, I have some real pretty lizard ones I can show you."

"We're really in a hurry," said Doc.

"Why, thank yeeeew," Jinx was saying to the Man in Tan who'd just carried out a tower of shoeboxes. "You didn't have to go to all that trouble."

"Jinx," said Doc. But she wasn't listening. And Doc didn't want to cause a scene. He was already making much more of an impression on the citizenry than he'd like.

"Here, sir, let me take those off for you." Cynthia was sitting on a stool before him with that tiny strip of silver stretched tight across her thighs. It was impossible not to look.

"No, thanks. I'll do it." He pulled off his boots and placed them carefully under his chair. Then he tried to look at her face as she handed him the boots.

They were a bit short in the toe and a tad too tight in the arch.

"Now, let's don't give up hope," said Cynthia. "We can do all kinds of tricks around here."

"They are *so* clever," Sam said, patting his arm. "I buy all my shoes here."

"You don't say," said Doc, looking down at her brown woven-leather loafers. Huh. Shoes were the first thing you looked at, you wanted to judge a potential mark. One of Pearsa's lessons. You take a man in a thousand-dollar suit, he's wearing cheap shoes, and *lots* of them do, you're not looking at a man with class. But a man wearing jeans and a blue denim shirt, a pair of Armani loafers, that's the man you zero in on. The money's all in the details.

So this broad had potential. Whereas Jinx, look at the flashy junk the woman was trying on. Catch-me-do-me stilettos. No wonder she didn't have any money. She didn't deserve any.

"So why don't you just slip those off, and let me take them in the back"—Cynthia was saying about the alligator Luccheses, when all of a sudden, Jinx started screaming. "What the hell do you think you're doing?" She jumped up out of her chair.

And then she was chasing the Man in Tan, who was running hellbent for leather toward the front door.

Jesus! Did he have her bag? Had he stolen the boodle in her wallet? The payoff for the scam? Jeeeesus!

Doc took off after them in the alligator boots.

The man in tan tore down the sidewalk past the Art Center, past a couple more galleries, and he was about to turn up the hill at the Chamber of Commerce when Jinx executed a flying tackle that was damned impressive.

"You filthy son of a bitch!" she screamed. She was sitting astraddle him in her little pink shorts suit.

"What did he take?" Doc grabbed the man by the neck and started throttling him. "What?"

"Nothing!" Jinx was breathing hard. She was red in

255

the face. "He was sniffing my feet. He was getting off on sniffing my feet!"

"Christ on a crutch!" Doc flung the young man down on the pavement. "Jinx, what the hell is wrong with you?" And then he grabbed her by the arm and dragged her the two blocks down the street and back into Frank's Shoes. The alligator boots were pinching the hell out of his toes.

He threw Jinx into a chair. "Just get some damned shoes, and let's get going."

Cynthia was wide-eyed. "I'm so sorry, sir. I'm so sorry," she gulped. "Is there any way we can make this up to you?"

Doc was pulling off the alligator boots. He reached over and grabbed up a box beside Jinx that the Man in Tan hadn't even opened yet. "She'll take these, and we'll be on our way."

"I'm afraid that'll be seventy dollars, sir. See, *she* wasn't the hundredth customer. You were. Now, could I show you some lizard boots we have in your size?"

"I don't think so," Doc hissed. He turned to Jinx. "Put those shoes on now. Right now." Then to Cynthia, he said, "I think, missy, you'll consider her shoes the Diamond Jubilee door prize and count yourself lucky that I'm not calling the cops and reporting this pervert you have working in your store."

"Yes, sir," Cynthia said. "I guess you're right. Thank you, sir. Thank you very much. And don't forget your boots." She was holding up Doc's old pair. Suddenly he felt nauseous. How could he? How *could* he have gone off and left his boots?

Doc snatched the boots out of her hand, jerked them on, and pushed Jinx out of the store. Sam and Cynthia ran to the front and watched him drag her down the sidewalk, then stop and point her around the corner and up toward Exchange. Jinx flounced on up the hill, and Doc slouched back toward the Mercury.

"We did it!" They hugged each other. "We did it!" Cynthia said, "Weren't we cool?"

And then Jethro the Iceman, Joey the Horse's precious gems fence and all-purpose jeweler, stepped from the stockroom. He was a dapper little man wearing a white linen suit and a handmade pair of brown-and-white spectator lace-ups that would have given Doc pause. He was carrying a smooth brown calf attaché case with serious combination locks. Jethro grinned. "Mission accomplished," he announced, then raised a hand adorned with four sparkling rings. He and the ladies slapped high fives.

35

THE WAY THE PRIEST AND THE JEWELER SCAM USUALLY BEgins is the outside man—who sets up the mark, in this case a jeweler—plays a priest who comes into a jewelry store and buys something not too expensive, but of a value to make the scam worthwhile, let's say a diamond bracelet for a thousand, maybe two thousand bucks. The inside man, who actually takes off the score, plays a cop who'll appear after the purchase.

But that wouldn't work in this particular situation. First, of all, Doc had to use Jinx because Mickey was dead and he didn't have another partner, and besides, Jinx gave him the access to her mother, the mark. Jinx would be the outside man, but she obviously couldn't play anyone other than herself.

And, if Loydell were cozy with the local cops, Doc

couldn't pretend to be one. However, he could be a U. S. Treasury agent, which is why he was wearing the cheap blazer and the ugly tie. Doc, like Mickey, had a whole wardrobe of costumes—which he'd be retiring very soon.

Now Doc was sitting in the Mercury on Central Avenue, right across from Bubbles, waiting for Jinx and Loydell to head for the bank. And here they were.

Jinx was mincing down the hill in her new navy high heels, which he had to admit, didn't go with her pink and daisy shorts suit nearly as well as her pink and yellow sandals, but, hey, he wasn't going to have to listen to her bitching about that very long, was he?

Beside her marched a little old lady in a red-and-white polyster pants suit. In her sensible white shoes, Loydell was about four steps ahead of her daughter. Doc gathered Loydell had believed Jinx's story about going back into the crystal altar business and wanting to buy Loydell's Arkansas diamond to be the centerstone of an altar called Hope that was going to be her reentry piece. Jinx just knew that altars of Arkansas crystal were going to be all the rage, and that's why she was willing to spend this last ten thousand dollars she'd tucked away. She'd won it at Oaklawn picking five out of six races in a Classix.

"What if she balks at the price?" Jinx had asked when they were rehearsing.

"What size *is* the rock? Show me again."

Jinx had made a circle with her thumb and forefinger. "It's about this big."

"Jesus! I'll be lucky if it's worth five thousand. Are you sure that's right? How long's it been since you've seen it?"

"Oh, it's been some time," said Jinx, making it up as she went along. "Mother hardly ever brings it out. She's kind of wacko about it. She thinks it has some kind of magical powers. I wouldn't be surprised if she didn't sleep with it under her pillow."

Doc had just grinned his wolfy grin. God, wasn't life funny? But that's why being on the grift was so easy: The infinite variety of humanity bent the envelope of possibilities in ways you just wouldn't believe—until you tried it.

Then he said, "This is an awfully cheap price for your boyfriend—you realize that, don't you? Your getting him back for a five-tops-ten-thousand-dollar piece of ice?"

"Oh, Doc," she'd said then, pressing her chest up against his arm. "I'm so grateful that you're letting me off so easy. I'll do this right, I promise."

"Remember to flash the cash in front of her. People see the green, they bite. Especially thousand-dollar denominations, they are *real* impressive. And then you remember that you recently heard that there were some counterfeit one-grand bills being passed at the track, and before you do anything to put your mom in jeopardy, you think they ought to take the money down to a bank and make sure it's the real thing."

"I insist on it—even if she's willing to just take the cash."

"Absolutely. You are determined that your mom gets the genuine jack."

So that's what they'd been doing, Jinx and Loydell, going to the bank. Doc had watched them march around the corner and down the sidewalk into the Hot Springs Amalgamated Savings, where an officer would swear on a stack of Bibles that the boodle was bona fide.

Because it was. A con man who worked any kind of scam involving currency always carried a stash of the real green.

Now here they were. Doc could hear them talking as they passed his car.

"Well, I feel a whole lot better that we did that, don't you, Mother?"

"I don't know. I'm sure Bo thought we were absolutely crazy." She shook her head, and the little gray waves marching back from her forehead didn't move an inch. Doc sure couldn't see any family resemblance between the two of them.

"Oh, he did not," said Jinx. "You know Bo's always been sweet on me. He'd do anything. . . ." And then the conversation trailed off as the two women turned the corner and headed back up the hill to Loydell's house.

Doc checked his watch. Jinx was doing swell. He'd give her ten minutes to have a Coke, schmooze with her mother, and then he'd make his move. He reached down and tapped on the heel of his right boot. He shook his foot, and he could feel Little Doc move inside the hollow heel. "Gonna bring you a little brother real soon," he said to the diamond.

Well, sort of a diamond.

Jack was sitting in his regular booth in Bubbles's front room, the one where folks could find him if they needed him—or needed a favor. It was table number one with a view of the street. He was drinking a cup of café au lait made with Community Coffee he had shipped up fresh from New Orleans once a week. Sam, across from him, was already too fidgety without the java. She checked her watch for the hundredth time. "Doc's been up at Loydell's for five minutes. How much longer, do you think?"

"Long as it takes, I guess."

"I hate it when you say things like that."

"You don't even know me well enough to know all the things you're going to hate, *after* you dump that fool down in New Orleans, the one who was stupid enough to let you out of his sight for even a second." Then he gave her a big wink.

Sam ignored that and drummed her fingers on the table. "I guess I ought to be pleased. It didn't take Cynthia but two minutes to talk those nice people who own Frank's Shoes into letting us use their store."

"Well, I did give 'em a free lunch for a sweetener while y'all were putting on your little show."

"And I thought we did real well. Doc seemed to fall for it."

"And Jethro did his thing."

"Cool as a cuke, your man Jethro. Not to mention the toe-sniffer. We didn't really have to use him, but I couldn't resist."

Jack finished off his coffee and leaned back. "So all we have to do now is wait for Jinx and Loydell to finish up."

"That's right."

"I imagine that's when Doc's going to come on over here and try to kill me, wouldn't you think?" With that, Jack pulled a beauty of an antique Colt revolver from where it had been resting beside him on the seat, and he laid it on the table.

Sam braced herself against the back of the mahogany and green baize booth. "Jack, have you gone crazy?"

"For wanting to defend myself? I don't think so."

"Wait a minute. The plan was, we finish the sting, then we sic the cops on him. Surprise, Doc! We've got your diamond, your money, and here's the blowoff— you're going to jail."

"And I said that wouldn't fly. He'll walk out, a free man, in five minutes."

"So instead you're waiting for Doc to come in here, to blast you away?"

"No, actually, I wasn't going to let him get that far. I was thinking more of meeting him out in the street."

"*High Noon?*"

"Something like that."

"Olive was right. You all can't help it. It's the testosterone backing up in your brain."

"You're a what?" Loydell was saying.

"Treasury Agent Dan Little, ma'am." Doc pulled out

his fake badge and ID and showed her. She didn't even look all that closely. Nobody ever did.

"Well, I swear. I never saw one of y'all before. Seen plenty of Fibbies. Yep, town used to be lousy with Fibbies, had one full-time there for a long while, J. Edgar sent down to torment Owney Madden."

"Mother," Jinx interrupted. "Mr. Dolittle, I mean Little, doesn't—"

But Loydell went right on. "That Fibbie stayed on, became sheriff. He's retired now. But a Treasury man? Nope. So what's your business here? I ain't robbed any banks." Loydell held her hands up in the air.

"I know that, ma'am." Doc gave her his best smile. "But it's banking, actually, that brought me here."

"I've banked with First National and Amalgamated Savings my whole life. They never sent anybody out to visit with me before."

"No, ma'am, I wouldn't think they would. But, you see, there's been this problem recently, people passing phony thousand-dollar bills at racetracks all across the South. I was just down in Shreveport dealing with the same thing."

"This is certainly is a coincidence. My daughter, Jinx, here and I were just down at Amalgamated having them check some thousand-dollar bills that came into her possession. But ours were real. You don't have to worry about us."

"Well, ma'am, that's the problem. See, I had called them over at Amalgamated not two seconds after you left the bank. I'd just flown into town and got myself situated and was starting to contact all the local bankers, when lo and behold, your names came up."

"Yes, sir," said Loydell, "we've got the real thousands all right. Or, I do. Now, Mr. Little, would you like a Coke?"

"No, ma'am. I don't want to put you to the trouble."

"It's no trouble. I'll be back in a second. You chat with my daughter, Jinx, here. She's single."

"Moth-er," Jinx wailed.

Doc winked at Jinx when Loydell left the room. Then he gave her the high sign, reached over and patted her on the shoulder. "You're doing swell," he whispered.

"Here's your Coke." Loydell bustled back into the living room. "So what exactly is it you want us to tell you about our thousand-dollar bills?"

"Well, ma'am, I'm afraid it's what *I* have to tell you. You see, I'm afraid they're not real."

"Not real! Why, of course, they are," said Jinx. "We just took them into Amalgamated, and my very good friend Bo, who's the president of the bank, he dealt with us personally, assured us our money was genuine."

Doc drew himself up, in a show of authority. "And where did this money come from?"

"I won it at the track," said Jinx.

"Wait a minute," the old lady interrupted. "What you're saying is, no matter what Bo said, this money of Jinx's that she just paid me for my diamond, it's not worth the paper it's printed on."

"I suspect that's pretty much the size of it," said Doc. "See, the thing is, these counterfeits are so good, you'd have to be a *real* expert to tell the difference. I mean, these are excellent fakes, not done the old-fashioned way with engraving plates, but on a color laser copier. And then the paper's aged. Here, let me see your bills, I'll show you."

Loydell reached in her white plastic handbag and found the long green envelope with the money Jinx had given her. She handed it to Doc. He fingered it, turned it over, pretended to examine it this way and that, all the while shaking his head. "It's amazing," he finally said. "Just amazing the work they can do with those laser printers."

"I swear!" said Loydell. Then she turned to Jinx.

"Well, hon, I guess you're out ten thousand smackeroos. Which is a real disappointment, but then, on the other hand, I guess you could say money won at the track is a kind of gift, anyway." She tapped Jinx on the arm. "Now, could you give me back my diamond, please?"

Jinx made a face, then rooted around in her huge yellow straw tote, pulled out a gray flannel jeweler's bag tied with golden cord, and handed it to Loydell. "Easy come, easy go," Jinx said with a sad shrug. "I guess that's the story of my life."

Doc had to give it to her. The woman was a good actor.

Then Jinx said, "Do you mind if I take another look at that money, Mr. Little? It sure *looked* like the genuine article."

"Sure thing." Doc handed Jinx the envelope containing his ten thousand in real bills. Then to Loydell, "And do you mind if I see your diamond, Mrs. Watson? If there's already been something of value exchanged for this counterfeit, it puts an extra twist on things."

"Why, I don't mind at all," said Loydell. "Hold out your hand."

Doc did, and Loydell untied the golden cord, turned the gray flannel bag upside down, and tumbled a breathtaking sparkler into Doc's palm. It was brilliant. It was gorgeous. And it was huge, *much* bigger than Jinx had led him to expect. It was, *Jesus*, thought Doc, it was the spit and image of Little Doc. A matched *pair* of premium quality diamonds like this, there was no *telling* what the value might be. It was all he could do to keep the excitement out of his voice as he said, "Gosh, ma'am, this is an awfully pretty stone."

"Well, I always thought so," said Loydell. "I found it myself, you know, over at Crater of Diamonds."

"You don't say," Doc breathed. He couldn't even look at Jinx. He was afraid he'd blurt, Hell, woman, you said it was a little thing. But then, she *was* dumb, barely had enough sense to come in out of the rain. Though, on the other hand, she hadn't screwed this scam up. Yet. He'd better get moving before she did.

"Now, ma'am," he said to Loydell. "What I need to do is this. Because there was something of value exchanged, I'm going to have to take your diamond along with this counterfeit down to the police department and have it photographed. That way, when we catch the counterfeiters, the charges against them will include the theft of your diamond."

"Really?" said Loydell. "Even though they didn't actually take it?" She reached out her hand for the diamond, and Doc handed it to her. She dropped it back in its little flannel bag.

"Well, they would have, wouldn't they, by passing this phony money, it would have amounted to the same thing? You would have been out your diamond."

"I never thought about it like that," said Loydell. "So, when will I get it back?"

"Oh, right away," said Doc. "Tell you what, I'll just take Jinx—did I get your name right, ma'am, yes, Jinx—along with me, and we'll shoot it, and then she'll bring your diamond right back to you. Of course, we have to keep the counterfeit."

"Maybe I ought to come along myself," said Loydell, rising.

"No, Mother." Jinx practically pushed her back in the chair. "I feel like this whole thing's my fault, and I don't want you to have to go to any trouble. You just wait right here, and I'll be back with your diamond before you can say Jack Robinson." She held out her hand, and Loydell gave her the gray flannel bag. Then Jinx tucked both the bag and the green envelope with the money in her straw tote and stood. "Well, Mr. Little?"

"Miss Watson." He nodded. "I guess we'd better go ahead and get this over with. I'm real sorry about your money."

"Not nearly as sorry as I am," Jinx said. "I'll tell you, this has been one horrible week." Her bottom lip was starting to tremble.

"Now, Jinx," said Loydell. "Don't burden the nice man with your problems. You just get on down to the police station and hurry back here, and then we'll go over to Bubbles, I'll buy you a nice lunch. Maybe that big Gulf shrimp salad they do. Won't that make you feel better?"

Bubbles, thought Doc. Bubbles, where he had an appointment with Jack Graham. Plus, now he had a *pair* of perfect diamonds, Little Doc plus this baby. A million dollars, they had to be worth a million, and that was probably on the conservative side. All of a sudden this whole thing was coming together better than Doc had ever dreamed. He could hardly keep himself from jumping up and down.

"Come, Miss Watson," he said offering Jinx his arm. "Shall we?"

36

"FROM WHAT I HEAR, THERE HASN'T BEEN A REAL GOOD shootout in the middle of Central Avenue for over a hundred years, not since 1883, Frank Flynn and Major Doran got into it over who was controlling the town's gambling," Jack was saying. "Of course, then, quite a few civilians were killed. We'll try to keep it among us bad guys, Miss Samantha." Then he nodded at his coffee cup to the waiter. Thank you, yes, he could use a refill.

"Do you think I'm going to let you walk out in the middle of the street with that six-gun like Wyatt Earp?"

"Why, Sammy," he reached over and covered her hand with his. "I didn't think you cared."

"That doesn't make the least bit of sense, Jack. I'd stop *anybody* from getting his head blown off." She paused. "Of course, I'd really rather you, specifically, didn't."

Jack leaned back in the booth and gave her his best grin. "Those are awfully sweet words to my ears. Almost as sweet as *I'm crazy about you too, Jack.*"

"I don't think the lady's likely to be saying that any time soon. Not if I have anything to do with it." It was Harry, Sam's Harry, glowering down at the two of them.

Doc unlocked the Mercury on the passenger side and said to Jinx, "Now, do you remember what to do?"

"Of course I do. I slide over, start the engine, and wait until you come back out of Bubbles. Then you'll take me to Speed. But what I don't understand is why you want me to keep the engine running. Are you going to rob the restaurant? Stealing my mother's diamond is one thing, Doc, but I don't want to be accessory to any robbery."

"There's not going to be any robbery, dimwit. Now get in the car." He grabbed her elbow and pushed her toward the door.

Jinx jerked away. "*Dimwit?* Dimwit! I have absolutely had it with people calling me names. Here, mister, you just take these." Jinx reached her right hand into her huge yellow tote and started rummaging around, talking all the while. "*Dimwit, stupid, dumb blonde.* I don't know where people get off thinking they can talk to me like that just because I was once a beauty queen. I own property. I have a business. I've raised a son who may not make straight A's, but he's not a juvenile delinquent, either. I am a person in the world, a registered Democrat, a citizen of the United States. Do you understand what

I'm saying?" Then she found what she was looking for and threw the green envelope and the little gray flannel bag past Doc through the open car door onto the seat. "Now, go screw yourself!" And then Jinx Watson, person in the world, registered Democrat, mother and property-owner, stomped into the middle of Central Avenue in her brand-new navy blue heels, right out in front of the same pickup truck that Jack Graham had cut off near the Kentucky Fried Chicken a couple of nights earlier, and for the second time that week, the driver of the pickup was real glad he'd let his wife talk him into that brake job.

"Besides," Jinx yelled back at Doc, who was standing there open-mouthed, staring at her from the other side of Central, "do you think I'm so stupid I really thought you were going to take me to Speed once you had your grubby hands on Mother's diamond? Up yours, Doc!" She punctuated her words with a stiffly crooked right forearm. Then Jinx took off running around the side of the Quapaw toward the back door of Bubbles, which was exactly according to Sam and Mickey's plan.

Sam could hardly take her eyes off Harry, she simply couldn't believe that he was standing there, but Jack kept tapping her on the hand. "Look!" he said, pointing out the window. "Jinx's doing it! Watch, watch, look, hon, there's the switch. See, just like Mickey told her, she tossed him the envelope with the fake money and the bag with Jethro's phony diamond, and now she's cross-ing the street. Here she comes. She'll be through the back door in half a minute. God, she must be pumped; she's gonna be screaming! Yes!" Jack slapped a palm down on the table, and his coffee cup jumped.

"Sammy," Harry said. "Sammy, I need to talk with you. *Now.*"

"Wait a minute." Sam still watching Doc, waved one

hand behind her. "Just a minute." Then to Jack, "Oh, God, is he going to look inside? What if he looks inside?"

"He's won't. Trust me. He's fallen for it hard, just like a rube would, because he *wanted* to believe it. He doesn't have a clue that Jethro replaced Little Doc with one of his fabulous fakes back in the shoestore."

Sam rubbed her hands together. "I can't wait to hear Loydell describe the look on his face when she handed him his own diamond and he thought he had twin Little Docs."

"Twin fakes." Jack laughed. "Jinx just passed him another one, now the man's got two magnificent chunks of cubic zirconia, one in his heel, one right there on his car seat, and we've got Little Doc and his ten thousand! God, I love it!"

Harry said, "I've come a long way to talk with you, babe."

At that, Jack slowly turned and gave Harry a lengthy look, starting with his worn-out running shoes, up his tattered jeans, took in his faded red-and-white polo shirt, his long curls, about a month past needing a trim, and said, "Son, if you're calling this woman babe, you wait right here. When I finish with that son of a bitch out there, I'll come back and attend to you." With that, Jack stood, picked up the Colt, gave it a gunslinger twirl, stuffed it into his belt, and pushed past Harry.

What the hell? The woman *was* stupid. Or was she? Now that Doc thought about it, what she'd done was save herself the bruising she'd have gotten when he shoved her out of the moving Mercury and, well, face it, who knows what else? Whatever it'd take for Doc to make his getaway.

He leaned into the Mercury and snatched up the envelope and the jeweler's bag and stuffed them both in his jacket pocket. Killing Jack was going to take only a minute, but there was no point in taking chances. Tourist town like Hot Springs, there were always thieves.

He relocked the car, straightened up, and stared at Bubbles across the street. He'd waited for this moment for a long time. Too long. He patted the Hardballer .45 stuffed in his belt. He took a deep breath. Then Doc counted, one, two, three, and started his slow march across the street.

"Jack!" Sam screamed. She was watching Jack, watching Doc, watching Jack. The restaurant had gone deathly quiet. It was like a freeze-frame in the movies. Everyone still. All eyes on her. "Jack, don't do it! Stop!"

Jack, who was halfway to the front door, paused next to a service station filled with chrome pitchers of ice water, cream, sugar substitutes, pickled peppers, quart bottles of tabasco sauce. His body stayed in place as his handsome silver head turned. He spoke softly from the side of his mouth, "He killed Olive, Sammy. Choked that sweet old lady dead."

"Let the cops deal with it, babe." She heard a small moan behind her at the *babe*. Harry. She shook her head. Not now. She couldn't deal with Harry now.

"And Speed. You know he killed Speed."

"It's their job, Jack. The cops' job."

"He murdered Lush Life. Remember that sweet filly, Sammy? You saw her. Such a pretty girl. Such a beauty."

"Hey, *I* remember that." That was Harry. He was right. He'd been there, too, at the New Orleans track, with Sam on his arm.

"He butchered my dogs, Sammy. He cut their heads off. He strung their guts around my yard like popcorn."

"Oh, babe."

"Early can tell you. Early saw them."

Now there was a thought. "Where is Early, Jack?"

"Early," Harry breathed. "Early Trulove, he's a friend of Lavert's. So who's *this* guy?"

"He's locked in my office downstairs. I didn't want Early to get into this."

"Jack, you've got to give this up," Sam pleaded. "It's nuts."

"Sweet pie, it'll be over before you can blink." Jack turned and stared out the window at the approaching Doc Miller. Then he stepped toward the door.

Doc placed his right foot onto the bottom of the Quapaw's steps. A little breeze ruffled the blue awnings. The sun was behind the building, in his eyes. He couldn't see into the big windows. But he knew Jack Graham was waiting for him in there. Jack, who'd humiliated him in front of all those tough guys. They'd laughed and called him names he still didn't like to think about, they made him feel so small. Made his guts curl. Then they'd turned their backs like he was a cat or a coon or something dead by the side of the road. Squashed and sticky and black and already stinking.

That's how he was going to leave Jack.

He took the next three steps in one swift glide and laid his hand on the brass door handle. Jack Graham was waiting for him, somewhere on the other side of the door's etched glass panel. Doc pulled the Hardballer from his belt.

"Jack! Jack! Stop!" Sam screamed.

But he didn't stop. He laid his hand on the brass door handle. He stood squarely in front of the etched glass panel. He pulled the Colt from his belt. He pushed his thumb on the big brass tongue of the door's release. The door opened slowly. One inch. Two.

And then Harry Zack—the Fastest White Boy in the South, they'd called him, not to mention the only white boy at Grambling State where he'd won a three-year track scholarship—took a running leap and tackled Jack Graham, hitting him right behind the knees. Then the *crrrrack* of a gunshot filled the silent room, and the big man crumpled backwards atop Harry. They crashed to the floor.

"No!" Sam wailed. "No, no, no!"

What the fuck? said Doc. The etched glass panel in the door shattered into a thousand pieces that held together, just like a windshield that'd been hit by gravel. Though that was no rock that made that sound. Doc knew the sound of a gunshot, but he hadn't fired. Then he looked down and realized that, Shit! He'd been hit—not by any piece of flying glass, either. He'd taken a slug. And he was bleeding bad.

Doc turned tail and ran toward the Mercury.

"Are you hurt?" Sam was on her knees.

"No!" snapped Jack.

"Are *you* hurt?"

"I think my leg's busted. Could you get this big old guy off of me?"

"Who the fuck are you calling old?"

They were okay. Sam stood and leaned across her two lovers and pushed the front door wide. She watched Doc unlock the dark blue Mercury with his right hand. His left was hanging at his side, blood dripping down the fingers. There was a trail of red, bloody spatters from the front step all along the sidewalk. Then it disappeared as Doc had crossed the dark pavement of Central.

He was in the car now. He'd slammed the door. In a second he'd start the engine, and he'd be gone. They had his money and his diamond, but still, Doc Miller would be on the road. On the loose. Free to kill again with no one to stop him. Sam whirled, stepped around Jack and Harry, and ran back through the restaurant and up the stairs.

*   *   *

"Oooooooowrunuhooooo," said Pearl sniffing the blood on the sidewalk. Then she looked back up at Bobby, searching his eyes, waiting for him to tell her what to do.

"Take this, too," Sam pressed all the cash she had in her wallet into Bobby's hand. They turned right when they hit the main sidewalk, about to head up toward the Palace Hotel and the parking lot and Sam's car. Across the street was an empty parking spot where Doc's Mercury had stood.

Pearl stopped. "Hooh hooh hooh," she cried, lurching toward the parking spot.

"The son of a bitch is going to have a fifteen-minute lead by the time we get your car and I head out after him," Bobby said. His face was white. His mouth was grim. Maybe they had conned the con man, thought Sam, but *this* was the man to kill the killer.

She said. "What else can we do? Let's go!" She took off jogging, with Bobby and Pearl right behind her.

Then a car horn sounded, and they turned. It was Loydell peering at them over the steering wheel of her ice-blue Chevette. "Where are you two racing off to? I gave up on waiting for Jinx to call me and tell me how it all turned out, thought I'd come down here and find you all. . . ."

"Miss Loydell," Bobby breathed, leaning on the side of the Chevette. "I need you to give me your car right now. The man who killed Mamaw has just drove off that way"—he pointed south down Central—"and I hate to be rude, but Pearl and I don't have time to stand around and chitchat."

Loydell didn't even blink. She just slid over into the passenger seat and said, "Son, you drive. Pearl can sit on me."

Bobby climbed into the Chevette. "Miss Loydell, I don't think you under—"

"I am just old, Bobby. I am not stupid." She reached

over and opened the glove compartment and pulled out her little .22 Jaguar Baretta. "Now hit it, son. The murdering bastard may run, but he can't hide from us. Can he, Pearl?"

"Yo yo yo yo," Pearl sang as if they'd already treed Doc and she was on chop, waiting for Bobby to blast his lights out.

Then Bobby did a smoking U-turn in the middle of Central Avenue, and he and Pearl and Loydell headed south. Sam waved them off. "Good hunting," she cried into the clear blue Arkansas afternoon.

37

"THIS CERTAINLY IS BEAUTIFUL COUNTRY," SAID MICKEY. The baby blue Mercedes she'd picked up at Hot Springs Classic Cars was cruising along Highway 270 past the western fingers of Lake Ouachita. They were about to enter the little town of Mount Ida.

"Isn't it pretty?" said Jinx. "You've never been here before? Well, just you wait until we turn up toward Fort Smith. That national forest up there is so beautiful. You know, we could keep going, on up toward Fayetteville, do a little turn back east and you could see Eureka Springs. It is so *cute* up in the Ozarks. They have all these darling bed and breakfasts in Eureka Springs. . . ."

"Jinx," Mickey interrupted. "Sweetie, I think we need to keep our eye on the prize here. Now, we've got the nest egg, we need to get a good running start on making you a crystal altar queen in L.A. We should get there and get started. You want to do sight-seeing, well, darlin', we can do some sight-seeing. We'll see London. We'll see France."

"We'll buy lots of lacy underpants." Jinx giggled.

Mickey turned and looked at her. Who'd ever thought that the main chance would come in the form of a ding-bat ex-beauty queen with one of the greatest legal scams in the world, who didn't know it? And who was also a natural talent?

"I'm telling you, darlin'," Mickey said, pushing the button that opened the sunroof. The wind rushed through their hair. Mickey's red curls looked like little pennants, bouncing around. "We're going to be rich. Rolling in filthy lucre. That crystal altar idea of yours, we take it to Hollywood, unh unh unh. You think those bored-to-death rich ladies in Texas are foolish, can spend some money, honey, you haven't seen *anything* until you've seen yourself some Hollywooders. That place is absolutely crawling with people so insecure, so nervous, so unhappy about one-half a pound of fat, one-quarter of a wrinkle, and that's just the actors. Then you take the agents and the producers and, my God, the *writers* everybody else treats like pond scum—those people need your help so bad. We're going to be bigger than Marianne Williamson. We're going to start small and exclusive, and then we'll branch until we're into television home shopping. With you up front and me behind the scenes, we're going to be colossal! Mega-colossal! And, furthermore, we're going to be legal!" Mickey reached over with her right arm and gave Jinx a hug. "You are one smart lady, Miss Jinx. God, I love you, you did such a beautiful job faking out that s.o.b., then faking out everybody else."

Smart. Mickey thought she was smart. Jinx sighed. God, she was happy. She couldn't remember ever being so happy. Then she slid down in the leather seat, propped her knees on the dash, and screamed through the sunroof: "Brace yourself, Hollywood!"

38

EARLY THE NEXT AFTERNOON, SAM AND KITTY WERE SITting on Sam's front porch. Snuggled between them on the wide slatted swing was Harpo, Sam's little dog, whom Kitty had brought home to Sam from her grandmother's.

"So then what happened?" asked Kitty.

"After I waved Bobby and Loydell off? I turned and walked weak-kneed back into Bubbles." Sam took a long sip of her iced tea. "You want some more?"

Kitty shook her head. "And?"

"And the two of them were sitting in Jack's booth having a beer and a chat like old friends."

"Man-talk?"

"Yep. Swapping lies about who'd lost the most money at the track, football, that kind of stuff."

"They weren't duking it out over you, in other words?"

"I don't even think they'd noticed I was gone. Though, Jack did say, when they finally looked up, that he'd seen Bobby take off with Loydell, and he figured Doc was about to get what was coming to him."

"How'd you feel about that?"

"Well, Oprah"—Sam held an imaginary microphone out in front of her—"as you can imagine, I felt like dog doo-doo, pardon my French, Harpo, I mean what the *heck* was going on? Wasn't Harry there because of me?

Hadn't Jack sworn undying affection? And they were talking *baseball?*"

"So you turned on your heel, marched back to the Palace, threw your stuff in a bag, and headed for home?"

"You got it, sport."

"You heard from either one of them?"

"Both. Multitudinously. Phone calls. Faxes. Telegrams. I expect a helicopter with leaflets any second. Both of 'em pitiful as hell. Seems I overreacted. Misunderstood."

"And what'd you say?"

"Didn't say a word. Not answering the phone—or any other form of telecommunication. Don't plan to answer my door, either."

"You going to hole up? Get real about writing your book? Become a big-time hermitess?"

"Looks like."

"I've got a hundred dollar bill that says you'll crack in less than a week. Furthermore, you'll come crying to me, Which one should I choose?"

"A *real* hundred?"

"Genuine."

Sam stuck out her hand. "You're on."

They swung silently for a few minutes, listening to the birds, the frogs in the bayou that flowed behind Sam's old house on the north shore of Lake Pontchartrain. The cumulus clouds blowing in from the Gulf were like gigantic puffs of whipped cream—which reminded Sam of Jack and that night in her hotel room. On the other hand, she and Harry had done some world-class smooching in this very porch swing.

Sam took another long drag on her iced tea. Then she said, "So, what do you think?"

"It's a tough choice. Very tough. You could make one of those lists. Line up all the pros and cons. Harry vs. Jack. Both have a lot to recommend them. Of course, you have a history with Harry. But then, he done you wrong. Jack, on the other hand. . . ."

"I could. I could do that. Or I could just flip."

Kitty pulled a quarter from her pocket. "Call it, girlfriend."

"Heads, Harry. Tails, Jack."

Kitty tossed the silver coin high into the warm afternoon air, where it caught the kiss of the sun before it landed on the sky blue floor of the old wooden porch and rolled and twirled and spun and whirled in slower and slower circles until it ran out of steam and came to a stop.